Grounded

Elemental Magic Unleashed

Book One

Serenity Ackles

Axellia Publishing

Grounded
Copyright © Serenity Ackles
All rights reserved.

First edition, September 2019
Published by Axellia Publishing

Print ISBN: 978-1-912644-52-0
eBook AISN: B086JZSVRT

Cover design by Moorbooks Design

Edited by Aethereal Press
Proofread by S. Harvell

All rights reserved. No part of this book may be reproduced, transmitted, downloaded, distributed, stored in or introduced into any information storage and retrieval systems, in any forms or by any means, whether electronic or mechanical, without express permission of the author, unless for the purpose of a review which may quote brief passages for a review purpose.

This book is a work of fiction. Any references to historical events, real people, or real locations are used fictitiously. Other characters, names, places and incidents are the product of the author's imagination. Any resemblances to actual events, locations, or persons – living or dead – is entirely coincidental.

CONTENTS

Dedication		i
Also by Serenity Ackles		iii
One	Battery	1
Two	Battery	18
Three	Battery	33
Four	DB	50
Five	Hunter	64
Six	Battery	81
Seven	Battery	99
Eight	Hunter	110
Nine	Zera	120
Ten	Zera	135
Eleven	Knox	142
Twelve	Zera	154
Thirteen	Zera	171
Fourteen	DB	190
Fifteen	Zera	199
Sixteen	Zera	217
Seventeen	Hunter	232
Eighteen	Zera	246
Nineteen	Knox	267
Twenty	Zera	277
Twenty-One	Zera	297

Twenty-Two	Hunter	313
Twenty-Three	Zera	326
Twenty-Four	Zera	341
Twenty-Five	DB	350
Twenty-Six	Zera	363
Twenty-Seven	Zera	380
Twenty-Eight	Zera	395
Twenty-Nine	Zera	417
Thirty	Zera	422
Thirty-One	Javion	443
Thirty-Two	Zera	465
Thirty-Three	Zera	477
Thirty-Four	Zera	495
Acknowledgements		505
Newsletter		509
About The Author		511
Ways To Connect		513

HEY, READER. . .

. . . Let me level with you. I created a pen name for a reason. That reason was because I don't want my mum, my dad, my sister—any of my family—or anyone I work with to read my books and think about exactly what research I did to write it. . .

So, if you do know me, do me a favor and return the book. It's cool, I forgive you. But I can't sit at the dinner table or in a meeting with you opposite me, wondering what sites come up in my search history.

It was bad enough when that person came running up to me to ask for my autograph because they thought I was on Game of Thrones. To this day, I can't help but wonder if they think they know what I look like naked, and I will never see them again. . .

ALSO BY SERENITY ACKLES

Elemental Magic Unleashed

Grounded

Coming Soon

Charged
Shocked

SERENITY ACKLES & J. S. LEE

The Goddess of Fate & Destiny

Cursed Luck
Stolen Luck
Twisted Luck

One

Battery

Please let today be the day I die.

That prayer was my only wish. It had been the same thing I'd wished for every day for twenty years.

My muscles were tense, contracting against the pain. The only time they weren't was when it finally became too much, and I passed out.

Like they had since the day after my 'gift' had

arrived, my wrist and ankles burned as the electricity surged from me, down the chains to the contact points on either side of my cell.

As time dragged on, the more electricity flowed through me, the more the constant thrum of pain ate away at me. Some days, especially the colder ones, the pain was unbearable. On those occasions, it was all I could do to remember anything about myself.

And I didn't remember much.

Not the place I lived in before I was put into this glass cage, although I remembered it was in the mountains. I didn't remember my family, either. Not clearly, anyway. Sometimes, I could see the image of a woman with dark hair like my own, who I assumed was my mother. In the memory, she was handing me a balloon.

That was the day my 'gift' had arrived. *That*, I remembered clearly.

The balloon was a present. A gold number five. It was tied around my wrist as I danced in the rain. It must have been my fifth birthday.

Lightning had struck me, and now, it was like the lightning never left.

I remembered screaming. I remembered blacking out, and when I had woken, I was in this box.

A bolt of electricity whipped off me, connecting with the contact points with a crack. The pain turned up a notch. My hand shot out, punching at the glass wall. The glass stayed unaffected.

My room—my prison—was a glass box. One of the few substances that didn't conduct electricity.

"It's resisting again." The owner of the voice was called Cliff. He was a short guy with a round belly. He'd let it slip once that he had two daughters. I found it hard to believe he was a father, but Cliff was mostly harmless. He would even angle the television so I could watch the blurry true crime documentaries he favored. Most of the time, he just continued doing his job.

I was just a job to him, and like the other people who worked here, they only ever saw me as a source of power.

"Of course it is."

The voice made my skin crawl. Its owner was the one in charge. He rarely came close to me, but when he did, I could always smell cigarettes on him. When it was just him, he would sometime smoke them as he watched me. I called him Bacco.

He had never shared his name. The others only ever referred to him as Boss. I hated him. I hated him and I hated the way my body would contract in fear when I saw him.

It only took a moment for my body to react to his voice. I winced and tried to move as far away from him as my chains would allow, despite the two walls of glass that separated us.

"Douse it in water."

Before I could object and tell them I wasn't resisting, a hatch opened above me and ice-cold water was dropped onto my head.

It burned like liquid fire.

I might have been able to generate electricity but when I came into contact with water, it electrified me like it might a human.

The lights in the room glowed and one of the bulbs exploded.

I was too busy dealing with the convulsions, trying to get my feet off the floor, and out of the puddle that my wooden stool sat in. My legs didn't want to comply with my silent prayer. They were painfully frozen as the electricity continued to surge through me.

"Go get another bulb."

I knew what was coming.

There was a pattern whenever Bacco was working.

My only relief came from the fact that I was lethal to him. I had no idea how many volts passed through me but being kept in a glass cage where no one else would enter was a good indication that I was as dangerous to them as they were to me.

My cage was in the center of a windowless room. It was never silent in there thanks to the constant hum of the electricity in the air, and the sound from the television. At the far end was the control room. The large glass windows were perfect for keeping an eye on their power source.

The moment Cliff stepped out of it, disappearing into the building my cage was in, Bacco locked the door behind him.

I wasn't naked, but I might as well have been.

I had a slip to wear. It was the same one I'd been wearing for about two years now. I probably smelled but after being stuck in a cage with recycled air and nothing to compare it to, I didn't know. I was also given an ice-cold shower on a regular basis which might have helped.

The threadbare slip was white.

As soon as it got wet, it went see-through.

"It's a fuckin' shame that body is wasted on a battery." Bacco grunted as he unzipped his pants. He pulled his dick out, already hard, and began rubbing his hand up and down his length. "If you weren't so untouchable, I'd fuck you." His gaze grew hooded.

"It's a good thing I'm untouchable," I spat back at him.

There wasn't much else I could do. My body was exhausted from the dousing and moving wasn't an option with the puddle beneath me. The length of my chains meant I couldn't cover myself no matter how much I wanted to. All I could do was sit there and be thankful that on this occasion, my slip hadn't ridden up to expose any more of me.

"Say what you will, but I'm the only man that will ever make you wet," he said.

It was like watching a play; he had the same lines, which he used every single time. And I knew what would follow.

I tipped my head forward, just in time for the next dousing of water. I forced back my scream, biting on the inside of my cheek to stop myself. Bacco liked to hear me scream, so I didn't want to give him that satisfaction no matter how much pain I was in.

"Now, that's not how we do this, Battery," he chided me. From the corner of my eye, I could see him continuing to pleasure himself.

The taste of blood in my mouth gave me a sense of satisfaction. He wasn't going to get off because of me—

not today.

Bacco caught me staring and blew me a kiss. He moved closer to the microphone. With the glass walls between us, the only way we could hear each other was through a two-way intercom. If I wasn't praying to die, I was praying for them to turn it off. Especially when it seemed to amplify Bacco's grunts as he jacked off to my pain. "Gimme your light show, Battery."

And then his hand slammed down on the controls.

Water poured over me in a constant stream. It was agonizing. My body contorted in pain. I tried to hold on, desperate to stop him from coming, but it was too much. A scream erupted from inside me. Another bulb blew as my back arched, exposing too much of me in Bacco's direction.

I passed out.

Unconsciousness offered only a brief reprieve.

I woke up, gasping in pain, my body wanting to shiver from the cold water still making my slip damp. The length of the chain didn't allow for me to stand, nor did it allow me to lie down.

At some point, someone had decided that sitting

on the backless stool was the perfect position to get the most electricity from me.

It was a new day, but I had the same wish.

Please, let today be the day I die.

Cliff had been replaced, this time, with Ruben. Ruben was a dick. If Cliff watched Netflix, Ruben watched Pornhub. The only person worse than him was Bacco.

If Cliff wasn't here, that meant we were somewhere into Ruben's first twelve-hour shift. I wasn't sure if it was day or night. I just knew Cliff worked a twelve-hour shift with his colleague, Kalif, each taking four shifts before they swapped for Ruben and Abe. It was the only way I could consistently tell time.

And time seemed to pass much slower when Ruben and Bacco were both working.

Please let today be the day I die.

"The levels have dropped again, Boss," Ruben said.

I finally opened my eyes, turning to stare at them. They were both fixated on the computer screen. "Fucking battery," Bacco grumbled under his breath. "Twenty fucking years. They'd last longer if they ate."

For the first time, their words brought me some comfort.

If I wasn't producing the same levels of electricity,

I was growing weaker. And that could only mean there was a limited amount of time before my prayers would be answered.

"She's going to have to last longer, Boss. This autumn is brutal. I can't sleep without the heating on," Ruben said.

Autumn. It was autumn?

It had been so long since I'd felt warmth.

"If people followed the pack rules and didn't run heating units on full through the night, we'd last longer." Bacco smacked the back of Ruben's head. "This is why the other one kicked it."

"When's that doc getting here?" Ruben asked, rubbing his head.

That perked my interest. A doctor? The only doctor I'd ever seen in all my years of being here were on the television. They worked in morgues and examined the dead bodies.

That sounded . . . promising.

And then, as though to remind me of where I was, the electricity surged through me. There was no point in getting my hopes up.

"Battery is awake."

Bacco looked over, meeting my gaze. "I bet when it's power is almost gone, it's gonna be fuckable."

"If it's the last thing I do before I die, I will zap your little dick straight off your body." I spat at him, my body betraying the strength in my words as it flinched away from him with an involuntary spasm.

"In your dreams, bitch."

I didn't dream. I was thankful for that. I don't think I'd ever truly slept, so much as passed out. But if I did, Bacco wouldn't be in them.

Not unless I was killing him.

"Get out." Bacco's eyes were locked with mine, but I knew he was talking to Ruben.

I could feel my already tight muscles constrict, bracing for the water I knew was coming.

Ruben let out a sigh but stood. He moved to the door and opened it just as Bacco's hands dove into his pants.

"What the hell is going on?" a voice demanded, turning both mine and Bacco's attention to the door of the control room.

Ruben was standing beside it, his hand still on the door handle. In the doorway stood one of the most beautiful women I had ever seen. Her skin was pale like the hair framing her face in a mass of golden corkscrew curls. She was tall and slim, her body hidden beneath a long white coat. This was the doctor they were expecting.

Completely unashamed, Bacco's hand remained in his pants. "Just getting my buzz, Doc. Want to give me a hand?" He grinned. "Or a mouth?"

'Doc' looked at him, her mouth pressed into a thin, unimpressed line. "I'd rather lick the bottom of a toilet."

At least I wasn't the only one who thought he was disgusting.

"That's not what you said the last time I saw you." Bacco let out a dirty chuckle.

"I say a lot after a bottle of sambuca." She snorted, turning her attention to me. And then her eyes widened. "What the fuck have you done to her?"

"She's been powering the town solo for the past year," Bacco responded, finally pulling his hand out of his pants. "It's not me that's been doing that."

"Did no one read the reports I sent back?" Doc asked. She stormed over to the door that would let her into the room my cage was in.

Bacco stepped in front of it, blocking her. "Yeah, and that's why we're down to one elemental."

"What the fuck did you do?" Doc demanded. "They're like us. They need looking after." Despite being half his size, she scowled up at Bacco until he stepped to the side. Shooting him a sour look, she pushed the door opened and entered my room, walking up to my cage.

I watched her, warily, too restrained to do much else.

Doc's gaze went to my chains. "Fuck's sake, Bentley. At the very least, you should have lengthened those chains and given her something else to wear. She's freezing; I can see her shivering. That's inhumane."

"And she's not human," Bacco shot back. He'd walked into the room behind her and was rolling his eyes behind her back.

Bacco's eyes narrowed, glaring at me before he looked at Doc. "You want to see how we get electricity out of her?" Without waiting for a response, ignoring Doc as she chased after him, Bacco marched into his control room.

Before I could look up at the hatch above me, he slammed his hand down on the release button.

I screamed as bolts of electricity shot out of me, bouncing off the walls, running down the chains.

This water burned.

This water was worse than any previous soaking.

The pain was constant and relentless. I could feel it in every cell of my body as my muscles contorted, unable to do anything else.

And then I tasted it.

Salt.

There was salt in the water?

I had no idea if this was how much water was usually poured on me, or if Bacco was doing it to prove some twisted point, but whatever the water was, this was the first time I was unable to pass out from it.

After an excruciating period where time seemed to stand still, the water finally stopped.

I slumped onto my stool, exhausted. My head fell forward, water still dripping from my hair, into my lap. My breathing was fast and shallow as I tried to get air into my lungs. I couldn't stop my body from twitching.

Please let me die.

My prayer wasn't answered, but the next best thing seemed to happen.

For the first time, *ever*, the chains holding my arms out relaxed. I fell off the stool, my face hitting the floor before I rolled over onto my side. I didn't have the energy left to cry despite the new pain I was experiencing. This came from my arms. A new tingling forced through me as blood seemed to flow differently.

I wasn't sure if it was the weight of the chains or the fact that my arms had been in that one position for so long, but I couldn't get them to work properly enough to even push myself up off the ground.

Instead, I laid there staring through blurred vision as the woman yelled at Bacco. I couldn't make out the words even though she was shouting so loudly.

Instead, I passed out again.

When I woke up this time, I was still on the floor, but for the first time, despite the puddle of water I was laying in, I didn't hurt as much.

No, that wasn't right.

There was pain, but this was a different pain.

This pain came from relaxed muscles which had spent too long in the same position, aching from not being able to move.

Still on my side, I moved my arms and groaned as I pushed myself into a sitting position.

"How are you feeling?"

My head whipped around despite my lack of energy.

Doc was crouched in front of my glass cage, peering at me in concern.

"I hurt," I told her. Everything hurt. Even my throat, which was making my words sound rough and gravelly.

"I've had your chains loosened. That should help. You should try to walk around a bit too."

I stared at her. Did she expect some award for that? I was still in chains, still trapped in a glass container, and still soaking wet from my last dousing.

Doc stood. "Bentley will not be responsible for you much longer," she continued. "The pain will ease." And then she walked out of the room.

I sat there and watched as she left the control room, flicking the lights off as she did. The control room went dark, and my area dimmed. It wasn't complete darkness, but it was the closest it had been in years.

I didn't like it. My eyes were used to the florescent lighting and now I could barely see anything other than a low voltage yellowing bulb on the other side of the room. That and little sparks of blue lightning bolts dancing across my skin, close to the areas where the metal lay.

For the first time in a very long time, I reached out for the small stool, using it to try and stand. It wasn't easy. My legs felt like they were going to snap while my arms felt like they were made of lead.

With effort that left me feeling winded, I was finally upright, clutching onto the glass walls to give me support. "Hey!" I croaked, slapping my palm against the glass. "Hey!"

Shouting was just as exhausting as standing, and I had no strength in my voice. I was barely loud enough to hear myself echo back at me, never mind anyone else in this place hear me.

"Hey!" I rested my forehead against the cool glass, watching as I fogged it up with my breath as I waited for anyone to hear me. "Just let me die. Please."

I didn't want a tease of freedom with this limited movement. I wanted full freedom. Freedom that I knew could only come from death.

"Please . . ." I begged as I slid back down to the ground.

Like death, nobody came.

I sat there for hours. As I slowly dried, a slight salty crust covered my skin, and the burning sensation lessened.

And just when I was beginning to feel drowsy, like I could actually sleep for once, the room exploded into light.

I could barely see anything in the dark, but the light was blinding. I curled up as small as I could and shielded my face from the light, trying to see what was happening through my squinting eyes.

"Trick or treat, Battery."

Two

Battery

"What are you doing here?" The rasping of my voice couldn't quite hide the quiver of fear, but I tried not to show it.

"Thanks to you, I got switched to the amp room." Bacco walked up to my cage, stopping about a foot away. "And do you know what I found out in there?"

I wasn't sure I wanted to know because whatever it was had put a look of sheer pleasure in Bacco's eyes. He stuck his thumbs into the beltloops on his jeans and gave me a toothy grin. "You're not enough to power the town and we're heading into winter. You're barely enough to power the experiments on this base."

"I hope you freeze to death."

His smile widened. As it did, I saw something I had never seen on him before: fangs.

Not the normal fangs people had, but sharp daggers.

With a quick inhalation of breath, I stepped backwards. "What are you?"

"Not what. Who."

Bacco tilted his head, cracking his neck. He slowly raised his hand. In front of me, it started to change, taking on a dog-like paw with long, sharp nails. "I'm the Lycan who gets to breed with you."

Terror shot through me, seeming to claw me from the inside out, choking my throat at the sound of Bacco's voice. Until the rational side of my brain became more vocal. "You can't," I told him. "I'll fry you the moment you come near me."

Relief at that realization washed through me.

Until I noticed the smirk was still plastered firmly on his face.

Bacco leaned forward, resting his palm on the glass.

He tapped at it with his long claw and shook his head. "I found something else out while I was in there, Battery. Did you know you used to produce a billion kilowatts a year? And then you got old and now you're producing half of that?"

I had no idea what he was talking about. I knew they used me to power their town, so I figured it was a lot, but if I had to guess, even half of a billion kilowatts was still going to fry his dick into a charred kebab.

Bacco pushed himself off the glass, his paw changing back into a hand. Without saying anything else, he turned his back on me and started walking to the empty control room.

As if they were anticipating what was going to come next, my muscles went tight, locking my body in place.

Inside the control room, Bacco finally turned back to me. That smirk was still there. "I found out some interesting things in the amp room. My sea water dousing produced the greatest yield of electricity to come from you in years. And when you're out cold, you can barely power a lightbulb."

That couldn't be true, could it? They made me pass out a lot, and no one had ever been in this cage since I'd been put in it.

"So I'm going to make sure our base batteries are charged for the next nine months, and then, when you least expect it, I'm going to join you in that hole, fuck you until you're pregnant, and you've produced your replacement."

Terror wrapped its fingers around my heart and squeezed. "Your child," I choked out.

Bacco's attention was on the computer, and he gave me a dismissive wave of his hand. "The only part of me in the monster you produce, will be the genes to heal quickly and last longer than you." He finally looked up at me. "You're nearly useless anyway. Once we have a backup, I can just keep fucking you and making you pop out these things until we can create dozens of powerplants."

The taste of bile worked its way up my throat. It was one thing for them to be doing what they were to me, but there was no way I would ever let them do that to a baby—even if that baby was half of Bacco.

If death was the thing that remained out of my grasp, then I was going to make sure the one thing I accomplished in this miserable existence was to never bear a child. "Fuck you."

"You're going to have to wait for that." Bacco sat down in a chair and swung his booted feet up onto the desk beside the computer. He unbuttoned his pants and pulled out his dick, running his hand up and down its length. "It's time to make it rain."

He tapped at the computer and the familiar whirring above kicked in.

I braced myself for the dunking that was about to follow.

What I got was worse.

Instead of one large cascade of water, it fell like rain. Big blobs of salted water fell over me.

Bacco's sick, twisted mind had come up with a way to make my torture worse.

The electricity crackled over my skin. The skin on my wrists, already raw and bleeding, burning where the metal wrapped around me, felt like a hot poker was being jabbed under it.

What was normally a short experience of blinding white pain had now turned down just a notch, but it was enough that my body continued to fight it instead of giving up.

I tried to hold out as long as I could, desperate not to give Bacco that which he was obviously wanting. His eyes were locked onto mine, and I could unfortunately see his hand pounding up and down.

There was no concept of time in prison, and I had

never before been more grateful than at that moment for the lack of a clock in sight. The water rained on me seven or eight times longer than it had in the past as the pain hovered just below the excruciating levels I was familiar with.

My neck muscles were locked up tight as my body objected, but it didn't stop the screams from escaping my throat.

And still, my body wouldn't pass out.

Instead, I witnessed Bacco jerking as he grunted out his pleasure.

Revulsion joined my pain.

And a second wish. Not a wish, a declaration.

I was going to kill Bacco before I killed myself.

I didn't see Bacco for a long time after that. Although I hoped he had been punished for coming back to me, I doubted that actually happened. His new method of extracting power from me must have worked because that water seemed to rain down on me for hours.

Carl, who had remained on the job, had me under it for half of the time he was on his shift. He would sit in the same chair Bacco had, watching his shows, alternating water with a break for each episode he watched.

Just before I would pass out, the water would stop. The pain would lessen but not completely dissipate, continuing to thrum high enough that I'd struggle to breathe but low enough that I wouldn't pass out.

I was exhausted, and I could sense myself getting weaker as each day passed.

Maybe mercy would be granted to me with the death I craved.

Then they would stop.

Then, for one day, just as I felt numbness settle over me and I got my hopes up that it was finally my time, they stopped.

The control room remained empty. Enough time would pass that my clothes and prison would be allowed to dry out. I would have the chains holding me in place loosen a fraction more. The lights would be turned off and I would be left in the blackness with only the sound of a drip from the back corner of the cell and the constant background thrum of the base.

That was the day I closed my eyes and passed out.

And every time, I opened them again.

It was on the fourth day of nothing that something happened.

I had been unconscious, rolled on my side in a ball, when something roused me. It was a glow coming from behind me. I stared at the outline of my shadow, the white light framing my body.

As my eyes adjusted to the glow, I rolled over, sitting up as I did. Facing the light, I squinted. It was too bright to see clearly.

The light began drifting toward me. The closer it got, the more I could see its human form.

A ghost?

Cliff's crime shows would occasionally mention ghosts. How they would be able to tell a thousand secrets, or how they should come back and avenge their murders. But from what I could gather, ghosts weren't real.

Maybe this was it?

Maybe this was a sign that I was finally beginning to die?

Whatever this thing was in front of me, I wasn't scared of it. And almost everything that walked through the control room door to the other side of my cell sent my heart into overdrive.

As I watched this thing continue to glide toward me, my heart slowed.

Calming and reassuring; that was what this spectral

figure did to me.

The ghost came to a stop just on the other side of the glass and looked at me. It had a slight flicker to it, but once I got more used to the brightness, I could see faint features.

A naked woman.

"What are you?" I asked. My own voice startled me more than she had. This was the first time I'd used my voice in weeks, and all the screaming had made it hoarse and strained. Speaking hurt, but not in the same way as the constant sharp jabs from the electricity which danced over my skin.

I shook my head. That wasn't the important question. "What do you want?"

"It's time for you to leave here," she said. Her voice was as quiet as mine, but soothing, like it carried a balm that lessened the pain levels in me.

The balm was hope.

"Is it . . . is it my time to die?"

The specter shook her head. "It's time to live."

Live? I might have been alive, but I wasn't living. *This* wasn't living.

Her words confused me. I was stuck in a glass prison, being drained of whatever this energy was inside me.

How could I live?

As though she heard my answer in the silence of the room, she gave me a soft smile. "You will live. You will escape here."

"How?"

The hope she had brought was having a strange effect on me. For the first time, something stirred in my stomach, making me feel both nauseous and restless. My urge was to pace, and had the chains not been holding me in place, I might have done so.

I glanced down at the chains and the little flickers of energy that ran up and down them before looking up at her. "How?"

"We're going to do this."

There was a familiarity about her, but she was a ghost, and I was a battery with no name. Full of power, but completely powerless.

"You will know," she said, like it was going to be the most obvious thing in the world.

She didn't have to survive whatever was out there. She was already a ghost—of course she wasn't worried.

"When you leave this room, go all the way to the end of the corridor to the last door. Go up *two* flights of stairs. Follow the next corridor all the way to the end and do not stop for anything until you reach a door with

351 on it. The exit is in there. Are you remembering this?"

I nodded. "Last door, two flights of stairs, door 351."

"Good. When you get out, don't stop. Don't stop running. They will follow."

Her form was growing dimmer and more translucent.

How was she going to be able to help me?

The room burst into light as the overhead florescent tubes flicked on. As they did, the specter disappeared.

I stared at the spot she had been hovering over. There was no trace of her left. At all. Was I hallucinating?

Whatever she was, it was pushed from my mind when Bacco strolled into the room and stopped in front of me. Rocking back and forth on his heels, he watched me. His tongue slowly ran over his lower lip.

My skin crawled as he eyed me like I was dinner. He already had an erection.

"Ten months, Battery." He jutted his chin out. "We got enough juice to keep us running for ten whole months. Which means, tonight is your lucky night."

The electricity running over my skin crackled. The

pain reminded me of my promise. The specter had gone, and no one was going to save me. I wished for death anyway, but if that was the price for never allowing another being to be subjected to what I had been, then I'd pay it and leave a tip.

I was taking Bacco with me.

Despite the pain, I straightened my back and looked him dead in the eyes. "Yes, it is."

Bacco chuckled. "I'm going to enjoy this." He turned his back on me and strode back to the control room with the same jaunt he walked in with.

I wrapped my hands around the chains, gritting my teeth against the burning sensation in my palms. I couldn't pass out. Not today. I needed to endure, and I needed to make sure there was just enough power left in me for Bacco.

I braced myself for the water.

Bacco's hand hovered above the control as his eyes met mine in a silent promise. He blew me a kiss.

The control room descended into darkness.

"Fuck's sake." He grunted and looked up at the lightbulb. His gaze flickered over to me and he smiled. "It's a neat trick, but it's not going to work."

I braced myself, clutching at the chains.

Then they went slack.

As they fell to the floor with a clink, the pain I felt from the electricity bouncing across my skin dropped.

I slumped to my knees, my eyes wide, my mouth gasping for air.

This was the first time my body felt like it could relax. That my lungs finally felt like they could fill properly and expand in my chest.

The shock of nothing was almost as painful as the constant charges.

"What the fuck?" I barely heard Bacco over the pounding in my ears.

Blood flowed through my veins as a new pain kicked in. My arms, no longer held in place at all, burned. Under the skin, in my muscles, especially at my shoulders and elbows, it felt like I was on fire.

"Get ready."

My head whipped around to the spot I had last seen the specter. There was nothing there, but her whispered instruction was clearer than Bacco's growling.

Bacco!

I turned my attention to my captor. He had just arrived at the side of the cell and was reaching for the instruments to extend into the cage and grab my chain without electrocuting himself.

Before the plastic claw grabbed at the chain closest

to him, I jerked it out of reach.

Bacco pulled the claw out and narrowed his eyes. "Look, bitch. Either we do this the easy way, or I douse you with a gallon of water."

There was a click.

Over my panting and Bacco's voice, the sound wasn't loud. But it was a sound which was out of place.

I looked around, trying to figure out where it had come from. When I glanced at Bacco and saw the color drain from his face, I knew what it was.

Not stopping to think about the trailing chains, I spun toward the door of my glass prison just as it popped open.

"Remember what I said."

I didn't acknowledge the specter's words, instead charging toward the door, racing Bacco.

He was bigger, stronger, and uninjured, but I had one chance.

I got to it just before he did, slamming into the door so hard that it hit Bacco. As he stumbled, I tore toward the door of the control room.

The handle rattled in my hand, but the door didn't open.

Bacco's laughter, cruel and gleeful, rang out behind me.

Whatever he was—whatever a Lycan was—was hurt by electricity, and I still had that flowing from me. Angry blue sparks started flicking off the end of the chains.

What had been the source of my captivity was about to be the source of my freedom.

I tensed, turning slowly, ready to attack.

Bacco aimed a hose at me. "Think again, bitch."

Three

Battery

I stared at the small black hole of the hose as a single drop of water leaked from it. My mouth went dry.

Bacco snarled, pulling my attention back to him. "Now, get your pathetic ass back in that cage before backup arrives."

Backup . . . that . . . that wasn't right.

"It's not coming," I said, tilting my head as realization washed over me.

Panic flashed through Bacco's eyes. It was brief, but I saw it. "There will be eight men—eight Lycans—pouring into this room any minute."

"No." I slowly, deliberately, took steps toward him. "They're not. No one is coming. Because no one knows that you're here."

"Bullshit," he snarled.

I took another step.

Bacco's hand trembled.

Something shot through me. It wasn't electricity, it was an emotion. Something so alien to me, I didn't know what it was until I smiled.

A genuine smile.

Bacco swallowed, reaching for the faucet. At the same moment he turned it, I raised my hands.

Water hit me, the pressure of it pushing me back and pinning me to the door. I screamed as all of the electricity focused on the center of my chest, a new location unused to the pain.

No sooner had the vocal anguish left my mouth did Bacco change his aim.

Water flooded down my throat. Instead of relief on the scarred tissue, it felt like a thousand shards of glass were being forced into my lungs as I inhaled.

I collapsed to my knees, trying to turn my head to

avoid the water, but whichever way I turned, Bacco followed. The flow was relentless. With each lungful of water I swallowed, the darker my vision became.

My knees and elbows gave out, and I fell face first to the floor.

Finally, as I lay there coughing and spluttering and unable to move, Bacco turned the water off.

"You're done for now, bitch," he growled.

I raised my head to look at him. I wasn't sure if it was a near-death hallucination, but I was convinced I saw his nose and jaw elongate. For a brief moment, as sharp teeth took form, I swore I was looking at something not human. *Lycan.* That's what he had meant when he said Lycan.

And then it was gone.

My head dropped back to the floor. My cheek rested in a large puddle of water as I watched Bacco walk toward me. All I could see were his boots, stomping so hard with each stride that the water he was walking through sent mini tsunamis racing toward the drains.

Maybe I needed to let the blackness win. Let this be my last breath. There was barely any spark left in me anyway.

"Don't give up. You can do this." It was the voice of

the specter. Or maybe it was my own inner voice.

Whoever said it, the urging made something inside me snap. I was not about to die without taking Bacco down with me.

Closing my eyes, I searched deep inside myself for that last ounce of power, desperation clawing at me as Bacco continued toward me.

And then, with him only a few paces away, I found what I needed.

My eyes shot open and I turned my head, locking my gaze on Bacco. "You're done for now, *bitch*," I told him.

I slammed my palm down into the puddle in front of me. One solitary spark left my fingertips.

Bacco arched an eyebrow. "Is that all you've got?"

Yes.

The lights in the room started flickering. Bacco looked up and let out a long sigh. "Scary."

The room descended into black. Black, apart from the white glow of the specter hovering between me and Bacco.

I could see through her. A dark patch appeared at Bacco's crotch, growing. He took several steps backwards.

"I'm fucking terrifying," the specter said.

The room exploded with light. I had a front row seat to the greatest show I could have ever dreamed of.

The water seemed to dance as sparks surfed along it. The first few sparks bounced off Bacco's boots and then they started racing upwards. Once they got past the rubber soles, Bacco contorted, his limbs locking in awkward angles.

He wasn't human. What I'd thought had been hallucinations hadn't been. Because there was no way a human would have survived the volts that she was pumping into him.

I could feel the power like it was an extension of me. It seized at Bacco, singeing the hair on his body and working upwards until the dark hair on his head went up like a candle. Inside, I could feel it doing the same thing, destroying his organs.

While his body went up in flames, the life inside of him was finally extinguished, even though his body remained frozen and upright.

Acrid smoke filled the room, but I couldn't tear my gaze away.

I'd wanted this for so long, and I was going to savor the moment.

Maybe I should have been repulsed at the sight in front of me. At the very least, I probably should have felt bad. I could have asked the specter to stop. We'd bounded past the fine line of overkill. Instead, the satisfaction was giving me a renewed feeling of strength.

As I eventually clawed myself into a sitting position, coughing and choking on the smoke in the air, I realized the specter was fading along with the power.

When there was barely a whisper of her left and her outline was nearly lost in the smoldering remains of Bacco, she turned back to me. *"Run."*

Running required energy I didn't think I had. I wasn't even sure that walking was a possibility, but as she finally disappeared and I saw how much smoke was in the room, I knew I had to try. I had to get out of there before someone smelled the charred remains of Bacco; before a fire alarm was set off.

I crawled over to his still smoking body with the chains attached to my wrists dragging behind me. They'd been attached to me for so many years that I didn't need to look at them to know they didn't have a lock. Getting them off would have to wait.

Although charred, most of Bacco's clothes were still intact. Whatever that specter had been, she was powerful and controlled. I searched his top pocket and pulled out the key. It was hot to the touch, but nothing worse than I'd experienced.

With my hand covering my mouth, still coughing, I pulled myself to my feet. My legs were shaky and not used to movement. I didn't stop, moving one foot in front of the other, back through the puddles to the door.

There was still some power left inside me. Intense shocks with every footstep made it feel like I was walking on razor sharp points. I gritted my teeth against it.

I was not giving up now.

The key turned in the lock, and I stumbled into the control room, the chains clanking angrily against each other. The floor in here was dry and with every step, the pain in my feet lessened.

Following the specter's instructions, I left the control room.

This was the first time I'd ever been on the other side of those doors. The hallway was long, with half a dozen doors on each side. Like the room my cell had been in, there were no windows, and the hallway was lit by the same artificial light.

There was something green glowing above one of the doors at the far end. I squinted as I peered down the hallway, but I couldn't make it out. That was the door.

Still exhausted from my encounter with Bacco, and

not forgetting that my legs were not used to walking, I stumbled down the hallway. My hands slid along the walls, helping me stay upright.

Outside on different flooring, the chains were making a shriek that had me wincing with every step. I glanced over my shoulder, terrified someone was going to come out of one of the doors.

Halfway down, I picked the chains up and gently laid them over each shoulder. I could feel the electricity in me travel along the skin where each one was draped over the thin fabric of my slip, but this was better than letting them drag.

I stumbled on, finally reaching the door. The green glow had been a sign, but even if I could make out the blurred letters, I couldn't read them. My doubt over it being the right door was driven away when I pushed it.

It opened easily into a stairwell. Steps ran both up and down.

As I took a step in, letting the door close quietly behind me, the lights switched on. I froze, hardly daring to breathe, much less move. Then, after a while, they switched off. When I moved again, and they turned back on, I sighed in relief. It was me making them turn on. No one knew I was here.

Yet.

Pushing on, I forced myself up the stairs. There weren't many, maybe ten, to a midway point before the stairs curled back around. Ten was enough. By the time I got to the top of the first set, I had sweat pouring down my back, and my legs were back to feeling like jelly.

I sank down to a step, catching my breath. This was the most I had ever moved. I was certain I would be able to curl up into a ball and actually sleep. Instead, I allowed myself a risky couple of minutes pause, and then continued up.

Two flights, the specter had said.

She might as well have asked me to climb a mountain.

At the top, I refused to stop. Not a second time. I needed to keep moving.

I pulled open the next door carefully. Another long hallway stretched out in front of me. This one had just as many doors down it as the last one, but it wasn't until I started walking along that I realized the doors had windows in them.

The specter had said not to stop for anything, but as I passed one, I couldn't help but take a step back and peer through the glass. Looking inside the room was like looking at the set for one of the shows Carl had watched. In the center was a bed—a table—and on either side were trays with tools on them. This was a room where bodies were cut up.

I bit at my lip, glancing down the corridor. What was this place?

One of those tools might have been helpful to have as a weapon, but the specter had never said to arm myself. My best weapon was the power inside me, even if it was weak.

I pushed on, trying not to stop too often to look inside . . . until I came to a room with someone in it.

Nearly at room 351, my exit—and freedom—in sight, I caught a glimpse of movement at the last minute. Flattening myself against the wall, my heart pounded.

I waited.

When the door didn't open, I inched my head forward, carefully looking in.

There were four people in the room. Two of them wore long white coats and were moving around. Another lay on the metal table. His bare chest was rising up and down.

The fourth was seated in a chair beside the table. It took a moment for the men in coats to move out of the way enough for me to be able to tell that the fourth was only a boy. His arms were tied down with thick leather straps.

The boy's skin had a strange appearance to it. I glanced down at my own arms, at the scars and burns that littered them. His arms were different than mine. I couldn't see it clearly, but it almost looked like scales.

I wanted to rub at my eyes, but I didn't dare move in case the chains dangling over my shoulders clinked. Instead, I squinted, peering into the room.

That intention was forgotten as I realized what I was seeing. I clamped my hands over my mouth to stop my horrified scream from escaping me.

The boy had no eyes.

Worse still, it looked like they had been gouged out.

Stuck in his mouth, strapped in place between his jaws, was a piece of metal. Poking over the top of it were two long fangs.

I didn't know what I was looking at, but I did know that Bacco wasn't the only monster who worked in this place.

Now I knew why the specter had told me not to stop.

I darted past the door, hoping the coated men hadn't seen me, and pulled open the door to room 351.

No sooner had I done so did I regret it. Once more, I clamped a hand over my mouth, this time, to stop something else from coming out. It was like I had been hit in the face with a stench so terrible that it made my empty stomach churn.

Death. That was the only thing I could use to describe the pungent smell. Not just odor, but I could practically taste it on my tongue.

While trying desperately not to throw up, I looked around the room for my exit. Like every other room, there was no window, and the only door was the one behind me. There was, however, a large circular wall in the center of the room.

I moved over, raising myself up onto my toes to try and look in without getting too close.

There wasn't a bottom. At least, not as far as I could see. Just a deep, dark hole. I had found the source of the smell.

That was not my exit. I was in the wrong room. I'd confidently told the specter I would go to room 351, but I couldn't read. No one had ever taught me that—why would they? Everything I had been 'taught' were through conversations and visual cues, and things I'd picked up from television.

I knew how to clean blood from clothes but unless a person read out the bottle labels, I wouldn't have a clue what I was doing.

An alarm sounded.

It was so loud, I instinctively jumped back, allowing the door to slam shut. The noise didn't stop, wailing overhead like an angry scream.

They'd found Bacco. They hadn't found me.

Yet.

My eyes darted around the room, hoping I'd missed something—something I could hide behind. There was nothing but the hole. Holding my hands in front of me, I stared at my palms. My weapons.

Did I have enough power in me to fight off anyone who came through that door?

No.

I had two options: go back in the hallway or go down the hole.

From somewhere outside the room, a door slammed, and heavy footsteps echoed down the corridor.

I moved back over to the wall surrounding the hole and peered down. There was nothing but black and the stench.

Either I had the right room, and this was the escape the specter was leading me to, or I had the wrong room, and I would finally have my prayers answered.

Making my choice, I climbed up and dangled my

feet over the edge. My heart pounded in my chest. I sucked in a deep breath, and just as the door to the room rattled, I pushed off.

My stomach felt like it had shot up into my throat as I fell through the air. My slip ballooned out, but the flimsy fabric wasn't enough to slow my descent. Instead, it whipped up, joining my hair in attempting to cover my face.

All of a sudden, I stopped, hitting the ground with no warning.

The ground was soft and lumpy, cushioning some of the impact, but my ankle twisted beneath me as I collapsed onto the ground.

I lay there, fighting back the tears from the fresh pain in my foot. Gingerly, I tried to wiggle my toes. They moved, but it hurt like hell.

"It went down there."

The voice sounded so far away. I stared back up the hole, the light shining down looked like a moon in the night sky. Or what I imagined it would look like.

"Don't be stupid. That's the disposal pit. It's got to be a hundred-foot drop."

A hundred feet sounded like a long way to fall.

Before I could process it all, a light was being shone in my face.

"There it is," came the excited shout.

I turned my head, trying to get the light out of my eyes, and saw what had broken my fall.

Bodies.

I was on a pile of bodies. Some looked human. Some had wings. There were a few animals too. All of them were mutilated; broken bones and innards ripped apart.

This was the source of the stench.

Rolling over, I scrambled off them, ignoring the protests from my ankle, and threw up.

I lifted my head as a cold wind blew down through whatever hell this was. It was fresh. There was a saltiness to it, but the air was icy and clean. A shiver ran across my body.

I didn't look back.

Following the fresh air, I stumbled along. The further from the bodies I got, the wetter the tunnel became until I was splashing through icy water, slipping over the rocks below in almost pitch black.

I knew my feet were ripped and torn. My ankle was causing so much pain that I could barely put my weight on it. And the water I was walking through—sometimes wading—felt like knives stabbing at the skin unlucky enough to come into contact with it.

Finally, there was a light at the end of the tunnel. The light was dim, and it only got bigger, not brighter, as I edged toward it.

The wind was colder, biting, numbing my body. It carried a sound I'd never heard before. It was like water was roaring, almost drowning out a high-pitched wail of an alarm. Wherever this was, I was still too close to the place I was trying to escape.

It wasn't until I reached the mouth of the cave and stared out at the angry black ocean that I realized I was free.

The area was lit by the moon. So big and yellowish, hanging in the sky as clouds raced over it.

I had never seen anything so beautiful.

But I wasn't going to remain that way if I stayed where I was. The specter had said to run and not stop. She'd not been wrong yet, so I pushed forward. Climbing over rocks, I bit the inside of my cheeks against the pain as they tore at my feet while water from the ocean sprayed over me.

My feet finally touched sand. It was soft, but just as cold as everything else.

I didn't stop.

Fueled by adrenaline, my ankle numbed from the water, and I pushed forward, trying to put as much distance between me and my former prison.

I was never going back.

Four

DB

A group of college aged students, not much younger than Hunter and Knox, ran across the street dressed as Scooby Doo and the gang. They were followed by a group of females dressed as . . .

I titled my head, unsure what I was looking at. Knee-high boots with chopstick thin heels, and tiny leotards, which covered their arms but not their asses, all in a variety of different colors. "I give up," I muttered to myself. "What the hell are they supposed to be?"

Beside me, Hunter finally looked up from his cell phone and craned his neck, staring after the females. "Hot."

"In those outfits, in this weather, in Maine? They're human, not supes. I promise you, they are anything but hot."

Hunter let out a long, suffering sigh and shook his head. "Come on, DB, I used 'hot.' That's from like, the last decade." He rubbed at the back of his neck as I gave him a blank stare. "Power Rangers."

"What are Power Rangers?" I held up my hand and shook my head. "It doesn't matter." I ran a hand over my beard as I returned to scanning the area. If Hunter knew what Power Rangers were, it was a sure sign I didn't want to.

"On our way back, we need to call in at Starbucks and get a Pumpkin Spice Latte . . . DB? Are you listening to me?"

"Starbucks. Got it." I looked over at my companion and saw his eyes light up before he punched the air.

"You need anything picking up, Javion?"

There was a brief crackle of static through the earpiece before Javion responded. "I wouldn't turn down some A Positive."

I tuned them out. While this wasn't a mission where we needed silence, but for now at least, I preferred it.

A group of zombies walked past us carrying a keg. I almost wished they were real zombies—not that zombies were real. The zombies' destination was a giant house on the corner of the block. The front yard had been dressed like a graveyard, and music blasted out from behind a tombstone.

These northern seafront towns were quite charming with their New England style architecture. Nothing like Castle Viegls, but few places could compare to home.

"Will you just get in the damn ball?"

For half a moment, I thought Hunter was talking to me until I glanced down at his hands and the phone in it. "Is that a new toy from Javion to help spot supes?"

Hunter's neck seemed to shrink into his shoulders as the tips of his ears turned pink. Slowly, he looked up at me. "I need more Magikarp candy to evolve my Shiny Magikarp to a shiny Gyarados."

"Put the phone away." I swear, if I saw him on Pokémon Go one more time, I was going to get Javion to hack his account and transfer all his Pokémon.

With his ears still pink, Hunter slipped the phone into the back pocket of his combat pants. No sooner was his attention not on the eight-inch screen, he shivered, running his hands up and down his arms.

I refused to comment. I warned him that Maine was a lot colder than South Carolina, but he insisted on only wearing a black T-shirt, claiming it was part of his 'costume.'

We were wearing the same clothes we wore every time we went out hunting. The only difference was this time, the pretty girls were out too, dressed as *Power Rangers*, and Hunter wanted to show his muscles off.

We'd only been in this town for a couple of hours now, but the conditions were perfect for the more unscrupulous characters of the supernatural world— ghouls, basilisks and as we were close to the ocean, the sirens— to be running rampant. This was a college town and most of the humans we passed were intoxicated— easy prey.

"Javion?"

"S'up, boss?" Javion's voice crackled through my earpiece.

"Where did you get your intel from?"

"Same place as always. The red web. So many flags on the search terms came up here on red web *and* the normal web. If you've got humans researching the same supes in the same town, there's something up."

"There's been nothing," I said.

"Unless there's something bigger scaring them away," said the final member of my team.

A grin spread across Hunter's face. "You're not here, baby brother."

"I'm only on the outskirts of this fucking dump." Knox growled at him through our earpieces. "I can be there in minutes and rip your wings off."

I pursed my lips. While Knox would never have hurt his older brother, there was a reason he was held back. Reason being if our target was here, he wouldn't hold back— not even in front of the humans.

That wasn't my present concern. There weren't many things that could scare off the basilisks, and the few that could meant we'd be better with both Knox and Javion here. "Javion?"

"Wrong climate for a cockatrice, and there's nothing in the search histories to hint at a leviathan— and you're at a seaside town," Javion replied.

A large wailing alarm suddenly sounded.

"The fuck is that?" Hunter asked, looking around.

There was nothing to indicate there was a car or house being broken into in this part of suburbia, but the alarm didn't sound close enough, not that kind of alarm. This was an alarm someone set off as a warning.

"Javion?"

There was a crackle of static.

"Javion?" I jabbed at the earpiece.

"He said he's checking," Hunter told me.

I turned my head in the direction of the alarm. There were too many houses dating back to the turn of the century, and too many trees, for me to see further. "Come on." Knowing Hunter would follow, I set off at a jog, heading downhill.

As we passed various trick-or-treaters, I knew something was wrong. While some, mainly the more drunken ones, looked irritated, most were hurrying in the same direction we were.

"—this, Boss." My earpiece crackled to life.

"Repeat that."

"DB, you're back."

"What did you say?" I asked. In front of us, the road opened up, revealing the ocean. The wind coming off the water was icy, but it wasn't stopping many humans from running out onto the boardwalk and looking to our left.

Hunter nodded at me and we followed, holding back. "It's from the nuclear power plant," Javion said, as my gaze landed on the two tall cooling towers across the bay.

"I know we have tough skin and quick healing, but I don't think that's going to help us. We should get out of here, DB," Hunter told me.

"We need to get to the bomb shelter," one girl wailed.

"Mandy, it's a fucking drill," a boy said rolling his eyes. "That's not going to blow."

I rubbed a hand over my beard. Hunter was right. We could survive a lot of things, but a nuclear power plant going up wasn't one of them.

But I was hesitant to leave all these innocent humans here.

"Forget about them," Knox said, as though he could hear my thoughts. "Humans have proven time and time again that they're fucking useless in a disaster. Those that want to live will go seek shelter, and the others, we should let Darwinism win out."

That didn't mean I felt comfortable leaving them. I glanced around the crowds. Some humans moved into town to where I presumed the shelter was. Others were dancing around as though their Halloween party had turned into an end-of-the-world blow out.

There was a crackle of static. "—nuclear."

"Say that again, Javion."

Javion let out a long sigh. "Will you please let me upgrade our comms? You are the cheapest person I know."

I jutted my jaw out. "Javion." My low tone was a warning.

There's a hierarchy in our team, and I was at the top of it. While I was happy for us to discuss plans as a team, ultimately, I was in charge.

Javion was bordering on disrespectful. Conversations with this tone were to be held when we weren't out on missions.

"I said it's not nuclear."

"The humans seem to think so," Hunter said, looking around.

"That's because it's being dressed up as one," Javion replied.

I nodded my head in the direction of the street, away from the boardwalk and the humans. Hunter followed after me until we were clear. "What does that mean?"

"I hacked it. It's definitely a power plant: it's been supplying that town with power for decades. But it isn't a nuclear power plant."

"Why would someone disguise a regular power

plant as a nuclear power plant?" Knox asked. "Surely, it should be the other way around?"

"Does it . . .?" I sniffed, raising my nose to the air. We'd moved away from the seafront, and the wind was blowing down the street from a different direction. It was faint, but the scent was unmistakable. "Lycans."

Hunter looked at me, mouthing the word before raising his head. "I don't . . . Shit. DB's right. It's Lycans."

Whether the power plant was nuclear or not was no longer the issue. I was staying even if that plant was ten seconds away from a meltdown.

"I'm on my way," Knox told me.

"Shit," Javion muttered. "Why did they have to be in Maine?"

"Don't worry, Javion. We'll bring one back alive." Hunter's promise echoed my silent one. We'd been hunting the Lycans for years, and this was the second time we'd stumbled across them.

The first time, we'd been unable to keep any of them alive.

Not this time.

This time, we were taking a prisoner.

I took off at a sprint, wishing I could spread my wings and fly, but if I did and one of those drunk kids caught it on camera, the council wouldn't forgive it.

The Lycans' scent was faint. Hopefully, they would be outside of the town and somewhere that would allow us to take advantage of our flight.

The scent—and the road—led us out of the town, along a seafront road, and toward the power plant. Away from the town, only the occasional streetlight lit the road. Just ahead, one was flickering, and the ones behind were out.

Maybe the power plant *was* failing?

A putrid smell hit me, mixing with the growing scent of the Lycans.

Beside me, Hunter stumbled. "What the fuck is that?"

"What?" Javion asked.

"The most rancid smell known to the world." Although he kept running, Hunter balked.

"Whatever it is, the Lycans have something to do with it," I said, certain of that fact. Their scent mixed in with the stench was strong.

The road leveled off to sea level, half hidden beneath sand. Under a flickering streetlight, I saw them. Eight Lycans surrounding . . .

"Is that a ghoul?" Hunter asked as we slowed to a walk.

I reached out and grabbed the sleeve of Hunter's T-shirt, keeping us back. Right now, they were focused on the thing. Eight against two was a tough fight. We needed Knox here too.

"Do you see that?" Hunter asked. There was a moment of confusion until I realized he was pointing at the ghoul.

The ghoul was fighting off the Lycans.

"It's not a ghoul."

It looked like a ghoul. Filthy, pale skin which hung over bones like it was the only thing keeping the body together. Hollowed out cheeks. Long dark, matted hair. The undeniable stench of death . . .

But ghouls had shuttering movements. They moved in short bursts of speed to capture their prey—usually human—before tearing the flesh off their bodies and eating it.

This *thing* moved differently. It had something—chains—and it was using them like num-chuks. Only with no grace or skill, swinging them wildly.

"I think it's human," Hunter muttered.

I looked down at him, just in time to grab his T-shirt once more. "It's not human," I said, still trying to work out what it was.

"Whatever it is, it's not going to last much longer."

A roar of an engine rang out across the night. From the road behind us, Knox shot in, revving the engine and aiming his pickup truck at the group of Lycans. They scattered, snapping and snarling, as Knox drove at them.

"Fuck's sake, Knox," I yelled. I'd wanted to assess the situation better and formulate a plan, not charge in, headfirst, to an uneven battle.

"No yelling on the comms," Javion shouted back.

I ran across, reaching the group as Knox spun the truck around and leaped out. With Hunter at my rear, we attacked.

My ears grew pointed as my hands turned into claws. Behind me, my wings shot out of the gaps in my jacket. But before I could get further than the closest Lycan, the ghoul screamed.

Human.

Female.

Not a ghoul.

I turned, ready to put myself between her and the Lycans, and found myself staring at the most incredible blue eyes I'd ever seen. They seemed to glow, alternating between blue and silver.

The scream wasn't one of terror.

The female raised her hands out in front of her,

aiming them at the Lycans—at me, Hunter and Knox.

It was like the Disney Fourth of July fireworks produced offspring with a thunderstorm. Electricity bolts and sparks shot out from the palm of her hands.

As they passed through the Lycans, her scream turned to one of rage and desperation. Sweat was beading along her forehead, and she had a slightly glazed look in her eyes. Over the stench—which was coming from her—I could smell her fury.

One by one, the Lycans dropped to the ground, dead, but their bodies twitching. When the power coming from her was no longer stopped by a Lycan, it came for us.

"The fuck?" Hunter turned his body, bracing for the electricity.

An electric bolt hit me straight in the center of my chest. It felt like a punch—one from Knox, and I staggered back but I didn't cower. "You can stop now," I called over to the female, as calmly as I could.

I took a couple of steps toward her, retracting my claws before I held my hands up.

"DB, what the fuck are you doing?" Hunter shouted at me.

I ignored him. "The Lycans won't hurt you anymore."

The female looked me dead in the eyes. "*No one* is going to hurt me anymore." She flung her arms up, and I had to dodge one of the flying chains.

And then her whole body started glowing. As her outline got whiter and brighter, a giant ball of energy hovered just above her hands, growing larger and larger.

I looked at her face. Her eyes were expressionless.

"Shit." I turned. "Hunter, Knox. Run."

Five

Battery

There was an explosion. The blast sent me soaring across the road and into the ocean. I sat up, coughing out seawater. *Fuck,* it was cold.

Feeling like I'd gone ten rounds with DB, Knox *and* Javion tag-teaming me, I dragged myself out of the water, searching for my companions.

"DB? Knox?"

"I'm here, I think." DB groaned. He rolled over

covered in sand, dry. "Or I just got railroaded into the next life."

"Knox?" I looked around for my twin, spotting a lump on the other side of DB. Ignoring my stunned alpha, I ran over to Knox and rolled him over. "Knox? Are you alive?"

"I fucking hope so, otherwise the angels are annoying as hell." He groaned, shooing me away.

"I love you too." I sat, leaning back on my hands, and stared at the carnage in front of me. The street, lit only by the moonlight, was littered with dead bodies of the Lycans, still in their wolf form. Thank *fuck* for our skin.

"What the hell just happened?" Knox asked. He rubbed at the back of his neck, wincing. Moving tentatively, he stood, stretching out his one good wing behind him. The other, damaged, hung against his back. He wrinkled up his nose as he retracted both his wings. "And what the hell is that stink?"

"I think . . ." I looked around at the air. "The siren stopped. Javion, what's happening at the power plant?"

There was silence. Not even static.

Scratching the receiver out of my ear, I blew on it before poking the small piece of technology back in. "Javion?"

"Mine's dead too." Knox reached down, offering me a hand.

I took it and allowed him to help me to my feet before turning to our boss. "DB?"

DB walked over, stretching his arms out like he'd spent hours in the gym. That was a thought that, despite our current situation, made me smile. Irony at its greatest, DB didn't do gyms. Not in the weight-lifting sense. He went running in the mountains around Castle Viegls, and he would spar with the rest of us. But DB did not work out.

"Comms are down." DB confirmed. "Seems like the coast is too."

I glanced behind him toward the town. DB was right. The only reason I could see it as well as I could was because of my supernaturally enhanced vision and the passing moonlight.

"Let the looting commence," Knox muttered under his breath.

I didn't doubt he was going to be right with that prediction.

"What the hell was that?" Knox asked. He was looking over the bodies. "It looked like a ghoul, but I've never seen a ghoul do that before."

"I think *that* was an EMP—"

"An electromagnetic pulse?" I pulled my phone out of my back pocket and hammered at the screen. Dead. "Fuck."

"Oh, woe is you, no more Pokémon." Knox folded his arms and rolled his eyes at me. "Looks like you might have to stop acting like a teenager now."

It didn't matter how many times I told him that people—humans and supes—of all ages played Pokémon Go, it never sank in. I opened my mouth to inform him that the game was played off a server and all I needed to do was log in on another device, when something dawned on me. "Pikachu."

"I swear to the gods, if you're going to spend the rest of the night going *Pika Pika*, I'm going to—"

"No, the *human* Pikachu," I said, pointing over to the pale piece of fabric blowing in the wind. Ignoring my brother's insult, I jogged over, avoiding the fallen Lycans. My nose turned up at the smell. Charred Lycan fur had been added to the stench of the female.

As I stood over the dead female, a hand covering my nose, DB and Knox joined my side.

"That was no human," Knox muttered.

"She's no ghoul either." I looked down, drinking in her appearance. I wasn't sure what I was looking at. Her body had collapsed, face first, onto a bed of glass.

"What's with the glass?"

"Fulgurite."

I looked at DB and arched a brow.

"Fulgurite is what is formed when lightning meets sand. They are the crystals which have formed." DB told us.

I glanced around at the ground. It spread out around her body, in an almost perfect circle, like dozens of lightning bolts. "Damn."

"We need to get the bodies disposed of before anyone ventures this way," DB said.

I looked over in the direction of the town. The wind was still blowing toward the buildings, and it wasn't going to be long before the smell drifted with it. For now, they would be occupied with the power cut, but they might soon come to the conclusion that the power station was out and head this way.

I walked over to the furthest Lycan, pulling out a small bottle of lighter fluid from one of my pockets and a lighter from another. Spraying its fur in a liberal dousing of the accelerant, I set the Lycan on fire.

It didn't take long for Knox and me to pull the other bodies over, piling them up into one giant wolfen bonfire.

"We should go," Knox said. "It won't be long until

someone spots this flame and comes down."

Thankfully, supernatural beings tended to burn hot and quick. Even if the humans left the town now, the bodies would be almost indistinguishable by the time anyone got here.

I nodded and walked back to DB. He was still staring at the female. "We need to add her to the fire and get out of here," I told him.

DB nodded. He dropped to a crouch and pulled her onto her back. Doing so revealed the chains around her wrists. I'd thought she'd been using them as weapons. "What the fuck?"

There was a scowl on DB's face as he lifted one of her wrists, gently turning it over. The skin underneath the metal cuff was a mess. A mixture of scar tissue, wet wounds, and burned flesh. She must have been in agony when she was alive.

"DB?" Knox asked, his voice low.

My attention switched to our leader. His hands were squeezing at the metal chain as it hung from her arm. "It's welded on."

"Well, this was a bust," Knox grumbled. He turned around and marched straight up to the last Lycan. There was a satisfying crunch as his boot slammed into the Lycan's face. "Let's get out of here." He bent down to pick it up and drag it to the fire.

The female moaned.

I thought I had imagined it, but then DB quickly brushed some hair from her face. Her lips were red, and there was a touch of color in her cheeks, barely peeking through the dirt on her face.

My mouth dropped open. "How is she still alive after that? What is she?"

"She's coming back with us."

Before I could process DB's words, he scooped her up into his arms. I was impressed at that. Not because she looked heavy. Quite the opposite. She was skinny. Hell, she looked malnourished—starved.

No, I was impressed because I didn't think I could get that close without heaving. I was certain I'd already lost a few nose hairs.

"Is that a good idea?" I asked, looking around. "I mean, she killed eight Lycans by herself. And the power to the town."

DB looked down at the female in his arms and nodded.

Knox folded his arms, nodding approvingly. "The Lycans wanted her. Either she knows their secrets, or they'll come for her."

DB whipped his head around to scowl at Knox.

"She's not bait. She's not a prisoner."

Knox arched an eyebrow. "Carter, she wiped out a Lycan team. We have no idea what she is, but I can tell you, she's dangerous."

"Didn't you come here with the same intention?" DB asked him.

"Exactly." Knox met DB's eyes before he turned and walked over to his truck. The blast had covered it in sand. He pulled open the door, jumped in, and slammed the door of the Dodge Ram behind him. I could see him attempt to start the engine.

It didn't even turn over.

Darkness filled his eyes as he jumped out. He scowled at DB. "We're taking her home and getting information out of her because that bitch has killed my truck."

"Knox." There was a warning in DB's growl.

"Are you sure it's dead?" I asked.

"No, I just thought I'd push the truck back instead of enjoying the ride."

"Leave the truck," DB told him. "It was a fifteen-hour drive anyway."

Knox folded his arms, defiance shining in his eyes. "No."

"It wasn't a request, kid."

I knew why my brother was being difficult, and I couldn't blame him for that. There was no way he'd ever allow me to carry him back—not when the reason for that was my fault.

The fact that we didn't have any Lycan prisoner would have also pissed him off. "I'll carry the female," I said, quickly. Letting him push the truck back would have given him time to cool off, but I didn't like when his anger caused friction with DB.

We'd been with DB for nearly a decade, so if he was going to throw us out, he would have done so by now. But there was always time.

Knox ignored me. "The truck is full of our prints, DNA, kit—I'm staying and getting it towed." There was triumph in his voice. He'd won.

"Burn it," DB said with a warning tone.

If either of these two had the ability to shoot lightning bolts out of their eyes, the other would be dead. Thankfully, that skill was reserved for the female in DB's arms.

"Knox."

Knox shot a look at me. "Fuck off, Hunter."

Without waiting for a response from either of us, he marched to the back of his pickup, pulled out a can of gasoline, and started soaking the inside with it. He tossed the empty can in the back seat before sparking his lighter. The lighter followed the gas can and in seconds, the cab was engulfed in flames.

Still seething, he marched over to me and folded his arms.

"Let's get out of here while we still have the cover of darkness," DB told us, Knox's near rebellion already forgotten about.

He spread his wings, adjusted the female in his arms, and took off to the skies.

The only way Knox would ever allow me to carry him like DB was carrying the female was if he were unconscious too. Instead, I hooked my arms under his shoulders before I took off, following DB.

I loved flying. It was one of the greatest feelings in the world: the wind in my hair, the moisture in the air caressing my skin, and the pure freedom.

With my face so close to my brother's, I fought to keep the smile from my face. Ever since he had lost the use of his wings, I'd hidden from him, how much I enjoyed flying, lying and pretending it was nothing more than a chore.

The lie had gotten a little easier to tell when he'd turned his attention to the other forms of transport and his wheeled collection had begun. But this close, up in the air himself, I knew the resentment was simmering inside him.

We'd both been robbed of things that night, but he'd also been left with a physical reminder.

I followed DB out to sea, away from the cliffs and the humans who lived along the coast. We were small enough that we rarely showed up as more than a blip on a radar, but the human eye was harder to escape from.

The drive to the small town in Maine had taken us several days as we had investigated a few soft leads in the process. It had been the longest we'd been away from Castle Viegls in several months, and we hadn't been planning on returning until the new moon.

The female had changed that plan.

I looked over at her. She was still unconscious in DB's arms.

Knox wasn't the only one who had been left with a physical reminder of the damage Lycans could cause. What had the female been through?

Flying back from Maine was a lot quicker than driving, but it still took several hours. By the time dawn broke, we were flying around the mountains, avoiding the small towns. Knox's bad mood had remained the entire way home, with barely a word uttered.

Even DB had his attention either focused on

getting back, or the female in his arms. In the end, I'd let them both be. Knox would talk when he was ready, and when I had tried asking DB a question, he'd merely sent me a stony glare and then nodded his chin at the unconscious female.

The November morning had mist rolling down the mountains and over the evergreen forests. Storm clouds were on the horizon, moving toward Castle Viegls from the southeast, but for now, the temperature was cool.

The castle itself rose from the ground on the side of a mountain, overlooking the valley below. Deep in a national park, it rarely got foot traffic, and those that did venture off the hiking routes were met with barriers put in place by witches a couple of decades ago. The protection spell didn't hurt the humans, but 'encouraged' them to change their route.

The sun crept around a mountainside, hitting Castle Viegls just as it came into sight. The dark grey stone still looked almost black in the morning light. It had frosted over throughout the night too, the layer of tiny ice crystals catching the sunlight and reflecting it back like a beacon calling us home.

I swooped in, enjoying the last moment of air rushing through my hair, and then landed on the grass in the courtyard. No sooner had Knox's feet hit the grass did he shake himself free and storm off into the castle.

Tucking my wings under, I shivered as my skin turned back to human-like and I could feel the crisp morning air. The grass beneath me was coated in frost, like the castle and it crunched as I turned around to watch DB land.

"Is she still asleep?"

"Asleep or unconscious," DB said, his voice gruff. Carrying her like she weighed nothing, but like she was made of glass, DB turned and walked into the castle, following Knox's footprints across the pale grass.

Inside, DB headed straight for the south wing. Although the castle was of reasonable size, it didn't have dozens of rooms like it seemed from the outside—just several large rooms.

The south wing had a couple of guest bedrooms—not that we ever had guests—and DB went straight for the biggest. I managed to get in front of him to open the large oak door and stepped back to let him in.

DB walked straight over to the bed, laying the female down on the immaculate white sheets. The bed was big enough that DB could have stretched out on it and not hung over the edge. The female looked lost in the middle of it.

"Is that you?" I heard Javion's voice from deep within the castle.

"In the guest room," I called back when DB didn't respond. He knelt beside the bed, the wrists of the female in his hands as he examined the cuffs around her.

"What the hell happened out there? Your comms went dead and the electricity in a forty-mile radius went down." Javion strode into the room. "I was worried—what the fuck is that?"

"A female," I replied.

Avoiding the sunlight that was beginning to stream through the window, Javion moved closer to the bed. "That's not what I had in mind when I asked you to bring back some A Positive." His hand went up to cover his nose. "Is it even alive?"

"She is alive," DB said.

"She doesn't smell like it." Javion turned and arched an eyebrow.

I silently pointed to DB and the wrist he was holding.

Javion followed my outstretched hand, scowling the moment he laid eyes on the chain. "What the fuck? Why is the human chained up?"

"She's not human," I said, remembering the electricity bouncing off her skin.

"She's an elemental," DB said. He gently laid the female's arm on the bed, placing the chain beside her.

"A what now?"

Javion shook his head. "You're stumbling into the made-up supernatural creature spectrum, Carter. Elementals don't exist."

DB stood, finally folding his wings away, and moved towards the window. "She is the cause of that blackout. That tiny little female, barely alive, killed eight Lycans and caused an EMP blast so powerful, it knocked out power for a forty-mile radius. You tell me what other supe can do that?" he asked as he closed the curtains, sending the room into near darkness.

Javion ran a hand over his jaw, staring at DB like he was speaking another language and his brain was trying to translate it. "Elementals don't exist."

DB gestured between the three of us. "To humans, we are little more than fairytales and horror stories. But we exist. Why can't an elemental?"

Javion's silver eyes dropped to the chain. "Because if she is an elemental, then those chains are on her for good reason. She should be in the cells, not the guest bedroom."

"If she does not exist, how can you know she is so dangerous?" DB asked.

"She was being chased by Lycans," I added.

"The Lycans she killed?" Javion asked, giving DB a pointed look.

"She didn't kill us."

If Javion had been there, he wouldn't have accepted DB's argument, considering she tried. It was only our skin that had protected us.

I glanced over at the female, hidden beneath years of dirt, blood, and who knows what kind of abuse.

No one is going to hurt me anymore. Those had been her last words.

Maybe her reaction was nothing more than that of a wild animal backed into a corner.

"If she is staying as a guest, we should do something about that," I said, gesturing to her, unable to pick a point to start with—there was so much. "Get the chains off her, clean her—"

"No," DB said, firmly. "We will not touch her until she awakens."

"Her wounds—"

"Hunter."

I turned as DB said my name, looking at the alpha in front of me. The idea of leaving her like that made me feel uncomfortable, and I wrinkled up my nose.

"Hunter," DB said, softer this time. "Whatever she

has been through, it has been a lot. I don't want to try to change her clothes or take those chains off her while she is asleep. If she wakes, she will be even more terrified." He started walking toward the door. "Let her wake on her own terms. It has been a long night. You should rest."

I looked once more at the female. I had no idea who she was, and only a vague idea of what she was capable of, but for some reason, I didn't want to let her wake up alone.

Six

Battery

New sensations greeted me as my body moved back into the realms of consciousness. The first was the silence.

For as long as I could remember there had always been noise. A droning electrical hum. Static electricity crackling across my skin constantly, the drip of water, movement in the control room . . .

Here, there was nothing.

No, not nothing. There was a gentle, steady ticking.

The second sensation was the softness of whatever I was lying on. My body had never sunk into anything the way it sank into this. Whatever I was lying on was warm, dry, and smelled incredible.

Of course, it took only a few moments of my body adjusting to these sensations before the familiar feeling of pain made itself known. Sucking in a breath through my teeth, I finally opened my eyes.

Almost instantly, I had to close them again as bright light—brighter than anything I'd ever experienced before—was shining in my face. I rolled over, hiding my head under my arm before finally peeking my eyes open again.

Everything was still bright and hurt my eyes, but I could make out unfamiliar shapes.

Where the hell was I?

I pulled back onto my knees, my face half hidden beneath my hair and the safe shadows it produced, then I looked around. The source of the light seemed to be coming from a window.

My mouth dropped open as I realized what it was. Sunlight.

I hadn't seen sunlight since . . . I scrambled off the bed. My feet touched something almost as soft as the thing I had been lying on—carpet—but I let out a cry of pain and collapsed to the ground.

Bathed in sunlight still streaming through the window, I curled around and stared at the new source of my pain: my feet. The soles were ripped to shreds, and although they were no longer bleeding, they were raw and tender. There were pieces of rock and sand embedded in them.

Before I could bring myself to try to do *something* with them, there was a soft knock. As my eyes fell on a wooden door, it opened. The most enormous man I had ever seen walked in.

He was so tall; his head just missed the top of the door frame. His hair was dark brown, but it was streaked with silver, especially around his temples. A light dusting of hair scattered under his nose and on his chin, with even more gray hairs. He had a strong, square chin and inky blue eyes.

A T-shirt which hugged his chest, showed off his broad shoulders and thick arms. He had muscles, but there was also something soft about them. They weren't quite defined enough.

Although he was older than me by quite a few years, he wasn't unattractive.

I frowned. His attractiveness wasn't the concern here.

My concern should have been the fact that I was in a place I didn't recognize with a man I didn't know.

Ignoring the pain in my feet, I jumped up, holding my hands out in front of me. The power was still inside me. I could feel it—see it—crackling across my skin.

Opposite me, the giant of a man held his hands up. "Now, now, Blue Eyes. I mean you no harm."

Sparks of electricity danced between my fingertips. "If you come any closer, I will kill you."

"I'm not moving from this spot until you say it's okay," the man agreed. He didn't move or even lower his arms. "But I would very much like to remove those chains from your wrists."

I glanced down at my wrists and the heavy metal that encircled them before looking back at him. "Why?"

The hands in front of him wavered. "Why wouldn't I? Only prisoners wear chains, and you're not a prisoner here."

My eyes narrowed as I stood up. "I'm not?"

The man shook his head.

Squinting, I glanced around the room again. It was still bright and there was a lot to take in. I was in a bedroom—that much was clear. "Where is here?" I took another step back, biting my cheek as the pain shot up my legs from the bottom of my feet.

Very slowly, the man lowered his arm to gesture to a small table, a chair on either side of it, against the far wall of the room. "I am happy to answer your question, Blue Eyes, but might we do it while you are sitting down? I will stay here, as I promised."

I stood there staring at him, trying to ignore the pain in my feet that was affecting my ability to think. I had no idea where I was or who this man was, although he looked vaguely familiar.

He didn't move, just waited patiently for me to make a decision.

"Why?"

"Why do I want you to sit down?" he asked, tilting his head. When I didn't answer, he used his chin to nod toward my feet.

I caught my lower lip between my teeth, glancing to the open door behind him. Sitting down would take me further from the exit.

"If you want to leave, I won't stop you. You can walk out that door now." The corner of his mouth turned up in a sympathetic smile. "I know you have no reason to trust me, but I would like to at least get those chains off you and dress the injuries on your feet first: give you a fighting chance."

Trying my hardest to hide just how much each step

hurt, I hobbled over to the table, never taking my eyes off the man. When I sat down, I couldn't keep the sigh of relief from escaping as I took the weight off my legs.

I could handle the constant pain from the chains around my wrists, the electricity as it crackled over my skin, but the agony in my feet was going to stop me from getting far.

"My name is Carter." He was still in the exact spot he had promised to stay in.

"Hey, DB, I have bandages and alcohol wipes and sterile—"

I leaped to my feet as a second man walked into the room.

He was shorter than Carter, but still tall. His hair had dark roots and sandy tips, and stood up in a way which looked like he'd ran his hands through it only moments before walking through the door.

Carter's hand shot out, only it moved toward the younger man instead of me, his hand falling in front of his chest, and stayed there. Although he never touched him, the younger man stopped in his tracks.

"This is Hunter, and as you can see . . ." he pointed at the green box in the man's hands. "He's here to help too."

I didn't drop my hands.

Carter inhaled a deep breath. "Hunter brought bandages and other medical supplies, but he's going to stay right here beside me until you decide to allow him to help you."

Hunter nodded enthusiastically, giving me a bright smile—but only after Carter had bobbed his head in approval.

There must have been fifteen or twenty years between the two men. Maybe enough for them to be father and son, but their features were too dissimilar for that. Hunter had more angles in his face, with sharper cheekbones and a more pointed chin.

Suddenly, I didn't care, and I sank back into the chair. As I did, the chains dangling from my wrists fell to the floor with a loud clank.

Both of the men winced.

"Please," Carter said, "let me get them off you."

I looked down at the arms in my lap, my gaze going to the chains. "I don't have the key."

"May I?" Carter asked.

Slowly, I shifted my gaze to him and nodded. He flashed Hunter a warning look before moving over to me. The whole time, his arms stayed out in front of him, palms facing me.

"Why do you do that?"

Carter paused. "Do what?"

"Hold your hands like that while telling me you won't hurt me."

Looking down at his palms, he tilted his head. "To show you they're empty."

I held mine up. Blue bolts of electricity danced across them. "So are mine."

Carter rubbed a hand across his jaw before lowering both hands. "I see your point, Blue Eyes." He moved over to the vacant seat and pulled it out. As he sat on it, it seemed to disappear beneath him. "Do you have a name?"

Battery.

My lips remained clamped together. Sharing of names seemed too . . . personal. All I had was the name Bacco had given me.

Bacco.

As I shuddered, a memory sparked in my mind.

"You were with them." I knew why he seemed familiar. He had been with the . . . what had Bacco called himself . . . Lycans.

Panic materialized from nowhere, climbing around my limbs, paralyzing me. It wrapped its tendrils around my windpipe.

Was he a Lycan too? Was he working with them?

Before I could get back on my feet, a voice boomed across the room. "*You* were the one with *them*."

My head snapped toward the door, and I found myself blinking rapidly. There were two Hunters in the room.

"And then she killed them, Knox," the original Hunter pointed out.

I rubbed at my eyes, unsure if I was hallucinating. They were wearing completely different clothes, but their faces were the same.

"We're twins." The one called Knox rolled his eyes. "Identical."

"I'm the older one," Hunter added.

I blinked a few more times as I squinted at him. They weren't identical. Hunter was wearing blue jeans that clung to his muscular legs like a second skin, with rips throughout the fabric to show off slivers of skin. Underneath an open red plaid shirt, he was wearing a white T-shirt. At the bottom, he had comfortable looking red shoes on with white toes.

Knox wore a T-shirt with no sleeves, but his arms were covered in drawings that disappeared under the fabric. The bottom half of him was completely covered in pants which were baggier with several pockets. Knox was wearing boots, laced up to his calves which shone in the sunlight.

Unlike Hunter's flyaway hair, Knox had kept his dark. It had been shaved more on one side, with thin horizontal lines cutting through. The rest was brushed over to the other side, a lock falling into his eyes.

But even if they had been wearing the same clothes, they wouldn't have been identical. They both had green eyes, but Hunter's seemed slightly brighter and full of concern. Knox... his were full of danger and suspicion, hidden beneath dark eyebrows, which seemed to join together. Especially for me.

I couldn't help but stare.

I had never seen two people who looked so similar.

"We are not with the Lycans," Carter said, drawing my attention back to him. "That is Knox, who, as you can tell, is Hunter's younger brother."

"Why are you telling her who we are, DB?" Knox demanded.

"I thought you said your name was Carter?"

Carter nodded. "It is. DB is a nickname these two call me."

"You have two names?" When Carter nodded, I looked at Knox and Hunter. "Do you two have other names?"

A grin spread across Hunter's face. "You can call

me Bae."

For some reason, the smile made bubbles appear in my stomach. My neck and cheeks felt hot under his gaze. I blinked a few times, unsure as to what the unfamiliar sensation was, but equally, not disliking it.

"Are you really flirting with that thing right now?"

Hunter turned around and punched Knox's shoulder. "Don't call her a thing."

"This is insane," Knox said. He shoved something at Hunter —I hadn't even noticed he was holding anything. As Hunter struggled to take the item and hold onto the box already in his hand, Knox shot me a murderous look before stalking out of the room. "Don't come crying to me when she kills you both," he called over his shoulder.

"Ignore him. He's got a stick up his ass." Hunter started walking over but stopped the moment I flinched back into the chair.

"Please stay over there," Carter told him, his voice calm while never taking his eyes off me.

"Sorry," he muttered.

"Okay, Blue Eyes. Before we were interrupted, I was going to tell you that we are not Lycan, nor are we working with them."

"Why were you there with them?"

Carter gave me a soft smile. "We have been tracking them for decades."

"Why?"

"To kill them," Hunter said with a shrug.

My eyes went back and forth between the two of them as my fingers curled around the chains. The electricity crackled over my hands. I winced.

"Please don't do that to yourself," Hunter blurted out.

"You're safe here, Blue Eyes," Carter told me, his eyes almost pleading. "Please, will you let me take those chains off you?"

My gaze dropped to my lap. I wasn't even sure they could come off. I couldn't tell why they cared so much to remove them. I did know that trying to come up with an answer to both was making my heart hurt in a way it had never done before.

"I'm not sure you can," I said. It came out like more of a whisper.

"I'll get them off." Carter slowly leaned toward me.

I leaped away, sending the chair falling to the floor as my chains whipped around me and smacked the table. "Don't touch me." One of the bulbs in the overhead light exploded, raining glass down.

Once more, Carter's hands shot into the air before

he suddenly flipped his palms to point at the floor. "I don't mean to hurt you. But I'm going to need to touch your arm to help you."

"I will kill you."

"I told you, Blue Eyes. I won't do anything that makes you feel uncomfortable."

"No," I said, half sobbing. "You don't understand. I don't *want* to kill you. Not right now, anyway."

"That's good to know," Carter said as a small smile appeared.

"I have an idea," Hunter said suddenly. He moved straight over to the table, ignoring the objection from Carter, and placed the items on top. Then he turned and ran out of the room.

My eyes went wide as I watched him go, and I turned to Carter. He shrugged. "I know you have your concerns, but I carried you here myself, and I'm still alive."

"It drops," I told him. "The power drops when I'm unconscious."

Carter nodded. "It also looks like it rises when you get agitated."

I looked up at the main light, at the high ceiling, the rafters out on display. Hanging from a rafter in the middle of the room was one of the most beautiful lights

I'd ever seen.

"That's an old chandelier, you know."

Guilt flooded me. "I'm sorry. I didn't mean to destroy it."

"Lightbulbs are replaceable. Why don't you sit back down? You keep putting pressure on those little feet of yours."

I diverted my attention to my feet. Carefully, I leaned down and put the chair back on its feet so I could take the weight off of mine. I sat there in silence, studying the man opposite me.

He seemed to be around the same age as Bacco—late thirties—but I didn't get the feeling he was the same as Bacco. I had only ever seen hate, anger, or a perverted lust in Bacco's eyes. This giant of a man had sympathy and something else that I'd never seen before but couldn't put a name to.

While I didn't completely trust him, I did feel at ease around him. I appreciated how he stayed back from me. If he wanted to, I was sure he could have leaped across the table and snapped my spine in two; I was in no doubt of his strength. Instead, I was certain he wanted to help me.

I just wasn't sure why.

Hunter soon reappeared in the room, only he was

wearing bright pink gloves. "DB, catch." He tossed a packet to Carter, who opened them and also put a pair on.

"You really think those flimsy things will stop me?" I eyed them in disbelief.

"They're rubber gloves," Hunter nodded. When I gave him a blank look, he wiggled his fingers. "Rubber does not conduct electricity, which means we should be able to touch you without you hurting us."

"Hunter," Carter said in a low warning tone.

Hunter shook his head. "It's okay."

I disagreed. "I don't think that's going to work."

Hunter and Carter seemed to have a staring competition before Carter sighed and looked back to me. "Would you allow me to try?"

Sucking in a deep breath, I held my hand out, resting it on the table. The chain clunked as it hit the wood. "It's not my fault if you die."

Carter reached over, his hand hovering over mine, before he gently lifted it and held it in his own.

My lips slowly parted. This was the first time anyone had ever held my hand. "They're really stopping me from hurting you?"

Carter slowly shook his head as he squeezed my hand. "You are not hurting me." Gently, he turned my hand over and looked at the chain cuffed around it. "Please, can I remove this now?"

I nodded.

"Thank the gods," I heard Hunter sigh. He moved over to the table and opened the box his brother had given him. From inside, he pulled out a funny looking pair of eyeglasses and held them out to me. "These will protect your eyes."

I stared at them before looking up at Hunter. "From what?"

"Knox has kindly leant us one of his tools," Carter explained, pulling it from the box.

The tool was cylindrical in shape, only a little larger than the hand wrapped around it. At the top was a thin metal stick, and sitting on top of that, a circle of metal about the size of a coin.

"*That* is going to get the chain off?" I asked, dubiously.

Carter nodded. "It might not look like much, but this will cut through metal."

"Yup," Hunter agreed. He was still holding the glasses out. "But it creates sparks, so you need to protect your eyes."

I raised an eyebrow. "I create sparks." When Hunter didn't give up, I took the glasses from him and put them on. They were big and covered most of the top half of my face.

Smiling, Hunter grabbed another pair and put them on. As he did so, he walked behind me.

I whirled around, ready to electrocute him.

"Hunter." Carter snapped at him, making the younger man jump back, even though there was no volume to his voice. "Tell the female what your intentions are first."

"Shit, sorry." He rubbed at the back of his head. "That thing is noisy. I was going to cover your ears." Hunter raised his hands, covering his ears.

I stared at him, searching his bright, green eyes for any sign of ill-intent, but found nothing other than something I didn't have a name for yet, but could only read as positive. I nodded.

"This might be scary, but I won't let it hurt you. If you need me to stop, just raise your other hand."

At first, when Carter started the small machine up and the sparks started flying, as the metal started to scream its protest, I could feel my heartrate start to rise and my own sparks appear on my skin.

But as Hunter gently held his hands over my ears, his fingertips also massaging my head, and while Carter was doubled over concentrating hard not to hurt me, I realized I wasn't scared.

No, I felt safe.

Seven

Battery

The second chain fell from my wrist, landing on the floor with a thud. Frozen in place, I could do nothing more than stare at my wrists, bare for the first time in twenty years.

My wrists were a mess. The skin was barely there, wounds weeping in red, angry welts. I could see flesh. Worse, I could see what I was sure was my own bone. The edges of the skin were burned from the constant electrical charge; black and swollen.

They hurt.

But the pain was still less than anything I'd been living with up to this point.

I wiggled my fingers, and for another first, there was no electrical spark dancing over the top of them. The power was still inside me. I could sense it. But nothing was forcing it out of me.

Drawing in a deep, shuddering breath, my lower lip wobbled, and I looked up at Carter. "Thank you."

Carter stared at me, his eyes turning stormy with anger. Standing abruptly, he scowled at Hunter. "Treat her." Without looking at me, he reached for the chains and stormed out of the room.

The door slammed behind me, making me wince.

"Don't mind DB," Hunter said, taking the seat Carter had left. He glanced over his shoulder at the shut door before looking back at me. "He, uh . . . he's not good with blood."

"He's not mad at me?" I didn't know why I asked that, but Carter had picked the chains up with rage, and for some reason, the idea that he could be mad at me brought a lump to my throat.

"Don't worry about him." Hunter busied himself with pulling items out of the green box. Rolls of bright, white fabric and several tubes of creams and liquids.

"What's that?"

When Hunter looked up at me, he wasn't smiling. "You really don't know?"

I didn't, but for some reason, I didn't want to tell him that again. It felt like the wrong answer.

Hunter pressed his fingers to the center of his forehead, his eyes closed, before he swept his hand through his hair. "The good news is that you're a supe. Now, I don't know your exact healing time, but I know it's going to be much faster than a human. The witches made the ointment to help with healing."

Witches?

With his lower lip caught between his teeth, Hunter lowered his head to examine my wrists. "I can't promise you're not going to scar from this, but you will heal." He looked up at me and gave me a bright smile.

From nowhere, a bubbly sensation appeared in my stomach.

"But it might hurt. So, I'm sorry."

With my free hand, I scratched at my chin. No one had ever apologized to me before they were about to hurt me . . .

The ointment burned almost as much as the cuffs had. I screamed, whipping my hand away, seconds before a bolt of electricity left it. The bolt hit the wall on the other side of the room, sending dust and pieces of stone showering across the floor.

"I'm sorry." Hunter's hands were up in the air, his eyes wide with horror. "Shit, I didn't mean to hurt you."

Moments later, the door to the room burst open, and Knox stormed in. Before I knew what was happening, Hunter was on his feet, standing between the two of us.

"It was my fault, Knox."

"It hurt," I whispered.

Ignoring his brother, Hunter walked over to me and crouched down in front of me. "You did nothing wrong. That one was on me."

"What was on you?" Knox demanded.

"I didn't realize how much the ointment would sting."

Knox joined his brother's side, standing above him and me, looking down at my arms. His face seemed to contort in pain, like he was the one with the ointment being rubbed into the wound.

"The Lycans did that to you?"

When I didn't answer Knox, he moved over to the green box and pulled out a small tub, which rattled. Holding onto it, he marched to a different door.

Moments later, I heard running water. Unable to

stop myself, I cringed, earning myself a curious look from Hunter.

Knox returned to the room, carrying a glass. He set it down on the table beside me and popped open the tub. Two white pills appeared next to the glass. "Take them. They will make you feel better."

"The witch's ointment made me feel better."

Skepticism washed over Knox. "You blew a hole in the fucking wall."

I shrugged. "It hurt. Now it doesn't."

Knox's jaw jutted out, but it was Hunter who spoke first. "Don't push her. Remember what—"

"—I remember what he said." Knox scowled at me. When I stared up at him, he turned on his heel and then stormed out of the door.

"Believe it or not, he's really like a cuddly teddy bear," Hunter said, lightly. When I shrugged, his eyes narrowed. "You know what a teddy bear is, right?"

"No."

Hunter's eyes darkened, and for a moment, he really did look like his twin. Almost as quickly, his eyes brightened, and he flashed me a smile. "Where have you been?"

I kept my lips clamped together.

The idea of trusting anyone felt alien to me. I also

wasn't sure if my judgment was good enough considering I'd never been in a position to trust anyone before. So far, Carter and Hunter had both helped me. *Maybe* they were two people I could trust. But they came with Knox, and he had my heart thumping in my chest.

For now, allowing these people to remove my chains and dress my wounds was the most I could do. I'd been held captive for a long time because of the power I possessed, chained up because I was dangerous.

They'd seen the damage I could cause, but they'd also found a way to help me without me hurting them.

What was to stop them from using that against me in the future?

"I'm sorry. DB said I shouldn't ask." He reached for the ointment and started screwing the lid back on.

"What about the rest of my wrist?" I asked, sticking the limb out in front of me.

Hunter arched an eyebrow. "You just blew a hole in the wall because that hurt you."

I shrugged. "I wasn't ready for it."

"I'm not prepared to hurt you like that again."

"Then give me the ointment and I will do it. I've felt worse."

Hunter closed his eyes and sucked in a deep breath. He held it for a few seconds before blowing it out.

Finally, he unscrewed the ointment jar.

This time, I prepared myself for it and the cold cream. With my hands tightly balled up into fists, Hunter finished applying the salve to my wounds. He didn't say a word despite the tension in his features. Once he finished, he wrapped the white fabric over the top of them.

"That feels . . ." I closed my eyes, realizing I didn't feel anything. No pain. I couldn't stop my smile.

"That ointment will need reapplying daily."

"Daily?" Did that mean they expected me to stay? Was I their prisoner?

"Let's look at your feet now and see if we can make walking around a lot easier for you." Hunter dragged his chair closer to me then he started to reach for my foot but stopped. "May I?"

Chewing at the inside of my cheek, I nodded. Why did he and Carter keep asking me if they could do things?

"How the fuck were you able to stand on these?" Hunter asked in disbelief.

I angled my body so I could look at them. There were no burn marks here, but there were still deep cuts with fragments of rock and rubble embedded there. "I didn't have any other choice."

Hunter sucked in a breath, whistling between his teeth. He shook his head, as though clearing his dark expression, because when he looked at me again, he was smiling. "Let's get these cleaned up and maybe they won't hurt."

Like my wrists, the 'cleaning' of my feet hurt just as much, but when the ointment started to take hold, the pain eased. By the time they were wrapped up in matching white fabric, the pain was barely noticeable.

All of my pain was barely noticeable.

I sat back in the chair, staring in amazement at my limbs. There was a dull throb from under each bandage, but otherwise, I felt . . . nothing.

"Are you okay?" Hunter peered at me.

"I don't hurt."

Hunter stood abruptly, making me jump as he dumped the leftover ointment and fabric onto the tables. "I'm done," he said, gruffly. He left the boxes on the table and left the room.

A new sensation hit me. This one ached as much as anything else had, but it seemed to emanate from my chest. I rubbed at a spot above my heart, wondering what had caused it.

Alone and trying to distract myself, I looked around the room. It was big enough that I could have fit a dozen of the glass prisons in there and still have space left over.

Aside from the enormous bed with four posts, there was the table and chairs I was sitting at, and a sofa. The walls were stone, but a soft brown color. And, as I tilted my head to make sure I wasn't seeing things, there were only three corners. One of the walls curved in a glorious arch, with most of the wall being taken up by the large windows that were letting light stream in.

I walked over to a window and stared out.

In front of me, for as far as I could see, stood trees rising up and down mountainsides. Their leaves were a mixture of colors; mostly dark green, pointy in shape, but interspersed between them were browns, golds, reds and yellows, like patches on fire.

Where was I?

I'd been left alone but been given no instruction to stay where I was. Expecting the door to be locked, I was surprised when it opened easily.

Outside my room, the corridor was long and dark. Smooth, dark wood lined the floors, and the same sandy stone made up the walls. I walked along, looking up at the fabric pictures hanging from the stone. They were mainly replicas of the sight I had seen through the glass, but impressive as they were, they didn't compare with the real thing.

I followed the corridor along until I came to a large staircase, spiraling down into an enormous entrance. The door looked solid, and big enough for a giant to walk through. Even Carter, who was the tallest person I had ever seen, would have head room.

Making my way down the stairs and toward the door, I tested it. Like the bedroom I had been left in, this door was unlocked.

If I wanted to, I could have left. Just like that.

My feet didn't move, though. I stood in the doorway, staring out at the stone path away from the building, toward my freedom, but I couldn't make my feet move.

It wasn't like I owed these men anything, but for some reason, I felt compelled to stay.

Goodbye . . . I could at least say goodbye to them, right?

Shutting the door, I turned back through the entrance and went back into the building. On this level, the floor was stone; the coldness seeping through the fabric bound around my feet.

As I wandered down the hallway, I caught the scent of something new.

Something which made my stomach ache.

Led by my nose, I followed the worn stone hallway until the scent was accompanied by voices. Carter and Hunter were in a kitchen, talking with Knox and a fourth man who had his back to me.

Whatever it was they were discussing was pushed from my mind as I stared at the new person. I had never seen anyone who looked like him before. His skin seemed to be the opposite of mine; dark and warm. Like Knox, he had drawings over his arms, but the pictures were almost lost in the darkness of his skin.

I had the urge to touch him, to run my fingers over his skin to see if it felt like mine.

He turned, locking eyes with me. His eyes were even more mesmerizing. They were silver, looking even bigger than they were behind his glasses.

Silver eyes filled with suspicion and disgust.

Eight

Hunter

"There was bone. I could see down to her fucking bones." I was ranting as I paced, but the other option was punching a hole in the wall and the castle had already acquired one of those today. "And how are you so calm?"

Calm wasn't quite right. DB was kneading bread like it had wronged him. "Did she tell you anything else?" His question was more of a demand.

Even though his back was to me, I shook my head.

Javion, who had been leaning against the wall with his arms folded and scowling at the side of my head, pushed away. "I went on the red web. I went on the dark web. I went on the damn human web, and there's nothing anywhere about elementals other than in fairytales. The kind of fairytales supes tell their kids to keep them in line. Elementals are the damn monsters that live under the monster's beds."

"She's not a monster." I'd seen many things in her, and most of them stemmed from fear. Which, considering she was most likely held prisoner by the Lycans, I wasn't surprised.

"No, she's a harmless glowstick who just happened to annihilate eight Lycans." Knox shot at me.

I sent my twin an irritated look. "Lycans who had been holding her prisoner. She was in those chains for so long, they had worn away her flesh to the fucking bone. Look at what they did to you: you'd gone there to do the same thing and destroy them too."

My words left my mouth before I could stop them.

Knox was in front of me in microseconds, wrapping his hand around my throat "And whose fault was that?"

Instead of grabbing his arms, I swung and punched the side of his head. Knox let go as he recoiled. "It was not my fault."

Once more, the words did more damage than my fists. Knox looked at me, despair and guilt in his eyes. "Knox, I'm—"

"Fuck off." He snarled. In an instant, his eyes had the cold glint to them that I was too familiar with.

I sucked in a deep breath as Knox moved away. There was no point in talking to him. He'd long since stopped listening.

"If she's not an elemental, what is she?" I asked.

"It doesn't matter what she is," Javion said. "The Lycans are vicious and ruthless, but they're not stupid. If they had her locked up, they did it with good reason. We should do the same."

DB turned around, launching his ball of dough in the vague direction of the trash can. It hit the wall beside it with a resounding slap. "Enough." He moved over and glared at the three of us. "We are not the Lycans. We are not locking her up."

"So what? You're going to let her stay in the guest bedroom?" Javion asked, squaring up to our leader.

Javion was old. Older than DB by at least twenty years. There was one time when we'd all gotten drunk, and Javion had let slip that he'd been turned in the early eighties, just after his thirtieth birthday. DB was closer to forty.

But DB was in charge: our alpha. Knox and I were the same kind of supe as him.

Perhaps that was why Javion pushed back so often.

"She is a guest for as long as she wants to be," DB told him. He looked at Knox, then Javion. "And you will both treat her like that."

"Is this because of Manon?"

DB's eyes narrowed, and the gap between him and Javion got smaller. "Enough," he said through gritted teeth.

Javion stepped back, tilting his head. "You're the boss."

"She is a guest," DB said, stressing the last word.

Knox walked over to Javion's side, pushing out his chest as his lip curled up at DB. "I agree with Javion."

DB pointed at the back door. "This isn't a democracy. If you have a problem with my decisions, the door is that way." He looked Javion up and down. "You can use it when the sun sets."

"You're serious?" Knox asked.

I didn't know why he bothered asking. DB rarely joked about anything, never mind our living arrangements.

"She's probably got a family missing her," I said. I

felt like opening the door just to let some of the tension out of the room. "I'm sure once she's had a sleep and something to eat, she's going to want to go home."

For some reason, that idea left a sour taste in my mouth.

"I don't know what she wants, or how she got to be in that situation, but she can stay here as long as she likes." DB stepped back, stalking over to the trash to scoop the mass of dough up from the floor.

"I don't know about what she wants, but I know what she needs." Javion's nose wrinkled up. "Dousing with a hose. Fuck me, that is one awful stench."

Spinning around, I found the female peering at us through the doorway, her blue eyes wide. How much of that had she heard?

I hurried over, opening the door with a warm smile as I fought to keep the revulsion from my face. Javion was right. She did need a shower. *Desperately.* "Come in."

The female inched in, but her attention was fixed on Javion, her eyes still wide. Had she heard what he said?

I glanced over at Javion, checking to be sure he wasn't flashing his fangs at her. He wasn't. He was, however, sending her a stony glare.

"Why are you on your feet?" DB demanded,

suddenly.

The female looked down at her bandaged feet before looking back at DB. "I can't fly?"

If that had been me, the statement would have been laced with sarcasm. The female was speaking like she was stating a fact.

DB moved over to the breakfast bar and pulled out a stool. "Please, sit."

We rarely used the kitchen for anything other than actually making our meals. There were plenty of other rooms in the castle for conversation, entertainment, or even sitting to eat. The only reason we'd ended up in here was because DB was taking his anger out on yeast.

The stool was tall, and the female eyed it warily before moving over and climbing onto it. As she sat down, I finally looked at her.

Until now, I had been focused on making sure her wounds had been dressed. I'd given her a sweeping glance and had acknowledged she was in a poor state, but I'd not allowed myself to see her properly.

Looking at her made my heart hurt. Her hair might have been black, or it might have been blonde. It was hard to tell considering how dirty and matted it was. Her hair hung down her back in a knotted lump. Rescuing that was going to take a lot of conditioner and patience with a comb, and even then, I was sure she'd lose several inches.

Once again, I found myself wondering where she had been and what she had been through if that was the state of her hair.

And her hair wasn't the worst of it. Her skin was covered in dirt, so dark and thick, that some places had crusted over. She had wounds on her wrists and feet, but there was also dried blood mixed in with dirt, which had me convinced there had been other injuries she'd endured.

But nothing made me as angry as her figure. The clothes—if you could call the disgusting *rag* she wore clothing—clung to her and did nothing to hide the fact that she was little more than skin and bones. It was no wonder we had thought she was a ghoul. She looked like the walking dead.

We'd been hunting Lycans for years with no luck, but just looking at her made me want to get back out there and find every last one of them just so I could pull their spines out through their throats.

Her blue eyes, squinting, were still fixed on Javion, meeting his own scowl head on. "That's Javion."

"What would you like to eat?" DB asked her, kindly.

The female's attention finally left Javion in order to look at our leader. She raised a shoulder, her face twisting in confusion.

Confusion?

DB leaned against the other side of the counter. "What's your favorite meal? Javion's a grumpy bastard, but he's a decent cook. He'll be able to whip up almost anything."

Javion arched an eyebrow but didn't say anything.

Javion didn't cook.

"I don't have one," the female replied.

"There must be something you like?" I asked her. "What did they feed you before?"

She turned to me and slowly shook her head. "They didn't."

I had suspected that I wouldn't like the answer to my question, guessing that the answer would be bread and water, or some other bullshit given her figure.

Her answer made my blood boil.

Behind her, DB's hands curled into fists. Even Javion seemed taken aback by her response.

"Not a single meal?" I asked.

The female shook her head.

Supes were different from human. We were stronger, bigger, and depending on what type of supe we were, we had certain traits and qualities specific to us, like the female's electricity or the rock-hard skin and wings that DB, Knox and I had.

We were also usually gifted with advanced healing abilities. Human disease didn't affect us, and we could recover from broken limbs in days instead of weeks.

It also meant that food and water weren't necessities for us. We could go a lot longer without, drawing energy from other resources. For us, it was the ground.

Javion . . . Javion was one of the anomalies . . .

But even Javion would have chosen to eat something after a while.

Yes, it was entirely possible that this female had never eaten a meal while being held captive—and still be alive—but a supe still needed some sustenance after a while.

I rubbed a hand over my jaw, trying not to react to her answer.

They hadn't fed her.

They hadn't fed her, *and* she couldn't tell us a food she liked.

How long had they held her for?

The door to the kitchen slammed shut before I realized Knox had left the room.

"I'll make you some pancakes," DB told her.

"No," Javion said, abruptly. He walked straight up to her, ignoring an earlier warning from DB to give her space, and stared straight at her. I couldn't help but be impressed when she stared back at him. "You have been fed nothing?"

"Nothing."

"Javion." DB said his name like a growl.

"Since when?"

"Javion." DB went to step around to the other side of the breakfast bar, but the female's words made him stop.

"Ever."

"Why?" Javion slammed his hand down on the breakfast bar, boxing her in. The second she flinched, I was at her side, just as DB grabbed Javion by the scruff of his collar and jerked him away.

"Back off," DB snarled, getting between him and the female.

Javion's hands flew into the air before he turned on his heel and marched toward the door. He opened it but paused before looking back.

"The only reason you don't feed a supe is to weaken them. You might want to think about why they chose to do that before you let her stay."

Nine

Battery

The door slammed shut, echoing around the large kitchen, but I was sure it wasn't as loud as the noise my heart was making inside me. Javion was beautiful, but there was also something inherently dangerous about him that I couldn't put my finger on. He had the eyes of a predator, watching me like he was seeking out my weak spot before going in for the kill.

Of the four of them, he was the one that scared me

most. Given the chance, I was sure he would be the one to turn on me.

It was abundantly clear I wasn't welcome here.

Closing my eyes, I tried to cast my mind back to when I was a child. The few memories I had outside of the glass prison. None involved food.

Inside the prison, there wasn't a memory of food, either. I'd witnessed Carl and the other guards eating on shifts, but even the smells hadn't made their way into the room I was in.

Of all the times I could remember, I hadn't had a bite of anything to eat. Had they really done that to weaken me? I could still take out a pack of Lycans in my 'weakened' state.

Javion was right to be wary of me.

I was dangerous.

The thought sent a pleasant thrum through me. Maybe I could find out just how dangerous I was. If I could find out what my unweakened state was, I could return to that prison and destroy it. And every Lycan in it.

"Are you okay, Blue Eyes?"

I opened my eyes and found Carter watching me. "He doesn't want me here."

"Don't worry about Javion. Let's fix you something

to eat." DB moved back to the other side of the counter and opened a cupboard, pulling out a small sack.

"Did you really have nothing to eat all that time?" Hunter asked.

I kept my eyes trained on DB, partly because I was fascinated with what he was doing, but also to avoid looking at Hunter. I wasn't sure why his questions made me so uncomfortable. "Yes."

Out of the corner of my eye, I could see Hunter open his mouth as though to say something, but he quickly clamped it shut. Instead, he moved to the seat next to me and sat down.

Hunter let out a long sigh before angling his body to face me. "What's your name?"

Carter was spooning white powder into a bowl, but I could tell he was listening. I chewed at the inside of my lip, watching as he went to the enormous fridge and pulled a long box and a bottle of white liquid out of it.

"Please?"

I turned to Hunter, regretting it as his green eyes captured me. "I don't know."

He cocked his head, frowning. "You don't know your name?"

"If I do, I don't remember it."

Hunter's head tilted in the other direction. "Do you

have amnesia?" He quickly shook his head. "You wouldn't remember if you did . . . how far back can you remember? They must have called you something."

"Battery."

Hunter's nose wrinkled up. He glanced over at DB, his eyes widening. "Oh, no, *batter*. He's making pancake batter."

"They called me Battery."

There was a crack and a wet splatter, and I looked up just in time to witness DB curse at the slimy yellow thing on the floor between his feet.

I shifted, feeling uncomfortable under Hunter's mortified stare. "You asked me what they called me."

Hunter stood, the stool screeching behind him as he did.

"Hunter, sit down," Carter snapped at him.

Without any hesitation, Hunter did as he was commanded. Refusing to look at either me or Carter, Hunter folded his arms and seethed at the worktop in front of him. "I am not calling you fucking *Battery*."

I lowered my head and stared at my lap. Hunter had asked what they had called me, and I had told him. Why was he angry with me?

Why did I care?

I didn't like being called Battery. I also didn't like

that I couldn't remember my name. But until now, neither had seemed really important to me.

Why would I want a name when what I had wanted was to die?

I sat upright, blinking rapidly; not because Carter had pushed a plate in front of me, but because I no longer wanted to die.

"It's a pancake."

"Where's the rest of them?" Hunter asked, turning almost horizontal as he stared at the plate in disbelief. "If the first food she's going to eat is pancakes, they need to be stacked high."

"It doesn't matter what the first food is that she eats. If it's the first thing she eats, she needs to eat a little at a time, or she's just going to throw it back up. Little and often."

The pancake was round and brown, and while it didn't look like much, it smelled incredible. My mouth watered, and my questions about my future disappeared.

I reached for the disc and picked it up. Almost instantly, I dropped it. "Ow."

"Here." Carter pushed a knife and fork toward me.

Without thinking, I reached for them.

Hunter's hand clapped down on them, stopping

them from coming close to me. "No." He gathered them up and dropped off his chair to walk to the other side of the kitchen.

Hunter opened a drawer and deposited the knife and fork in them before dropping to his knees and almost climbing into a cupboard. He reappeared a moment later with a packet of white knives and forks. Extracting one of each, he handed them over.

Carter watched with mild amusement.

"What?" Hunter asked.

"I don't think cutlery is going to be an issue."

"They're silver. It's one of the most conductive metals on the planet," Hunter said, looking at Carter like he was an idiot. "We can't give her metal."

Somehow, Carter didn't seem offended. He only smiled. "And yet, she managed to open every door between the bedroom and here."

Both Hunter and I turned to look at the door. Carter was right; I had opened all of the doors by their handles, and they hadn't affected me. But everything metal that I had touched since escaping the glass prison had made the electricity whip across my skin.

My gaze dropped to my bandaged wrists. They were the only thing that had changed, but now, aside from the dull throb beneath the white fabric, nothing hurt.

"Don't worry about it now," Carter said, gently. "Eat up."

My eyes drifted slightly higher to the plastic utensils in my fists. I'd watched people use these on the unsolved murder reenactments I would watch with Carl, usually before they ate a meal laced with . . .

"Is there poison in this?"

Carter scratched at the back of his head while Hunter's mouth dropped open.

"You watched me make it, Blue Eyes."

"Why would DB want to poison you?" Hunter blurted out.

I bit at my lip and thought about it. So far, Carter—and Hunter —had only tried to help me. "It's a common way to murder someone."

"What? With flour, eggs and milk?" Hunter's eyes were nearly bulging out of his head.

Carter grabbed a fork from the drawer before walking over to cut a bit off. Without any hesitation, he ate it. "Feel better?"

I could feel my face getting hot, and I dropped my gaze. Maybe I shouldn't have asked, but the people on these shows always ended up dead. I didn't want that anymore.

"Okay, wait," Hunter said, suddenly. He went into a cupboard and produced a bottle with golden liquid in it.

"Hunter, maple syrup is going to be too rich for her." Carter sighed.

Hunter shook his head and walked over to the counter. "I know, but just a little. It's a pancake. It's her first meal in who knows how long. She can't just have her first pancake without a little sweetness. Everyone's first time has got to be special, right?" He looked up at me and winked.

As Carter rolled his eyes, Hunter leaned over and poured a little bit of the gold liquid over the pancake. Next, he wiped his finger around the lip of the bottle lid and stuck it in his mouth. "And I promise, it's not poisoned either."

The sweet aroma flooded my nose. Once more, my mouth started watering.

Unable to wait any longer, I dug into the pancake.

It was like heaven in a bite. The pancake was no longer hot—it was barely warm—but it was light, fluffy, and the maple syrup was so sweet, it made my teeth tingle.

I was glad I'd never been given food because having eaten something like this and then not being able to eat it again—that would have been almost as unbearable as the current passing through my body.

It didn't take me long to devour the pancake. Halfway through, I abandoned the knife and fork—they were too awkward—and just used my fingers. I finished every last bit on the plate before I sat back.

When I finally looked at Carter and Hunter, they were both watching me with raised eyebrows. "What?"

Hunter opened his mouth, but Carter responded first. "If you enjoyed that, I will make you a second, but I think we should then wait a while before you have more. Your body is not used to food, and I don't want to make you ill."

I nodded, eagerly. "Yes."

While Carter went to make a second pancake, Hunter came back and sat down beside me. "What are your plans?"

"What do you mean?"

"Where were you going when we found you?" Hunter asked.

I wasn't *going* anywhere. I was leaving somewhere.

Things had been happening so quickly that I didn't know what I was doing. I wasn't sure how long I'd been in this place, but the last time I had woken up before this, I had wanted to die.

Then I had wanted to live.

Now . . .?

"I don't know," I admitted.

"No one is forcing you to make any decisions now," Carter told me. He put a cover over the leftover pancake mix and put it, and the other ingredients away. "You can stay here for a while."

I started to nod but stopped. Doubt flooded me. I didn't know these people, and they didn't know me. So why would they let me stay here? They had seen what I was capable of, and I was sure that was beginning.

Or was that *exactly* why they were allowing me to stay? They knew what I could do, and they planned to use me in the same way the Lycans had?

My gaze dropped to the empty plate in front of me, and then to my bandages. The Lycans had never fed me. They'd never dressed my wounds. Hell, they'd never taken the chains off my wrists.

The truth was, I knew nothing.

I had lived in a glass house for most all of my life.

I didn't know how the world worked or how to survive in it. The shows I had watched, which had given me a glimpse into what the world was like, were full of things I didn't understand. People had homes—how did you get one of those? Or even just shelter.

The only thing the Lycans and the television shows had consistently taught me was that everyone either wanted to kill me or fuck me.

The smart thing to do would be to stay. Stay for a few days while I healed. Eat their food and see what that did to the electrical energy inside of me. Learn as much as I could to survive.

Then I could get the hell out of here.

I finally looked up at Carter, meeting his dark blue eyes. Neither he nor Hunter had spoken while I'd been thinking. Instead, they waited patiently for me. "I will stay until I have healed."

"Great," Hunter said loudly. He leaned back in the chair. "Now we're going to give you a name."

"Hunter." Carter was using his warning tone again.

"I can't keep calling her *her*, and I'm not calling her Battery," he said, his lips contorting on the last word like it had put a foul taste in his mouth.

Carter sucked in a deep breath, clutching at the edge of the counter. "You can't just *give* her a name." He exhaled and then looked at me. "You have no recollection of your name at all?"

I shook my head.

"Then is there anything you would like us to call you?"

There weren't many names that I knew. Most were of the guards, and I didn't want to be called anything remotely close to them. From the documentaries, there were only a few I could recall.

"Carol?" I suggested.

Hunter made a face. "You don't look like a Carol."

"You can look like a name?" I asked, confused.

"Yep," Hunter said with a nod. "And while I don't have anything against the name, Carol, you don't look like one."

"Dorothea? Myra?"

Carter and Hunter shared a look. "Do you . . . do you like those names?" Carter asked.

I shrugged.

"Maybe we could come up with something until she remembers her name?" Hunter offered.

"Great idea," Carter quickly agreed.

Hadn't that been a bad idea a few minutes ago? Were my name suggestions really that terrible?

Carter looked me up and down. "Sapphire."

Hunter shook his head. "She's not a Sapphire."

Carter leaned forward. "Tempest."

This time, it was me who shook my head. It wasn't that I didn't like it, but it didn't feel like me.

"Pikachu," Hunter said with a grin.

With an irritated sigh, Carter stepped back and swiped at the air just in front of Hunter's head. "We're not giving her the name of a goddamn Pokémon."

"A what?"

"Elektra," Hunter said, ignoring my question.

Carter fixed him with a glare. "Is that a Pokémon?"

"A Marvel character and a Greek goddess, depending on how you spell it."

Pinching the bridge of his nose, Carter rocked back on his heels. "Hunter." That low warning tone was back.

"Oh, come on. It's better than *Tempest*." When Carter lowered his hand to scowl at the younger man, Hunter shrugged. "Fine."

"It doesn't really matter," I said, feeling bad that they were now arguing over what to call me. It wasn't Battery. If Carter liked Tempest, I'd go with Tempest. It was only going to be for a few days, anyway . . .

"Zeraora," Hunter said, suddenly. "Zera."

"I like that," I blurted out.

Carter turned to me and gave me a gentle smile. "Your name does matter, Blue Eyes. You need to like it."

"But I do like Zera," I told him. "Zera." The name rolled off my tongue. That was much better than the other suggestions.

A big grin broke out on Hunter's face, lighting it up. "You do."

Carter tilted his head. "You do?"

I nodded. And then I yawned.

"You look surprised," Carter said, leaning forward to rest his weight on his forearms as he watched me.

"I am . . . tired?" I asked, unfamiliar with the sensation.

"You've been through a lot, and your body wants to heal. It's not surprising, really. Even for supernaturals like us, we still need to rest and allow our bodies to recover."

"I haven't until now."

The happy expression on Hunter's face slowly disappeared and was replaced with thinned lips. "Recovered or rested?"

My eyes once again drifted to my bandaged wrists. "Both."

"I swear to the gods—"

"Not now, Hunter." Carter's warning tone was back.

I looked over at Hunter and found him scowling at the counter. I didn't like the way his forehead wrinkled like that. Lightness was a better look on him.

"Worry not, Zeraora," Carter said, dragging my attention to him. His face carried no frowns as he looked at me, but his body was tense. "While you stay here, you may rest when you need, and eat and drink as you need."

Eat and drink as I needed?

Leaning to the side, I glanced behind him at the kitchen that was so big, his enormous frame didn't look lost in it. Unlike me: I had no idea where to start in there.

"One of us will be around if you want anything," Hunter added. "All you need to do is ask."

I dropped my head again, not wanting them to see my face. I didn't know enough in the world to be able to trust myself, never mind them. The last thing I needed was to have that trust used against me.

But if they kept saying things like this, I was going to want to stay.

Ten

Zera

Sleep was as wonderous an experience as eating. After all the years I'd been held prisoner and only ever lost consciousness, I'd assumed it was the same. It was indeed similar, but the feeling of waking up was incomparable.

When I'd regained consciousness the day before, I hadn't fully appreciated the bed I had been lying in. Now, I stretched my arms out, allowing my fingers to drift over the fabric. Soft.

For the first time, I also wasn't experiencing pain so bad that I wanted to die.

I'd never realized before, how much of me had been consumed by that pain. It had taken over my mind so that, not only were my thoughts ruled by it, but I hadn't been able to focus on anything else around me, never mind being able to form thoughts.

This wasn't the time for complacency.

Relaxed and comfortable as I was in this bed, this was only a temporary situation. I needed to use this time to plan my next move and prepare for it.

I needed to learn.

Yawning, I sat up and stretched. There might not have been the constant excruciating pain, but there was still a dull ache, my muscles protesting.

I pulled back the covers to get out of the bed, and a gasp left my mouth. "No," I muttered, scrambling off the bed.

The pale bedsheets were filthy. Dark smears stained the fabric where I'd been lying.

Had that come from me?

Of course the dirt had come from me. It was obvious from the outline in the bed.

Hanging on the wall opposite the door was a large mirror. I walked over and stood in front of it.

Back in my prison, I'd caught rare glimpses of my reflection in the glass, but I'd never really cared about how I looked. Color-wise, it was hard to tell where the slip I wore ended and my skin began.

If it wasn't for the water stains on my arms and legs, I would have assumed gray-brown was the natural color of my skin. In some places, the dirt was thicker and darker.

The dirt was broken up with red marks, dark scabs, and some mottled patches of blue and purple bruises. Most of these injuries were obtained when I escaped.

Hunter's hair seemed to bounce when he walked, and Knox's danced as the air brushed through it.

My hair hung down my back in one thick, dark, matted clump. I couldn't even push my fingers through it.

Behind me, there was a knock at the door. I turned and waited. There was another knock.

After the third knock, it opened, and Knox stepped in. The concern on his face was quickly replaced with narrowed eyes. "What are you doing?"

"I'm trying to work out what I look like."

"A stinking mess?"

I raised my arm and brought it to my nose. *Do I smell?*

Knox rolled his eyes. "Considering you look like you've not had a shower in weeks, I doubt you're going to be able to smell the stench." He walked over to the bed and dropped a pile of things onto the bedspread, spotting the dark smear on the bedsheets. "You might want to consider one of those pretty fucking quick."

"How do I do that?" I asked him.

Knox turned back to me, arching an eyebrow. "Shower?"

I nodded.

He pointed at the door in the corner. "Turn it on, step in and use a shit-ton of soap. And when you think you've used enough, double up and use more, because I promise you, you need it."

For some reason, his words brought a lump to my throat.

On the list of things that I cared about, my appearance had never been there. Trying to die had taken a greater priority. Plus, there was also the hope that looking how I did would have stopped Bacco from jerking off because of me.

I glanced over my shoulder into the mirror. My reflection made me wince, but not as much as Knox's words did. Driven as much by the desire not to have Knox look at me with revulsion as well as my own need to see what I really looked like, I headed to the bathroom.

I stopped in the middle of the bathroom. This was another room that was bigger than my prison had been. The whole room was covered in white tiles with an occasional blue tile. The wall opposite the door was almost entirely a window made up of small pieces of diamond-shaped glass.

Outside I was rewarded with a similar view to the one from the bedroom: miles and miles of trees and mountains. I wasn't sure of the time, but it was light out, even though the sun was hidden behind dark clouds.

Inside, there was an enormous bathtub in front of the window.

"I wouldn't bother with that yet," Knox told me.

Turning, I looked at him. "What?"

"The bath. You're just going to end up sitting in your own dirt. You need a shower." Knox pointed to an alcove.

I stepped closer to take a better look. It was just a square area.

And then Knox reached over and opened a glass door. The glass had been so clean that I hadn't even noticed it.

Blood felt like it was rushing to my feet as my lungs

seemed to stop filling. "No." I wasn't even sure if the word left my mouth.

Knox leaned in and flipped something, and water started gushing out.

All of a sudden, I was back in that glass cell.

My wrists felt heavy and when I looked down, the bandages had been replaced with shackles. Electricity erupted from my skin under the metal on one hand, rushing across my skin, stabbing me as it moved. When it hit the other shackle, I dropped to my knees.

All I could hear was the water hitting the floor and the crackle of electricity in the air.

Let me die.

Protecting my head with my arms, I closed my eyes. In the deepest part of my mind, it registered that was odd, but it was quickly drowned out by my body reacting to the agonizing feeling of the power whipping it.

Not again.

I couldn't face this again.

Let me die.

I sensed something in front of me, and I opened my eyes to see boots there.

Bacco.

No.

I screamed.

Electricity poured from me. It whipped and cracked through the air in large arcing bolts.

On the far side of the room, the window exploded. Glass flew through the air.

At the same time, the figure in front of me shot backwards, slamming into the wall.

My vision cleared.

I wasn't in the cell. I was in a bathroom. The bathroom of the people who tried to help me.

Electricity continued to crackle over my skin until I looked at the figure.

Knox.

He was slumped against the wall.

My mind went blank as the power in me cut out. I didn't have a ghost telling me to escape. This time, I was on my own.

Wind whipped in and I turned to face the hole which had once been a window.

Another hole.

I ran toward it and leaped.

Eleven

Knox

"She called herself what?"

Hunter gave me a smug smile which made me instantly suspicious. "Zeraora. Well, Zera."

I narrowed my eyes. I knew my brother too well to know that there was more to that name. However, I didn't dislike it. There was a spikiness to it that suited her.

"She will be staying here for a while," DB said.

"You've said that." I reached for my coffee and

took a sip. *Twice.*

"Just making sure it's abundantly clear." He stirred the contents of the pot on the stove. Oatmeal. We'd not eaten oatmeal in months, and I was sure this morning's breakfast choice had something to do with the female—Zera.

It *was* abundantly clear. It had been yesterday when he'd said his piece.

But like yesterday, I still hadn't decided how I felt about it. I'd spent the night with Javion, and we'd done our research on elementals. There wasn't much out there, but the little that there was?

She was dangerous.

Fuck, I'd witnessed her wipe out a pack of Lycans firsthand. Of course, she was dangerous.

But the female was so small. Not just in height, but in mass.

It wasn't that I thought her size made her harmless. It was *why* she was so slight.

She'd been used by the Lycans. There was no doubt about that. Apparently, everyone thought elementals didn't exist anymore because they had been used as power sources until they died out.

If she was an elemental—and I was happy to accept that fact—it sounded exactly like the kind of sick and twisted thing the Lycans would do.

Collectively, we agreed that she had been held by the Lycans for a long time. Too long.

The length of time for that amount of torture didn't leave anyone without scars. And not just the physical ones.

You could see it with the questions she asked. She wasn't . . . right.

But neither was I.

Which was exactly why I didn't trust her.

"Then she needs to take a fucking shower," I said with a grunt.

"You're not wrong," Hunter said, sitting at the table opposite me.

As he sat, I stood.

"Where are you going?"

"To make sure she gets that shower. I'm not eating breakfast with something that smells like a sweaty sock that's been fermenting in a dead skunk's asshole." I swear I could smell it down here, either lingering from her presence yesterday, or seeping through the house now.

If it was the latter, her mattress was going to need burning.

"Knox, do not upset Zeraora."

I looked over at DB and waved the back of my hand at him. "Relax. I'm going to give her some clothes and ask that she showers before she joins us."

Okay . . . maybe I was going to *insist*.

"I have some clothes on my bed for her," DB said just before I closed the door.

Out in the corridor I arched an eyebrow. Either DB had found an old T-shirt for her to wear as a dress, or he'd . . . *no*. I shook my head and hurried upstairs to DB's room.

The door was ajar, and I walked in.

I'd never met his late wife, but she lingered in the room. Feminine touches here and there which, over time, I'd learned had definitely not come from DB.

The floral netting which hung from the four-poster bed. Perfumes and jewelry that still sat on the dressing table. In the bathroom, the second toothbrush beside the twin sink.

Her face had gone. I'd never seen a single picture of his Manon in Castle Viegls. But her ghost seemed to remain. Which was why it surprised me that the clothes DB had left on his bed were probably hers.

I picked up the floral dress and wrinkled my nose, trying to picture the woman who would have worn it. The image I conjured wasn't the filthy female in the guestroom.

Then again, it also wasn't a woman I pictured with DB.

I left the room and went to mine. While I didn't have a mysterious woman in my past—none would touch me—DB hadn't left any shoes. Although I figured most of my shoes would swallow her feet, I had some flipflops.

I'd seen the state of her feet, and she shouldn't be walking around on them barefoot.

Bent over and reaching for the shoes in the back of my closet, I frowned. Why did I care about her feet? I shook my head and grabbed the shoes, then headed to her room.

She was still there. The pungent smell of stale body odor, old blood, and what I could only attribute to decay, seeped out from under the door. I covered my nose with the back of my hand and knocked.

Nothing.

I knocked again. And again.

Fine . . . if she didn't want to invite me in, she could skip the clothes and breakfast. But as I started to turn, another thought hit me.

What if something had happened during the night?

I wasn't sure why that bothered me, but I pushed

open the door, expecting to find her on the floor.

She was in front of the mirror staring at her fucking reflection.

"What are you doing?" I demanded, waiting for my racing heart to calm.

Her eyes met mine through the mirror. "I'm trying to work out what I look like."

What the actual fuck? How could she not know what she looked like?

I dragged my eyes over her body. She was far too skinny, to the point that simply looking at her arms and collar bones made me uncomfortable. Cuts, bruises, and wounds fueled my hatred for the Lycans even more, like pouring gas on burning rage. Big eyes stared at me with a mixture of innocence and devastation.

"A stinking mess?"

Those eyes filled with confusion and then she started sniffing herself.

"Considering you look like you've not had a shower in weeks, I doubt you're going to be able to smell the stench."

She'd need to soak in a tub for days to even begin to counteract that offending aroma. I took a step forward and almost gagged.

Fucking hell . . . I was not going to stick around for

this. I was quickly losing my appetite. Moving to the bed, I placed the dress and shoes on the corner. And then I saw the state of the sheets.

The female was so fucking filthy she'd left an outline on the bed like something out of a crime scene. Maybe her state wasn't her fault, but she wasn't there anymore.

The only thing that could help in this situation would be taking a shower, and I would drag her into one if that's what it took. "You might want to consider a shower pretty fucking sharpish."

"How do I do that?" she asked.

It took me a second even process the question. Did she not understand me, or had she never used a shower before? For some reason, I figured it was the latter. "Shower?"

When she nodded at me, her eyes wide, it took everything in me not to react. I'd assumed that I had reached my anger limit when it came to the Lycans, but right now, they were proving that wrong.

Very slowly, trying to keep the rage from making my arm shake, I raised my arm. "Turn it on, step in and use a shit-ton of soap. And when you think you've used enough, double up and use more, because I promise you, you need it."

I'd kept the anger from my arm, but not my voice. My words came out in a growl.

Certain I saw tears forming in the corner of her eyes, I followed her to the bathroom. Probably not the right move given the circumstances, but guilt flooded me at the mere idea that I had upset her.

She needed to be protected.

I needed to protect her.

Where the fuck did that come from?

"What are you doing?" She had stopped in the middle of the room and was looking around like she'd never seen a bathroom before.

Probably hadn't.

Her gaze lingered on the bathtub. Visions of her in it flooded my imagination.

The fuck, Knox?

This female was dangerous, and these kinds of thoughts needed to stop. I was not about to let myself get distracted by a pair of legs that wouldn't even look twice in my direction.

"I wouldn't bother with that yet," I told her. "The bath. You're just going to end up sitting in your own dirt. You need a shower."

I pointed to the shower and held the door open as she came near. She stopped some feet back, and I let out an irritated sigh. Why was it so damn hard to get her to clean herself?

Reaching in, I turned it on, checking the temperature of the water. The old boiler was in the basement on the far side of the castle. It worked well; I'd made sure of that. But it also took a little bit of time for the water to work through the pipes.

Finally, it came out warm. I stepped back, ready to leave and let Zera shower—or push her under if needed—and found her on the floor.

She was crouched down, hands over her head, and rocking. She was shaking. Huge, wracking tremors.

"The fuck?" I muttered under my breath. "Zera?" I stepped forward, my hand hovering above her shoulder.

Electricity sparked over her skin.

Before I could back away, she screamed.

Simultaneously, the electricity crawling over her body seemed to ignite. Like a thousand whips lashing the air. Shooting out in all directions.

As one hit the window shattering the glass, another hit me square in the chest.

I was flung backwards, across the room until I hit the wall.

Sliding down it, my body jerked as electricity played

havoc with my nerves.

This was worse than the last time she had exploded. Whether it was the small area, or the fact that I was the only living thing around to take the brunt of the hit, I'd taken more power than if I'd been shocked by an outlet.

And I'd experienced that one before.

Thankfully, my skin, though scarred and disfigured, was still tough enough to withstand it. The stone in me grounded the electricity just in time to see the female leap out the window.

She was absolutely batshit crazy.

"Zera," I yelled, getting to my feet.

Slow and stumbling as my body kicked back into gear, I ran to the missing window and stared down.

Castle Viegls was built on the side of a cliff made of granite. The south side didn't open up to a garden, but a sheer drop.

Thirty feet and then nothing but forest floor. I could survive this drop. My body was toughened and made of a harder substance when in my true form.

Elementals were not . . .

Only questioning my action when I was halfway down, I leaped out of the window and followed her.

I expected to find her on the ground, dead. There was nothing.

Nothing but her pungent scent.

Following my nose, I tore after her. It didn't take long to catch up. She'd gotten to the bank of the lake. From this side, the ground was above, jutting out on a rock. Her head was turning from side to side as she stared out across the water.

With her back to me, I approached carefully. "Zera?"

The closer I got, I realized she was still shaking. I was sure it wasn't from the cold mountain air.

"Zera?"

She finally turned. Her blue eyes were glowing.

The shaking wasn't cold or fear.

It was rage.

"I am going to kill them all," she snarled at me as though I was stopping her.

"Kill who?"

"The ones that did this to me. The Lycans."

Suddenly, standing in front of me wasn't a weak, small female. She was dangerous, just as I'd suspected. But in the most glorious way possible. There was beauty in that pain, and anger.

And I wanted it.

I stepped forward without thinking about what I was doing.

The anger in her eyes evaporated and was replaced by fear. "Don't touch me," she yelled. She stepped backwards. And then she was falling backwards.

My hands reached out, but they weren't quick enough. Her body slipped through my grasp, off the small stone ledge, and hit the water.

I pulled my jacket off, throwing it to the side, then dove in after her.

The water was icy and even with my toughened skin, it felt like I was being stabbed all over. She was just in front of me, thrashing around in a cloud of bubbles.

Wrapping my hands around the rag of a dress she was wearing, I pulled her upwards. We broke the surface and I sucked in a deep breath.

I pulled us both to the bank, out of the water and onto the grass. Making sure she was laid down gently, I then flopped to the side, lying on my back as I tried to catch my breath.

Beside me, she sucked in a breath. I didn't know what it was about that action, but it made me lose my shit.

My fists hit the ground beside me and then I rolled over, a hand on either side of her head. "Are you fucking insane?"

Twelve

Zera

Too many thoughts and sensations were attacking my mind and body at once. The icy water had shocked me, and I could barely move.

Water.

I fell into water, yet I was alive.

My body was in pain, but it wasn't from electricity. I hadn't even felt a single charge. It hurt in my chest. My lungs. They were struggling to fill with air, but the cold air was scratching my throat.

The pain wasn't from electricity.

That made no sense.

My whole life had been spent wet; either from water pouring over me or puddles on the cell floor that were never let to dry.

I sucked in a breath, oxygen and relief finally filling my lungs.

The next thing I knew, Knox was hovering over me. "Are you fucking insane?"

I froze. If I moved an inch, we would be touching. And that . . . I didn't want to kill him.

"Who the *fuck* jumps out of a window?"

Knox's face was inches from mine. Despite the fact that he was shouting at me, I barely heard him. I was too distracted by his face.

It was like seeing him for the first time. I could see detail. The green in his eyes wasn't just green. They were ringed in black, which was what made them look so dark.

Black hair, water from it dripping onto my face, was brushed to the side, revealing a metal bar punctured through his eyebrow. More metal lined his right ear. And when he spoke, I kept seeing flashes of two metal balls.

More distracting than that were three scars that started above the pieces of metal above his eyebrow and stretched down his cheek.

Claw marks.

"Zera." His fist slammed down on the ground next to me. "Are you fucking listening to me?"

I blinked as volume seemed to rush back in. Before he could repeat his question, my brain seemed to process it. "No," I told him, truthfully.

Knox stilled. He scowled while his teeth caught the first of his tongue piercings between them.

My gaze drifted to the bar, unable to look away. How could he have so much metal in him?

Feeling cold was no longer a problem.

"I asked you why you jumped out of the window."

My mind flashed back to the shower. As it did, I could feel the electricity crackling at my palms. "You need to get away from me," I whispered.

He'd saved my life, so I didn't want to take his.

"You need to answer my fucking questions."

"I will kill you." It wasn't a threat, but a fact. "You're not the one I want to kill."

Knox cocked his head, sending another drop of water splashing on my cheek. "You want to go after the Lycans? By yourself?"

I hadn't realized it until now, but I did. No longer did I wish to die. I wanted the Lycans to die. Every last one of them.

Thanks to them I had no idea who I was or where I was from. I was alone. I didn't know if I had a family.

For decades, I'd been their prisoner—their power source. A commodity.

And I wanted revenge.

"I want to make every last one of them suffer."

A growl erupted from the back of Knox's throat as he lowered his head toward mine.

"Don't."

At the last minute, he stopped. His lips were millimeters from mine. "Zera, I'm claiming you as mine, which means I'm not going to hurt you, and I'm not going to let any other fucker hurt you."

His words and the intensity in his eyes had heat pooling between my legs. As if my brain had relocated to my vagina, it was screaming out at me to act on that. His lips were close enough that I could claim them.

The electricity crackled in my palms, and I closed my eyes, fighting against the charge.

I could feel Knox move away, and when I opened my eyes, he was sitting beside me, running his hand through his hair. I sat up, keeping a safe distance between us. "Knox?"

He waved his hand, refusing to look at me. "It's fine. I get it. I know what you see." Taking a deep breath, he rose to his feet. "I won't touch you, but I'm still claiming you as mine."

I watched him walk away to pick up something off the ground—his jacket. He returned moments later and draped the jacket over my shoulders. The weight felt reassuring. It also provided me with the instant warmth I needed.

"Can you walk?"

Knox offered me a hand, but I refused to take it. Instead, I scrambled to my feet. My legs felt weak, like they were going to give out if I stood there too long. There was also a new pain in my heels from where I had landed when I jumped out of the window. "I can walk."

With each step we took, the grumpiness seemed to settle over Knox like a shield. I had made him angry.

That was okay; it was better to be angry than dead.

Knox walked by my side, keeping a safe distance. The silence broke on occasion when he muttered under his breath about me being out in 'my condition.'

I wasn't really paying attention. Most of my energy was spent on walking. My body was cold, and my legs didn't want to cooperate. As I clutched at the soft leather of his jacket, keeping it wrapped tightly around me, my mind was preoccupied.

The jacket smelled of him. There was something almost mechanical about the smell that I couldn't name.

Every so often I would send sneaky glances in his direction. With the distance between us, I could no longer see the scars on his face. I kept squinting, trying to see them, but if my gaze lingered on his face for long enough, Knox would turn and give me a scowl.

I had zero experience when it came to men.

Considering my ability to fry people, it was going to remain that way.

But I wanted to know what he had meant when he said he was claiming me.

It wasn't a long walk back to his home. Eventually, we returned to a dirt track and the building was finally revealed to me.

Thoughts of Knox were pushed to the back of my mind as I gaped up. "You live in a . . . a . . ."

"This is Castle Viegls."

It rose like a dragon, half hidden in the shadows from the mountain around it. Dark stone like the rock it sat on made up the walls. We had to pass through a gate in the center of the wall.

Inside, the gardens were well kept, with all kinds of

colors bursting out the borders. Past the gardens and at the end of the drive, Castle Viegls, with its two-story building complete with cone-topped towers and painted-glass window, stretched out in either direction.

Knox didn't wait for me. He strode toward the main door, picking up his pace, and I hurried to catch up with him.

As I walked inside, Hunter was walking down the stairs. "What the ever-loving fuck happened?"

"It was nothing," Knox said with a dismissive wave of his hand.

"Nothing?" Hunter's eyes almost bulged out of his head. "Nothing? Knox, half of the fucking bathroom is missing. Meanwhile, you and Zera waltz in like you've been having a fucking swimming lesson. In *November*."

"It was my fault," I offered. "Don't get mad at Knox."

Knox's shoulders tensed. He looked at his twin, pointedly ignoring me. "She needs a bath. Don't you dare try to use the shower or your bathroom will get remodeled too."

As Hunter gaped at him, eyes wide, Knox strode down the corridor. Slowly, Hunter turned to me and then he did a doubletake. "You look . . . cleaner." He shook his head. "You look freezing. Come with me."

Making sure I was following him, he led me upstairs and in the opposite direction to the room I had been staying in. As he did, he pulled a phone out of his pocket and held it to his ear. "She turned up with Knox." He glanced over his shoulder at me. "Cold and wet . . . Go ahead. I'm going to make sure she gets a bath." With a nod of his head, he slipped the phone back into his pocket.

Before I could ask him what that conversation meant, he stopped outside a door. He pushed it open and walked in.

I stood in the doorway, peering in. Hunter's room was a little bigger than the one I had been using. It had the same wooden floors and the same stone walls, but that was where the similarities ended. It was full of shelves lined with toys.

Although he didn't invite me in, I entered anyway, drawn to the collection of toys above a desk. They had little bodies, fat head, and big eyes. Strange looking as they were, they were cute.

"That's my Marvel Funko Pop collection," Hunter told me, joining my side. "And I'm more than happy to let you look, but you're cold and shivering. So how about a bath first?"

Like the bedroom I had been using, the door to the

bathroom was in the same place. Hunter walked over to the bathtub and started the water running.

The sound sent tremors running down my spine and made me feel light-headed. I closed my eyes and clenched my fingers into fists, squeezing so hard, my nails dug into my palms.

It was over there. I was over here.

I wasn't locked in that cage.

The water wasn't being poured over my body.

"Zera?"

I opened my eyes as Hunter shut the door to the bathroom behind him, blocking the sound of the water.

A shuddering breath escaped me. How would I be able to destroy all of the Lycans if I was scared of water?

"While that's running, why don't I check under your bandages?" Hunter asked. "In fact, why don't you look at the models. I'll be right back."

Nodding, I watched as he hurried out of the room, leaving me alone. My feet carried me over to a wall of shelves covered in more toys and books. I scanned the sides of them, but unable to read them, carried on examining the room until I came to a drawing of a man with orange clothes and strange, spiky black hair. Someone had scribbled over the top of it.

"That's Goku," Hunter told me, reappearing in his

room with a collection of items in his hands. "And it's signed by Sean Schemmel."

I had no idea who either were, but I nodded.

Hunter set the items down on his desk and walked into his bathroom. Moments later, I heard the water stop. He reappeared and gave me a bright smile. "That's ready, but bandages first."

"You can't touch me," I warned him.

His hands went behind his back, and when he pulled them in front of me, he was holding his bright pink gloves. "I came prepared."

The sight of them made me feel a little more relaxed, so I sat down in the chair at the desk.

"Feet first," Hunter said as he kneeled in front of me. He picked up a foot, gently unwrapping the bandage.

It was no longer white.

Once off, he tossed it in a trash can before peering at my feet. "Aside from the fact we need to get you some shoes, they're healing quickly." He reached for the other foot, repeating his actions. "Or they would be if you didn't run around outside on them." Once finished, he held out his gloved hand. "Time for the wrists."

Unlike my feet, it hurt when the bandages came off, peeling away from the damp skin. I winced.

Hunter looked up, his eyes full of apology. "I'm sorry. I'm trying to be as gentle as I can."

My wrists were beginning to heal, but I could tell it would be a long process. The skin surrounding the worst of the wounds was still charred, and further out, red and angry. Bone was no longer visible, but the flesh was still wet.

While Hunter reached for the witch's ointment, the door opened and Carter appeared. "Thank the gods," he muttered as his eyes fell on me, drinking in my appearance. "What happened? Why are you wet? Your room . . ."

"I didn't mean to destroy it."

Carter shook his head, walking over to me. With his long strides, it only took a couple of paces to join us. "I'm not worried about the damn building, Zeraora. What happened to you?" He glanced over his shoulder at the door, his expression darkening. "I'm going to murder him."

"It wasn't Knox's fault," I said, firmly. "I will fix the damage."

Slowly, Carter turned back to face me, his eyebrow quirking up in amusement. "You know how to fix a window?"

I didn't know how to read, never mind fix anything,

but I held my head up.

A chuckle escaped the giant man. "Why don't you worry about fixing yourself and I'll worry about the window." Carter's gaze finally dropped to Hunter and the pink gloves he was wearing. His eyes narrowed. "Why are you wearing those?"

"So I don't get killed."

"Hunter."

There it was again. That low warning tone.

Hunter sighed, allowing his weight to rest on his ass as he let go of my wrist and turned to look at Carter. "It makes her feel better."

I looked up at Carter, my eyes going wide as my heart seemed to quicken. "I don't want to kill any of you."

"We're fine, Zera," Hunter said, patting my knee.

"Hunter."

"It makes her feel better, DB," Hunter said, this time through gritted teeth. "Let's just allow Zera to bathe and then we can have a nice conversation later. She's cold and wet." Without waiting for a response, he turned back to me, picking up my wrist and the ointment. "This may sting again."

I closed my eyes and braced myself.

Hunter was right. It didn't hurt any less than it had

the night before. But like last time, the ointment quickly soothed the raw wound.

With just as much care, Hunter wrapped fresh bandages around my wrists. "You're going to need to be careful in the water."

"Take your time in the bath," Carter told me as he started to walk to the door. "I will have some food ready for you when you are done."

I stood, taking Knox's jacket off, just as Carter stepped outside of the room. Although Hunter's room was much warmer than it had been outside, the air was cool on my damp skin.

Hunter's eyes seemed to bulge out of his head. He stood, reaching for a strange tube, refusing to look at me. "You need to keep the bandages as dry as possible, so I'm going to wrap this around it."

I wasn't sure what the tube was, but clear plastic unraveled from it as he wrapped it around my wrists, covering the bandage. He tore it off, flattening it over the fabric, and then did the same to the other arm.

When both were covered, he led me to the bathroom. Before he walked in, he turned back to me, his eyes fixed on my face. "I put in extra bubble bath, so it should cover you. I'm not sure what it is that you don't like about bathrooms, but I'm not going anywhere. I'll keep the door open a little, and I'll be here, on the other side, if you need me. Okay?"

I nodded and stepped inside the bathroom. Purposely refusing to look to my side where the replica of my former cell lay, I walked past it.

Hunter's bathtub was as big as the one in the other bathroom. This one was now full of water, white frothy bubbles sitting on top. It also smelled heavenly.

With the floral scent and the white frosting, the water didn't look terrifying.

"The lake didn't hurt you," I said to myself, then took a deep breath. "This won't hurt you either."

Knox had said I should take off my clothes when I showered so I pulled the slip off over my head and discarded it. With another deep breath, bracing myself for the electrical shocks, I dipped my toe into the water.

Nothing.

No sparks dancing on my skin.

No pain.

Carefully, I lowered my foot in. There was tingling where the warm water met the cuts on the soles of my feet, but that was manageable.

The rest of me followed. The water was comfortably warm. It also felt . . . silky.

I'd thought the bed was wonderful, but nothing

compared to the feeling of this water surrounding me. I let out a moan and closed my eyes.

"There's a new sponge and some soap," Hunter called through the open door. "It's all yours."

Taking care not to let my wrists drop into the water, I lathered up the sponge and set to washing my skin. The sponge was slightly rough to the touch, but as it passed over my body with a little pressure, the dirt started to go away.

Having a bath was the best experience of my life. There was nothing that could top this.

Slowly, the water turned a murky brown—not unlike the lake water. As it did, the pale pink of my skin was revealed.

"Zera?" Hunter called through the door.

"Yes?"

"There's a towel on the side when you're done," he told me, as though he knew the water was turning cold.

I climbed out of the bath and wrapped myself in the towel. It was large and fluffy, and felt like I was being wrapped in a hug.

There was a soft tap at the door. "Can I come in?"

"Yes."

Hunter walked in and stopped dead, his mouth dropping open. "Fuck, Zee. You're beautiful."

I turned, finding my reflection in a mirror above the sink. My eyes were wide and blue, my lips were far too big for my face, and now that my skin was clean, it was very evident that my skin was clinging to me, and I looked more like a walking skeleton than a woman.

At best, I was striking—and all for the wrong reasons.

Or was this just because I was now clean?

Yes. That made more sense.

The silence in the room grew until Hunter hurried over to the bathtub. "I just came to drain the water and to let you know that there are some clothes for you on the bed."

I nodded.

"There hasn't been a female staying in this house for some time, so we don't really have much for you. DB found a dress, but if you prefer pants, I dug out some old sweats that might fit if you tighten the drawstring." Hunter moved toward the door. "I'll be downstairs in the kitchen. I'll let you get dressed in peace."

I waited for the bedroom door to close before I left the bathroom. As promised, there was a small pile of clothes on his bed. I looked down at the two completely different options.

Was there a right option?

Would Carter be upset if I picked the sweatpants?

Would Hunter be disappointed if I chose the dress?

I chose both.

Before I left Hunter's room, I took another walk around it. I had no idea what any of the things were on the shelves, but they made me feel . . . happy.

I made my way downstairs, but instead of retracing my steps to the kitchen, I stopped. The opposite direction was the one Knox had gone.

I'm claiming you as mine.

From nowhere, his words echoed in my mind. Like I could hear them calling me down the hallway, I walked the way he had gone.

The hallway led to more stairs, this time, going down. Unease settled over me, making my stomach churn as I carefully walked down them. Down here there were no windows.

It was like being back in that place.

My feet finally stopped moving.

Just as I was about to turn around and head back up, I heard a sound.

A moan of pleasure.

Deep, throaty, and masculine.

Thirteen

Zera

I recognized the moan as being Knox. Curious, I moved to the open door where I could hear the sound coming from.

The room was dark; the only light came from a lamp beside an empty bed. The moan was coming from the other side of the room. Knox was completely naked, the profile of his pale, bare ass in front of me.

His hand was bracing himself against the wall, the muscles in his back were tight.

Pressed up against the wall was Javion, also naked.

Between them, their hands wrapped around each other's dicks.

Mesmerized, I stood there. Watching.

A warmth grew in the apex of my legs as I stared. The little I could see of Javion's body was flawless. Dark skin flexing and contracting as his hand worked Knox's dick.

Knox's skin was less than perfect. I hadn't been able to see the scar on his face until I'd gotten close, but even from here I could see the angry slashes along his side, long since healed but not gone. They stretched around his back, the worst being in the spot between his shoulder blades.

I couldn't see Knox's face. His head was turned away, resting on Javion's shoulder. I could hear his moans and gasps. Each one making me feel hotter.

Javion's moans were muffled, his mouth clamped down on Knox's neck.

I'd witness Bacco jerk off more times than I wanted to remember, and not once had it ever had this effect on me. Even thinking about it had the bile burning in the back of my throat.

But this was nothing like that. This was . . . beautiful.

Javion stilled. His mouth left Knox's neck, just long enough for a low cry to escape.

I caught a glimpse of his mouth. Sharp fangs tipped in blood were on display. My breath caught in the back of my throat.

Lycan.

Before I could get my breath back to warn Knox, Javion clamped them down on Knox's neck.

"Oh, fuck, Jay." One of Knox's hands shot up and fisted Javion's hair.

All of a sudden, from that spot in the center of Knox's back, two giant wings shot out. They were almost the length of his body, with points at the ends of each arm that looked sharp enough to rip the skin off an animal. There were no feathers, but gray membranes. There was something wrong with one of them. That one hung low and close to his back, part of the skin torn.

What the hell is he?

Whatever this was, I no longer wanted to be near it. I could feel the electricity crackling in my hands, so I quietly backed out of the room.

Knox had pulled me from the water and claimed me as his own. I still wasn't sure what that meant, but I was not going to be shared with a Lycan. The only thing stopping me from destroying Javion was the fact that Knox was there.

I took a few steps down the corridor as Knox's cries of pleasure echoed off the stone.

Then there was silence.

I whirled on the spot, ready to go running in there to help him. Javion was in front of me, still naked. Blood trickling from his mouth. A drop ran off his chin and landed on his chest.

"Did you like what you saw little female?" Javion was still breathing heavily, but the lust in his eyes had been replaced with anger and suspicion. "I can smell your arousal."

"What did you do to Knox?"

Javion's eyes narrowed. "I should be asking you the same thing." He took a step toward me. "You don't get to invade this castle and hurt him like that."

I hurt him?

"*You* were the one biting *him*," I pointed out.

Javion's lips twisted up in a smirk, showing off one of his fangs. "He asked nicely."

The gap between Javion and me was getting smaller. I refused to move, standing my ground. Lycans terrified me, but I could take Javion out. Especially because Knox wasn't here.

"What did you do to Knox?"

Javion leaned in, his eyes scanning my face. "I made him very, *very* happy. Why? Do you want to try it too?"

"I know what you are, and I will destroy you." As if to emphasize my point, electricity crackled across my skin.

He didn't move. "I'm dead, and I've just fed. It's going to take more than your static shock to stop me."

I slapped my hand against his chest, sending a charge of energy along my fingers.

Javion shot back and slammed into the wall behind him.

"Not bad for static, huh?" I asked, tilting my head.

The next thing I knew, Javion was back in front of me. He wrapped his arm around my throat, lifting me off the ground. "Do not underestimate me, female," he snarled.

I clawed at his arm, unable to breathe. "Let go."

"Not everyone wants you here and as soon as DB sees what you really are, you'll be gone faster than the lightning you can create." The grip around my neck tightened. "I see through your act. No one escapes from the Lycans unless they let them."

Black dots started dancing across my vision. I was too focused on trying to get him to release me than to really pay attention to what he was saying. The electricity churning inside of me was building. "Let go," I gasped.

Something inside me snapped.

This was no different from being back in my cell. I decided that I wanted to live, and *if* I was going to die, it wasn't going to be at the hands of a Lycan.

I pushed the energy out of me. Just as it escaped, a goliath appeared out of nowhere—Carter.

He launched himself between us. Javion let go as Carter fell on top of me. Wings spread out, his body taking the brunt of the power.

The hallway went dark.

Dark except for the small glow coming from me. Carter's eyes, shining onyxes in the dark, were locked onto mine.

"DB?" Javion yelled, scrambling over.

Carter ignored him, gently reaching up and brushing some hair from my face. "Are you all right?"

"Are you shitting me?" Javion demanded. "She EMP'd the place."

Finally turning his head, Carter frowned at Javion. "And whose fault it that?" He pushed himself up, then leaned down to help me to my feet.

Dizzy from using up all of my energy, I stumbled

into him. Carter's strong arm wrapped around me.

"I swear to the gods, if she's fried my computers, I'll—"

"You'll what?" Carter asked him. "If you're that worried about your computers, go and check on them." He looked the man up and down. "And put some pants on. Zeraora doesn't need to see your dick."

"Didn't stop her before," Javion grumbled. He stepped toward me but stopped when Carter moved slightly in front of me. "You may have DB under your spell, but I've got my eyes on you."

I watched as he stalked off down the corridor, disappearing into the darkness. My glow dimmed, and I slumped against Carter.

Carter scooped me up in his arms. He carried me past Javion's room and up the stairs to where natural light was illuminating the hallways. He didn't stop until he walked into the kitchen.

Still holding me tightly, he opened up the cupboards, pulled out things and stuffed them into his pocket. Then, with a can in his hand, he walked straight back out.

This time, he walked to an enormous room with a huge fireplace. The fire wasn't lit, but he sat down on a couch opposite. What was it with the rooms? This one was big enough that there were three separate sitting areas, broken up by stone arches holding the ceiling up. In each central part hung an ornate chandelier.

I was still in his arms, too busy looking around to realize until he was gently rubbing my arm. "You can't do this," I said in alarm, struggling to get out of his grip. "I'm going to hurt you."

Carter let out a long sigh but didn't let go of me. "I think it's time we had a talk."

"Let go of me," I begged.

With a gentle nod, Carter set me down on the couch beside him before walking over to the fireplace. It was so tall, that his head was level with the top of it.

I still felt dizzy, but no longer in Carter's arms, I felt less panicked. "You shouldn't do that." I leaned forward, resting my head in my hands, willing the lightheadedness to go away.

"Please accept my apologies for Javion's behavior."

"I wouldn't expect anything less from a Lycan," I muttered.

"A Lycan?"

I looked up at the surprise in Carter's voice. "I saw what he did to Knox."

Carter cocked his head, and then realization set in. He moved back toward me, sitting on the adjacent couch. "There are more supernatural beings in the world than just Lycans."

"He's not a Lycan?" I asked, dubious. He had fangs. Bacco had fangs.

Carter slowly shook his head. "Javion is a vampire. What you saw . . ." he ran a hand through his silver-edged hair. "That's between him and Knox to explain, but Javion is not a Lycan. They are his enemy as much as ours."

Vampire.

I'd heard the word before, but I didn't know what one was.

"Are you angels?" I asked. "Knox has wings."

That earned me a small smile. "No, not at all. In some cultures, our kind is considered the opposite. Knox, Hunter, and I are gargoyles."

I stared blankly at him.

"Zeraora, can I ask you some questions?" Carter asked, gently. "If it is too uncomfortable, you do not have to answer."

"Okay."

Instead of asking me anything, he reached into his pocket and pulled out the can. Opening it, he handed it over to me. "Go steady with it."

I sniffed at the opening before taking a sip. I nearly

spat it out, not expecting the bubbles or the sweetness of the liquid. As soon as I swallowed, I wanted more. I drank greedily while Carter watched.

The sweetness left my teeth tingling, but I could feel the dizziness start to disappear. "I like that."

Carter rubbed at the back of his neck. "And I'm going to get you addicted to junk food like Knox is." He pulled a small bar out of his pocket and ripped open the covering before handing that over.

I had no idea what it was, but it was delicious too. Not quite as sweet, but filling.

"The place where the Lycans held you," Carter said, eventually. "How long were you there?"

Chewing at the bar, I swallowed before answering. "I don't know. I was a child when I went in."

I could almost see Carter process my answer and try to pick his next question.

"Do you know what you are?"

For the longest time, I had assumed I was human. With the electricity in me, it sounds strange, but I hadn't known anything else had existed. It had only been in recent years that Bacco had mentioned 'others' like me—or at least, one other. I slowly shook my head. "Not human."

"No, you're not," Carter agreed. "Humans

dominate this world, oblivious to the fact that there are supernatural creatures living amongst them—often in plain sight. I am almost certain you are an elemental."

"I'm an elemental, Javion is a vampire, and you are a gargoyle." I still had no idea what they were, other than supernatural. The way Carter was talking, I wasn't sure if I was supposed to be scared.

I wasn't.

They were supposed to be scared of me.

"Javion thinks I'm dangerous."

Carter let out another sigh as he nodded. "There are things I will talk about and things I won't. With Javion, it's up to him to tell his story. What I will say is that he has been with me for several decades, and he is loyal. I trust him."

"Javion is right."

"Maybe," Carter agreed. "I don't doubt that you are one of the most powerful supes out there, but you're not so dangerous that you could hurt so easily. We're made of stronger stuff."

I didn't know much about the world, but there was one thing I did know. "There's not much that can stop electricity."

"Given that I carried you into this room, I would say I'm one of them." Carter stood and moved next to me on the couch. He kept a small distance between us, but he held out his hand. "Gargoyles are born of stone. Our bodies are harder than diamond."

I narrowed my eyes at Carter's hand, eyeing it warily. His hand was enormous, like him, but there was nothing special about it.

"We don't need gloves to protect us," he said when I continued to hesitate. "I apologize for allowing Hunter to mislead you, but he did it with good intentions; to reassure you."

"DB," Hunter's voice echoed down the hallway. "Everything is dead. Is Zera—"

I looked up as Hunter entered the room; his eyes went wide when he saw the two of us. My hand was hovering over Carter's.

"Yes," Carter said, calmly. "Zeraora had a little incident with Javion."

Hunter stared, blinking rapidly. "Is Javion okay?"

I gave Carter a meaningful look, withdrawing my hand.

"He is fine." Carter nodded his chin toward me. "I was just explaining to Zera how we're all a little tougher than we look."

Hunter hurriedly nodded, moving to take the seat on the couch on the other side of me. "You can't kill what's already dead."

Carter let out a harassed sigh. "Hunter."

The younger man fell silent, folding his arms.

There it was again. That single utterance of a name, which seemed to hold some control over the person he spoke of.

"What is that?" I asked.

Hunter cocked his head. "What?"

I pointed at Carter. "You say their name, then everyone stops."

"DB's our alpha," Hunter answered, as though that explained everything.

Sensing neither of them were going to elaborate more on that, I left it. I had a lot to learn, but I would. As far as I could tell, *alpha* meant Carter was in charge.

Carter reached his hand toward me. I flinched, and he paused, but then, moving slowly, he tucked my hair behind my head. "It's nice to finally see you without all that dirt in the way."

Even though Carter had carried me into this room, I still found myself breathing a sigh of relief when I didn't kill him.

"If it's okay with you, I'd like to try to brush out your hair," Hunter said.

Grasping the ends of my hair, I pulled it toward me.

While my body felt clean, my hair didn't. When I nodded at Hunter, he gave me a grin and disappeared from the room.

"Zeraora," Carter said, bringing my attention back to him. "What are your plans?"

Kill all the Lycans.

I didn't say that out loud, even though it was the truthful answer. Something told me it wasn't the answer Carter would approve of. I stared at him. "I want to find a place to call home. I won't stay longer than I need to."

The corners of Carter's mouth dipped down. "As I said before, you're welcome to stay with us for as long as you need." He shifted his weight and leaned forward. "Actually, I would like it if you stayed with us for a month or two."

"I don't know how long that is." Now that I was out of the Lycan's possession and I could see the sky for the first time, I could also see the sun rise and fall. I could see the seasons I'd heard about. But that still meant nothing to me.

Carter rubbed his hand over his jaw, making a soft scratching sound over his facial hair. "Stay with us until spring. Snow has already fallen on the tops of the mountains, and it will soon reach this castle. We may live in a southern state, but the winters can still be cold, especially when you have nowhere to go."

"Why?"

"Because we're at a higher altitude. Although, if you're set—"

I shook my head. "No. Why do you want me to stay here? You don't know me."

Carter's dark eyes never left my face. "I'm not going to pretend to know or understand what you've experienced under the Lycans, but it's clear you don't know much about the world—supernatural or otherwise. The supernatural law states we cannot reveal ourselves to the humans. We must keep our existence a secret. I don't think you know enough to be able to survive in the human world. Worse, I'm not sure you can survive in the supernatural one."

"I will kill anything that tries to hurt me," I pointed out as I folded my arms. I might not know much, but I could do that.

With a patient smile, Carter nodded. "And that's part of the problem. Zeraora, you don't hurt me with your electrical charge, but I can feel it. You're not safe around humans right now. One touch could be fatal for them."

"If they try to hurt me—"

"What if they try to help you?"

"Why would they do that?"

Sadness crept into Carter's eyes. "I know given what you've been through, that your ability to trust has been broken, but I promise you, not everyone wants to hurt you. I want to help you learn to control your powers, and to also learn how to trust."

There was a lot I didn't know. Carter was right; I didn't know much about trust. I wanted to trust him, though. I did feel safe around him.

My gaze fell to the bandages around my wrists. Were his words just another way of keeping me prisoner?

Before I could give him an answer, Hunter returned, placing some items I didn't recognize onto the couch beside me. One was a bottle of something, and the other . . .

"It's a brush," Carter told me. At Hunter's arched eyebrow, he stood, pulling him to the other side of the room. Whatever he told him, it was too quiet for me to hear, but it earned him a look of surprise from Hunter.

While Hunter walked back to me, Carter left the room. "DB's going to help Knox out with the generator," Hunter explained, picking up the bottle. "Your powers include EMP bombs—electromagnetic pulses. You have the ability to kill all electrical devices in quite a wide radius. It's pretty impressive."

"I didn't kill anyone?"

Hunter shook his head. "Nope. Just a bunch of the devices in the house. Once Javion gets over it, he'll be able to fix most of them."

"I can kill things as well as people?" I looked down at my hands, not sure if I liked that revelation. When I'd discovered I couldn't kill any of these men, I felt relieved. But now I had to be careful not to kill their belongings?

"Disable," Hunter said, making me look up at him. "You've not killed them, so much as disabled them. Your powers send a surge—an electrical pulse. The electricity finds the shortest route to being grounded, and if it finds something like a wire, it travels along that. Whatever's attached gets circuit boards and microchips frazzled. The good news is that Javion is an electrical tech genius. He spent years building his computers and servers, to the point that he kept frying circuits. We learned not to leave most things plugged in, and the few that did, he's got spare microchips for."

Maybe I hadn't destroyed everything, and the idea of inconveniencing Javion so that he had to fix everything made me smile.

"Oh wow, a smile like that needs a warning,"

Hunter said, clutching at his heart. When I didn't say anything, Hunter climbed onto the couch. "This is going to take a while, so get comfortable." Moving behind me, he started squirting the liquid onto my hair. "So, this is conditioner that I'm applying. Normally you put it on your hair after you've shampooed it, which is done when you're showering. Or bathing, in your case."

"Did I do something wrong before?" I asked, alarmed.

"Not at all," Hunter assured me. The bottle continued to make slurping sounds as he squeezed the contents out. "You have a lot of hair, and it's not in a great condition, so this was always going to be easier if someone else did it. But once we get all these knots out, next time you bathe, you can do this part."

I nodded. Shampoo and conditioner on my hair. *Check.*

Hunter fell silent, rubbing the cream into my hair. It smelled nice. Like Hunter. Fruity.

After a while, he picked up the other object. Holding out his arm over my shoulder, he held it in front of me. "This is a brush. You're going to need to use this daily." He brought his hand back and then started running it through the ends of my hair.

I'd never used a brush in my life. If it hurt this

much, I wouldn't be using it again. But as Hunter was trying to be as gentle as possible, and because it didn't hurt nearly as much as it had when the chains were clamped around my wrists, I didn't say anything.

I brought my knees up under my chin, wrapping my arms around my legs.

Spring.

Could I stay here until spring?

Fourteen

DB

"Wherever she was, she'd been locked up there for a considerable length of time," I told Hunter.

There were many questions I had wanted to ask Zeraora about what happened to her, but I refrained. The destroyed bathroom told me she had been through something horrific, and she'd relived enough of it for today—for a lifetime. My questions could wait, at least while I was capable of reading between the lines.

"I figured as much," Hunter agreed, his voice low as we tried to keep our conversation from Zeraora. "She seems to know about some things, but she's missing out on basics."

"She's not ready to leave. She's either going to hurt herself or someone else. I need to speak to Knox and Javion. Can you keep her out of the basement for a while?"

Hunter set a hand on my shoulder. "DB, have you seen that hair? I'm going to be combing that hair out long after it gets dark. So, if you could get Knox to hurry up on the lights, that would be appreciated."

I glanced over at Zeraora. Even before she had bathed, I was mesmerized by her blue eyes. Now that she was clean, I was struggling to keep my eyes off her. There was something about her that made me want to protect her.

Like with Manon.

"Keep an eye on her, and make sure you explain everything you do," I told Hunter before I could let my mind drift to Manon.

I left Zeraora with Hunter and hurried back down to the basement.

I felt terrible lying to Zeraora. I'd told her a half-truth, and that was as good as a lie.

Ignoring the fact there was something compelling me to help her—protect her, I had another reason to get her to stay. Whatever she had escaped from, the Lycans were sure to hunt her down and take her back.

If the supernatural world caught wind of Lycans hunting elementals, they wouldn't be the only ones who would be hunting her.

The basement was as cavernous as the castle. When it had been built a couple of hundred years ago, it had been used as a dungeon. When I'd inherited it, I'd converted most of it myself.

The basement was Javion's domain. Being a vampire meant the large windows in the castle were problematic for half of the day. Deep underground, he was safe.

He also had appalling taste in music—it was noise—and down here, I couldn't hear it.

I knocked on the open door and poked my head in. Javion had left some candles burning on the bedside table. Knox was still passed out on Javion's bed. I walked into the room, over to him.

I'd seen Knox's scars before, but they never failed to raise my blood pressure when I did. Just one of the reasons I was determined to stop the Lycans.

Pulling the silk sheets free, I covered Knox's naked

body. I didn't expect Zeraora to wander back down here, especially with Hunter occupying her time, but I knew Knox would appreciate it.

The younger man let out a sigh in his sleep, turning his head. Even now, he was frowning. I reached over, brushing his hair off his face.

The endorphin rush from a vampire bite was addictive and orgasm inducing. There had been a time when I had suspected Knox had been using that like a drug addiction, but I'd eventually seen there was more to their relationship.

I left Knox sleeping. I'd check on Javion first and then wake him.

Javion was in his 'office' if that was what hackers called their workspace. The room was warm and stuffy from all the computers in there—and probably from the rage radiating from the vampire.

Ironic considering his normal body temperature.

"I'm going to kill that fucking female," he was muttering to himself as he worked, ignoring me. I knew full well that he was aware of my presence. Even if the door hadn't beeped when I'd walked in, his hearing was impeccable.

He'd managed to pull on a pair of jeans which hung low on his hips. A torch was shining on one of the many desks, light aiming at a motherboard of a dissected computer tower. "Fucking fried."

"Computers are replaceable."

Javion continued to ignore me.

"Are the servers okay? Or is she too strong for you?"

Finally, Javion's back straightened, and he turned and scowled at me. "The server room was built within a Faraday cage *and* reinforced concrete walls. My servers are protected better than the NSAs."

I raised a shoulder. "I'm fairly certain the NSA is prepared for an EMP."

"It wasn't an EMP. She hit the castle's electrics with an electrical surge."

"Then what are you worrying about?" I asked.

Javion's eyes narrowed once more. "An electrical surge can be just as damaging as an EMP if the devices on the receiving end are fried."

I glanced around the room. It was one nobody other than Javion rarely entered. Whenever the team needed to plan anything, we used one of the upper levels. Javion used a laptop that was hooked up to his personal supercomputer. These things were like his children—I sometimes wondered if they would have been cherished more than a computer had he ever actually had kids.

The server room was next door. Floor to ceiling, stood stacks of drives and processors. Not that I could tell the difference between the two. I left that to Javion.

This room had several towers on one side—computers, not servers. I couldn't tell the difference between those either. Behind a long desk was a wall of monitors. There was one central 60-inch beast, surrounded by a dozen other smaller ones. Only one of them was turned on, showing a dial with a percentage slowly increasing below it.

"I thought as your set-up started getting more elaborate and began constantly blowing the fuses, that you installed surge protectors. In fact, I distinctly recall you saying that even a direct lightning strike wasn't going to harm your computers."

Javion's eyes narrowed once more. "She's not a fucking lightning strike, Carter. She's like eight. All at once. Standard surge protectors aren't going to protect equipment from that. Like all the hardware in this fucking room. She's violated my domain." He stood and took a few steps toward me, pointing his finger. "Do you know how much this is going to cost you?"

"At least you get new comms."

"Which you will have to keep replacing because

they can't be protected from surges and EMPs."

I leaned back against the wall and folded my arms. "She shouldn't have seen what she did, Javion."

"She shouldn't have been in the fucking basement," he snapped back. "She shouldn't be here at all. If you want to adopt a stray, let's go to the fucking pound."

I ran my tongue over my teeth as I waited for Javion to finish. It wasn't often that we disagreed. While he skirted the line of disrespectful when he did, right now, I wanted to punch him.

"She's a liability, Carter. The Lycans will . . ."

"Will what?" I asked when he didn't finish his sentence.

Javion picked up a screwdriver and doubled back over to the computer. "Forget it. She's a guest. Whatever."

I'd expected it would take longer than that for him to listen, but I was glad. I didn't have the energy to waste on arguing over this. "Work out what is needed for replacing and get it ordered."

"You tell the female to stay out of the basement."

Pursing my lips, I pushed off the wall and left. As I walked back toward Javion's room, the door opened and Knox walked out. He was wearing a silk bathrobe, which seemed more like Javion's thing than his. As he usually did after Javion had fed from him, Knox looked settled. The endorphins were still kicking around.

Knox stretched as he saw me. "What time is it?"

"Midday. Get dressed. Zeraora and Javion had run in; she sent an electrical surge through the place and knocked almost everything out."

Rubbing at his forehead, Knox arched an eyebrow. "Why?"

"Javion was being Javion, and she thought he was Lycan."

Whatever endorphins were in Knox disappeared. "Shit."

"She's with your brother at the moment. We need to get the electricity back on."

While Knox left to get dressed, I went outside to the backup generator. With a home in South Carolina's Blue Ridge Mountains, we'd gotten a generator installed decades ago. It had been serviced a few years ago, so I was sure it would kick in when I turned it on.

My concern wasn't even the power.

It was, as it was frequently becoming, Zeraora.

The guest room's bathroom looked like a warzone, and she'd killed the electrics in the house.

If we didn't help her, she was going to kill a lot

more than just the power.

Fifteen

Zera

Hunter liked to talk. A lot.

Even though I didn't understand much of it, I didn't mind. Just having someone talk at me—to me—was a nice feeling.

At some point while he was telling me all about a superhero who had gotten his powers from being bitten by a spider, the lights came back on.

"Looks like you didn't take the generator out," Hunter declared happily.

A shiver ran down my spine, but this one was from the temperature. The castle was enormous and a little drafty. Combined with the wet hair and the damp patch on my back where Hunter was brushing it out, I had gotten cold a while ago.

"Are you cold?" Hunter asked, instantly.

"Yes."

Hunter set the brush down and got up off the couch. "You need to tell me these things. You shouldn't be cold."

"I'm used to it." Bacco had never checked the temperature of the water before he'd poured it over my head, and no one had ever made sure my cell was at an ambient temperature.

Hands grabbed mine before I could stop him. Even though Carter had promised that I couldn't hurt them, it didn't stop my heart from leaping into my throat.

"You're like an ice cube," Hunter muttered, shaking his head. Abandoning my hands, he moved over to the enormous fireplace and started throwing logs onto it from a pile beside it. He pulled a small box out from behind the logs and added in some white cubes, which smelled funny.

And strangely pleasant.

They reminded me of Knox.

The next thing I knew, there was fire licking at the logs.

Hunter stood and turned back to me. In his hands, he held a small box, the contents rattling as he moved it from palm to palm while he watched the fire. As the flames slowly started to take hold, he set the box down on the mantle and returned to me. "At some point I will teach you how to make a fire, but for now, if you get cold, you call me."

I nodded, barely listening as I watched the fire flicker. The fire was small, but I could already feel the heat from it. The sensation was as pleasant as the bath had been.

Hunter sat back down beside me, once again, taking my hands in his. Gently, he clasped them together and then started to rub his hands over the tops of them.

Biting the inside of my cheek, I watched the motion.

"We need to get you a better wardrobe," Hunter muttered.

I looked at him, finding him staring at the dress I was wearing. "This is nice." The dress was dark blue with tiny white flowers over it. The sleeves ran to mid forearm—just above the bandages. The sweatpants were big and warm too.

His hands paused. "That's not what . . ." he looked down at my bare feet. "Are your feet as cold as your hands?"

I nodded. "I'm used to it."

A small growl erupted from the back of his throat. "Okay, Zee, it's time for ground rules. Number one: you have to look after yourself, even if doing so feels unnatural to you. If you are cold, we get you warm."

Hunter stood and pulled his shirt off. He had beautiful arms. Unlike his brother, I couldn't see any drawings on them.

Distracted by his golden skin and muscles, I didn't notice as he draped the shirt over my shoulders. "We're taking you shopping to buy you clothes." He frowned. "When did you eat last?"

"Pancakes," I told him, not knowing when that was, but what it was.

"Rule number two: you eat regular meals." He gently pulled me to my feet, but he didn't step back as he stared down at me. "I know you said you survived this long without food, but it shouldn't be like that."

Taking my hand in his, he led me to the kitchen, not letting go of me until I was sitting on one of the tall seats beside the counter.

There was a bowl at the end of the counter. Hunter leaned over and plucked several items out of it, placing them in front of me. "Apple, pear, grapes, plums, nectarines," he said, pointing to each of them. "These fruit, you can eat as they are. Some have hard cores inside them so be careful."

"What are you doing?"

Hunter leaned against the counter and tilted his head as he looked at me. "I'm assuming, if you've never been fed, that you don't know what most foods are, never mind how to eat them?"

"Yes."

He closed his eyes, but not before I saw the wince. I wasn't sure why, but I got the impression that even though he'd asked the question, and correctly predicted the answer, that wasn't what he wanted to hear.

When he opened his eyes again, it was with a smile. "If you're hungry, come and eat the fruit. DB washes it all before he puts it in the bowl." He turned and pulled the remaining unidentified fruit out of the bowl. "Orange and banana. You need to take the skin off these, otherwise, you're fine."

I picked a grape off the stem and popped it into my mouth. *Juicy.*

While I ate the grapes, Hunter worked his way

around the kitchen, showing me things that I could eat and drink without needing to prepare them. I probably should have felt embarrassed about the gaps in my basic knowledge, but because Hunter was so patient, I didn't.

"And now I'm going to introduce you to cinnamon almonds," he said, grinning. From one of the cupboards, he pulled out a pan and put it on top of the stove. He drizzled in some oil before lighting the ring.

As the oil started to crackle and spit, he pulled a bag of almonds from the pantry and tossed several large handfuls in. Shaking the pan occasionally, he sprinkled cinnamon sugar on the top.

Very quickly, a sweet aroma filled the kitchen, making my mouth water.

As the almonds cooked, Hunter poured some almond milk into a different pan, tossing in a cinnamon stick. He looked over at me. "This is the best winter treat."

Finally, the nuts were in a bowl, and the milk had been transferred to two mugs. Instead of handing them over, he led us back to the fire in the other room, waiting for me to sit down on the couch before he let me have a mug. "Blow on it because it will be hot."

The fire was roaring now, fat flames licking at the hole above. I did as Hunter said before taking a sip.

Forget the pancakes.

Forget the bath.

This was the greatest thing ever.

I moaned.

Hunter sucked in a sharp breath. "You need to stop doing that, Zee," he muttered.

Unsure what he was talking about, I lowered the mug from my mouth. "Did I do something wrong?"

"Nothing. Enjoy your drink." Hunter set the bowl of toasted almonds by my lap and then set the second mug on the small table beside him. He gave me his bright smile. "It's going to take me ages to finish your hair, so I figured we could incorporate Netflix into the equation."

Netflix. I knew this one. It was what Cliff watched his crime shows on. "Netflix and chill?" That was always Cliff's plans for his days off. Netflix and chill with his girlfriend.

Hunter froze, his mouth slowly dropping open. Just as slowly, he moved his hand to his jaw, rubbing at it. "You're killing me."

Eyes wide, I leaped up. While the nuts remained in the bowl, the same couldn't be said about the milk as it slopped over the edge. Electricity crackled across the back of my skin.

Hunter was on his feet in an instant, hands in the air. "I'm fine, Zee. It's just an expression. You're not really killing me."

With my heart pounding, I stared at him. "Really?"

He nodded. "You surprised me with your knowledge about Netflix." Hunter turned, pulling some tissues from the box on the table beside the couch. He moved over and dabbed at the spilled milk.

"Do you really not feel it?" I asked as I watched the crackling electricity zap at him as he cleaned up my hand.

Hunter looked up, meeting my gaze. "I feel it, but it doesn't hurt."

"Because you're a gargoyle?"

He smiled, tilting his head. His green eyes seemed to sparkle in the light. "Our kind was born from the earth—from the rock, like that which the castle is sat on. We still feel things like touch, water, temperature, and even electricity, but our skin is like a shield. You can see it when we're in our true form."

"Can I see it now?"

Hunter closed his eyes, taking a deep breath. He shuddered, his muscles rippling. "Not now." He suddenly balled the tissue up and threw it into the fire. "Sit."

I did as he said, moving back to where I had been, but Hunter remained standing. "I think today calls for Captain America."

"What is that?"

Hunter's buoyant mood appeared from nowhere, and he bounded across the room to a large cabinet. He pulled the door open, revealing even more thin books. Carefully, he slid one out, closed the cabinet door, and walked over to a different cabinet. He opened the . . .

"That's not a book." I realized.

Hunter looked down at the item in his hand and then slowly shook his head. "This is a Blu-ray. And I'm hoping that if the lights are on, the television will work. I just need to plug it in."

I couldn't see what he was doing in the cupboard but moments later, he rejoined me at the couch and handed over the Blu-ray case.

"The books are in the library. I'll let DB show you that at some point, because that's his second favorite place." Hunter sat down beside me.

"Where is his favorite place?" I took a sip of my drink.

"I'll let DB show you that too." Hunter leaned over, picking something up off the side table, and pointed it at the big black painting above the fireplace.

I nearly choked on my drink. The thing I had assumed to be a strange painting of black was a television. It was about as wide as Carter was tall. "It's massive."

Hunter nodded, sinking into the couch beside me. "That's what she said."

I looked over at him. "Huh?"

"Nothing," he replied, laughing to himself.

Making myself comfortable, I curled my legs up underneath me and watched the movie, drinking my milk and nibbling at the almonds. I had been happy talking with Hunter, but the movie was like nothing I'd ever seen before.

At some point Hunter left me there, returning, holding a plate with a sandwich on it.

Sandwiches were amazing.

I was quickly coming to the conclusion that food, in general, was the best thing ever. In addition to my goal of destroying the Lycans, I was going to try every food I came across.

Every so often, I would hear Hunter quoting scenes in the movie as they happened. Even though he was half-watching the movie, I could tell he was taking care with my hair as he worked out the knots.

He finished before the movie did, but I was so

engrossed in what was happening, I barely noticed.

As the film ended, I stared at the television, allowing my brain to process everything I had seen. There was so much to learn, and half of the film had apparently been set in the past.

"Your hair is done, Zee," Hunter said. "We need to rinse the conditioner out."

Abandoning the living room, we returned to his bedroom. I paused, looking over at the shelves I had earlier thought to be books. "Are they all Blu-rays?"

"Blu-rays and DVDs," Hunter replied. "I get that I can watch most of them on Netflix now, but I was collecting these when Netflix used to mail you a disc. . ." he glanced at me and shrugged. "I collect things." He looked at the bathroom door before looking back to me. "Wait here for a moment."

I did as he requested while he disappeared into the bathroom, pulling the door closed behind him. While he busied himself in there, I occupied myself by staring at Hunter's collections. Now I recognized some of the items on his shelves.

A short while later, Hunter reemerged, only to lead me into the bathroom. There was a small pile of towels on the floor in front of the bathtub and he pointed to it. "Can you sit there, your back to the bath?"

I did as he requested. Although the bath was deep, the rim of it settled into the crook of my neck.

"Normally, I'd suggest you have a shower, or even use the shower attachment on the bathtub, but we're going to have to go old-school and use a jug." He picked a jug up off the side as though to demonstrate.

Hunter lowered himself to his knees beside me. He'd been filling the bath with water while I'd waited.

I was grateful he'd done that behind a closed door.

The idea of him being so close to me and water still made my heart race though. Even though Knox had pulled me from the lake, and even though Hunter had promised it hadn't hurt, I still couldn't shake the feeling that I was going to cause them pain.

"Relax, Zee," Hunter said, gently. I looked up just as his hand cupped my cheek. "I won't hurt you. And you won't hurt me," he added before I could.

I brought my knees up to my chest and wrapped my arms around them.

Hunter's hand disappeared from my face and I instantly missed it, craving the warmth.

Maybe that was what scared me more. Not hurting him, but not being able to have someone touch me again.

Warm water touched my head as Hunter started

pouring it over my hair. As his fingers worked through my hair, massaging my scalp in the process, I felt myself relax. I wasn't in pain, and neither was he. If anything, this was enjoyable.

After years and years of water being poured on my head, I didn't think I would ever be able to get used to water being poured on me, but Hunter did it in a way that didn't feel like it was being dumped onto my head.

Finally, he squeezed the water out and wrapped my hair in a towel before helping me to my feet. The water in the tub was as dark as it had been after I bathed earlier. There was also an unpleasant smell to it again.

"Honestly, I think it still needs a hairdresser to work their magic, but this is as good as I'm going to get it," Hunter told me as he rubbed my hair dry. "We also don't have a hairdryer in the house, so we'll have to make do."

He took another run at it with a brush before finally letting me look at my reflection.

I ran my hand through my hair, marveling at the ease my fingers slid through. It was soft. Best of all, it smelled clean—fruity.

I didn't recognize the woman staring back. My hair was almost black, but it seemed to have a blue tint to it that shone under the bathroom light. It hung down to my stomach, the ends curling out in all directions.

Because it was so dark, it made my skin look even paler. There was finally some pink in my cheeks, and my lips looked red.

While my reflection had improved, being clean hadn't performed any miracle and I still wasn't anywhere near as attractive as the women I had seen in the movie.

Hunter's phone beeped, and I watched him in the mirror as he pulled it out to read a message. "Dinner's ready."

We went downstairs, only this time, Hunter led me to a different room. Like every other room I had been in so far, it was enormous and seemed much bigger than it needed to be. A long table stretched down the center of the room with a lot of chairs, but the places were set all at one end.

"I'll go help DB dish up and bring out food. You go and sit down. We'll be in soon."

Hunter left me in the doorway, and I walked in, taking one of the seats. It had long since gone dark, and out of the enormous windows which I had chosen to sit opposite of, I could see nothing but blackness and my own reflection.

There was something homey about the table,

despite its grandness. The wood was worn with dings and scratches in the surface. At the far end of the table, there was a small pile of papers, and just in front of them, a tray of small plants.

The windows were lined with thick curtains, some with the ties holding them back, some without. Underneath them, a long radiator stretched out with several items of clothing hanging over it.

There was a second doorway at the opposite end to the one I'd used. This one held a double door made almost entirely of glass. The room on the other side was dark, but the little which had been illuminated from the dining room showed a couch.

I was busy guessing who the T-shirt belonged to when one of the double doors opened. From the second living room, Javion walked in.

My body tensed as my eyes narrowed. In my lap, my hands fisted the fabric of the skirt. As though remembering his hand wrapped around it, the skin on my neck tingled.

Javion might not have been a Lycan, but he had attacked me. If he came near me again, I would have no hesitation on cooking his dead ass.

The vampire scowled back at me. "That's my chair."

Briefly, I contemplated moving, but decided against it. "Shame."

"Dropping the damsel in distress act already?" He moved toward the table, never taking his eyes off me. There was something in his eyes which was almost predatory.

"I might not know much, but I do know I'm not a damsel in distress. I've rescued myself once, and I will do it again." I lifted my hand and let the electricity crackle around my fingers. "Or do you need reminding of that?"

A small smile appeared on Javion's face. A smile with a deliberate showing of a fang. "I see exactly what you are, *Zera*, and it will only be a matter of time before you slip up and show your true intention to the rest of this household because you won't be able to help yourself."

"And what would that be?"

"The Lycans."

My breath caught in my throat. Did Javion know I planned to destroy the Lycans? Before I could tell him otherwise, the door opened, and Carter walked in pushing a cart. Whatever was on it smelled delicious and my mouth started to water.

"Has someone called Knox?" Carter asked, but he

was looking at Javion.

"I'm here," came Knox's gruff voice before he appeared behind Carter. He had a streak of something dark on his cheek and he looked tired. "Please tell me I can smell burgers?" He slipped into the room and stopped short when he saw me, glancing back at Javion.

Carter pushed the cart over and started unloading the dishes onto the center of the table. "Pick another seat, Javion," he said, without looking at the vampire.

With his jaw jutting out, but not taking his eyes off me, Javion took the seat opposite me. Finally, he turned his attention to Knox, fixing him a pointed look. Whatever it was he was trying to silently tell him, I figured Knox understood it as he sat down beside Javion and the vampire shot me a smug smile.

"I have drinks." Hunter announced his presence, a tray with multiple beverages on them.

My eyes lit up when a glass of almond milk was deposited under my nose. Moments later it was accompanied by a plate of food from Carter.

"Burger and fries," Carter told me. "If you don't like anything, don't eat it. And if you start to feel nauseous when eating, don't finish it." He took a seat at the head of the table as Hunter sat down beside me. "You've not eaten much before now, so don't force yourself. I don't want you to feel ill."

I grabbed a fry and pushed it into my mouth.

Okay, so maybe I didn't *need* to eat food, but I had been missing out.

I'd eaten most of the fries and half of the burger before I realized that the room was silent. I looked up and found everyone watching me, their meals barely touched. "What did I do?"

Javion blinked. "I'm sorry, I couldn't hear that over the food in your mouth."

It was only because Knox's nose had also turned up that I swallowed the food in my mouth and sat back. "What?"

"Nothing," Hunter said, hurriedly placing a second burger on my plate. "Eat up."

Sixteen

Zera

The longer I stayed at Castle Viegls, the more I realized just how much I had to learn about the world outside its walls. For six weeks, my teacher was Netflix, Hunter, and Carter.

Mainly Hunter and Netflix.

Carter, I discovered, was a multi-talented individual. He'd spent a week fixing the bathroom, fitting new glass so I could return to the room. My room, as he had declared it.

The only time I saw Javion and Knox was at mealtimes.

One of the things I'd noticed, thanks to my Netflix education, was that four men living together was highly unusual. So was eating meals together. Hunter was happy to explain most things as we watched them, but he'd never commented on that.

Seeing Javion three times a day was three times too many, but with Knox, I was both curious and irritated.

He had declared me his and then barely spoke to me.

I still wasn't sure what he meant by that declaration, but we'd never been alone long enough for me to ask him. Given that he was always with Javion and doing his best to avoid me, I was sure this was a 'brush off.'

Finally, I found one morning where I didn't have Carter or Hunter for company. I wasn't sure if they were aware of that fact considering I suspected they were conspiring together to make sure I was never left by myself.

It wasn't long after breakfast, and as I sat in the living room trying to pick something to watch, I realized Hunter hadn't appeared.

I hadn't intended on seeking Knox out. Instead, I wanted to go outside. I loved the grounds of the castle.

It was also Carter's favorite place. He'd given me a tour of the gardens and explained how he'd spent the better weather days gardening.

Today, everything was white.

Snow.

Over breakfast, Carter had said it was the first snow to fall on the castle. It had covered the grounds like I was looking at a blank canvas, hiding so much of the greens and browns.

I walked through the snow, amused that my steps left a path behind me. My feet had quickly gone cold and wet in the flipflops I was wearing, but I didn't want to go back inside despite how cold I had become.

With the grounds no longer looking as I remembered, I took a wrong turn. Just as I realized and was about to follow my footprints back, I heard music. I followed the sound to a large building I'd not seen before. From there, the castle was blocked by a line of trees.

There was also a trail of footprints coming from another direction, leading to a door on the side of the building. As I got close and the angle changed, I discovered the building was a garage.

I pushed opened the door and was greeted by loud music. The garage was warmer inside, but it still didn't have the heat of the house. Shivering, I wandered in, my mouth falling open at the number of cars in there.

I knew enough about cars now to be able to tell the difference between a car, an SUV, and a pickup truck, but after that, I was clueless. There were maybe a dozen different vehicles in the garage, of varying kinds and ages.

Four vehicles down, propped up on a stand, was an older looking car. Two black, denim-clad legs poked out from underneath.

Knox.

I walked over, stopping a few feet away. "Knox?" I called. My voice wasn't louder than the music, and he didn't hear me.

Glancing around, I tried to figure out where the music was coming from. It wasn't one of the cars, but instead, hanging from the rafters were several black speakers. Unsure where the control was for them, I abandoned the idea of trying to lower the volume.

Instead, I found my gaze drifting back to Knox's legs. They were muscular. Even lying down, his thighs filled the denim out well.

If I was Javion, I would have bitten him there.

I cocked my head at that thought. I wasn't a vampire, but would he let me bite him there anyway?

Knox slid out from under the car, spotting me right away. As he got up, he pulled his phone out of his pocket and then the music suddenly stopped. "Zera?" He opened his mouth, but stopped, tilting his head. Slowly, he started to walk toward me, stopping just inches away. "What's that look for?"

"What look?" There wasn't a mirror close to me, and the shiny finish of the cars wasn't enough for me to be able to see my reflection.

"What are you thinking?" He was close enough that I could see the scars on his face again. "Your eyes are filled with naughty thoughts."

I raised a hand, pressing the back of it to my cheek. It was a little warm. "I want to bite your thigh."

Knox went still. The only movement was his tongue as he ran the ball of one of his tongue piercings over his lip. Finally, he let out a breath and stepped back. "What are you doing out here?"

"I went for a walk, and I ended up here."

"And what about Hunter? I thought he was supposed to be with you."

I shrugged. "I waited for him and Carter, but I haven't seen Carter since breakfast and Hunter disappeared a while ago."

"DB went to . . ." Knox frowned. "He went to run

an errand. He won't be back until late this evening."

"What are you doing out here?" I looked down at all the vehicles. There were so many different kinds. "Are they all yours?"

Knox glanced over his shoulder before looking back at me. "Mostly. The F-150 is Hunter's and one of the bikes is Javion's."

"Is it broken?" I pointed to the one he had been under.

"The Mustang?" Knox led me over to it, running his hand lovingly over the grill. "I've been restoring and building her for the last few years."

"It takes that long to build a car?"

"It does when you're trying to source original parts. I've had to compromise with some because the rubber and plastic hasn't survived as well over time, but I've been making those parts myself."

I edged up to the car and peered in, not really understanding what I was seeing. The outside was definitely nicer to look at than the engine. I moved along, stopping at the door. It wasn't the interior that stopped me. It was the smell. Pushing my head to the open window, I sniffed.

There was something missing.

As Knox followed me in mild amusement, I

wandered further back, stopping at a bench with bottles and rags. When I picked up a rag to sniff, Knox shot in and took it from me. "You can't just go sniffing random rags in garages—or in general. You don't know what's on them."

"What is that?" I asked, pointing to the rag.

Knox glanced down at the rag, and then back at me. "Polish."

That was it. The last part of a smell I identified as Knox: cars and musk.

Satisfied with my investigation skills, I didn't complain when Knox set the rag back on the side. "Can I watch you work for a while?"

Confusion knitted Knox's brows together. "Really?"

When I nodded, Knox stepped up beside me, cleaning off a space on the workbench. He turned, wrapped his hands around my waist and lifted me onto the area he'd just cleared. "Don't touch anything. It's dangerous in here."

Our eyes were at the same level and my attention drifted to the piercing in his brow. Without thinking, my hand drifted toward it, but I stopped at the last moment as the smallest spark appeared at my fingertips.

Aside from the time Javion wrapped his hand

around my throat, I'd managed not to short out anything electrical, nor had I shocked any of the men in the castle. My skin got sparky around water, but otherwise, my power had been humming away at a low level just below the surface.

Until now.

Hunter had been adamant—daily—that I had yet to hurt him because his skin was tough enough to protect him. But Hunter didn't have pieces of metal piercing his skin.

I dropped my hand.

Moving sharply, Knox stepped back, a frown on his face.

"What's wrong?" I asked him, panicked that I'd shocked him and hurt him.

"Fuck what he said," Knox growled before marching straight up to me. His hand slipped behind my head, holding me in place as he brought his mouth to mine.

There was a firmness to his kiss, but it wasn't harsh. His lips moved against mine, over mine, capturing the lower lip between his before he released it to repeat it again.

I did my best to mimic what he was doing, hoping I was doing it right. The movies I had been watching had given me a basic guide, but they failed to point out how easy it was to get lost in a kiss.

Knox's other hand settled on my thigh, his touch burning its way through the material of Hunter's sweatpants.

In response, mine reached forward, pushing under the jacket he was wearing. My fingers splayed out over his T-shirt covered chest. He was solid, but just as hot as his hand.

I spread my legs, grasping at the T-shirt to pull him closer, and then he brushed up against me. I gasped, my grip of him tightening at the sensation.

Knox's tongue dove into my mouth like the noise had been an invitation. The softness of it contrasted with the hard balls of his tongue piercings. I swear, my mind and body were beginning to turn to mush.

And then it was suddenly being taken away from me.

Breathing heavily, a hand raking through his hair, Knox stepped away, turning his back to me.

I clutched at the worktop, feeling sick. Had I done it wrong? Had I used my powers without realizing? Had Carter been wrong and I *could* hurt one of them? Their skin protected them, but the inside of Knox's mouth wasn't skin, and he had metal running through him.

Knox looked back at me, wincing, before moving closer. Only this time, he stopped just out of reach. "Have you ever been with a man before?"

I shook my head. "Can you tell?" My voice was barely louder than a whisper.

Swiping his hand across his jaw, Knox groaned; a sound of anguish, not pleasure. "Fuck, Zera. It wasn't you."

His answer didn't make anything clearer.

"That wasn't fair to you. Fuck him for being right, but that wasn't fair to you."

"I don't understand."

"My point exactly," Knox muttered. "You've been locked up for who knows how long. You don't know what you want, and I took advantage of that."

I frowned. "I didn't want you to stop kissing me."

Knox closed his eyes and hung his head as he rubbed at the back of his neck. When he looked at me again, his eyes were full of guilt. "You don't know what you want, Zera. Fuck," he muttered. "That's the name Hunter gave you because you don't know your name. You're not even wearing your own clothes."

I looked down at the outfit I was wearing. It was another dress, pale pink with white flowers. It was still too big for me, but it didn't hang as much as the clothes had done a couple of weeks ago. Underneath, held up by the thin string ties, was a pair of Hunter's sweatpants. Finishing it off were Knox's flipflops.

Was that the problem? My outfit?

"Oh," I said, surprised it was that simple. I grabbed at the bottom of the dress and started tugging it up off over my head.

"What the fuck?" Knox asked as he bounded over. His hand grasped the bottom of the dress, holding it in place. "What are you doing?"

"If you don't like it, I will take it off," I replied with a shrug.

Knox's palm flew to his forehead. "Zera, you can't just take your clothes off like that." His hand went up into his hair as he stepped back. "I can't believe I just said that."

I let go of the bottom of my dress, feeling lost and confused.

"Fuck, don't look like that," he said, raising my chin to look at him. He suddenly pressed the back of his hand against my cheek. He let go and grabbed my hand. His face darkened as he frowned at me. "You're freezing. Why aren't you wearing a coat? Why the fuck did you take a walk through three inches of snow in those shoes?"

"Why are you getting mad at me?" I demanded. "You gave me these shoes."

"Not for walking in snow," he yelled.

I flinched. The electricity in me bubbled to the surface.

Knox took a few deep breaths before holding his hands up. "Enough of this. We're going to buy you some clothes. Fuck what DB said."

He picked me up off the worktop and set me down on the ground. Taking my hand in his, Knox led me to one of the SUVs. Just as he unlocked it and the little orange lights on the side flashed, the door to the garage opened and Hunter burst in.

"Knox have you . . . Zera? What are you doing here?" He looked at the flashing lights. "Where are you going?"

"She was walking around in the snow in these shit-ass shoes and no coat. We're going shopping."

Hunter stopped, shook his head, and then held up a hand. "Hold up. *You* are going shopping? *Clothes* shopping?"

"Fuck off, brother. She can't keep wearing some dead woman's clothes."

"What?" I asked, staring down at the dress. "Dead woman? Who died?"

"I know that, but DB said not to leave the grounds," Hunter told him. "I know it's not ideal, but we have to wait."

"Why do we?" Knox demanded. "And don't give me that bullshit about the sanctity of Castle Viegls. I'll drive us to Atlanta."

"Castle Viegls is safe. There are wards—we're protected from other supes here. Atlanta will be teeming with them."

"Exactly," Knox nodded, finally letting go of my hand. "There are that many supes there, what is three more going to do. In a different state?" He waved his hand in my direction without looking at me. "And didn't you say she deserved to be Pretty Womaned?"

"Yes, but the point was if she's here, it doesn't matter if she lets off an EMP because we're in the middle of the boonies and no one is going to know, even if hikers did manage to stray past the wards." He put his hands on his hips and glared at his brother.

Even though they were identical, somehow, Hunter's frown wasn't as intimidating as his brother's.

"She's managed six weeks. We can't keep her locked up forever."

"I want to go," I said.

Hunter looked at me, chewing on his lip before

pulling his phone out of his pocket. "DB won't have arrived in Raleigh yet," he said, slowly. "If we left now, we could get to Atlanta and back."

Knox walked over and clapped his hand on his twin's shoulder. "That's what I'm talking about."

"I'm only saying yes because I know damn well that you'll go even if I tell you not to," he muttered. Hunter looked back at me, his gaze dropping to my feet as he sighed. "And you're right, she does need clothes."

Knox turned back to me and nodded his head at the SUV. "Climb in. We're going on a road trip."

I climbed into the back of the SUV and looked around. The inside of the vehicle was big enough to fit a bed in.

Before I could close the door, Knox was there. "Seatbelt," he said, gruffly, leaning over me to strap me in.

The two men got into the front of the vehicle, leaving me wondering how we were going to get out until Knox pushed a button and the door rose.

Although there were a couple of inches of snow on the ground, the SUV drove over it with ease. I had my face almost plastered to the window as we drove along the drive and through the main gates. The thin track down wasn't as snowy as the grounds, protected from the giant evergreen trees which loomed overhead.

The further down the mountainside we travelled, the less snow there was until we hit a busy road. Despite the weather, there were a lot of vehicles on the road, and I stared at them all as we drove past.

At some point, one of the twins had put some music on, probably to hide the conversation they were having. I was so fascinated by everything outside of the vehicle that I wasn't paying much attention to what was happening inside.

Seventeen

Hunter

I had wanted nothing more than to take Zera shopping and get her some clothes and personal belongings, but leaving the castle left me feeling nervous.

As much as I could be a smartass sometimes, I rarely went against what DB said. Six weeks without Zera shorting out the castle or sparking unnecessarily wasn't really a long enough time to establish whether or not it was safe to let her leave the castle. She felt safe enough around us, which was great. But we'd not put her under any form of stress-test like DB wanted to do first. As far as he was concerned, she wasn't ready for that.

I wasn't sure how long we needed to wait. DB hadn't given any specific timeline, other than it being too soon.

But Knox was also right about her needing clothes. Zera didn't even own any underwear. And while I was comfortable letting her use all of my bubble bath, and wash products, she needed her own . . . scent. Something that was distinctly her.

There were also a few other things I wanted to fix for her. Knox was right about me wanting to go Pretty Woman on her. Even though I'd been able to restore her hair, it still needed cutting.

I pulled my phone out of my pocket and scrolled through the contacts until I found Liberty's name. I quickly tapped out a message.

"Are you texting DB?" Knox asked me.

I glanced over and shook my head. "Just because I came doesn't mean I think this is a great idea, but I'm not about to tell DB. Better to ask for forgiveness than permission, and all that."

"You could have stayed home."

I could have, but Knox's mood bounced all over the place on a good day. On a bad day, if someone looked at his scars funny, we were lucky if the police weren't called.

Between him and Zera, I wasn't sure who was the most unpredictable.

And we'd chosen to go to Atlanta.

This had disaster written all over it.

My phone finally beeped at me and I read Liberty's answer. "Liberty can fit us in this afternoon."

Knox glanced over before returning his attention to the road. "Liberty? You told a fucking witch that we're coming with an elemental? And not just any witch, but your nutjob ex?"

I turned in my seat and flicked the radio on. "First up, she's not my ex. We only hooked up a few times, and that was during our assignment in Atlanta *six* years ago. You know as well as I do that she's not exactly the popular one in her coven, and even if she was, she's loyal to the Benjamins. Therefore, I trust her."

Knox snorted. "If we can buy her silence, what's to say someone isn't going to pay more to break it."

"Who else knows about an elemental's existence other than the mortal enemy of the witches?" There were very few supes who didn't hate Lycans. They'd burned those bridges decades ago. "Besides, I never told her Zera's an elemental. Just that she's someone under our protection."

"You'd best be right about that, brother."

I'd been a little quick to defend Liberty because Knox wasn't exactly wrong when he said she was nutjob. There was a reason why she wasn't popular with her coven.

But I did trust her.

I turned in my seat, watching Zera. She was staring out of the window with her blue eyes wide. It was almost like seeing her watch the television.

More than a month had passed since we brought her home, and I'd been fighting with myself on a daily basis not to ask her questions about her past. Her wrists were still healing, and it made me want to stick a Lycan's dick in an outlet every time I had to apply the cream.

"We should stop for food," I told Knox as we approached the outskirts of Atlanta.

Three large meals a day was slowly starting to have an effect on Zera. I suspected most of her energy was going into healing her wrists and whatever internal injuries she might have, but she was starting to change.

She'd finally gone from far-too-skinny to too-skinny. It didn't sound like much, but she no longer looked like a ghoul.

Knox pulled off the highway and parked outside a restaurant. The lunchtime rush was dying off and more people were leaving the parking lot than were entering.

"Are we here?" Zera asked, looking up at a billboard.

"You haven't been shopping with Hunter before," Knox told her, killing the engine. "We need to eat otherwise you're going to be passing out on the floor."

I stepped out of the car and reached up, grateful to stretch my back. The temperature in Atlanta was a lot warmer than home with no snow in sight. I glanced up at the dark clouds. If we were lucky, we would avoid the rain, at least until we'd bought Zera a coat.

The three of us walked over to the restaurant and were led to a booth by the window. Zera slid in, but Knox sat down beside her before I could. Frowning, I slipped in opposite them. *Okaaaaay.*

"Welcome to Randalls," the waitress greeted us, sliding a menu in front of each of us. "I'm Amber and I'll be your server this afternoon. Can I get you some drinks while you look over your menus?"

I looked up at the blonde. She was pretty in that country-girl way but paled compared to Zera. Her gaze was fixed on Knox and the scars that marred his face.

Him sitting next to Zera made no sense. He *always* made the effort to sit so his scar was hidden from the room.

"We'll get three Cokes," I told her before Knox noticed her staring.

Blushing at being caught, she gave me a polite smile and hurried away.

"What do you want, Zera?" Knox asked, opening the menu for her.

Zera glanced at him before picking up the menu. A pink blush started to creep up her neck and to her cheeks as she glanced at the menu.

"You can have anything that you like the look of," I added.

She stared at the menu, shifting uncomfortably before I realized something that made my breath catch in my throat.

Zera didn't have a clue what anything on the menu said.

How could she? She'd never been treated as a person. If no one had ever taken the time to see to her injuries, when would anyone ever have taught her to read?

Which meant she had been held captive by them for a lot longer than I'd imagined.

I closed my eyes. Underneath the table, my hands balled into fists. If I ever caught the person who captured her, I was going to lock him in a cage and make sure he spent the rest of his life begging for me to end it.

"What's it gonna be?" Knox asked, still oblivious.

Zera shifted again, chewing at her lip. "I . . . I don't know. There's too much to choose from."

I leaned over and tapped one of the pictures that formed the border. "I'm stuck between this meatloaf. . ." I pointed at another picture, "and this shrimp, bacon and broccoli pasta. Do any of the pictures look appetizing to you?"

A small sigh escaped her lips.

Bingo.

Eyes narrowing, Zera leaned over, examining each picture.

I cocked my head, watching her. The pictures weren't the greatest, but her nose was almost touching the menu.

That didn't escape Knox's attention. He watched her before looking at me, an eyebrow arching. He discreetly pointed at his eye before nodding his chin in her direction.

Motherfucking Lycans. As soon as we got back

home, I was going to make sure Javion was still hunting leads to their bases because I was going to annihilate them.

Supes had good hearing and eyesight. Better than humans. For the most part, we were predators with advanced healing abilities. We weren't shortsighted.

Not unless something had damaged our eyes beyond repair.

Considering Knox's whiplash mood, he hadn't worked that out yet.

I flattened my hand, wiping my palms on my thighs. If I got worked up over this, Knox would want to know what was up, and then he would be in a foul mood for the rest of the day.

"That one," Zera said, straightening her back as she pointed at one of the pictures.

I quickly lined it up with the menu in front of me. Chicken strips.

The waitress returned with our drinks, and I gave her both mine and Zera's order. Knox, unsurprisingly, opted for a burger.

"Are you two related to Carter?" Zera asked, suddenly.

"No," Knox replied.

"Then how did you end up living with him?"

I looked over at Knox, but his gaze was fixed on the table. Rubbing at my chin, I frowned. There wasn't a simple or short answer to that. I'd fucked up, Knox had been irreparably hurt from it, and . . .

"Why don't you ask Hunter?" Knox said, stirring the straw around in his drink as he fixed me a stare, practically daring me to tell her the truth.

I hung my head. "I got captured by the Lycans."

"Hunter here decided that he was brave enough to take out a Lycan clan by himself. Figured that he was old enough and strong enough to take them out without any help. Instead, he got our whole family wiped out."

I turned to look out the window, shame burning my face. He was right. I'd been a cocky asshole back then. There was nothing I could say to disagree with him without lying.

The waitress chose that moment to return with our food. I wasn't sure if it was a blessing or not.

I did know that I'd lost an appetite for meatloaf.

Knox took a few bites of his burger before shoving the plate away from him. "I'm going to wait in the car." He was gone before I could stop him.

Zera watched him leave for all of two seconds before she started to follow after him. I stuck my hand out and gently grabbed her sleeve. "Let him be alone,

Zee," I told her. "He needs some time to cool off." I pointed at her plate. "You should eat something, anyway."

Zera gave the door one last look before turning back to her meal. She picked at the chicken, eating a few pieces before folding her arms and resting them on the table. "What did the Lycan clan do?"

"It's not worth worrying about," I told her. "It's in the past."

"We spend our time watching superhero movies, and even then, I can tell that what we are isn't considered real to most humans."

I looked around the restaurant, thankful that it had emptied out considerably, and the only people who were close enough to hear our conversation were busy arguing over the results of the weekend football game.

"Supes—supernatural creatures—must follow the law of the supernatural council. As far as humans are concerned, we don't exist, and we need to keep it that way."

Zera popped a fry into her mouth and chewed it slowly. "Okay, but does that mean you can't talk about it with other supes?"

I shook my head. "Not at all."

"Then why don't you talk about it with me?"

Zera's eyes seemed to burn into mine as she waited for an answer. I wasn't sure I really had one. "I guess because we were just busy talking about other things?" I offered. "And some of it is unpleasant."

That earned me a dark look. "I've been through unpleasant things. I doubt what you say could be worse than that."

My gaze fell on her bandaged wrists. I didn't doubt that. Which was precisely why I wasn't in any hurry to discuss anything further with her. She'd seen and experienced enough.

"How does keeping things from me help me?" she asked, as though reading my mind. "Isn't not knowing more dangerous than knowing?"

She was right. Of course she was. But it didn't mean that I wanted to tell her.

"So, what did the Lycan do? There must have been a reason for you to go after it by yourself."

"What . . . ?" I sucked in a deep breath. Picking up my fork, I started jabbing it into the mashed potatoes on the plate in front of me. "I was eighteen, and it was just after my *aibidh*."

"Your what?"

"*Aibidh*. It's when a gargoyle reaches maturity," I said. "Usually around their eighteenth birthday. As children, we look like humans, but when our *aibidh* arrives, so do our gargoyle traits."

Her mouth formed an 'o'.

"We were living in a small town in North Carolina—the only supes in town. Gargoyles are rare over this side of the Atlantic. Not as rare as elementals though."

"Do you know any elementals?" Zera asked.

Slowly, I shook my head. "Just you. You're rarer than a unicorn."

Zera sat back into the booth, nibbling at the fries on her plate. A sliver of satisfaction ran through me at that. Food would make her grow strong.

"My best friend at high school was a human named Chad. One day, he went out hunting deer and he never came back. The police found his body four days later, apparently killed by a wolf."

"Lycans?" she asked.

"Back then, we didn't think it was Lycans. The Lycans had been in trouble with the council a few years before and most had gone to Canada. Or so my dad said. DB has a theory that they never left but hid."

"Why?"

I glanced out of the window at Knox's 4Runner, still parked in the lot. There was a fair chance that Zera was the only reason he hadn't driven off and left me here.

"We don't know why," I admitted, glancing down at the plate in front of me. It looked like mush that even a baby would turn down. "They're good at covering their tracks and when supes go missing, they rarely come back." I set my fork down and pushed the plate out of the way.

"I can believe that," she muttered, darkly.

"The town was worried there was a wolf in the area and set up some hunting groups. I volunteered to go—my *aibidh* had happened, so I was suddenly invincible with my stone-like skin and claws. Of course, I couldn't show this to the humans I was with, so I went by myself. That's when I discovered it wasn't a wolf we were hunting."

"A Lycan."

I nodded. "It was in its wolf form and tried to bite me. I was in my true form, and it stopped the bite from going deep. Got a good scratch in its side too. The wolf ran off. At the time, I thought it was because it was injured. But I went home, and it followed me."

"And it attacked?" Her hand, which was holding several fries, sparked.

Glancing around the room, I leaned over and

covered her hand with mine. "Not here. And yes. They attacked. Knox and I managed to get away, but no one else survived. He got hurt really bad too—he was in the middle of his *aibidh*. Couldn't heal properly."

"Is everything okay over here?" Amber asked, suddenly appearing at the table with a bright smile on her face. "You've not touched your meals. Is there a problem with them?"

"We just weren't as hungry as we thought. Can you box them up for us?"

"Of course I can, sugar." The waitress picked up our plates and disappeared into the back.

Zera sat in silence, staring at me as she processed what I had told her. Finally, she shook her head. "I don't think it's your fault. You didn't know it was a Lycan when you went after it."

I shrugged. "Still led it back to our home."

Eighteen

Zera

The rest of the drive into Atlanta was subdued. Even though I had so many things to keep me occupied outside of the SUV, I was more concerned with what was happening on the inside.

Which was currently nothing.

Ever since we left the restaurant, neither Hunter nor Knox had said a word to each other.

Hunter had been eager to drop the conversation

the moment the waitress returned with our meals in boxes, and outside, Knox was in the car, glaring at the steering wheel like it had personally wronged him.

The more I replayed the conversation, the more I was certain Knox's hatred and blame was misguided. How could anyone know Lycans were going to find them and follow them?

How would I know?

That thought hit me hard, and I gasped before I could stop myself.

"You alright, Zee?" Hunter asked me as Knox glanced back at me through the rearview mirror.

I bit the inside of my cheek instead of answering. The two men had already been upset enough for today. I didn't need to add to their worry.

But I did need to learn more about the Lycans.

"If you don't feel comfortable, I'll turn the car around now," Knox offered.

Quickly, I shook my head. I'd been at Castle Viegls for a few weeks. If any Lycans had followed me, they would have attacked it by now. If they didn't know I was there, then they didn't know I was coming to Atlanta.

As Knox pulled the SUV up in front of a row of shops, Hunter turned in his seat. "My friend Liberty is going to cut your hair for you. She's a witch, and we've worked with her before but—"

"—but don't tell her what you are," Knox cut in.

I nodded. The fewer people who knew what I was, the lower the chance of the Lycans finding out where I was.

Knox's instruction earned a frown from Hunter, but when he looked back at me, his usual smile was back on his face. "I've already told Libs that she's not allowed to use the shower to wash your hair because you've got a phobia. She's normally closed today, so it will be just us. We're not going to leave you, but I want you to know you're safe."

"I'm safe, so please don't cause a blackout in the salon?" I asked, wearily.

Hunter and Knox shared a look. "Well, yes," Hunter said, a slight wince in his tone.

I'd managed two weeks without even blowing a bulb. I could do this.

Despite the sign saying closed, the door was unlocked. Stranger still, Hunter and Knox didn't seem alarmed by this. Clearly, they hadn't watched the same shows as me.

Liberty was not what I had imagined. She was tall and slim, tan skin and full lips. But the most striking thing about her was her hair. It was longer than mine and the most beautiful colors I'd seen. It started off pink at the top, went to purple about halfway down, before turning blue at the ends.

She gave Hunter a wide smile before wrapping her arms around him. For some inexplicable reason, my stomach twisted at that sight.

"If it isn't my favorite Carraig twins. I've missed you both," she said, although the statement seemed to be directed at Hunter.

"This is Zera," Hunter said, moving beside me.

Liberty turned, finally seeing me. Her mouth dropped open. "Holy shit on a stick, what did you do to your hair, Zera?"

Even though I knew it wasn't pretty, I instinctively curled it around my hands.

"You remember what I said, Libs?" Hunter asked.

The witched rolled her eyes. "No questions, I get it. But I'm asking about her hair. I need to know what has been on it to make sure I don't do something to fuck it up." She moved in closer, picking up a lock of it and examining it. "These ends are fried." Her eyes met mine. "Girl, you've got to stop putting a flat iron on your hair."

I nodded, even though I had no idea what on earth

would possess anyone to put an iron on their head.

"I've got some treatments which will work wonders for most of it. The rest," she held the hair up again before looking at me. "How do you feel about losing six inches?" she held up the amount.

How did I feel? It was just hair. I glanced over at the twins.

"Cut off what you need to," Hunter answered for me.

For the briefest of moments, Liberty's blue eyes flashed hot pink. She turned to Hunter and poked a finger in his direction. "When I'm cutting your hair, you can tell me what you want taking off. Zera is the one who must live with it." She turned back to me, her eyes blue again. "We can take a big chunk off, or, if you like your long hair, we can do a bit now, and a bit another time."

"No, it's okay," I said, hurriedly. "You can cut it. It's just hair."

"Follow me," she said as she nodded her head.

With Hunter and Knox right behind me, Liberty led me to the back of the shop where there were several strange shaped sinks with chairs in front of them. She wrapped a towel over my shoulders before getting me to sit in one.

"Hunter told me about the ablutophobia," Liberty told me as she bustled around.

"What's that?" I asked.

Liberty cocked her head. "Ablutophobia? It's a fear of showers or showering." She gave me a curious look, then continued. "I've got some water in the back, ready, but this will take a little bit longer than normal because of it."

I nodded, not caring. Instead, I closed my eyes and tried not to think about the water being poured on my head.

Even though I had been bathing daily—I loved the feeling of sitting in a hot bath—water going over my head still left me with a racing heart and a chill down my spine. I'd learned that wetting or rinsing my hair was easiest if I sank down into the water and tipped my head back.

A hand clasped mine, and I opened my eyes to find Hunter in the seat next to me. "I'm right here."

Between him and Liberty, the whole experience wasn't as bad as I was expecting it to be. By the time I'd had the treatment washed from my hair and Liberty had sat me down in front of a mirror, I was starting to feel better.

"How are things going with the coven these days,

Liberty?" Hunter asked my hair stylist.

"Great. They continue to tell me I'm a waste of space and I continue to ignore them," she said. Catching my surprised expression in the mirror, Liberty paused in cutting. "I'm a kick-ass hairdresser, but magic is a little sketchy with me."

"You're a fantastic tracker too," Hunter said, flashing her a smile which had my insides clenching again.

Instead of listening to him, however, Liberty was staring at an empty corner. "I did tell you. Twice . . . She's cursed, okay . . .? And you still haven't paid me, so why don't you fuck off to her house and see how that curse is going for her."

I looked over at Knox and Hunter in time to see Knox using his finger to circle the air in front of his ear.

Hunter shot him a glare before he looked over at the witch, his expression softening. "Are you okay over there, Libs?"

Liberty turned back to him, her cheeks going pink. "Yeah, just a ghost being a bigger pain in the ass than a dragon shifter's dick." She shot the empty corner a pointed glare.

Knox snorted. "You would have experience with that."

Without saying a word, Liberty raised her middle finger at Knox.

"Ghosts don't exist," Hunter said.

"I wish they didn't exist," Liberty muttered, sending the corner another frown. "Not even if you were the only ghost . . . oh, shame."

Hunter and Knox shared another look. "Hey, Liberty, we have to get a few things done while we're in Atlanta. Are you going to be much longer?" Hunter asked.

"Ghosts do exist," I blurted out. "I've seen one."

"No," Knox said, firmly. "Ghosts don't exist. Not real ones, anyway."

"But I saw one."

"Can you see Liberty's?" Hunter gestured to the empty corner the witch kept talking to.

I caught Liberty's eye in the mirror before slowly shaking my head.

"Where's fuck iz all the fucking Ginot Prigio?"

The new voice had me looking around the room.

"Don't move like that," Liberty shrieked. "I'll end up giving you a bob if you're not careful."

Seconds later a weird looking skunk staggered into the room, clutching at an empty bottle. "Where's its bitch?"

Liberty's hand wrapped around the scissors like she was holding a knife. "I don't know?" she responded through gritted teeth. "Maybe in your stomach?"

The skunk threw the bottle across the room. It hit the wall where Liberty claimed her ghost had been. "I haven't drunken its all. You stole its from me."

And then, waving its arm so vigorously it spun on the spot, the skunk collapsed on the floor.

"Your familiar talks," Knox said, flatly.

"I thought it would be a good idea. I forgot my spell skills weren't great." Liberty rubbed at her temples.

Hunter arched an eyebrow. "Um, Libs, with all due respect, how do you forget you're not the best with magic?"

"Absinthe. A whole lot of Absinthe." She glanced at the skunk and winced. "Who knew honey badgers had such bad attitudes?"

"Liberty, it's a fucking *honey badger*."

"You mean it's not a skunk?" I asked, staring in amazement at the animal. Now that it was asleep, it was kind of cute.

"No, but they do have a gland at the base of the tail which can spray a similar, pungent liquid," Liberty replied. She shot a dark look at the unconscious honey badger. "Which Pinot likes to do because he's a fucking asshole."

"Because it's a *honey badger*," Knox said, stressing the words.

Liberty calmly stuck her middle finger up at him before resuming cutting my hair.

"Is he okay there?" I asked, giving the honey badger a sideways glance.

"You couldn't pay me to move him, and I'm broke."

I was so busy staring at the strange creature, which was now snoring, that I didn't see Liberty move beside me to pick something up until the most horrific noise was whining in my ears.

Instinctively, the electricity crackled across my skin and with a loud pop, and the store fell into darkness, the noise stopping at the same time.

"Well spank my ass and call me Anastasia," Liberty muttered, her eyes wide. She took a step back, watching me warily. "*That's* why you didn't want me to ask any questions."

"Liberty, you can't say anything," Hunter told her.

"Who am I going to tell?"

Knox gave her a pointed look.

"I said I wouldn't say anything, and I won't." She ran a hand through her multicolored hair. "That's two supes that don't exist."

"Ghosts don't exist, but Zera does." Hunter walked over and placed his hands on her shoulders. "You really can't say anything."

"I *won't*. Jeez, I have enough on my plate with the ghost—which does exist—and I don't need any other supes turning up on my doorstep." She glanced up at the light before sighing. "I'm going to check the fuse box."

I waited for Liberty to disappear into the back before looking at the twins. "It scared me."

Hunter moved behind the chair, looking at me in the mirror as he played with my hair. "It's a hairdryer. I'm sorry; I should have said what it was. It's noisy, but it won't hurt you. It just blows warm air out."

"You think we need to go check on the witch?" Knox asked, directing the question at his brother.

Sucking in a breath, Hunter shook his head. "I trust her."

The lights flicked on and moments later, Liberty reappeared. "Thank fuck, because my landlord is desperate for a reason to kick me out." She walked back to me and arched an eyebrow at Hunter. "You want to do my job?"

Hunter moved out of the way as Liberty reached

for the hairdryer, flicking the switch. Nothing happened.

"Did I break it?"

"It might just be the fuse," she said, thoughtfully. Liberty unplugged the hairdryer, set it on the side, and then grabbed one of the hairdryers from the other side of the room. She plugged it in, but paused, holding it up in front of me. "Are you going to fry this if I turn it on? Because one is easy enough to replace, but after that it's going to start getting pricey."

I shook my head but braced myself.

Aiming it up in the air, Liberty turned it on. While the noise startled me, because I was expecting it, I managed not to destroy another hairdryer.

Liberty quickly clipped part of my hair back and then got to drying it. I'd gotten used to letting my hair dry naturally, but this was much quicker.

Finally, she turned the appliance off and set it down. "All done."

Running my hand through my hair, I discovered it felt soft and silky. It fell around my face, hanging down to my breasts in soft waves. The hair didn't feel as heavy, and it smelled heavenly.

I stood and turned to face the twins. Knox was rubbing at his jaw while Hunter was giving me his bright smile. "Liberty, you may be a shit witch, but you are the best hairdresser."

Hunter handed over a pile of money before the three of us headed for the car. "Where are we going now?" I couldn't stop touching my hair.

"I was going to suggest Lenox Square," Hunter said.

Knox shook his head. "Are you serious? She freaked out over a hairdryer. She's not ready for the biggest mall in the city."

"It's the second, actually, but you're right."

"I know a place," Knox muttered.

Hunter shot him a look. "You know where to shop?"

"No, that's why I walk around naked," he replied, deadpan.

Despite Hunter's questioning, Knox didn't let on to where or what his place was. Instead, he drove us there, finally pulling up to a parking lot.

"A strip mall?" Hunter sighed and shrugged. "Good call." He turned to me. "You can go in as many stores as you like. We've got plenty of time. Don't settle for the first thing you see—find something you love."

Something I loved? I thought to the shows I had been watching, a few outfits standing out in my mind.

"Okay."

"And we're starting with underwear," Hunter said, pulling me toward one of the stores.

That was a whole new experience.

Apparently, if I was going to try clothes on, I would need underwear. Hunter marched straight up to a woman and got her to measure me. Hunter and Knox stood back, watching me hold up bras, not knowing what to do with themselves.

I was surprised at how much I enjoyed seeing their cheeks turn pink.

But I was more interested in their expressions. I'd seen the same look in Knox's eyes before he had kissed me. Every so often, I would catch him rubbing at his jaw, not hiding the fact he was staring at me.

Hunter, on the other hand, would look away when I looked at him. But he had the same expression Knox did.

I just couldn't figure out why he was trying to hide it.

Wearing one of the underwear sets under my clothes, I walked out of the store feeling incredible. I left the store with more bras and panties than I thought I really needed, but I wasn't complaining.

Finding clothes wasn't as easy.

All the clothing stores seemed to hold clothes in the same style and as pretty as they were, I didn't *love* them like Hunter wanted me to. Given how both he and Knox would turn their nose up at my half-hearted suggestions, I knew they didn't love them either.

Shopping with Hunter and Knox was an interesting experience. The two men were exceptionally good-looking and even though there weren't many people around, almost everyone turned their heads to look at them as they walked past.

After watching one woman react the same way everyone else had, I could feel myself growing irritated, and I fought with my body not to zap her.

It wasn't the staring. I couldn't fault anyone for that because they were handsome. It was the double-take and the follow-up sneer of disgust when they saw the scar on Knox's face.

In the daylight, it was easier to see, although I still didn't think it was that noticeable. At first, I thought I'd gotten it wrong and something else was causing the stares, but I heard the woman talking to her friend on the phone. "Why didn't he get plastic surgery? He'd be hot as hell if he did that."

If it weren't for the fact that I had promised to try not to draw attention to myself, I would have zapped her. While I didn't particularly care if she survived the shock or not, a dead person wasn't being discreet.

Unfortunately.

Instead, I tried to be less picky and attempted to hurry up. We'd worked our way through nearly all of the stores when an outfit in a window caught my attention. Without a word, I walked into the store, knowing the twins were following me.

One of the most beautiful women I had ever seen walked up to me. "Hey sugar, see anything you like?"

I nodded, pulling several items off the shelf. Ignoring the surprised expressions both Hunter and Knox had, I gathered up the clothes, the assistant helping me find the right sizes.

Finally, she led me to a room at the back to try things on. "I'll be right here. You holler if you need any help."

I stepped into the changing room and started pulling clothes on. I knew as soon as the supple leather pants fastened that these were the clothes I loved. This was almost like what the superheroes were wearing in all the movies I'd been watching.

Although I wasn't entirely sure how bodices protected the women, I loved how I looked in it. I'd put on a little weight, and I was starting to look a lot less skeletal.

Having tried on everything and loving it all, I stepped out of the changing room wearing one of the outfits: black leather pants and a black and red bodice.

"I don't know what to put back," I told the assistant.

She arched an eyebrow. "I promise you, when you walk out there, you're not going to put anything back on the rack." She took all the clothes off me and led me out.

Knox was stretched out on a chair looking at something on his phone, while Hunter was busy inspecting a dress. Knox looked up first and dropped the phone.

Hunter glanced down at the phone on the floor. "What's up with . . . gods above . . ."

"I love this," I told them, firmly.

"You're not the only one," Knox muttered, staring at me, unblinking.

"DB is going to have an aneurysm." Hunter rubbed at the back of his neck.

"Does that mean I need to find something else?"

"Like fuck you do." Knox was on his feet, taking all of the clothes off the assistant and marching to the checkout before I could tell him he had forgotten his phone.

I bent down and picked it up, looking to Hunter who was staring at me like he had never seen me before. "I love it," I told him, firmly. "You told me to find something I love, and I did."

Hunter slowly shook his head. "Zera, you look like. . . you."

Folding my arms, I squinted at Hunter, trying to understand what he meant by that. Was that an insult or a compliment? The way he said it made me think it was, but the look in his eyes, like this was a bad idea, told me otherwise.

"I am so screwed," he muttered, walking away.

I glanced down at my outfit. Was this really going to upset Carter that much?

The last thing I wanted was to put them back on the rack, but I also didn't want to upset the person who was letting me stay in his home.

"Zera," Knox called, waving me over.

Having already paid and the items in several bags, he didn't give me the chance to change my mind.

With a big smirk on his face, I followed Knox out of the store. "I think we should celebrate with ice cream," Knox declared.

"Excuse me."

I turned, trying to work out where the voice had come from, before realizing the owner was a child. "Hi."

"You're really pretty."

"Lewis, don't bother the lady," a woman chided him.

"What's your name?" he asked, ignoring her.

"Zeraora," I told him.

The kid's eyes went wide before turning to his mom. "Mom, she's named after a Pokémon," he yelled.

Knox's head whipped around. "What?"

I shrugged. I had no idea what he was talking about. Hunter, on the other hand, was scratching at the back of his neck with a sheepish expression on his face. "Zera chose it," he protested.

"Zera doesn't know what a fucking Pokémon is."

"Knox; children," Hunter hissed at him as the woman dragged her child off.

"I don't give a fuck about children. You named her after a fucking Pokémon."

"Zeraora is a legendary tiger Pokémon," Hunter corrected him. He folded his arms and scowled at his brother. "And Zera picked it."

Without another word, Knox turned on his heel and stormed off, still carrying half of the bags of clothes.

Hunter gave me his familiar, friendly smile, and took my hand. "Ice cream."

The ice cream store was almost empty. Hunter led me to a table in the back and sat me down, leaving the dozens of bags by my feet. While he went to the counter, I sat chewing at my lip.

Carter wouldn't like my clothes and now Knox didn't like my name.

I had no idea why that upset me. I would be leaving soon anyway.

But my chest hurt, and I could feel a lump in the back of my throat.

When Hunter returned, I was still frowning. "Are you okay?" he slid a bowl of ice cream in front of me.

"Not really," I said as I started to shake my head.

Hunter's phone rang. He pulled it out of his pocket with an irritated sigh and pressed something, making it go silent. A second later, it started ringing again. This time, he answered. "Knox, you . . . the ice cream store. . ." And then he was on his feet, looking around.

"What's the matter?" I peered toward the door, expecting to see Knox.

"We'll meet you back at the car . . . yes, I know that." Hunter hung up and turned to me. "We're leaving now."

"But what about the ice cream? What happened?" There was a knot forming in the pit of my stomach. I didn't care about the ice cream, but if Hunter was ready to abandon it, something had happened.

Was Knox okay?

Hunter looked at me as we walked toward the door.

"We've been followed."

Nineteen

Knox

Pokémon?

He named her after a fucking *Pokémon?*

I couldn't be mad at Zera because even if she had picked the name, she didn't know what a damn Pokémon was.

The most annoying part was that Zera suited her.

Fuck it all, I wanted to punch something—Hunter being top of the list.

DB had given her a home, and Hunter had given her a name. What the fuck could I give her?

I was past the point of trying to deny my attraction. That had been abandoned when I had kissed her.

And that kiss also made no sense to me.

Why me?

Why had she kissed me back?

It was clear I was ruined goods. I wasn't the kind of person a woman like her should have by her side.

Hell, I spent half my time arguing with myself that Javion saw me for more than a blood supply. At least that attraction had grown over time.

But Zera, she had . . .

I wasn't someone a person fell in love with at first sight.

Turning my head, I caught my reflection in a store window. Without the scars on my face, it would be handsome. You only had to look at Hunter to see that. These weren't scars that made a person look attractive. Lycan claws were tipped with toxins which stopped supes healing properly.

A gargoyle's indestructible skin was one of the only things which could protect against it—provided the gargoyle had gone through their *aibidh*.

I'd been attacked when I was still going through the

aibidh. For a brief moment I had tasted freedom in the air. Now my wings were useless, claw marks covered my body, and my vision was in grayscale. The claws had caught my left eye and in addition to giving the left side of my face a permanent sneer, the trauma from the fight had left me unable to see in color.

I knew what colors were, and I saw them in my dreams sometimes, but awake, everything was black, white, or gray.

Something sparkling in a window display caught my attention.

Diamonds.

A bracelet sat twinkling at me under the store lights. It was beautiful. Something that would look good on Zera, especially with one of the dresses she had bought.

Her clothing choice surprised me. Although Hunter had muttered the colors of the outfits that she had shown us, it hadn't been that which had surprised me.

It was the style.

I didn't need to see the color to know she was wearing a lot of tight-fitting leather. While some of the bodices showed off how deep the recess in her collarbones were, there was something about them which showed off her confidence.

She still hadn't revealed exactly what she had been through, but her still-healing scars told me it was enough that most females would be retreating into themselves.

Looking up, I caught the expression of a store employee watching me like I was about to put my fist through the window and take the jewelry.

Fuck her.

And fuck the bracelet.

It wasn't Zera's style: too dainty. And she wouldn't want to put anything around her wrists anyway.

But if the store employee—a human female—could look at me and see the danger, why didn't Zera?

Why had she kissed me back?

Better yet, why had I kissed her? She was still an unknown. She was still as dangerous as I was.

It wasn't even like I was starved for attention. I had Javion.

Finding myself at the far end of the strip mall and a supe owned biker bar, I stepped inside. Although I had my own collection of bikes and an appreciation for them, I'd never joined a club. There had been times when I was tempted, but no matter how much I hated my twin some days, he was still my blood.

The Outpost Pride was run by a bunch of cats. The 21s' president was a lion shifter called Hamilton. I hadn't seen his bike parked up outside, and he wasn't in the bar when I walked in. I stalked up to the bar and took a seat, dumping the bags of shopping on the floor beside me.

"Hey Knox, it's been a while," Quinn greeted me, already pulling a beer out of the fridge.

I liked Quinn. She was a shifter of some description. I wasn't sure what, but I was almost certain it wasn't feline. Quinn didn't belong in a place like this. She was too soft and gentle for the clutter that was the 21s.

"Holy shitters, Knox, you got a girlfriend, or have you got a new nighttime hobby?"

"Girlfriend? She blind?"

All of a sudden, I didn't want the beer.

I ignored the laughter from the two panther shifters, members of the 21s. and focused on the bottle.

"Garret, Alec, leave Knox alone," Quinn told them. Although she was softly spoken, the two bikers listened to her.

"You were up in Maine on Halloween, right?" the more muscular of the two, Garret, asked. He slid onto the stool beside me. Of the two, he had the lighter hair.

It wasn't as light as Quinn's, which I guessed was either white or platinum blonde. But close.

I had been going to leave; pay for the undrunk beer and get out of there . . . "Maine?" I asked, reaching for the beer and taking a sip.

"Well, rumor has it that the seaside town of Cape Clovelly has a Lycan pack living there, or it did until someone destroyed their power supply," Alec continued. He stood beside Garret; his dark eyes fixed on me. "And we all know how you and the other residents of Castle Viegls have been hunting the Lycans."

"Our hunting of the Lycans has never been a secret." I shrugged. "But we're not the only ones who suffered at the hands of the Lycans."

"No, but there was a burnt-out Dodge Ram left in Cape Clovelly with absolutely no identification in it."

I turned, arching an eyebrow. "If there was absolutely no identification left on it, I would say the owner of the vehicle had done a superb job of not having it tracked back to him or her."

Garret held his hands up. "Mate, I'm just saying, there was a burnt-out truck and the fact you guys have been after the Lycans, combined with half a pack being wiped out, means you might want to watch your back.

You've been hunting the Lycans, and now they're hunting you."

"Or whoever left that burnt-out truck," Alec added with a roll of his eyes as I turned back to the bar.

I stared at the bottle of beer in my hands, not really seeing the label. For years, this was what we wanted: to lure the Lycans out of hiding. Considering how monstrous they were, and how many supes they had kidnapped to have half of the supernatural world wanting them dead, they had done a fine job of hiding.

Under normal circumstances, this would be ideal.

Now it forced a knot of fear in the bottom of my stomach. They weren't after us.

They were after Zera.

While a heightened sense of smell was usually reserved for the animal shifters, gargoyles had their own ability to sense other supes. Annoyingly, it wasn't as specific as scent, but it was enough for me to know there was a different supe present.

As I took another sip of my beer, the hairs on the back of my neck stood on end. I glanced over my shoulder at the newcomer.

A female.

She wasn't the same type of shifter as Quinn—whatever she was—nor was she feline. Her hair was cut short in a harsh line under her chin, but it had two contrasting streaks on either side. Given her wardrobe choice, she had probably been shopping in the same store Zera had.

"Who are you?" I asked as she draped her arms over Garret's shoulder.

"Caitlyn," she responded, ignoring the fact Garret shook her off him.

"Can I help you?"

"I heard their power supply was an elemental." She almost sounded like she was purring, but she definitely wasn't a feline shifter. As her glossy lips curled up, I realized she was trying to flirt with me.

"What time did you start drinking, kitten?"

Caitlyn arched a perfect eyebrow. "Kitten? I'm not a cat. I'm a mongoose."

And there it was. The weasels of the shifter world. Scavengers who called themselves bounty hunters but would sell their 'bounty' to anyone who outbid the original offer.

"The Lycans sent you after their elemental?" I asked.

She cocked her head. "I might have a slight incentive on that. I'd be willing to share it with anyone who could give me some information."

I turned fully to face her. "I can give you some information." I leaned forward. "Elementals don't exist."

Caitlyn leaned forward, and then glanced over my shoulder at the shopping bags. "Then who is the lucky lady?"

Without answering, I threw some money down on the bar and stood, scooping up the bags. "See you next time, Quinn."

The moment I got outside, I pulled my phone out, calling Hunter. "Where are you?"

"The ice cream store—"

"I've been at Outpost Pride. The Lycans know we were in Cape Clovelly. There's a mongoose shifter asking questions about Zera. Get out." I glanced over my shoulder just as Caitlyn walked out of the bar.

"We'll meet you back at the car," he told me.

"Be careful." I hung up, put the phone back in my pocket, and walked in the opposite direction to our car. I knew she was following me.

I didn't stop until I hit the street and hailed a cab. Sliding in the back, I asked the driver to take me downtown—just in case—and called Hunter again.

"We're at the car," he told me.

"I'm heading downtown," I muttered, glancing out

the rear window. "I was being followed and didn't want to risk it."

"Knox, you have the keys."

I rolled my eyes. "No shit, Sherlock. Get far enough away to get a taxi and come join me downtown."

"Why don't we just meet back at Liberty's hair salon?" he asked.

"Not a chance. You think it's a coincidence that after only a few hours in town, there's a fucking mongoose shifter tracking us?" I kept my voice low and covered my mouth as I kept an eye on the driver. He seemed too distracted by the traffic to notice my slipup.

"I don't think—"

"I don't care." I snapped. "I don't trust Liberty and I'm not willing to risk it. Meet at Woodruff Park at that Phoenix statue."

I sank back into my seat, rubbing my hand over my face.

Why had I thought coming here was a good idea?

And we still had to get back to Castle Viegls before DB got back.

Fuck.

Twenty

Zera

It was the Lycans. It had to be.

I could feel my heart pounding in my chest, blood pumping around my body. For some reason, it didn't feel like it was taking the oxygen with it. I felt weak.

"Hey, Zee?" Hunter's face appeared in front of mine. "Zee?"

Was this it? My chance to destroy the Lycans?

"What did he say?"

We were at the SUV, waiting for Knox to appear. He was nowhere in sight.

"We're going to meet him downtown," Hunter muttered, tilting his head as he looked at me. "Are you okay?"

"I'm fine," I said, barely paying attention as I looked around for anyone who could possibly be a Lycan. "Why do we have to go downtown? What's wrong with here? There's hardly anyone around."

"Exactly." Hunter transferred all of his bags to one hand, and then took mine in the other. "We're going where the people are so we can hide amongst them. The more people there are, the easier it is to get lost."

He started pulling me toward the street on the far side of the parking lot, but I stopped, forcing him to turn back. "Why would I want to hide from them?"

Hunter's mouth slowly fell open. "Zee, they're dangerous."

"And so am I."

Sucking in a deep breath, Hunter shook his head. "With a new hairstyle and a kickass wardrobe, you look ready to take on anything, but you're not. Especially not the Lycans."

"I've done it before." I pulled my hand free of his and narrowed my eyes at him. "I can do it again. I have been getting stronger."

"Is this your girlfriend, Knox?"

At the sound of the woman's voice, both Hunter and I turned. She was crazy beautiful. She was also not alone.

"Oh, you're not Knox. You must be the twin." She looked at me and smirked. "Sharing the girlfriend, I see. I thought that was a Lycan thing, but . . ." she shrugged. "I guess she spent a little too much time with the Lycans."

Before I realized what he was doing, Hunter had moved in front of me. "I take it you're the mongoose shifter?"

"Caitlyn." She looked at me again. "And that's the missing elemental?"

"Elementals don't exist." Hunter scoffed.

"You might want to tell the elemental that." Caitlyn laughed, pointing at me. "I can see the sparks from here."

I glanced down at my hands. She was right: I was sparking. I flexed my hands before raising them in her direction. "If you know what's good for you, you'll leave now."

"Oh wow, that's kinda cute." Caitlyn turned to the two men flanking her. "Show her the neat weapons you have."

Although their imposing height made them hard to ignore, I'd been keeping my attention on Caitlyn. When they started advancing toward us, I switched my gaze to them.

The two men made Carter look short. They had to be seven feet tall with broad shoulders and thighs that were thicker than my waist. Their hair was fiery red, with matching beards hanging down to their chests.

"Shit," Hunter muttered under his breath.

He might have been worried, but I wasn't. Considering Caitlyn had told them to show me their weapons, their hands were empty. Unless their hands were their weapons . . .

My weapon had range.

Calling the electricity to my hands, I aimed them at the closest man and let it rip.

The charge bounced off his chest and hit Knox's car.

Before I could work out what had happened, I was being flung backwards as the car exploded. My body slid along the asphalt. While the leather of my clothes gave the majority of me some protection, my bare arms weren't.

As I let out a cry of pain, Hunter's arms wrapped

around my arms, pulling me to my feet. "Run." He started pulling me away from the two advancing men.

"Why didn't I shock them?" I asked as I tore after him, trying to ignore the pain in my hip from where it hit the ground.

"They're ogres. They draw their power from the ground like we do. Electricity won't do shit to them."

"How do we stop them?" I glanced over my shoulder in time to see them both breaking into a run.

"We don't. We get the hell out of here."

I didn't want to. I was certain they could be stopped with a large enough blast.

Hunter didn't give me the opportunity to find out, as he pulled me to the road. Just as I thought he was going to make us run into oncoming traffic, he reached out, grabbing the edge of a flatbed truck.

With a cry of exertion, he heaved us both up onto the back of it, just as one of the ogres wrapped their hand around one of the shopping bags Hunter had somehow managed to hold onto.

As the bag ripped, sending some of my brand-new bras flying into the ogre's face, Hunter and I landed heavily on the truck bed, just behind a stack of crates. More specifically, Hunter landed on the truck bed, holding me in his arms to make sure I'd landed on him.

I lay there, staring down at him as my hair seemed to create a curtain around us. His bright green eyes were lined with a ring of brown I'd not noticed before.

Hunter reached up, brushing my hair back from my face. "Are you okay?"

Pressing my hands onto his chest, I started to push myself up, but Hunter wrapped his arms around me. "Stay where you are until the truck stops."

As one of his hands went back to my face, cupping my cheek, the idea seemed tempting. Hunter was comfortable.

"You should have let me kill them."

He shook his head. "You couldn't have. Not with just the spark in you."

I snorted. "It's more than a spark."

"Not against an ogre."

My gaze dropped to Hunter's neck and the curve down to his collar bone. His skin was flushed, but it looked as normal as mine. "Does their skin protect them like yours?" I asked, running my fingers along the curve of his neck.

"No." His voice, barely above a whisper, was hard to hear over the noise of the truck engine. "Ogres are just mean, dumb brutes who draw strength from the ground. My claws would be able to rip them apart." He reached up and grabbed at my hand, holding it firmly in his. "Yours would be less effective, but with a manicure, you might get in a decent scratch."

Electricity danced over our hands, but I wasn't sure why it was there.

"Then why didn't you do that?" I asked, trying to ignore the sensation.

"If it had been just me, I might have, but with that mongoose shifter, there were three of them and I couldn't risk anything happening to you."

Despite my irritation at not being able to destroy the ogres, I had the overwhelming urge to kiss Hunter. Just as his lips parted a fraction and I started to lower my head, the truck jerked to a stop.

My mouth barely brushed Hunter's as he caught my weight and pushed me up. "We need to get off this truck."

I had no time to think about what had happened—or nearly happened—as Hunter pressed me against his waist and jumped off the back of the truck. To the soundtrack of horns blaring, he set me on the ground, and we hurried through the paused traffic toward the sidewalk.

As Hunter looked up and down the street, gathering his bearings, I watched the gargoyle in disappointment. We had escaped the ogres, much to my annoyance, so there had been no need for us to get off the truck.

Unless he needed it as an excuse.

Was that his way of letting me down?

In some respects, I couldn't blame him. The Lycans had sent ogres after me.

I tilted my head to the side as my thoughts drifted down another path.

The Lycans had sent ogres after me.

They knew I had escaped and were actively trying to find me. If I could use that to my advantage, I wouldn't need to figure out how to track them down. I could just wait for them to come to me.

"Zera?"

I turned and found Hunter holding open the door to a yellow and white car which seemed almost toy-like compared to his build. He beckoned me over, and I slid in after him.

We didn't drive for long before we were dropped off at a giant garden surrounded by a street and tall buildings that stretched into the sky. As Hunter paid the taxi, I stared up, my head going almost vertical to see the top of the buildings.

Being up there I would be able to touch the sky.

"This way." Hunter slipped his hand through mine.

The area was full of people, unlike the strip mall. For such a small place, the crowd was bigger than I expected. With the tall buildings surrounding the garden, it made me feel uncomfortable. Like I was back in the small glass cage.

A shiver ran down my spine, and I moved closer to Hunter, wrapping my arms around his.

"What's up, Zee?"

"I feel like I'm back on display in the cell," I muttered, too busy watching people stare at us while we walked by to care what I was saying.

Sensing Hunter's eyes on me, I looked up and found him watching me too. "You are someone who naturally draws attention, regardless of what you're wearing," he told me.

I glanced down at my new clothes, already a little disheveled. "There's something wrong with what I'm wearing?"

"Not at all. People dress in clothes that match their personality. Bold, colorful, mature, playful, sexy . . . you picked something which matches you, even if you don't know who you are yet, so don't worry about it."

I wasn't entirely sure what my outfit choice said about me, but I straightened my back.

Hunter led us along a path to the opposite end where we had started. Below a canopy of trees, even though they had lost their leaves, the world seemed a little less overwhelming.

I spotted Knox quickly. He was underneath a small covered structure, staring at the back of a statue of a woman holding a bird. He still held all of the bags from shopping.

As though he could sense us, he turned before we got close and hurried over.

Stopping a few feet in front of us, his brows knitted together as he stared at me—at my scratched arms still wrapped around Hunter's. "What the fuck happened to your arms? Are you okay?"

"The mongoose shifter wasn't alone. She was accompanied by ogres," Hunter told him, after a quick cursory glance to see who was nearby.

The effort was wasted. "Ogres?" Knox repeated, so loudly, a dozen heads turned in our direction.

"Fuck's sake, Knox," Hunter hissed at him.

Knox grimaced then shook it off, taking a step closer to me. "What the fuck did they do to your arms?"

"They didn't. I threw a bolt of electricity at them, and it bounced off and made the car blow up," I told him, still bitter about that. "Because I'm not made of stone, I went flying."

The younger twin unthreaded my arms from his brother's and turned them gently. The blood was beginning to dry, but there were still wet areas. I glanced at Hunter's sleeve, spotting blots of blood on his checked shirt.

"Does it hurt?" Knox asked.

I thought about it before nodding my head. "I guess."

"You . . . guess?"

Hunter put his hands on my shoulders and turned me to face him. "Are you hiding your pain from us?"

"No, I just . . ." I shrugged. "I guess I'm used to it."

I watched as Knox's blank expression gave way to rage before he turned and stormed off. Seconds later, he was spinning on his heel and marching straight back. "Don't you ever hide the pain from me. Stay here."

Knox took off again, and I gave Hunter a helpless look.

"He can get a little protective," Hunter said, leading me over to a bench. He waited for me to sit down before looking at the cuts and grazes along my arm.

Before I could respond, my attention was snatched away by a sound that made my heart pound.

A bark.

I looked up, seeing an enormous dog charging across the grass.

There was just one, which wasn't ideal, but it was going to be one less Lycan to worry about by the time I'd finished.

As I leaped to my feet, I drew all the electricity in me, bringing it to my fingertips before letting it fly.

The bolt barely left my personal space before Hunter dove in front of it. His action wasn't enough to stop the shock completely, but it was enough to knock Hunter off his feet while sending the electricity off course. The bolt of energy soared through the air before hitting the statue beside us with an almighty bang.

I looked up in time to see the Lycan running in the opposite direction. "What did you do?" I demanded, frowning at Hunter. I could feel the electricity crackling over my skin, but the feeling wasn't painful for once.

"That was not a Lycan," Hunter told me as he scrambled to his feet. "Zera, you need to stop with this electricity before someone sees it. Now."

I stared at the retreating dog, a young man chasing after it. "It looks like a Lycan."

"It's just a dog. A big dog, but a dog." Hunter looked over my shoulder and winced. "Shit." As I started to turn, he grabbed my hand. "Don't."

"Why?"

"He has his phone on you. The last thing we need is your face ending up on the internet. Or worse: the red web."

I had no clue what the red web was, and the only thing I really knew about the internet was it seemed to hold a lot of information which, once it was on there, stayed there.

But it also needed energy to power.

Well, I knew how to take that away.

I closed my eyes, concentrating.

"Zee, what the f—"

I let the energy inside me burst free. It was like an explosion of white light and pressure, and when the light cleared, I seemed to be the only one still standing.

For the briefest moment, there was silence. No one spoke, no sounds came from vehicles—not even a chirp of a bird.

And then, like a switch had been flipped, there were bangs, crashes, and people screaming.

Groaning, Hunter sat up, blinking at me as he held his head. "Oh, Zee, what did you do?"

"You didn't want my face on the internet, so I destroyed it."

Hunter's mouth dropped open as he stared at me, now no longer blinking. "Fuck me, did you EMP Atlanta?"

"I think it came from her." The accusation came from behind me from a voice I didn't recognize.

After a quick scan around me, I realized there were a number of people looking in my direction.

"Fuck." Hunter grunted. He gathered up the bags which he had dropped and then wrapped his hand around mine. "We need to get out of here."

He started pulling me in the direction that Knox had gone as more and more people started to point fingers in our direction. "I've got enough power left in me to take them out too," I offered.

Hunter stopped suddenly, turning on the spot so quickly that I couldn't stop myself from colliding with his hard body. He stepped back and narrowed his eyes. "Do not use your powers on innocent humans," he told me.

"Hunter? Zera?" We both looked over at Knox who was running across a road littered with crashed cars, trying to avoid the collisions. "What the ever-loving fuck happened?"

As I pointed at myself, Hunter gritted his teeth. "Exactly what you think happened."

Knox nodded. "We need to get out of here, now."

"And how the fuck are we going to do that?" Hunter asked him. He gestured to the dead vehicles in the road before flinging his arms up at the traffic signal. "Even they are dead."

Without responding, Knox took my other hand and started jogging away from the garden, weaving through traffic. "We couldn't stay there. Too many people staring at you. We need to get lost in the chaos and then figure out what we're going to do."

Chaos was a good word.

The streets were full of so many people who seemed to be walking in circles, either in a panic or having a meltdown. There were some trying to help those that had been injured, or calming down people that were overreacting with fear.

All I'd done was kill the power. Why was everyone having such an issue?

As we ran past a store, a window exploded. I screamed, the noise making me jump, and found two men climbing through broken glass, grabbing at items on display.

Were the doors suddenly broken?

And then the area seemed to descend into madness. More screams filled the air as fires and fights broke out.

Both Hunter and Knox gripped my hand even tighter. We ran through the crowds, avoiding the patches of violence and defunct vehicles, until I stumbled. I'd spent a lifetime barely moving. I wasn't ready for this much movement.

I never hit the floor—both Hunter and Knox's strong arms stopped me from falling. The older twin swooped around and picked me up; the bags he was still managing to hold onto crashed into Knox.

Although neither spoke, Knox let go of my hand and took the bags from his brother, allowing Hunter to carry me easily.

I collapsed against Hunter's chest, trying to catch my breath, while cursing the fact that I was unable to run. I shouldn't need to be carried around like this.

As I clung onto Hunter, watching the madness erupting around us, the two gargoyles ran along the street, dodging more cars as we ran under the interstate, until finally, in a more residential part of the city, we ducked into a cemetery.

Hiding behind a thick tree, Hunter set me on the ground. Although the pair of them were breathing more heavily than usual, both looked like they would be able to continue running for some time if needed.

I glanced back in the direction we had come from, the twilight sky lighting up from below by glows of red and orange.

"Now what?" Hunter asked his brother.

Knox swept a hand over his hair as he looked at me. "What happened?"

"I only did it because Hunter told me to."

Hunter's mouth fell open as he gaped at me. "The fuck?"

"There was this guy with a phone, and you said I couldn't have my face on the internet." I shrugged. "I stopped the internet."

Knox, who's eyes had been flicking between the two of us held up a hand. "What? What the fuck did you need to stop the internet for?"

"Oh shit," Hunter muttered, pinching the bridge of his nose. "Zee, that's not what I meant, and you didn't stop the internet. That's impossible. I mean, not single handedly anyway—it would take many of you . . ." he shook his head and looked at Knox. "She did her electric bolt thing, and I tried to stop it but ended up destroying the Atlanta From The Ashes statue. Someone was filming, and I saw them point it at Zera, so I told her not to look and let it get on the internet."

Knox's eyes drifted up, and I had to tilt my head to

see if he was staring at anything in particular before I looked down and found him watching me. "So naturally, your reaction was to do your little EMP trick and wipe out the power—no, anything vaguely electrical—in the whole damn city?"

I shrugged. "I didn't end up on the internet."

"Look, I know you—"

Knox's laughter echoed out around the cemetery.

Both Hunter and I turned, only to watch him double over, clutching at his stomach. "And people think *I* have anger issues? That's the most nuclear reaction to *anything*."

I folded my arms, chewing at my cheek as I watched him. Both of the men were not reacting in the way they should.

"Fuck this," Hunter grumbled. "I'm going to see if that works." He pointed at something outside of the cemetery but walked off before I could see what.

As he disappeared, Knox finally straightened, wiping under his eyes with the back of his hand. "I'm sorry. I'm not laughing at you. But fuck a duck in the ass . . ."

I narrowed my eyes at him. He'd best not be laughing at me. "I only did it because Hunter said not to let my face get on the internet."

With two strides, Knox was in front of me, brushing my slightly sweaty hair from my face. He leaned down and kissed me before stepping backwards.

"What was that for?" I asked.

Knox's mouth quirked up in the corner as he gave me a wry grin. "I need a reason?"

I thought about it, and then shook my head.

Once more, Knox stepped forward, capturing my lips with his. This time, his tongue swept over them before easing into my mouth. His hands settled onto my shoulders before gliding down my body and stopping just under the swell of my breasts.

They were no good there.

I pushed my chest up toward him, taking his hands and placing them on my breasts. The heat seemed to sear me through the leather, but it was Knox who groaned into my mouth.

All of a sudden, he pulled back, shaking his head. "I am down for some funky shit, but even I've gotta draw the line at going past second base in a fucking cemetery."

"I don't see a problem with it," I told him, although I had absolutely no idea what bases he was talking about.

Knox let out a bark of laughter. "Doesn't surprise

me, Tric." He laughed again. "You managed to turn Atlanta into some fucked-up apocalypse and all I can think about is desecrating graves just so I can see you light up when you come."

Half of what he said still didn't make sense, but with the heated look he gave me, I didn't care.

"Phone box is dead," Hunter announced, reappearing. He looked at the two of us, arching an eyebrow at Knox. "Are you still laughing at that?"

Knox gave him a dismissive wave of his hand. "Of course, the phone box won't work. In about half an hour, we're going to see just how dead this city is."

"And we need to get out of here before the monsters come out to play."

"The Lycans?" I asked, hopeful.

"Humans," Hunter said, slowly.

Twenty-One

Zera

"Humans?"

Hunter nodded. His eyes didn't leave me as he watched me.

I wasn't sure what response I was supposed to give him, so I just stared back. "They're worse than the Lycans? Or the mongoose woman and her ogres?"

"In this situation, yes," Knox answered for him although his attention was on scanning the surrounding area.

I looked around into the darkness. From the way Hunter spoke, I was expecting crowds of humans to start falling from the sky.

"When humans get scared, they do stupid shit and turn on each other. And when it gets dark, they get even more scared," Hunter told me as he gathered up the bags from the ground. "We need to get out of the city as quickly as we can."

"What about Caitlyn? Don't we need to worry about her anymore?"

"Oh, we still need to worry about her. And she's probably not the only bounty hunter out here. At least the one advantage to this blackout is that their communication is blocked too." Knox glanced at the city before glancing back in the opposite direction. "If the last blackout is anything to go by, we need to get to Gainesville before we're going to see power again."

"Didn't Javion say it was a forty-mile radius?"

Knox looked at his brother and shrugged. "I'd say Gainesville might be generous considering she passed out after the last one, and she's still up and walking after this one." He looked around again before shaking his head. "We should wait for darkness and then you should get her out of here."

"What about you?" If the place was teeming with

dangerous humans, surely Knox shouldn't stay here alone.

"Don't worry about me, Tric. The quickest way for you to get out of here is with Hunter."

"I can't carry both of you."

I turned to Hunter and pointed at the dozens of bags that neither of them had given up on. "I don't need them."

"It's not about these. I physically can't carry the both of you."

"Then we walk to Gainesville together." I folded my arms and stared at them both.

"I will be perfectly fi—"

Gunshots rang out across the night, and the three of us dove behind some gravestones. "I thought your skin was rock hard."

"In our true form, it will stop a bullet. In this form, it will hurt like a bitch." Knox grunted and poked his head over the tombstone to look around. "I don't think anyone is firing at us. Yet."

"Then turn into your true form and let's all get out of here together."

"We can't just turn into our true form," Hunter said, he ran a hand through his hair. "Rules still exist for supes, and the big one is not exposing ourselves to humans."

"Fine, but this isn't getting us out of here," I muttered, standing. "And you don't need to carry me. I can walk."

"I wasn't planning on walking." Hunter rose to his feet and then reached for my hand. "No point in sticking around. Let's see if we can find something that will get us all out of here."

"Hold up." Knox began emptying the contents of all the bags onto the ground in front of him.

"What are you doing?" Hunter asked.

"Trying to shove as many things into as few bags as possible."

I shrugged. "I don't mind carrying them."

Knox raised a shoulder. "It's fine. But they take up less space this way."

When Hunter started doing the same, I arched an eyebrow. "If they're that much of an issue, leave them."

"The whole reason we're here is because Knox wanted to get you some clothes."

Knox grunted. "You've been wanting to play dress-up Barbie, so don't spout any bullshit." He thrust a bra and panty set into a bag and then stood. "We came to get you clothes, and unless we *need* to ditch them, I plan on getting them—and you—back to the castle."

Moments later, Hunter had also managed to downsize the number of bags. Slinging the remaining bags over his shoulder, he started to lead me back to the entrance of the cemetery.

It was almost completely dark now, with most of the moon and starlight being cut off by thick black clouds. The temperature had dropped a few degrees, but the air smelled of a city being burned to ashes.

"Come on," Knox muttered. He took over the lead, taking us along the streets. The further away from the city we got, the fewer vehicles we passed that had been abandoned in the middle of the road, but there was still a lot of people.

Despite the fact that they didn't scare me, Hunter and Knox made sure that I was always between the two of them, making sure that any passersby were put off by the menacing looks they were sending.

The groups of people did look like they were out for trouble. Most were carrying weapons—mainly bats or planks of wood. They seemed happy enough to attack the abandoned cars, but for some reason, they stayed away from the houses.

They also seemed to keep a large distance from us, even though we were unarmed. It was as if they sensed the tall men and I would be able to do them harm.

I liked that feeling.

We walked for two hours. Every time I looked at either Hunter or Knox, I got the sense that they would be able to walk all night. Although there had been no more running involved, and walking was a lot less strenuous, I wasn't sure I was going to be able to continue for much longer.

Sweat was running down my back, I was desperate for a drink, and my feet felt like they were on fire. I was also really struggling to see in the darkness, relying on the nearness of others to guide me.

And then I stumbled over a crack in the sidewalk. If it weren't for Hunter holding onto me, I would have fallen completely.

"Fuck, we shouldn't be doing this," Hunter muttered. "Knox," he said, louder. "We need to stop."

Knox glanced back at his brother before looking at me. With a frown, he nodded. "This way."

We ducked into an alley. I leaned against the wall before lowering myself to the ground. Even though there was a cool wind blowing down the alley, my face felt hot.

"We can't keep on like this. Look at her. And she can barely see where she's going," Hunter said to Knox.

"It's dark," I pointed out.

Hunter sighed before crouching down in front of me. "I can't do anything about it now, but I'm going to help out with that when we get back home. I promise."

A metallic jangling had me leaning to the side to watch Knox. He was shaking a gate, the chain wrapped around it, making the noise as it clanked against itself. "What are you doing?"

"Thinking."

I glanced at Hunter who shrugged. "You want to elaborate?"

Knox turned back to us. "Wait here."

Offering no further explanation, and despite his brother's protests, Knox jogged out of the alley.

With a long sigh, Hunter twisted his body so he could lean back against the wall beside me. "Of course."

"Don't we need to go after him?"

"I doubt you would keep up," he muttered.

Crossing my arms, I turned my head and frowned at the empty darkness of the alley. Alright, so I was currently useless, but I hated feeling like this. Even more, I hated the idea of Knox being by himself. What if that shifter appeared again?

What if the Lycans did?

Was I going to miss out on an opportunity to destroy them by being left behind in this alley?

"What's the matter, Zee?" Hunter asked me, softly.

"I hate the fact that I'm like this."

There was a moment's pause and then Hunter took my hand, pulling it into his lap. I turned, finding him tracing his finger along the edge of the bandages that wrapped around my wrists.

"You've not said much about what happened to you, but from what I can tell, you were chained up for a long time." His fingers stilled. "Chained up with limited ability to move. It takes a long time for it to affect us—more than it would a human. You're doing fine. You're doing a lot better than I think most would, given the circumstances."

"Do you want to know what happened to me?"

"Only if you're comfortable sharing," he said, slowly turning to look at me. In the darkness, I could just about make out the glint of his eyes.

I chewed at the inside of my cheek. Part of me wanted to put that part of my past behind me, but at the same time, until I had killed all the Lycans, I wasn't sure I would be able to. "Not now."

Hunter reached up, draping his arm over my shoulder and pulling me to him. I leaned against his chest and sucked in a deep breath. Even after all these hours, he still had a hint of fruit and spice.

More importantly, he felt like safety and security.

"No matter what happens," he murmured into my hair, "I want you to know that you can tell me anything—even the bad things. I'm going to do everything I can to protect you."

"I don't need protecting."

Hunter's hand started stroking my hair. I closed my eyes, enjoying the sensation.

"Protecting you doesn't just mean kicking the ass of anyone who tries to hurt you, although I would, even if you could take them out with a bolt of lightning. Protecting you means making sure you're safe. I'll make sure you have a roof over your head, clothes on your back, and food in your belly. And I'm going to do everything I can to make sure that you can do all that without me, so that one day, when you find yourself out in the world without me, you will survive."

When I'm out in the world without him?

For some reason, those words made my chest hurt.

Staying at Castle Viegls was temporary. I knew that. When spring came, I would be doing exactly what he said—going out into the world alone—but for the first time, I wasn't sure I wanted to.

I pushed the ache down.

No, I had to leave. I had to destroy the Lycans. My

desire to die had been replaced with a desire to kill. Revenge was what kept me going.

"I accept," I told him.

"What do you mean?" Hunter asked, leaning back to try to see me.

"I accept your protection. I want to learn. I want to grow stronger. And I really want to know how to survive."

Hunter chuckled, but his laughter didn't sound like he had thought I was being funny. The opposite, actually. "You don't have to . . ." He lowered his head and pressed his lips against my forehead. "I'll protect you."

Couldn't he see very well in the darkness either?

"My lips are here," I said as I lifted my head and allowed my mouth to find his.

Hunter froze, and then his hands were on my shoulders gently pulling me away. "What are you doing?"

This was the second time I had kissed someone, and the second time my actions had been questioned. Knox had said I was doing nothing wrong, but here was Hunter, pulling away.

With my lip clamped tightly between my teeth, I ducked out of Hunter's arms and stood, moving away from him. I could feel my cheeks burning.

Kissing had seemed simple, but here I was, getting it wrong.

"Okay, woah, Zera, you gotta stop right there," Hunter said, scrambling to his feet behind me. "You can't just kiss a guy out of nowhere like that."

Was that where I had gone wrong? I needed to tell them I was kissing them? I turned to face him. "Oh. I didn't know."

Hunter let out a long sigh as he ran his hand through his messy hair. "That's the problem." He walked over to me. "Look, just because a guy offers to do something nice for you, it doesn't mean you have to repay him with a kiss."

"I wasn't," I said. "I was doing it because I wanted to."

"But I thought you liked . . ."

I tilted my head. "I like you."

This time, Hunter sucked in a deep breath. He ran his hand through my hair until he had a large lock of it in his fist. "Zera, baby, I'm not sure if you do. It's only been a few weeks, and this is probably the first time someone has ever done anything nice for you."

"So what if it is?" I crossed my arms, rubbing at my upper arms. "I might be experiencing a lot of things I've never done before, but I can tell you what I like and what I don't like. You're one of them."

"Zee," Hunter whispered. "I'm trying to do the right thing here. Because I like you, but I can only barely hold onto my self-control when I'm around you as it is."

Hunter's actions didn't match his words. If he liked me, he would kiss me, not pull away? I fought against the wave of uncertainty. Uncrossing my arms, I placed my hands on Hunter's hips. "I'm going to kiss you now."

That was enough warning, right?

I stood on my toes and leaned up to his mouth. I was just too short to reach, but as my balance wobbled, Hunter's strong arm wrapped around my waist, bringing me flush up against him.

Hunter dipped his head and claimed my mouth with his.

Considering how identical he was to Knox, his kisses weren't. Hunter's lips were soft and hot. They moved against mine, sucking at them like he was trying to taste them. Hunter tasted like blackberries.

As Hunter's hand settled on the small of my back, his cool fingers slipped under the waistband of my pants. The sounds of the suburbs attacking itself seemed to quieten, and all I could hear was the sound of our lips and our breathing.

I reached up, threading my hand through Hunter's hair. As I brought my fingers out, my palm ran over something hard.

Before I could work out what it was, a guttural groan escaped Hunter and the next thing I knew, I was being pushed backwards and pinned up against the wall behind me.

With no space between us, I was also very aware of another hard thing pressed up against me.

Hunter pulled back. I could barely see him in the shadows, but his silhouette had changed slightly. Just beside where my hand was hovering, a small point had appeared—a horn. There was one on the other side of his head too.

"They're . . . sensitive," Hunter said, his voice husky and breathless.

"Did I hurt you?" I asked, alarmed.

"The opposite."

It took me a moment to understand what he was saying. Then, before I could stop myself, I wrapped my hand around it. It wasn't big, barely filling my hand. It was smooth, and strangely cool, with a sharp point to the end.

Hunter's weight pressed up against me as he

moaned. The sound sent heat flooding the area between my legs. I collapsed back against the wall only for Hunter to return his mouth to mine, this time, slipping his tongue in.

As I reached up, taking the other horn in my other hand, Hunter's hands cupped my breasts.

There was no metal in Hunter's tongue, but it felt as good running up and down my tongue as his hands did, gently squeezing my breasts.

Hunter's hands moved south, pulling the buttons of my pants open. When I clutched his horns tighter, he ground up against me, but his hands returned to my breasts.

Before I could complain, wanting his hands between my legs as much as I needed them on my breasts, something slid under the waistband of my underwear and down between my legs. The cry that left me as it rubbed at that sensitive area was swallowed up in Hunter's mouth.

Electricity cracked in the air around us and the familiar scent of ozone filled my nostrils.

Whatever was between my legs was cold and rough, but at the same time, soft, moving with the dexterity of a finger. I gasped, breaking the kiss, needing oxygen.

"You are so beautiful," Hunter murmured into my

ear. "Come for me."

In all honesty, I was barely aware of what he was saying, much less able to understand his request. Just when I thought I couldn't feel any more amazing, the thing rubbing up against me pressed firmer. With no warning, the most intense wave of pleasure hit me.

Bolts of electricity seemed to explode out of me, shooting in all directions. Before I closed my eyes, I watched as one hit a nearby streetlight. It burst into light and then exploded, raining glass on the sidewalk below.

My legs felt weak, and I could barely catch my breath. The only reason I was still standing was because of Hunter. The only thing that seemed to work, with a will of their own, was my hands rubbing at his horns. I could feel the electricity in the tips of my fingers, vibrating away.

And then Hunter was cursing in my ear, nipping at the soft skin of my neck. His hands gripped at my side, holding himself up as much as me.

It took him a few moments to catch his breath, and then he stepped back. As he did, the thing between my legs slithered out of my pants, giving one last caress on the way.

A shiver ran down my spine as I slumped back against the wall, trying to focus on it. I'd known from the way it moved that it wasn't his hand, but I wasn't expecting to see a tail twitching beside him—as much as I could see in the low lighting.

How I desperately wanted to be able to turn the lights back on so I could see him.

"Fuck, I'm sorry." As Hunter's tail disappeared, he stepped forward and started fastening my pants up. This close, I could see the horns had gone too.

"Why?"

"I lost control. A gargoyle's horns . . ." he shook his head. "No, it's not an excuse. I shouldn't have done that."

The pleasurable sensation I had been riding on seemed to evaporate instantly. "Why not?" The words sounded choked.

"Because your first orgasm shouldn't have been in the back alley in a sleazy part of a rioting city. It should have been somewhere I could take your clothes off and worship every part of your body."

"You call that an orgasm?" a voice asked from above.

Twenty-Two

Hunter

Zera and I looked up at the roof of the building opposite us and found two women watching.

The hair of one was styled in a ponytail scraped onto the top of her head, falling down midway between her chin and her shoulders. The hair on the other woman was hanging loose, curling around her breasts.

"Baby girl, if you want an orgasm, we can give you one," said the one with the ponytail. "Irina will lick your pussy while I drain your blood."

Vampires.

How long had they been there?

Too long.

This was precisely why I shouldn't have done that with Zera.

But the moment her hands wrapped around my horns? I was a goner. The stone demon in me wasn't going to let me stop until he had come—at least I'd managed to keep my cock out of it, otherwise there'd be a whole sticky mess in my pants right now. Instead there was still a hard-on and an ache that wasn't going to be soothed anytime soon.

Now was not the time to be thinking about my dick.

There were two vampires across the street, and I knew damn well that was no coincidence.

Stepping to the side, I put myself between them and Zera.

That was a waste of time. Seconds later, Zera was at my side. "I have no complaints with the one I just had, thanks."

I couldn't keep the smirk from my face as I straightened my back. Much as I should have kept control and not laid a finger on her—or tail—at least I had done her right.

"Shame. I figured we could have some fun before we killed you," Irina said. Both she and the other woman jumped off the two-story building and landed on the sidewalk across the street.

I'd sparred enough times with Javion to know vampires were strong and fast. With two of them, there were good odds on me beating them, but with Zera here, like with the ogres, our best chance was to run.

Only, Knox hadn't returned yet. If we ran now, we'd likely remain separated.

"Zera, no matter what, do not use your power on them," I whispered, hoping it was quiet enough not to carry over to the advancing vampires.

"I can take them out." She huffed.

"They're vampires, like Javion." I turned my attention back to the two women and stepped forward, putting some space between Zera and me. Clear, I gave the gargoyle in me the release. My wings uncurled, my skin hardened, and the horns which only moments ago had Zera's small hands wrapped around them, pushed out.

"He's a fucking gargoyle, Aella," Irina hissed at the one in charge.

"Then you're in for a treat because gargoyle blood

makes human blood taste like toilet water."

Did that mean they thought Zera was human?

I wasn't about to let them get any closer to find out.

Supernatural laws be damned, I stepped out into the street. Thankfully, the blackout and the clouded night sky meant visibility, for most humans, was going to be limited. So long as none came down this way, we would be okay.

Even if they did, it was unlikely they were going to be able to prove anything they saw. Not tonight, at least.

Without giving the vampires a chance to even change their minds, I charged at them, swinging a punch at the one with the ponytail. She dodged it, as I expected, but not the jab to her kidneys.

Just as Aella fell to her knees, the other—Irina—jumped on my back, attempting to slash at my neck.

I wasn't sure what weapon she was using, but I felt it tear through the skin of my wings.

Some weapons existed which could cut a gargoyles skin; usually ones enchanted by witches. But a gargoyle's wings weren't the same as the rest of the skin covering my body. It couldn't be: not if we wanted to fly.

A roar of pain escaped me. I reached over my shoulder trying to shove her off, but she clung on, evading my claws.

The vampire on my back moaned. "Unholy shit, that does taste good."

"I am not your fucking food," I snapped. She hadn't bitten me. I knew she hadn't, otherwise I'd be on my knees coming in my pants. Her teeth weren't strong enough to penetrate my skin while I was in this form.

With the other vampire starting to get to her knees, I ignored the leech on my back and punched the side of her head again. Then, as the weapon sliced through my wing, I turned on my heel.

I jumped in the air and allowed myself to fall backwards, slamming the full weight of my stone-like body down on Irina and Aella.

Something went clattering to the side, and I turned my head to see a long blade slide under a parked car. The hands holding on to me went limp.

"Hunter." Zera shouted my name and started to run toward me.

"Stay back," I snapped at her.

Zera stopped, let out an exasperated sigh, but did as I said. Albeit with a scowl on her face.

Let her be mad at me. Over there, she was away from the vampires and safe.

I rolled onto my knees and looked down at the pile of them. They were still alive—or rather, undead—just unconscious. To kill a vampire, you either needed sunlight, decapitation, or fire.

Annoying as they were, at this moment in time, they didn't pose a threat. Seeing as how they didn't know who or what Zera was—they were just opportunistic vampires out for a bite to eat—I didn't want to kill them in front of Zera.

Zera had already seen enough terrible things.

Getting to my feet, I tucked my wings away and returned to my human form. Although my wing would heal much quicker in my gargoyle form, I couldn't risk staying like this. Even with the cover of darkness, humans had a habit of being in places they shouldn't, seeing things they shouldn't.

When Knox got back from whatever crazy idea he had, I would get him to check it over. For now, I would grin and bear it.

I turned, seeking Zera out. Just as I realized that she wasn't where I had told her to stay, a blinding pain hit my leg.

As I let out a roar of pain, I turned and found a blade sticking out of my thigh. The first vampire, Aella, wasn't unconscious anymore.

Out of nowhere something flashed in the brief moonlight, and then I was staring at a headless vampire.

Aella's head, now a few feet away, blinked at me for a couple of seconds.

Standing over her body, Irina's blade in her hand, was Zera.

The look in her eyes sent a shiver down my spine. She was far too calm about a decapitation for my liking, instead, staring at Irina's unconscious form as though she was contemplating doing the same.

"Don't," I said, quickly.

"They hurt you." Her eyes were still on Irina, but she was hesitating.

And then the street burst into light as a car rounded the corner.

Shit.

I got as far as grabbing Zera's hand and started to pull her out of the way, ignoring the agonizing pain as I tried to move my leg, when the car squealed to a halt.

"Hunter."

Relief flooded me at the recognition of my brother's voice. I stopped and turned back. It wasn't a car, but instead, a very old Jeep. The thing looked like it had been built during the Vietnamese war, so I wasn't sure how it was still working, no thanks to Zera's EMP.

Knox jumped out of it, leaving the engine running. He took a few steps toward us and then stopped. His gaze drifted from the vampires in the middle of the street, to the blade in Zera's hands, to the one in my thigh.

"Don't ask," I muttered.

"Don't ask?" Knox's eyes went wide.

"No." I hobbled over to the Jeep, placing both hands on the side as I braced myself. "Let's get out of here and then I'll fill you in." Sucking in a deep breath, I gritted my teeth and took hold of the handle of the blade, yanking it out of my thigh.

I tossed the sword in the back of the Jeep before resting my head against the support bar. *Fuck, that hurt.*

From the corner of my eye, I caught Knox hurrying over to Zera, easing the blade out of her hands. She was still glaring at Irina.

Turning, I leaned back against the car. "Leave her, Zee," I called over. "There's no need to kill her too."

Knox's eyes seemed to bulge out of his head before his expression turned to one of awe. "You killed the vampire?"

Zera pointed at me. "They hurt Hunter."

"You know you have to tell me everything, right?" Knox said.

"We need to get out of here, first." I took a couple of steps toward them, but then stopped when I nearly keeled over. With a grunt, I pressed my hand against the stab wound.

Pulling it away, I tipped it, staring at my palm in the headlights, then my gaze dropped to my thigh. There was more blood there than I expected.

"Shit," Knox muttered. He turned to Zera. "You need to get in the car."

Zera gave him a cursory glance before walking over to me. "Are you okay?" she asked, her voice barely above a whisper.

"I'm right as rain."

She blinked, looking up at the sky. "Why is rain right?"

Hell if I knew. My mom used to say it all the time, but I'd never questioned it. Even now, my concern was on the fact that Zera suddenly looked terrified.

I reached out and took her hand in the one that wasn't covered in blood. "It's going to be okay. *I* am going to be okay. I heal fast, remember?"

Turning my body so it wasn't in the light, I was suddenly grateful for the lack of power in the area. At least for a few minutes so Zera couldn't see it.

The Jeep Knox had acquired was one of those with no roof. It probably had a soft top cover that you had to pull on yourself somewhere, but either Knox had taken it off, or it was never on when he stole it.

With no door, nor a step, I put my hands around Zera's waist and picked her up. Keeping my weight on my good leg, I turned and deposited her in the driver's seat. "I'm going to need you to hop in the back. I'm too big to fit back there."

That and with the lack of door, I was going to feel a lot easier about her sitting where she couldn't fall out easily.

Knox appeared next to me, the few bags of Zera's shopping in his hands. "Just be careful with the electrics," he told her.

My gaze dropped to the wires hanging out underneath the steering wheel. "How did you manage to find a car that would work?"

"It's too old to have a computer in it," Knox explained. "That's what fucks most cars over. I lucked out that this thing was still running." He waited for Zera to slip into the back seat before leaning over and putting the bags on the floor beside her.

"We could have left them."

Knox rolled his eyes. "This whole thing started because of those fucking things. At this point, I'm as determined to get them home as I am us. So, get your ass in the car before either your undead girlfriend wakes up, or the engine draws attention over here."

I heaved myself up and over, collapsing into the passenger seat. "Let's go home." I sighed. Until Knox got in and put the Jeep into gear. The horrific screeching noise had me wincing. "Is this thing even going to get us home?"

Keeping his eyes on the road, Knox nodded. "They built these things to survive a warzone."

"They built this to survive a warzone fifty years ago."

"And yet it's still running. Our bigger problem is whether the gas is going to last us until we get out of the blast zone."

For the most part, the streets Knox stuck to were the backstreets. There were still a fair number of vehicles on them, and because it was a more residential area, also enough humans about to watch us with curiosity, but we managed to navigate them anyway.

I'd not paid attention to how many times I'd relied on the GPS to get us somewhere. Hopefully Knox had some internal GPS wired into him, and we were heading toward South Carolina, at least.

Considering the horizon behind us was still glowing from various fires, and the roads ahead were lined with less houses, I was feeling relatively confident in my brother.

"Are you ever going to tell me what happened?" Knox asked.

I poked an eye open—I'd had them closed for the last few miles—and turned my head. "Honestly, there's not much to tell. Vampires stumbled upon us, decided they were hungry, and I attacked."

Knox leaned over and poked at my thigh, just missing the healing wound. "Looks like they attacked you," he said over my yelp of pain.

I returned his poke with a punch to his arm, regretting it the moment the Jeep swerved, and a muffled 'ouch' came from the back.

"Dumb asshole." Knox looked in the rearview mirror. "You okay back there, Tric? Warm enough?"

We were slowly starting to head up into the mountains, and combined with the night air, it was getting colder. I'd made sure to turn the heat on full blast when I'd gotten cold—I'd left my jacket in Knox's SUV. I'd also made sure that Zera found one of the new jackets we'd bought her and put that on.

"Is Hunter's leg okay?" Zera asked.

"Don't worry about me," I said, giving her a bright grin. "As soon as we get some place I can clean up, I will."

"What about your wing?"

"What *about* your wing?" Knox demanded, shooting me a questioning look.

"Vampire got my wing too." Given that the throb behind me was getting less with every mile, I was sure it was healing. Even my thigh wasn't bleeding as much as it had been.

Knox let out a small growl before putting the Jeep back in gear. "Fucking idiot," he muttered under his breath.

Twenty-Three

Zera

This drive wasn't nearly as interesting as the drive to Atlanta had been. Darkness prevented me from seeing anything outside of the strange car with no windows, and the radio was just giving off static.

Knox had said something about the radio being a POS because the radio waves should have still been able to be picked up—whatever that meant.

All I knew was that I had nothing to distract me

from the fact that I desperately wanted to head back to the city and take care of that other vampire.

How *dare* she hurt Hunter like that?

Cutting the head off the first hadn't been as hard as I expected it to be. Actually, it had been satisfying. And reassuring to know that I didn't have to rely on my power to kill someone, especially when it didn't work against certain supernatural creatures.

My gaze kept drifting to the sword-like weapon Hunter had tossed in the back of the car.

Would they let me keep it?

On top of that, my body had already forgotten about the pleasurable sensation Hunter had caused and instead, it was hungry. Hungry as I was, I didn't say anything. I figured the others were hungry too, and it wasn't like there was a store anywhere nearby.

Finally, we saw light in the distance.

"Thank the gods," Knox muttered.

It was a streetlight, which turned into a second, and then a third. Eventually, it led to a gas station.

A closed gas station.

Knox pulled in, muttering curses before turning to us. "That gas light has been on for ages. I don't want to go much further in case the engine—"

There was a spluttering noise then the car fell silent.

Hunter looked at the dead dashboard before turning to his brother. "That has to be *the* best timing I've ever seen." He pointed to the side of the gas station. "I'm going to phone DB." He made to move, and then winced.

"*I'm* going to call DB. You stay here."

He hopped out of the car and jogged over to the phone, leaving Hunter and I alone. "How is your leg?"

"Getting better, don't worry." He shifted his weight. "Knox is making it out to be worse than it is."

"How mad is Carter going to be?"

Hunter let out a dry chuckle. "You don't need to worry about that either."

Knox hung up and hurried back to us. Instead of getting in the car, he stood outside and ran a hand through his hair. "Well, the good news is that DB left Raleigh as soon as he heard about the EMP—"

"He heard about that?" I asked, surprised.

"Ah, Zee." Hunter sighed. "You wiped out a whole city. I guarantee you that made the news worldwide."

I looked at Knox who nodded.

"He was already back at Castle Viegls when I called. We're actually past Gainesville. DB said he can be here in about ninety minutes."

"So we have an hour and a half to kill?" Hunter

asked.

Knox nodded. "Javion did a trace on the number. Turns out if we walk about ten minutes in the direction we were heading, there's a diner which should be open. Think you can make it that far?" he asked his brother.

"I'll be fine." With a grunt, he heaved himself out of the truck and put tentative weight on his bad leg. "Might take us twenty minutes though."

When he tried to lean in and take the bags, I batted his hand away. "I can carry them."

There weren't many. Plus, I'd slipped the blade in there . . .

It was a slow walk, but I didn't mind. I just wished that Hunter would let one of us help him.

He was wearing dark jeans but every time we passed under a streetlight, I could see the bloodstain. It looked more brown than red, but it was still wet. As I walked just behind, I kept looking for his tail and wings, but neither made a reappearance.

The light from the diner soon shone in front of us. My stomach let out an appreciative grumble. Now that I was eating regularly, I couldn't begin to imagine not doing again.

But we stopped just before we left the sidewalk. Hunter turned and held his hand out for a bag. "I'm going to need those now, Zee."

"Why?" The blade was hidden in there.

"Humans don't like blood. I can hold the bags up against it."

Reluctantly, I handed them over. As Hunter took them, Knox replaced the bags with his hand. "Let's go eat. I'm starving."

I had no idea what time it was, but there were only a handful of cars outside, and just as many people inside. Most were at the counter, watching an enormous television hung on the wall.

Everyone turned to look as we walked in.

Hunter ignored them, heading straight for a booth. He slid in, wincing slightly before making sure the bags were blocking his bloody leg. Like with dinner, Knox ushered me in first before sitting down beside me.

Moments later, an older lady came over. She smelled of cigarettes and cheap perfume which tickled at the back of my throat in an uncomfortable way. "I've not seen you around here before," she drawled.

"That's because we're not from around here," Knox said, shortly.

Hunter shot him a dark glare. He quickly turned it into a smile as he looked at the older woman. "Our car broke down. We've got a friend coming to pick us up."

"Heading outta Atlanta?" she asked, her eyes narrowing in suspicion.

"Out?" Hunter shook his head. "No, ma'am. Quite the opposite. We're heading in that direction."

The woman jabbed her thumb over her shoulder in the direction of the television. "Haven't you heard about what's going on there?"

"Why do you think we're going?" Knox muttered.

Hunter shot him another dark look. "We're going to help. It seems they need it."

The woman's suspicious look turned on me. "In that outfit?"

"Can we get three coffees and some menus, please?" Hunter asked before I could send a little shock in her direction.

It was my turn to frown at Hunter. "What's wrong with my outfit?"

"Nothing," Knox responded.

"It's the South. The more rural you get, the less accepting people can be."

"You live in the middle of nowhere and you don't care."

Hunter sighed wearily and rubbed a hand over his face. "I know."

The woman came back with three cups of coffee

and the menus, setting them down on the end of the table. Without waiting for a response, she walked off.

"Can I give her a little shock?" I asked.

"How little?" Knox asked.

"No," Hunter said, firmly. "You've used enough of your power for today, Zera. Let's try to go at least twenty-four hours before we blackout the entire state."

"Relax, Hunter. I don't think she was planning on zapping her into dust." Knox reached for the coffees and handed them out.

I glanced over at the woman. She was behind the counter, but her attention kept switching over to us. "Maybe not dust . . ."

Hunter rubbed at a spot in the center of his forehead. "She's human, Zee. We don't hurt humans."

"Let's just get something to eat. With any luck, by the time we settle the bill, DB will be here." Knox handed the menus out.

There was only one page of meals, but looking down, all I could see were blurred patterns on a page. I lifted it up, using it to hide behind as I pretended to read what was on it.

There were no handy pictures this time.

"I think I want pancakes."

I lowered the menu and found Hunter watching

me. I nodded. "Me too." Setting the menu on the table, I reached for the coffee. Back at the castle, I'd favored cold drinks, so I'd never tried a coffee.

Until I wrapped my hands around the cup, I didn't realize how cold I was. It was like a mini heater. It smelled good, but the dark drink didn't look appealing, despite the fact the Coke I drank all the time was a similar color.

Coffee tasted like shit. The first mouthful I had made me want to wash my mouth out. It was bitter and nasty.

Knox took a sip before smiling at me. "Yeah, that will put some hairs on your chest."

I pushed the cup away from me and then glanced down at my breasts. "I don't want hair there."

Knox chuckled into his cup. "No, I guess that'd ruin things."

Hunter let out a long sigh. "Well that's my fault. I probably should have gotten you coffee from *anywhere* else to let you try something decent on your first try." He reached over for the sugar dispenser and poured some in. "Pass the creamer, Knox."

His brother complied, passing a small jug over. "In fairness," he told me, "Hunter's right. This is terrible coffee." As Hunter stirred the creamer, he picked up the sugar and poured more in the cup.

Hunter slid it back to me. "Try it like this."

Taking the cup back, I gave the beigey liquid a suspicious look. It didn't smell any different. I took a sip.

While it was an improvement on the first try, it still had me wrinkling my nose up in disgust. Thankfully, when Hunter ordered pancakes for me, he also ordered me a Coke instead.

I was glad I'd tried Carter's pancakes before I had those too. Even Knox who loved burgers seemed to eat it automatically. "At least we've eaten," he grumbled, pushing the empty plate away from him.

"How is your leg?" I asked Hunter.

"I'm more concerned about your arms." He looked at my jacket. When I rubbed at my wrists, he shook his head. "You scratched the shit out of them."

Knox's eyes suddenly went wide. "Shit. I went to get first aid supplies."

And then I knocked out the power to the city.

Considering the only part of my arms which had any pain were under a bandage, and that was only a low dull throb now, I was guessing that my supernatural healing ability was starting to kick in.

I rolled up a sleeve and discovered I was right.

Knox reached over and took one of my hands, turning it slightly. "That looks better than I expected."

Headlights shone into the diner as a large SUV pulled into the parking lot. I knew it was Carter before Hunter and Knox stood. As Knox dropped a wad of bills on the table, Hunter gathered up the bags, keeping them held against him as he slid out of the booth.

"Thank you," he called to the grumpy waitress as we walked out.

The temperature had dropped another few degrees, and I shivered as we walked over to the SUV. Halfway over, the driver's door opened, and Carter jumped out. He marched straight over to us, his hands in fists.

Neither twin moved as he brought his hands up. At the last moment, he opened his hands, smacking them upside the head. "I should leave you two here and let you walk home."

"You shouldn't be mad at either of them. I'm the one who—"

Carter turned and stared down at me, his height and broad shoulders making me feel like I was four feet tall. "Get in the car, Zeraora."

"Hunter's leg is injured. If you're going to make him walk home, I'm walking with him."

"Get in the car, Zee," Hunter muttered, giving me

an appreciative grin. It disappeared when he shot Carter a sideways glance and found him frowning at him. "It's fine."

I shook my head. Beside me, my fists were sparking. "No, it's not fine. None of you have the ability to wipe out power to a city, so if Carter is to be mad at anyone, it's me."

Carter rubbed his hand over the whiskers on his chin. "Despite the fact I would love to leave him here, I'm not going to. Get in the car, please? We will discuss this at home."

Part of me wanted to stay there and make sure Carter didn't leave Hunter and Knox there, but I didn't. Trusting Carter, I walked over to the back of the SUV and opened the door.

It wasn't until I had slid over and settled on the edge of the seat, peering out of the window that I realized I wasn't alone in the car.

Slowly, I turned my head to the front, finding Javion in the passenger seat. He was looking at me like he wanted to rip my throat out. "They should have left you in Atlanta." He snarled, showing off his fangs.

"Shut up," I muttered, turning my attention back out the window. Sadly, supernatural hearing had never been in my repertoire of abilities. Nor had lip-reading.

While Hunter's head was bowed, looking at the floor, Knox was staring defiantly at Carter, his arms folded.

"They're in trouble, and it's all your fault," Javion continued. He stretched out, lifting his feet and crossing them on the dashboard. "And I'm just going to wait patiently until we get back to Castle Viegls because then I'm getting the popcorn out."

The only time I had popcorn was when I was watching a movie with Hunter, but I had a feeling that wasn't what Javion was talking about.

As though he sensed my knowledge gap, he slipped his hands behind his head and grinned at me. Those fangs were back on display. "If DB has any sense, he will lock you in the dungeon and use you as the new generator."

Javion settled back in his chair, closing his eyes. I, on the other hand, was frozen in place on the edge of my seat.

Just the fact that Javion was suggesting it had doubt and fear flooding through me in a wave so overwhelming, I wasn't sure how to breathe. I clutched at the seat, my nails digging into the fabric as I fought against the nausea.

No.

Carter, Hunter, and Knox—they'd all told me I was safe with them. Being safe meant not being in a prison. It meant not being used for my power.

So why would Javion even suggest it?

If there was one thing I knew with every fiber of my being, it was that I could *not* go back to that.

Before I could get my body to respond to me—to get out of the car and get out of there because, as my brain was rationalizing, it wasn't even worth the risk that could happen—the door opened, and Hunter heaved himself up into the seat next to me.

Behind us, the trunk opened, and Knox set the few shopping bags in there. And then the door on the other side of me opened and Knox was there.

"Scoot over, Zee." Just as I looked Hunter in the eye, seeing the weariness and pain he was in, his arms wrapped around my waist and pulled me across the seat to his side.

Carter climbed into the driver's seat and backed out of the parking spot without looking behind. Moments later we were on the road, driving back to Castle Viegls.

My chance to escape was gone.

The drive back was awkward and uncomfortable. Unlike the drive into Atlanta, Carter didn't have the radio on and for the most part, there was no conversation.

That didn't bother me. I was mentally planning my escape—if I needed it—when we got back to the castle. If it came to that, I would throw myself out a window again.

The tension in the back was palpable, and I was sure most of it came from me. No matter how far we drove, I couldn't get my heart to slow. It was just enough to stop myself from not sparking the car and killing it like I had the city.

In the darkness, Knox's hand slid over, settling on my thigh. I could feel the heat of it through my pants, and I appreciated it. Somehow, that small gesture was finally enough to make me realize that Knox would never allow me to be locked up again.

And then Hunter's hand sought out mine. He brought it to his leg, holding it tightly as his thumb circled the back of my hand.

Hunter wouldn't allow it either.

Javion was a dick.

I knew this.

But even if he hadn't realized it himself, he'd found the one thing that was eating me up. Because despite the twins sitting on either side of me, reassuring me without knowing it, I still couldn't shake the doubt.

Especially because they had seen what I was capable of.

If the Lycans, and the Marvel and DC Universes had taught me anything, it was that people wanted power.

And I had a hell of a lot of that.

Twenty-Four

Zera

I wasn't sure how far away from Castle Viegls we were, but we had been driving for over an hour. The clock on the dashboard told me it was nearly midnight. I was exhausted, but my body couldn't relax.

"Are we really going to get all the way home without someone saying something?" Javion asked.

"Yep," Carter replied.

"She wiped out the power for everything in a sixty-mile radius of Atlanta." Either Javion wasn't picking up on Carter's 'stop what you're doing' tone, or he didn't care.

"Not tonight," Carter said, this time, through gritted teeth.

"The only reason the humans aren't hunting her is because they don't know supes exist, and even if they did, it's not going to stop them calling it a fucking act of terr—"

"Javion! Drop it!"

Carter swung the car over so that I went flying into Knox, despite the fact that I was wearing a seatbelt. His arms wrapped around my waist, holding me upright.

"We are not having this conversation in the damn car. We're not even having this conversation tonight," Carter said. "We are going to get home, and I am going to bed because I have already had a shitty day and that was before I had to spend half of it driving halfway around the damn Bible Belt."

I shifted back into my seat, chewing at the inside of my cheek.

"You hear me, Javion?" Carter pressed.

Javion glared back at Carter. His silver eyes had a slight red sheen to them. "You're a fool, and if I didn't know better, I'd say you were thinking with your dick, too. She took out *Atlanta* and you're still bringing her back to the castle?"

"Javion—"

"Don't bother," Javion said with a shake of his head. Although he didn't look in my direction, he pointed a finger at me. "She is worse than a liability. She's a fucking timebomb. If you had any sense in you, you'd drive her back to Maine and let them have the problem back. Instead, you're going to bring them here."

Before anyone could say anything, Javion jumped out of the car, slamming the door behind him.

There was a roar from the engine and then I was flung back as the car shot off, leaving Javion at the side of the road in a cloud of smoke.

We weren't far from the drive into the castle. Carter took the corner sharply, and I would have gone flying again if it weren't for Knox's arms still around me.

It didn't take long for us to arrive at the castle gates. I was fully expecting Carter to send the SUV straight through them instead of waiting for them to open, but he surprised me by bringing the vehicle to a stop. The drive to the garage was much calmer.

Carter killed the engine, but he didn't move. "I'm going to bed. We will discuss this tomorrow." Without turning back, he got out of the car and walked off into the darkness.

Finally, Hunter turned to me. "It's not your fault. DB had a job a couple of states over this morning, and it already put him in a bad mood. He will be fine after some sleep."

"You should go do the same," Knox said.

"What about you two?"

He shared a look with his twin. "I get to stick a band aid on Hunter's thigh, and then we're going to bed too." Knox got out of the car. He helped me out and then walked around to the back. "Can you take your bags up yourself?" When I nodded, he opened the trunk, pulled out the bags and handed them over.

I left the twins there, heading inside alone.

The house was almost silent, but Carter had left the lights on when he came in. Ignoring the loud voice in the back of my head which was yelling at me to get out, I went upstairs to my room.

After this, I still had that unshakeable doubt that maybe Javion was right. They had all been upset about me using my powers—even though I didn't think it was *that* big of a deal.

But they did.

And I'd never seen any of them this angry with

each other before.

Even the image of Javion being left on the side of the road left me feeling uneasy. And I didn't like Javion at all.

Yet I couldn't help but feel conflicted about him being left out there. These four men had seemed close until . . .

Until I arrived.

Catching sight of my reflection as I walked past the mirror, I stopped.

"Enough."

I may have been short and still far from regaining the muscle my body needed, but I wasn't a pushover. Sure, a ghost may have helped open the door to the cell, but it was me who got me out of the Lycan's secret base, and it was me who killed their retrieval pack.

My plan hadn't changed.

I was still going to leave this place. I will find the rest of the Lycans and make them pay for what they did.

Because *I* had the power to do that.

Being able to trust myself and my instincts was something I was still learning, but I'd never had anyone to trust before.

I liked Hunter and I liked Knox. I also liked Carter.

My instinct was telling me they were people I could

trust.

But my instincts had been in constant battle with that voice in the back of my mind since Javion had given it the words to become vocal.

My biggest fear wasn't dying. It never had been.

It was going back in a cage.

"Enough," I said again, louder this time. "If they try to put you in a cage, your instincts were wrong. They didn't like you . . . and even if your electrical powers can't kill them, a surge big enough will knock them down long enough to escape."

My reflection nodded resolutely, back at me.

I wasn't going to be a power source for anyone.

I didn't sleep well.

Despite repeating to myself several times over that I would do what I needed to get out of Castle Viegls if or when the time came, the idea of hurting Hunter, Knox, or even Carter left my stomach feeling like someone had twisted a knife in it.

I woke long before dawn and unable to fall asleep again, I took a bath. My hair was finally feeling soft and easy to wash.

After emptying the contents of all the bags onto my bed, I rebandaged my wrists, dressed and then put the remaining clothes back into the bags. I wasn't sure what was going to happen later, much less if I would have the chance to come back and get these things, but at least in the bags, they were easy to carry.

With the sun finally starting to lighten the gray sky, I left the room and walked down to the kitchen.

Although it was still early, everybody—including Javion— was in there. Fresh coffee was brewing, and the three gargoyles already had a mug in front of them. Javion's mug, I'd learned over the previous weeks, contained blood.

The look he gave me when I walked in told me he wanted to drain mine and let it drip into his mug, drop by drop.

"Morning, Zee," Hunter greeted me with a smile, which was far too enthusiastic to be believable.

"How is your leg?" I asked him.

"All fine." As if to prove a point, he started doing squats in the middle of the kitchen.

Apart from the wounds under the bandages on my wrists, mine had healed too, but I was still relieved to see that he seemed better.

Before I could walk over and join him, Carter

stepped out in front of me, handing me a can of Coke. "We need to talk."

Carter moved past me, back into the hallway. I followed him, aware that Javion was just behind me, and Knox and Hunter were right behind him.

We were led to the library. Although books were wasted on me, I liked this room. There was something that felt . . . safe. This was one of Carter's sacred places, and in here, I was sure nothing bad would happen.

The older gargoyle left the door open as he walked over to the windows that stretched up from the floor to the ceiling. This room was as tall as two stories, with bookshelves covering every free space on the walls. The second floor was a balcony that ran around the room so people could get to their books easily.

Although the light had barely broken, Carter pulled across the heavy curtains, making sure they were closed properly before he turned and moved over to the fireplace.

Like the living room, the fireplace was almost as big as me, but the room was warm enough that Carter didn't need to light a fire. Instead, he stood in front of it and gestured to the worn armchair beside it, which he usually favored.

I sat down, crossing my legs. While Javion stayed

back, leaning against one of the bookshelves, Hunter sat down in the other armchair and Knox perched on the arm.

Carter closed his eyes, rubbing at the silver whispers of the beard that covered the underside of his jaw. Finally, he took a deep breath. "Okay. Let's hear it."

"She walked into the garage in my flipflops and one of Manon's dresses," Knox said before I could speak. "There was half a foot of fucking snow out there."

Slowly, Carter dragged his eyes away from me to look at Knox. "Online shopping, Knoxlyn. That is what we agreed."

"You can't get a haircut online though."

Carter folded his arms, kissing his teeth. "Hunter did a good job at cleaning her hair. As I've told you many times, outside of this castle, Zeraora is at risk. She can't control her powers, as was proven yesterday."

I interrupted him. "I knew what I was doing."

Twenty-Five

DB

The indignation in Zeraora's voice had me turning back. Her blue eyes were giving me such a fierce look that I was almost reluctant to correct her.

"Zeraora, you wiped the power and destroyed just about every object with a microchip or electrical charge within a sixty-mile radius," I told her, as gently as I could. "Did you honestly mean to cause that much disruption?"

"Hunter told me not to let a man get a photograph of me, and that's exactly what I did."

Hunter's wince had me turning back to him. "I did say that, but I didn't mean for her to . . ." He winced. "She stopped the photograph being uploaded."

"Why was . . .?" I held up a hand, silencing myself. "I'm getting ahead of myself." I looked to Knox. "Atlanta?"

Knox waved his hand, vaguely. "I figured it was far enough away from here that if something did happen, it would throw anyone off our trail."

While I understood that decision, his casual declaration made me want to punch him for the insubordination.

He was right. I had told him many times that it wasn't safe for Zeraora to leave the grounds, and yet he went to Atlanta *knowing* that—knowing that his decision to go to that city had been based upon that knowledge.

The only thing that was keeping me from punching him were the soft glances he kept shooting in Zeraora's direction. I'd caught them last night too.

Somehow, in only a few short weeks, this woman had managed to get Knox to care about *something*.

No, that wasn't fair. Even though they had a love-hate relationship at times, love did win out between

Knox and his brother. And there was no denying the attraction between Knox and Javion. The two had been together for years, and before now, I was sure that Javion was his true mate.

Cross-species of mates existed. As did same-sex mates, especially with vampires who were one of the few species that didn't conceive to create the next generation, but instead turned them. They were also one of the species that would take multiple mates—betrothed, as they called them.

There had been a lot of moonshine consumed one night, and Knox had told us he was choosing Javion.

Gargoyles had one true mate. Usually, the pull was to the opposite sex because of the need to reproduce. Hunter had said later that wasn't an option for Knox anymore, and at first, I'd wondered if it was going to be permanent. Javion had a personality of a wolverine half the time, and Knox was so similar that I was sure they would destroy each other.

Turned out they saved that for the bedroom.

But if I didn't know any better, I'd have said Knox liked Zeraora.

That was a whole other problem that I was not about to dive into today.

"So; you took her to a hair salon owned by the

Daughters of the Twilight Goddess?" I arched an eyebrow.

"It's Liberty—she's sound."

I had to stop myself from asking Hunter whatever *that* lingo meant.

"Everything was fine at Liberty's," Knox agreed, reluctantly.

Javion rolled his eyes. "Then when did everything go to shit with sparky over there?"

I shot Javion an unimpressed look, knowing full well that wasn't a term of endearment. But it was also a question I wanted the answer to. I turned to Knox and Hunter, giving them both a pointed look.

"A fucking mongoose shifter turned up."

A bounty hunter? Dammit.

But Hunter's answer didn't trouble me as much as Knox's expression did. As I stared at him, he subtly shook his head. I narrowed my eyes, but I turned my attention back to Hunter as he continued to tell me about the ogres and Zeraora blowing up Knox's car.

Whatever it was that Knox knew about the mongoose shifter, he would tell me later.

"And that was what resulted in the EMP?"

"Actually . . . no." Hunter rubbed at the back of his neck. "That was because I saw someone pointing a phone at Zee, and I told her not to let herself get filmed."

Folding my arms, I arched an eyebrow at the older twin. Something didn't add up. "Why would you have to tell Zeraora that?"

Hunter shifted uncomfortably. "Because she tried to kill a dog."

"A dog? She's a fucking lunatic," Javion burst out. "How many times do I have to keep telling you guys she's—"

Before I could speak, Knox was standing in front of the vampire, his forearm pressed on his throat as he pinned Javion against the bookshelf. "Shut the fuck up, Javion."

"Stop it. Both of you," I shouted at them. I'd hit my limit on the bullshit behavior level I was prepared to tolerate from Javion. And tempted as I was to let Knox continue with his symbolic action—vampires were already dead so choking them wasn't going to work—I was not going to allow us to descend into mindless violence against each other like a Lycan clan would.

Knox relaxed his hold just enough for Javion to shove him away.

"It was a Lycan!"

I turned just in time to see Zeraora leap to her feet,

the electricity already crackling over her knuckles as she scowled at Javion.

"A Lycan? In wolf form? Surrounded by humans?" Javion sneered. "And here she continues to provide more evidence that she is nuts and needs to be locked up."

"You will not lock me up again," Zeraora shouted. Before I could stop her, she'd sent a bolt of lightning across the room. There was a loud crack as it narrowly missed Javion's head.

"Bitch, I'm dead. You can't hurt me with that."

"Then I'll do what I did with the last vampire," she snarled.

She leaped toward him, but I reached out, grabbing her and wrapping my arms around her. "Enough, Zeraora."

Her body was trembling, and I could feel the buzz of power as the electricity made contact with my body.

But so help me, as I inhaled and somehow breathed her in, my heart did something it hadn't since Manon. It pulled toward her.

"What vampire?" Javion asked, snapping me out of my daze.

"The one I killed last night."

I took one look at Hunter, seeing her words were

true, and then turned to Javion. "Get out of here."

Javion took half a step toward her. "What fucking vampire?"

"I didn't ask."

Javion's fist slammed into the bookcase, and then he turned, swiping them on the floor.

"Javion, get out of here, now," I told him, holding onto Zeraora.

The vampire took a couple of steps toward us before Knox was in front of him, pressing his hand against his chest.

"The vampire attacked me." Hunter jumped in, pointing at his leg. "That's how this happened. Zera saved me."

"Saved you?" Javion sneered. "Are you honestly trying to convince me that *you* couldn't take a fucking vampire by yourself without killing him?"

"She was protecting me," Hunter said through gritted teeth.

"Enough," I yelled.

He swung around to face me, jabbing his finger at me. "And you're protecting her too? You're going to let another . . . ?" Javion shook his head and shoved Knox's arm away. "I'm done with this bullshit. You're all too stupid to see what that is in front of you, and I'm done arguing with you. Fuck the lot of you and don't come crying to me when the rest of the supernatural world turns up on your doorstep."

Javion stormed over to the door, slamming it so hard behind him that it bounced back open.

With an apologetic look to Zeraora, Knox ran his hand through his hair and then hurried out after his mate.

Feeling Zeraora trembling in my arms, I looked over at Hunter. "Tell me you at least bought her a coat yesterday?"

Hunter nodded. "Yeah. Why?"

"Go get it for me."

"DB, you can't kick her out!" Hunter cried, his mouth dropping open in horror. "She was protecting me."

I pursed my lips and tilted my head as I gave him a pointed look. "Hunter?"

Although I saw a flicker of doubt, the younger gargoyle nodded before leaving Zeraora and I alone.

Finally, feeling as exhausted as I had last night, I let the female go, stepping in front of her. Only to find it wasn't fear or even distress that was causing her to shake. The look in her eyes was nothing other than venomous. "Zeraora?"

"They were attacking Hunter," she said with a coldness which sent a shiver down my spine. "I don't care if they were vampires or not. I will destroy anyone who dares to hurt me or the ones I care about."

I stepped forward, putting my hands on her shoulders.

She scowled up at me. "And if that means you're going to throw me out, so be it."

Frowning, I tilted my head. "No one is being thrown out. I said you were welcome to stay here, and I mean it."

Hunter appeared in the doorway with a long leather coat draped over his arms. With one look, he walked over and held it up.

I nodded to the coat. "You and I are going for a walk, but I want you to wear a coat. It may have warmed up out there, but there is still snow on the ground."

Although she gave me a suspicious look, Zeraora turned and slipped her arms into the coat.

The clothes they had bought her were far from the dresses of Manon's I had given her. For a fleeting moment, I suspected Hunter or Knox had led her to that style choice, but then I remembered Zeraora's sparky, temperamental personality—much like her powers—and realized the decision was more likely hers.

I'd let her have some of Manon's clothes because she didn't have any of her own . . .

That wasn't entirely true. I'd also wanted to see them put to good use after all this time but seeing them on her hadn't felt right.

It was like I had brought a ghost back to walk the halls of Castle Viegls.

"Come on, Blue Eyes." I led her back to the kitchen, only realizing as I pulled my vest from the hook by the door that Hunter had followed us. "Just us," I told him, firmly.

I stepped outside, holding the door open for Zeraora. Her face was still tensed up with anger, but she followed me out. Leaving Hunter to shut the door behind us, I started walking toward the ground's wall.

We were having one of the rare pockets of 'warmth' that occurred in December. The temperature had been rapidly dropping for the last few weeks, and snow had fallen and settled on the ground. Today, the dark clouds were low, but a high pressure swell from the south meant snow wouldn't be falling today, while the earth was so frozen that the snow wouldn't melt.

These were the kind of days I loved to go walking through the forests. The clouds stopped the sun from reflecting off the snow and dazzling us. Hell, looking at the clouds, I knew I could have left the curtains open in the library without worrying about Javion, but I would never take that risk.

I did not do exercise—not in the way the other three did. Hiking and gardening—and of course training and fighting—meant that I was fit. My love for cooking and eating had rounded out the hard lines my figure once had several decades ago.

As I led Zeraora out of the castle grounds and into the forest, I kept my eye on her, eventually slowing my pace. Despite the rage which still seemed to swirl through her, she was struggling with the hike.

Hiking was how I burned off my anger, and I was hoping it would do the same for her.

After only a couple of miles, I realized she was going to collapse from exhaustion before that happened, and I altered my course. A short while later, the forest opened up in front of me.

In the summer, the view was incredible from here. Not quite as good as further up the mountain, but impressive, nonetheless. Today, with the low clouds, visibility was limited.

That didn't mean the view of the Blue Ridge Mountains was any less beautiful.

I led us close to the edge of the cliff edge and

sucked in a deep breath of the cold mountain air.

"So you're not just throwing me out of the castle, but off a cliff too?"

I almost choked on the air.

"What the hell, Zeraora?" I spun around to face her. "I'm not throwing you off the cliff. I'm not even throwing you out of the castle."

The dark look in her eyes lessened a fraction. "You're not?"

"Do you honestly think I would do something like that?"

Zeraora looked down at her feet before shrugging. "I hope not," she said in a small voice. "I like being at Castle Viegls, even if it is only temporary."

Her words cut me. Somehow, I had managed to make her think that, not only was she not welcome, but I could do her harm.

Javion had done nothing but warn me about how she was going to be our demise for the last few weeks, and hell, he could have been right. But right or wrong, there was something about the tiny female that made me want to do everything I could to protect her.

Even if it did mean my demise in the end.

The fact that she thought I could harm her . . .?

"Zeraora?" I said softly, waiting for her to look up

at me. When she did, I shook my head. "I'm not going to hurt you."

Twenty-Six

Zera

A wind blew across the mountainside, blowing my hair back from my face. It wasn't cool, despite the snow, and it smelled of the pine trees we were walking through. A bit like Carter, only he had a touch of cinnamon mixed in. As he moved in front of me, I smelled it.

"I brought us up here because I thought you might want to get some fresh air. Not to kill you," Carter told me.

I wanted to tell him that I'd never thought that, but the truth was, in the back of my mind, a part of me had.

"Nor am I throwing you out of my home. I told you that you were welcome to stay here until at least the spring, and I mean that. But I think it's time we had a conversation about what the expectations are of you being here."

And here it was.

"I will never be your power source," I told him.

Carter's eyes widened in surprise as he took half a step back. "Our . . . No, Zeraora. Never."

"That's not what Javion has been saying."

A low growl erupted from the back of Carter's throat. "Javion's saying things that he has no right saying. I thought I'd made that clear to him before but evidently not. Zeraora, you are *welcome* in our home and *no one* is going to turn you into a power source . . ." Carter's eyes went wide again. "Wait, is that what the Lycans did to you? Is that why they were keeping you chained up?"

I looked away, as a strange sensation washed over me. I wasn't sure what it was, but it left my skin tingling, my stomach churning, and the strange desire to cry.

And then I felt it.

A drop of water on my face.

It wasn't tears.

I looked up, just as the rain started to fall from the sky in big, thick, heavy drops.

My mind and my body shut down, and once more, I was back in the last place I ever wanted to be, with Bacco pouring water over my head. Even though the clothes I wore offered much more protection, it was like they weren't there. The rain seemed to sear through the leather, burning at my skin.

The scream left me before I could stop it. My body doubled over as I tried desperately to stop the pain that was firing at all my nerve endings.

Time had passed. It wasn't much, but it was enough that my body had begun to forget this agony. The rain brought it all back, and twice as bad.

I could feel it—the power in me surging to the surface, trying to break free.

Why was it when I used it, this power didn't hurt, but something as simple as water could make me feel like my skin was being pulled off from the inside out?

Something wrapped around me.

Something solid and stone-like, but at the same time, soft and comforting.

And then the rain stopped.

I opened my eyes, breathing heavily, to find I was

in Carter's arms, pressed up against his chest.

His skin had changed. There was a dull shimmer to it that, depending on how you looked at it, made it either look like stone or skin, but with a dark gray tint to it.

Above us, like a giant umbrella, were his wings. They seemed more bat-like than bird-like, but they were enormous. As they wrapped around us, barely any light, and thankfully little rain, got in.

"You're safe, Zeraora," Carter muttered. It took me a moment to realize he had been repeating that, but my brain hadn't quite registered the words.

And then we were moving. Safe in his arms he carried me somewhere, walking slowly as the wings blocked most of his view.

Finally, still cradling me, he sat and lowered me between his legs, never letting go of me, and never opening his wings.

It wasn't dark. My body was creating a soft glow of blue-white light.

I might not have wanted to be a power source, but right then, I was a damn lightbulb.

As a shiver ran down the back of my spine, I huddled up into Carter's torso, grateful that he wrapped his arms around me.

"Are you okay?" he asked, his voice barely above a

whisper.

Outside of his umbrella wings, I could hear the rain lashing against them. My body let off some involuntary sparks of lightning which hit Carter's body, and with each mini flash of lightning, I could see the glass cage and Bacco's twisted smile as he got off from my pain.

I clung at Carter's clothes, holding my hands over my ears as I tried to block out the sound of the rain and Bacco's grunts.

And then a new sound seemed to break through. I wasn't sure how long it had been there until I realized it was singing.

Carter.

I couldn't understand what he was saying as it wasn't in English, but the melody, the vibrations in his chest, and the way his warm breath danced on the back of my neck all started to make the visions of Bacco fade away.

The tremors took longer to stop than the glowing of my skin, but finally, it settled into a near darkness under his wings, and the sound of the rain had returned to just that.

"What was that?" I asked after Carter stopped singing.

"An old French love song."

I nodded, my face rubbing against his chest.

"Zeraora, I've avoided asking this because . . ." Carter took a deep breath, exhaling softly. "What did they do to you?"

My wrists were just in front of my nose, as though emphasizing to me exactly what Carter was asking of me. Although they were healing and the pain in them had lessened, right now, they were throbbing. Pulsing.

"If I don't tell you, will you throw me out?"

The arms around me tightened as Carter rested his cheek on the back of my head. "Never. And if you really can't talk about it, I understand, but I'd like to know. It started raining, and you were screaming like you were being tortured."

"Normal people don't do that, huh?"

I asked the question not really expecting an answer, but behind me, Carter nodded. "I don't like the term normal, but it's not usual for many people to react to bad weather that way unless they've been through something."

I closed my eyes and chewed at the inside of my cheek. "I don't know anything," I said, eventually.

"You've forgotten?"

I shook my head. "I was little when I went in there. I think it was my fifth birthday."

Beneath me, Carter tensed. It was like I was suddenly resting against stone. "Five?"

"I remember a balloon in the shape of a five. I think it might have been my birthday." I closed my eyes and screwed my face up, desperately trying to dig through the recesses of my mind for something more, but like always, that was it. "They took me and the next thing I remember was being in a cage with glass walls."

"The Lycans?"

"I didn't know what they were until recently. I'd never seen their true form until Bacco . . ." I shuddered.

Carter growled, the sound low and angry. "Who is Bacco, because I'm going to rip him apart with my damn hands."

"He was the one in charge, but he's dead." There was still an enormous sense of relief and satisfaction as I said that. The only thing I regretted about his death was that a ghost killed him and not me.

"Good." Carter grunted.

"Do you know what a kilowatt is?" I asked, suddenly.

"It's a unit of measurement for electricity," Carter said, carefully. He lifted his arm and gently brushed some hair out of my face. "How do you know what a kilowatt is?"

"Apparently I used to produce a billion of them a year."

"Produce . . .?" Carter's hand paused just behind my ear. "When you said that they called you Battery, do you mean they had you powering something? Since you were five years old?"

There were times when I was aware of my power because it seemed to hover in the air like a tangible entity. Right now, Carter was producing his own, fueled by anger. I was sure that if I reached out, I would feel it, heavy, and consuming the little cocoon we were wrapped in.

"Yes." I closed my eyes, pressing my head against Carter's chest, seeking out the rhythmic beating of his heart instead of the rain that continued to fall outside. "They chained me up and poured water over me. Eventually one of them—Bacco— realized that if it rained on me instead of being poured, it produced more power, and I didn't pass out."

"Zeraora, I swear to the gods that I am going to find those Lycans, and I am going to pull their spines out of their throats."

I pushed myself away from him so I could look at him as I wildly shook my head. "You can't do that."

"Do not tell me that despite all of what they did to

you, that you have some form of positive feelings toward them." Carter's eyes looked like inky pools of liquid rage in the dim light.

"No. You can't do that because I am going to hunt them down and kill them all myself. If they want my power, they're going to feel every single kilowatt of it as I fry them from the inside out." My words came out as a snarl as my sparks fell from my fingers.

"Oh, Zeraora." A bark of laughter left Carter before he pulled me to him, holding me against his chest. "You don't need to go near the Lycans ever again."

I pushed myself away once more. "But I want to. I want to destroy them all. I am going to make them pay for every day I was chained up in that cage. For every gallon of water that was poured on me. I'm going to find them, and I'm going to obliterate them."

Carter rubbed a hand over his jaw. "Oh, Blue Eyes. . . They're more dangerous than you think they are."

Staring back at him, I pushed out my shoulders. "So am I."

"I don't doubt that . . ." He sighed, glancing up at his wings above us as though seeking something in the veiny skin. Finally, he looked back at me. "Okay . . . Zeraora, I need you to promise me that you won't go and seek the Lycans by yourself. It seems like they're already looking for you, and I know you're just as deadly as they are, but they've spent their lives training and hunting, and you've spent it . . ."

"I can handle them," I said, stubbornly. I'd wiped out eight of them already. I would wipe out eight hundred more.

"*Alone*, Zeraora. I'm just asking you not to do it alone."

I frowned. "You want to . . . help me?"

Carter reached for my hands, holding them firmly in his. "Promise me."

Staring into the dark pools of his eyes, I was torn. I had no idea where to start when it came to hunting the Lycans and some help would be nice. The fact it was Carter offering help made a warmth radiate from my chest. But somehow, at the center of it, was a shard of ice. I didn't want him to get hurt.

"Okay." Though I honestly wasn't sure if I meant it.

Carter continued to stare at me as though he was trying to work that out himself. Eventually, he nodded, pulling me back to him.

I wasn't sure why he kept doing that, but I couldn't fight it. His arms were warm, strong, and a physical representation of something that I craved. There was a pull toward him, like he was my center of gravity, and I couldn't explain why.

"I'm sorry that I brought you up here," he said, his hand was back to pushing hair out of my face. "And I'm sorry you've had to go through all that you have." He looked over my head and smiled. "It stopped raining though. Let's go back home."

Slowly, he lowered his wings. The little bubble we had been in popped with a flood of cold air that showed my breath when I breathed out.

But with it came light.

My mouth fell open as I finally saw Carter in his gargoyle form. He was already tall and broad, but he somehow seemed bigger and more imposing. His body had bulk which was normally curved and softer looking, but like this, there were edges to his muscles.

There was definitely a grayish hue to his skin, and like Hunter, he had a horn protruding from each temple. I couldn't stop staring at them, wondering if they would elicit the same response as they had from Hunter.

"Ah." Carter glanced over his shoulder at his wings before shrugging. "I guess you've never seen me in this form."

I shook my head, stepping forward.

As if I were a wild animal he didn't want to startle, Carter stayed so still he could well have been made from stone. He didn't move until I reached up toward a horn, and then suddenly his hand was wrapped around mine, pulling it down.

"A gargoyle's horn is . . . that's something only a mate should be touching, Blue Eyes." Before I could say anything, he turned and started leading me back toward the castle.

I was expecting his wings to return to wherever they hid, but he kept them out, occasionally glancing up at the sky as we walked. It wasn't until we reached the kitchen door that he let them disappear through two slits in his vest, shrinking away to nothing. When I looked back at him, he was normal again.

We walked into the kitchen and were pounced on by Hunter. "Thank fuck. I saw the lightning. Is everything okay?"

Carter glanced at me before nodding. "Nothing to worry about. Do you mind fixing Zeraora some breakfast? I want to catch Javion before he sleeps for the day."

Hunter shifted on the spot, rubbing at the back of his neck. "You might want to wait until tonight. I went down to talk to him, and I think Knox is . . . um . . ." he looked at me before sighing and turning back to Carter. "They're occupied."

Occupied? "They're fucking?"

"Well, yes . . ." Hunter rubbed at the back of his neck again.

I shrugged, walking over to the fridge to grab a can of Coke. My walk through the woods had made me thirsty.

Or maybe that was the memory of the noise Knox made as Javion had his cock in his hands.

I shut the fridge door, frowning as I did. I hated Javion, so why was I remembering that? I didn't need to remember his beautiful naked body. *Ick.*

"Fix her some breakfast," Carter said, breaking my thoughts. "I've got things I need to do." With no further explanation, he left the kitchen.

Hunter stepped in front of me, cupping the side of my face. "You okay, Zee?" he asked me.

"I'm hungry."

"Thank you for protecting me from that vampire," he said, softly. He leaned over and pressed his lips against my forehead. "And don't worry about Javion. He gets defensive whenever anyone talks shit about vampires, but there's a reason why he's with us and not them."

I wasn't worried about Javion, but I certainly didn't trust him, nor did I like him.

I tilted my head upwards to look at Hunter and he lowered his, this time, claiming my lips. His hands slid under my coat to settle on my hips as mine draped over his shoulders, still clutching at the can of Coke.

I didn't see Carter, Knox or Javion again for the rest of the day. Once Hunter had filled me up with pancakes, we ended up in our usual spot on the couch, watching episode after episode of television shows.

This was going to be the last day of doing just this. Although I was learning through watching these things, the cast of Supernatural—which we were currently watching because there were a lot of supes that were almost accurate to real life—weren't going to help me.

Although I wasn't going to turn down any help from Dean or Sam Winchester if they ever turned up at Castle Viegls . . .

While I might have been packing enough power to do some damage, something Carter said had stuck in the back of my mind. The Lycans were more dangerous than I thought. They'd already shown me that by getting that mongoose shifter and her ogres to help her; supes that weren't affected by my abilities.

I needed to know how to fight them without zapping them.

And currently, I couldn't walk up the side of a mountain without almost keeling over.

Tomorrow, whether Hunter wanted to watch movies or not, I was going to work on improving my non-existent fitness, stamina and strength.

"You're quiet," Hunter muttered. His arm was draped over my shoulder as his hand twisted a lock of my hair between his fingers.

"I'm tired."

Hunter glanced at his phone before nodding. "It's late. Why don't you head up to bed?"

I nodded and stood. Seconds later, Hunter took my hand, pulling me onto his lap. "What are you doing?"

"Getting my good night kiss." Hunter reached up and gently turned my face to his before his mouth covered mine.

His tongue gently urged its way between my lips, while his arms wrapped around me, hands resting on my hip. My hands went up, settling on his cheek. It was rough with the prickle of a beard that hadn't been shaved that morning.

Hunter pulled me closer to him, moaning as I shifted in his lap. The sound was as pleasurable to me as the feel of his tongue running over mine. The last time he'd made that noise had been in the alley before his horn and tail made an appearance.

I reached up, feeling at his temples just as a small bump appeared.

And then, before I could work out what had happened, I was deposited on the couch and Hunter was beside the fireplace with his hand on the mantle, breathing heavily. "I think you need to head up to bed now," he muttered, his attention on the glowing fire and not me.

"Did I do something wrong?"

Hunter sucked in a deep breath before turning back to me. "Not even close. That was my fault, and I had to stop things before I lost control again."

"I liked it when you lost control last time." And if that was him losing control, I was all for him losing it again.

"Go to bed, Zee." Hunter turned his back on me, his shoulders hunched.

I ran a tongue over my lower lip before leaving him. Men were complicated, and I was going to add 'figuring them out' to the list of things I wanted to accomplish while I was here.

The irritation stayed with me until I got in my room and went to get a nightdress from the shopping bags. Only when the silky material was covering me did I start to feel a little calmer, like the softness managed to smooth over my feelings as well as my skin.

I walked into the bathroom to brush my teeth, stopping a couple of paces from the door when I knew something was different in there.

Twenty-Seven

Zera

It took me a moment to realize that the thing that was different was me. Every time I went into the bathroom, the hairs on my arms stood on end and an involuntary shudder would always run down my spine.

Even though I knew it was tucked in the corner and I could walk past it freely without ever needing to step into it, the large shower had always spiked some anxiety.

Today, that feeling was gone.

I turned to the corner of the room, my mouth dropping open.

The glass door was gone. As was the showerhead and the control. In its place were several tiles a few shades lighter than the ones around it with bright white grout holding them in place.

In the center of what had been the shower was now a tall planter filled with bright red, star-shaped flowers.

This was what Carter had needed to do?

I walked out of the bathroom, straight through the bedroom and into the corridor.

Hunter had taken me on a tour of the castle when I'd arrived, so I knew where everyone's bedroom were. Carter's room was at the opposite side of the castle to mine, overlooking the main entrance and the gardens that lay between the house part and the gate.

But Carter's bedroom was not my destination.

It wasn't that late, despite Hunter's insistence on sending me to bed, and I was certain that Carter was going to be in the library.

Sure enough, there was a light shining out under the large wooden door. I pushed it open and walked in. Almost instantly, I was hit with an icy breeze which whipped the door out of my hands and closed it behind me with a thud.

Shivering, the thin nightdress offered little protection from the cold. I took a couple of steps into the room and looked around. The fire was lit in the fireplace, but it seemed pointless considering the windows were wide open.

Every time I'd been in here previously, I'd never noticed that the central windows weren't windows—they were doors.

After establishing Carter wasn't in the room, I walked toward the door. They led to a patio the length of the windows and about half as deep. They were surrounded by stone railings that came up to my waist to stop anyone from falling over the cliff edge the castle sat on.

Perched on the corner, looking out across the moonlit mountainside, was Carter. If it wasn't for the jeans he was wearing, I would have thought he was a . . . a gargoyle. Even his hair was barely moving in the ice-cold wind howling around the mountainside.

He was crouched down, toes hanging over the edge of the railing, his chin resting on the back of his fist as though he was contemplating jumping off. No doubt, his wings would stop his fall and instead make him soar into the air.

Carter let out a long sigh. "Are you just going to

stand there or—" His question died as he turned and saw me. "Zeraora? What are you doing here?" He jumped off the railing and onto the balcony, hurrying over to me.

I threw my arms around him, making him come to a dead stop.

"What are you doing?" he asked as his hands awkwardly patted my back.

"Saying thank you. I saw the flowers."

His palms settled on the small of my back. "It was nothing," he said, gruffly.

"It was everything."

Carter let out a long sigh before tightening his hold around me. "If I'd have known, I would have removed it sooner."

The wind picked up, blowing flurries of settled snow around us and I shivered, cuddling more into the older man.

"Zeraora!" he exclaimed, suddenly. "What are you wearing? What are you doing out here?" Suddenly, his hands settled onto my hips and he picked me up. I clung to him, not liking the wind when it got between us. He marched inside, still holding onto me as he shut the doors. Then, he moved toward the fire, setting me down in front of it.

He stepped back, putting some distance between us. I stared up at him, still in his gargoyle form, marveling how the light from the fire danced over him.

Although the stone-like finish to his skin gave him the impression of harder lines, there was little definition in his stomach. My Netflix education had given me enough shows with abs to know he didn't have any—just a slight roundness to his stomach.

Seeing me stare, he glanced down before giving me a wry smile. "There's a reason they call this old man DB."

I continued to stare at him. I'd noticed that I was the only one who called him Carter, but I'd never worked out why the others called him DB, or even what it meant.

"Dad bod?" he supplied, as though that explained everything.

With a soft groan, he sank down into the highbacked armchair, reaching for the half full glass of whiskey beside him.

As though in a trance, I watched him, first curious about how his wings seemed to curl up behind him and allowed him to sit, and then at the lump in his throat that bobbed up and down as he swallowed his drink.

Finally, he pulled the glass away, looking at the

liquid and shaking his head. "Maybe I've had enough of this." He turned his gaze on me, inhaling deeply. I didn't miss how his eyes worked their way up my body, settling on my breasts, before continuing up. "Was there something else you needed?"

The chill that had set in me from those few minutes outside disappeared under the heat of his gaze. In all my time here, he'd never looked at me like this.

Slowly, I moved toward him, my footsteps silent until they left the rug and hit the stone floor in front of him. I sat down on his thigh.

"What are you doing?" he asked, although his hand seemed to instinctively move to the small of my back.

The truth was, I wasn't entirely sure.

I raised my hand, placing it over Carter's heart which I could feel beating strongly.

Carter's hand came down on mine. "If this is about the shower, you don't need to pay me back."

Tilting my head, I pulled my attention to his face. "I didn't realize I owed you a debt."

"You don't."

I shrugged. "Then this isn't me paying you back for anything." As he kept his hand firmly over mine, I lifted the other, reaching for one of the horns on his head. I wasn't sure why I always had the urge to touch them, but it felt like it was calling to me.

Just as I got close, the hand on my back shot up, pulling it away. "Zeraora," Carter said, saying my name like he was scolding me. I didn't flinch. The heat in his eyes was contradicting that. "I told you; you can't just touch a gargoyle's horns like that. It's like touching—"

I slipped my hand out from under his, removing it from his chest so I could take his hand. I pulled it to me, settling his palm over my breast.

Heat seared through the thin silk.

Carter's breath caught as he looked at it. "What are you doing?"

"It's like touching me here, right?"

Slowly, Carter nodded his head.

The nightdress was a simple slip of black silk that clung to my body like it was water and had done nothing to protect me from the cold. Right now, it was doing nothing to hide my nipples.

His thumb moved toward it, brushing over the top. His touch was gentle, but it didn't stop my gasp. Carter closed his eyes, but his hands gently squeezed as his thumb made another pass over my nipple.

I let go of him, allowing him to move more freely as I arched my back and pressed my breast up against his palm.

As the most incredible sensations seemed to radiate from there, down between my legs, I resumed my mission of touching his horn. My fingertips barely touched the top before his hand was clasping mine again.

"It's not just like touching your tits," he said, roughly. "They heighten everything we feel, and things like control get dampened."

"So?" Stopping me made me want to touch them even more. There was a pull to this man, and I was in no mood to fight it. If he wanted to lose control, he could.

"So? I'm not a man. I have gone a long time without a female's touch, and I'm trying hard not to let the stone demon in me take control and take you right there on that rug. The longer you go, the harder it is. You're not ready for me to claim you like that. Knox or Hunter—"

"I want you." I tried to push past his grip, but he remained firm.

"Gods be damned, I know you want me. I can scent it all over you."

My hand went limp.

"You don't want me."

That was why he was trying to send me to the

twins.

"Oh no, don't you dare look like that." Carter growled. "Make no mistake, you are a beautiful woman, and I would love nothing more than to have your pussy contracting around my cock as you scream out my name, but I want those screams to be pleasure and not pain. You've been through enough of that."

"So, you do want me?"

I could hear the growl in the back of his throat as he let go of my hands, only to wrap them around my waist as he picked me up. "Yes, I want you." He dropped to his knees before lowering me backwards on the rug. "And so help me, I know I shouldn't, but your scent is driving me crazy."

I frowned. "My scent?"

That was the second time he had mentioned my smell, but I was bathing daily. Did that mean I wasn't doing that right either?

Before I could ask, I was distracted by his skin returning to normal and the horns disappearing back into his head. "What are you doing?" My eyes went wide.

"I don't trust you not to touch them, and I sure as hell don't trust myself to let you." He leaned forward, placing a hand on the rug, on either side of my arms. "If

I can't take the temptation from in front of me, I can take it from in front of you."

He closed his eyes and let out a long breath. I could almost taste the whiskey in the air.

"If you don't want to—"

"Gods be damned," he said, his words almost a snarl as he opened his eyes. Carter dipped his head, his lips meeting mine. Considering how in control he normally seemed, I wasn't surprised when his kiss was like that too.

Strong and guiding, but gentle. Now I really could taste the remnants of the whiskey on his lips.

And then they were gone, moving to my neck, along my collar bone, and down my chest. Finally, without bothering to remove my nightdress, Carter's mouth closed around my nipple, sucking hard as he ran his tongue over the tip.

My hands curled into the rug as my back left the ground.

I swear the temperature of my body shot up twenty degrees.

Carter moved to the other nipple, replacing his mouth with his hands. As he gave the other the same attention, his fingers splayed out over my breasts before he captured my nipple between his finger and thumb.

He squeezed, gently pulling as he bit down on the other.

Oh yes!

Then, as my eyes felt like they were going to roll into the back of my head, Carter moved lower.

He pulled the short skirt of the nightdress up and hooked his fingers under the elastic of my panties. As he pulled them down my legs, he followed them with his mouth. The coarse hair of his beard tickled my sensitive skin.

Once off, he repeated his action in reverse up the other leg, until he came close to the apex between my legs. Then he sat back on his knees.

"Zeraora," he said, using the same tone he always used on the others.

"Carter."

"You are beautiful," he murmured.

I wasn't sure what to expect, but it wasn't Carter's head diving between my legs. I giggled as his beard tickled me, despite the weird sensation of his tongue running the length of me.

And then, *oh my*, he reached that sensitive area.

Forget weird, it was incredible.

As I squirmed in pleasure, his hands grabbed my thighs, holding them open and in place.

My hands left the rug to dive into his hair. His hair was too short to hold onto properly, but I didn't want that tongue leaving me any time soon . . . until he slipped lower, pushing it inside me before returning it back to my sensitive spot.

With each lick and suck, I responded involuntarily with a moan or gasp. And each time, I felt the pressure growing inside me.

Carter's tongue was both skilled and relentless, working me into a frenzy that I was dying to release.

"Oh, Gods. Oh, my gods." Electricity crackled over me, only this time, it made my skin feel like it was buzzing.

Then it stopped. Carter lifted his head, despite me desperately trying to hold him in place. "It feels good?"

"Yes," I shrieked, half-hoping the short answer would get him to resume what he was doing.

Carter chuckled. "You want to come, my Zeraora?"

Electricity sparked as I nodded. "Don't stop."

Thankfully, Carter dipped his head.

I dropped back to the floor, trying to remember to breathe as Carter focused his attention back on my sensitive spot.

And then there was an explosion.

A metaphorical one and a physical one.

Orgasms. Orgasms were the best thing in this world. I'd be able to cope without television or food but locking me away again to never experience this—that would be the worst thing.

As intense pleasurable sensations radiated out from the area Carter's tongue was all-but assaulting, to every extremity of my body, they seemed to continue further. Lightning bolts shot from my fingertips, zapping various things around the library.

It was the one which hit the chandelier that exploded, raining glass down on the far side of the room.

Carter finally moved, this time, heading back up my body until his head was hovering above mine. "I take it that my little Zeraora enjoyed that?"

I barely had the energy to open my eyes, never mind nod my head. "Mmmm."

His lips were on mine, along with a new taste—me. "You-taste-so-good," he told me. Carter rolled onto his side, pulling me to him. I sighed, content. "There must be a catch."

Sleep was trying to take over my body, but I poked an eye open. "What catch?"

"I don't know." He nuzzled his chin against my collarbone, the action making me smile as it tickled.

"But I feel like I've been given a second chance, and I've always been told that's not possible."

Second chance . . .?

I couldn't get my mouth to open and ask what he meant as I finally lost my battle and fell asleep.

I was alone when I woke up, and I was also in a bed. Half asleep, it took me a while to realize it was mine. About then, I also realized I wasn't alone.

The other person wasn't Carter. Nor was it anyone in the bed with me.

It was a ghost.

Sitting bolt-upright, I rubbed at my eyes, trying to scrub the sleep away, along with the disbelief. "You?"

"You remember me. Good." It wasn't just any ghost, but the ghost who helped me escape the Lycans. She was much fainter this time. I could barely make out the nose on her face. "You need to trust them all."

"Trust who?"

She took a step forward, but instantly halved the brightness. "Carter, Hunter, Knox and Javion."

"Javion?" I scoffed. If there was anyone I didn't trust, it was Javion.

The ghost was fading quickly. "Trust him, Zera. It will take all of them to . . ."

"To what?" I asked the empty room.

I flopped back onto the bed, yawning. She was already seeming like a remnant of a dream. Maybe she was.

But trust Javion?

Rolling onto my side, I pulled the sheets up to my neck. Javion had made it perfectly clear, his opinion of me. Was I to trust he didn't like me?

Whatever.

Yawning, I closed my eyes. It was still the middle of the night, and I was exhausted. This was something to think about when I was awake.

Twenty-Eight

Zera

Sunshine was already streaming in through the castle when I woke. I stretched out, wiggling my toes as my body gave me happy flashbacks of what had happened in the library with Carter.

After making my mind up that I was going to get Hunter to teach me to fight yesterday, I was still determined to accomplish that today.

I picked out an outfit from my bags of clothes, dressed, and hurried down to the kitchen. It wasn't until

I sat eating some cereal that I noticed the time—it was early afternoon.

Surprised that no one had woke me before now, I finished off my breakfast and loaded the empty bowl into the dishwasher. I walked into the living room, but it was empty.

Where was Hunter?

Puzzled, I headed upstairs to his bedroom, but found that empty too. I worked around the first floor, checking each room methodically, but each was empty.

Downstairs was no different.

Although it was possible that they had all gone out, something told me there was no way they would have left me alone. *Someone* would be here to keep an eye on me.

I glanced at the corridor to the basement and Javion's domain.

Someone other than Javion.

I'd found Knox out in the garage before. Maybe he was there now?

More snow had fallen while I'd been asleep, and the temperature had dropped again. My breath was coming out in small clouds, hovering in the air in front of me until I walked through them.

As I got near the garage, I discovered fresh tire

marks leading away, down the drive to the gates.

Someone had gone out.

Seeing as though I could hear music as I approached the garage, I suspected it wasn't Knox.

I walked into the garage, but the music wasn't coming from in there. Following the music past all the cars, I reached a door at the end. Pushing it open, the music got louder. There were no lyrics, just an electronic sound that rang out over the through the room.

This room was a gym. There were all kinds of machines: benches and weights, and in the corner, swinging back and forth, a punching bag which was almost the same size as me.

Knox was alternating between punching and kicking it like it had personally wronged him. I hung back by the door to watch him. His workout involved him wearing grey sweat pants and nothing else. His hands and feet were bound up by some tape or bandages, but he wore no shoes or gloves.

I could also finally see his wings.

One hung properly, reacting with his body as Knox pounded the bag. The other looked withered and hung limply against his back, occasionally knocking into the good one. That side of his body was also covered in scars. Parts of his skin looked like they had once been ripped apart and then stuck back together with glue to create ridges and craters that ran the length of his spine. Between them all were the black lines of his tattoos.

Knox's skin glistened. Sweat was running down the lines in his back. If it didn't drip onto the mat, it collected around the waistband of the sweats.

Despite the obvious old injury, there was still muscle and raw power in the gargoyle. It was a beautiful sight to behold.

And wow, it made me want a drink.

Finally, Knox stopped, clutching at the punching bag as he caught his breath. He took a step, reaching for something—a water bottle—before turning and finally seeing me. He gave me a crooked smile. "When did you get here, Tric?"

I shrugged. "A while ago? Where is everyone?"

The smile slipped. "Javion is asleep for the day. DB and Hunter went out on a grocery run. Which reminds me; wear that pretty red dress for dinner tonight, okay?"

I hadn't chosen many dresses when we'd gone shopping. In the back of my mind, I had been thinking about the fight scenes in the movies, and how everyone always appeared to go rolling over the floor or through walls. It seemed to me that keeping covered might help a little.

Taking a couple of mouthfuls of his drink, Knox walked over to me. "You need something?"

I glanced around the gym before nodding. "I want to know how to fight."

Knox burst out laughing.

For some reason, that pissed me off. I curled my hands into fists as I frowned at him. "Why is that funny?"

"Because you pack enough of a punch with your lightning bolts, that I can't imagine your fists coming close." He reached down and took a fist in each of his hands. "What do you need to learn to fight for anyway? You're safe here where we can protect you."

"Like I was in Atlanta? Because ogres don't feel my power, remember?" Seething, I cocked my head, pulling my hands free to set them on my hips. "Oh, no. You weren't there."

"Ouch," Knox muttered, moving back. "But that won't happen again."

"Taking me to Atlanta, or being chased by ogres? And what about vampires?"

Knox rubbed at the back of his neck. "Zera, you're safe here."

"What about Javion?" As I asked the question, it sparked at something in the back of my mind, but like I was grasping at smoke, it disappeared.

"Javion?" Knox shook his head. "Look, I know he has been a complete and utter dick, but he's not going to hurt you. I spoke to him yesterday—and DB did too."

"Javion wants me gone." I pointed out, folding my arms. "He doesn't like me . . ." A thought occurred to me. "Is it because you claimed me? Is he going to make you unclaim me?"

"Unclaim you?" Knox's eyes widened. He quickly shook his head. "Why would you . . .? Do you know about me and Javion?"

I nodded. "I saw you and him together when I first arrived. Javion saw me watching. That's why he attacked me, and we had the power cut." I frowned. "I thought he was a Lycan."

Understanding washed through Knox's eyes. "No one ever told me you'd seen us together. I thought it was Javion being his usual dickish self. Shit." He looked away, sucking in a deep breath before looking back to me. "I have no intention of 'unclaiming' you . . . we call it rejecting . . . and I have no intention of rejecting you either."

"And he doesn't care?"

Knox ran a hand through his hair, scrubbing his

fingers against the back of his neck. "I wouldn't go that far, but mates are different with vampires."

I stared blankly at him. The television shows only ever showed human relationships, and they seemed messy as fuck. They called them girlfriends and boyfriends, not mates.

"Most supes take a female mate. That's what we call them: mates. Vampires call them their females betrothed, but they can also take multiple mates in any sex." Knox shook his head. "The point I was trying to make is that Javion doesn't give a fuck about that. That's not why he hates you."

As Knox clamped his mouth shut, I arched an eyebrow. "But he does still hate me."

"He just doesn't trust you."

There it was again: that wisp of a memory.

"If you're not going to teach me, I'll wait for Hunter to get back."

Knox poked his tongue out to capture the first piercing between his teeth. "Okay, little elemental. Come with me." I followed him over to the punching bag, bringing my fists up in front of me like I had seen him do. "Not so fast," he muttered.

"Why?"

He jogged over to a cupboard and pulled out a pair

of gloves before returning to me. "Just because you got the quick healing gene doesn't mean we don't need to protect those hands."

I took them from him but didn't put them on, instead, I stared pointedly at his bandaged hands. "What about you?"

"I've spent a lot longer fighting than you. I know how to punch properly." He folded his arms and stared down at me. "If you want to learn, you wear the gloves until I tell you otherwise."

I put the gloves on.

"Okay, let's see what you've got." He nodded his chin in the direction of the punching bag.

With a satisfied smirk, I stepped up to the punching bag and slammed my fist into it.

It barely moved.

When Knox had been hitting and kicking it, the thing had been bouncing around on the chain it was suspended from.

What was worse, my knuckles hurt from hitting the bag.

"What is that thing made from?"

When I looked at Knox, he was now the one smirking. "I hate to break it to you, Tric, but that's sand. It's just a normal, 'human' punching bag."

Sand?

"Look, it was your first punch, and you're not close to being able to hit that properly. I just wanted to check if you're left or right-handed." He picked up one of my hands. "You're a leftie, by the way."

I pulled my hand free and narrowed my eyes. "I can punch."

Knox put his hands on my shoulders and turned me to face him, away from the punching bag. "How you stand will help with how you hit, how you block, and how you take a hit. You want to be light on your feet, but you need to be steady. Have your feet a shoulder-width apart."

Looking down at my boots, I spread my legs slightly.

"Good. Now, you're a leftie, so you need to lead with your right foot, so take half a step forward."

Again, I did as he said, and then turned my attention back to him.

Knox moved closer to push my shoulder. "See? Now you're more stable." He took a few steps back and then mimicked my pose, only leading with his left foot. "You need to be light on your feet, able to rock back and forth like this."

On the balls of his feet, he did as he was describing.

And then my attention span flatlined, completely distracted by the thing swinging between his legs against the fabric of his sweats.

I licked my lips.

"Zera?" Knox clicked his fingers in front of my face. "Focus. If I attacked you, you'd be on your back now."

"Is that a bad thing?"

Knox's rocking slowed. "Do you want to learn to fight, or do you want to take your eyes and your mind off my dick?"

I looked up, finding a smirk on his face. I wasn't sure which one I wanted to answer yes to. Sucking in a deep breath, I shook it off and started rocking back and forth.

"Shame," Knox muttered under his breath as he moved back over to the cupboard. He returned with some tape and used it to mark a cross over the faint impression I'd made when I'd punched it previously. "All I want you to do for now is to hit that cross."

The task sounded far too easy . . . until I started doing it. I wasn't sure if I was struggling to see the white cross on the black bag, or if my aim was *that* bad, but I rarely hit the same spot twice in a row.

It didn't take long for my arms to tire. Sweat was

already building up in the small of my back—it was no wonder Knox only wore sweatpants. Next time, I wasn't wearing leather.

"Let's leave it there for today." Knox suggested.

Stubbornly, I shook my head. I had barely lasted thirty minutes.

I took a few more swings at the bag before Knox stepped forward and caught my hands. "Don't be disappointed. You did well."

"No, I didn't." I snorted.

"This is the first time you've done this, and you've got no muscle mass or stamina. We need to spend a bit of time working on those next time. As they improve, so will everything else."

The last thing I wanted to do was admit that I was already tired.

Instead, I held my hands out and waited for Knox to release the Velcro straps. He stepped forward, releasing one. He pulled the glove off and tossed it to the side, but he didn't let go of my hand. Instead, he reached for the bandage.

"What are you doing?" I demanded.

"It's been nearly seven weeks. Are these still hurting? I shouldn't have strapped the gloves over them if they are."

"They don't hurt," I said too quickly.

Knox looked up at me. The pierced eyebrow disappeared under his hair. "Why are you still wearing the bandages?"

"To hide what's underneath."

My wrist injuries *had* taken a lot longer than anything else to heal. But the truth was, when I'd checked them before we'd gone shopping, they were mostly healed.

In their place I had been left with a thick red welt that completely encircled my wrist, with lightning bolt marks firing off from them.

"Would you mind if I looked at them?" Knox asked, softly.

"Yes."

The piercing was caught between his teeth again as he tilted his head and looked at me. "Can I ask why?"

I shrugged. "They are hideous, and I don't want to see them."

He straightened, releasing my hand. "Is that what you think of mine?"

"Your what?"

Knox pointed at his face, and then at his side. "My scars."

"No!" Unless I was up close and squinting, I could

barely see the ones on his face. And until now, the ones on his body had largely been hidden away under his shirts. But even if they hadn't, like now, they didn't repulse me like mine did.

"Then how are they different?"

"How?" I tore the second glove off my hand and flung it by my feet. "Because looking at them just reminds me of what had been there before. I had chains around my wrists for nearly twenty years of my life, and I couldn't do anything to stop it."

"Hey." Knox stepped toward me and placed his hands on my shoulders. "That sure as fuck is not something to blame yourself for."

"It doesn't mean that I want to look at them." I wiggled myself out of his hold and moved away. Trying to put some distance between us—or at least *something*—I moved behind a weight bench and found myself staring at my reflection.

My appearance had changed from the first time I looked at myself in a mirror. Aside from the missing dirt, grime, and dried blood, there was now color in my cheeks. My skin had remained pale—much whiter than Knox or Hunter's. I'd also put on a little bit of weight, although I still looked, as Hunter had once said, like a good burst of wind would blow me away.

The problem wasn't what was on the outside. It was what was on the inside.

The more television I watched with Hunter, the more time I spent with all of them, the more I realized there was something different about me.

Javion was constantly saying I was dangerous, and I'd always thought he was right.

But I was sure he didn't really know how dangerous I was.

"What's all this about, Zera?" Knox asked, appearing behind me.

Looking up, I met his gaze in the mirror.

I think they might have been right to keep the chains on me.

Although it felt like my mind was ready to shout this out, my lips remained clamped together.

The only things that were locked up in this world were the unsafe things. Lethal criminals in prisons, dangerous animals in cages . . .

When I was with Knox or Hunter or Carter, I was able to act 'normal.' Someone could look at me and see a short, skinny woman, who looked harmless. And with the guys, I sometimes felt like I could be harmless, especially when my powers didn't hurt them.

But it slipped.

I saw their reactions when I'd said I would destroy

the Lycans. Or how zapping a guy's phone and setting an EMP off in a city was an acceptable level of action. Even Hunter's face when I'd decapitated that vampire—and I hadn't wanted to stop. I had been more than prepared to take the head of the other one too.

Those weren't normal responses to any of those things.

Somehow, I had become stuck in a situation I couldn't see a way out of.

Being with them felt right. And when I was with them, I wanted to be someone they would want to be with too.

But there was going to come a point when they would see what Javion did, and they would realize that I either needed to leave Castle Viegls, or I would need to go back into a cage, just like Javion said.

And whenever I looked at the scars on my wrists, I was reminded of this, and it made me feel like my insides were eating themselves up.

The Lycans had taken everything away from me for the last twenty years. The last thing I wanted was for them to take my mates away from me too.

"Tric? You're worrying me."

I zoned back in just in time to see Knox step up behind me and wrap his arms around me.

"If you don't want me to see under your bandages, you don't have to show me."

I relaxed back into him and nodded.

"And I know today didn't go exactly how you wanted it to, but we can come out here every day and work on building up your strength and stamina while working on your fighting skills."

While that made me feel a little happier, I still couldn't shake my uneasy sensation. As Knox was watching me, expectantly, I gave him a smile before he could tell something was still eating away at me.

Instead, I turned my attention to his face. "How come you don't have horns?"

Knox blinked before looking away. "My *aibidh*."

"That's when you become a gargoyle, right?"

"We're always a gargoyle. It's the time when we are able to transition into our true form. This one." He opened up his good wing, bringing it around to wrap me up like it was a blanket.

Like the rest of his body, it looked like it was made of stone, but when I reached out and ran my hand over it, it felt like leather.

"It's more like puberty. The change can take a few months. So, along with squeaky voices, wet dreams, and the joy of shaving, we also have to deal with spontaneous wing reveals—which are painful as fuck—sensitive horns, and gravel skin."

I looked up at him. "Gravel skin?"

"I'd rather acne."

My powers had been present since the lightning bolt had hit me, and I'd not been tracking time well to know exactly when my breasts had started to grow, but their appearance had changed Bacco's attitude toward me.

I shuddered and instantly, Knox cracked a crooked grin. "Gravel skin sucks."

"Yeah," I muttered, unable to meet his gaze.

"The Lycans attacked me while I was midway through my *aibidh*. My wing was damaged so badly, it never recovered, and my horns never appeared."

"If you don't have horns, does that mean you can't. . . you know . . ."

"I know?" Knox stepped back and turned me around so that he was looking at me and not my reflection. "Fuck's sake, Tric. I thought you said you'd seen me and Javion together? My cock works perfectly fine. I might not be able to fly, but I sure can still fuck."

That was true. Knox certainly seemed to be enjoying himself, but the way Hunter and even Carter had reacted, I just felt like he might be missing out.

Knox turned to the side and let out a long sigh, rubbing at the back of his neck. "Everyone makes such a big deal out of not having horns, and maybe I am missing out on something, but from everything we're taught growing up, at least I can keep control of myself, even when I'm in this form." He gave me a sideways glance. "I'd have enough restraint to keep *you* begging all night long."

Electricity crackled across my skin, earning me a smirk. "Begging for what?"

Knox chuckled. "I can smell your arousal. You know damn well what."

"I thought you said I didn't know what I wanted."

The piercing was back between Knox's lips. Slowly, like a cat stalking his prey, he moved over to me. "What do you want, little Tric?"

Knox, Hunter, and Carter.

Seeing as it was just Knox in front of me, I stepped up to him and placed a hand on his chest. Taking my time, I ran my palm across his torso, tracing the indentations of his scars.

Knox didn't move. His breathing became heavier, but he stayed perfectly still.

When my fingertips ran over his nipples, his breath caught.

Remembering how it had felt to have Carter's lips around my own, I stepped on my toes and brought my lips to it. Knox's hands settled on my waist, helping me balance, but he didn't stop me. Instead, as I ran my tongue over it, he groaned.

The sound made me feel more powerful than the electricity inside of me. Taking hold of that power, I let my hands continue their exploration downwards, until they found the waistband of Knox's sweats.

"You don't have to do that, Tric."

"It's what I want," I whispered.

As Knox sucked in a large breath, I hooked my fingers in the waistband and tugged them down, crouching to my knees as I did.

Knox's erect cock greeted me, bobbing in front of my face, and my mouth dropped open. He was huge. I'd gotten that impression from when I'd seen it bouncing against his sweats, but I wasn't expecting something quite so . . . long.

"Tric, baby, you can't just kneel in front of my cock with your mouth open and not put it in there. So, if this is too much, just—"

I leaned forward and took the end in my mouth, running my tongue around it.

"Oh, fuck yes." Knox hissed.

I wasn't entirely sure what I was doing, but I took that as a good sign and started taking more of him in my mouth.

"Use your hands too."

I did exactly as he said, wrapping my hand around his shaft. The other went to his thigh, helping me keep my balance as I started moving up and down. Looking up, I found his dark green eyes fixed on me.

Keeping my eyes locked on his, I started changing my pace, trying to discover what it was he liked. My tongue around the head of his cock was one thing and judging from how his hands threaded through my hair as I took as much of him as possible into my mouth, he liked that too.

It took a while to figure it out and find my rhythm, but Knox didn't complain once. And then I heard the sharp intake of breath.

"I'm close."

Angling my head slightly, I took him deeper. The grip on my hair tightened, and for a moment, Knox was almost moving me along his shaft. And then he grunted and tried to stop me.

I slapped the back of his hand.

"Zera, I'm going to come." His words sounded almost desperate as he stared down at me, gently shaking his head.

Refusing to stop, I kept my eyes locked on his. He jerked, twice, and then something hot and thick hit the back of my throat. I pulled back, just enough to be able to swallow all that he offered me.

Finally, I sat back, releasing his cock from my mouth to look at Knox properly. His eyes were closed, and he was hunched over, his shoulders shaking with the deep juddering breaths he was taking. "Was that okay?"

Knox's eyes flew open and he leaned over, sliding his hands under my shoulders to pick me up. "You were fucking perfect," he declared before kissing me. I could still taste him in my mouth, but that didn't stop his tongue from diving in, rubbing against mine.

Just when I was starting to go lightheaded, he pulled away. Breathing heavily, he rested his forehead against mine. "Absolutely fucking perfect."

As sparks started dancing over my chest, I ducked out of his arms. "Good."

"Where are you going?"

As I got to the door, I looked over my shoulder. "To take a bath before dinner."

Knox arched an eyebrow. "DB and Hunter aren't even back yet. What about you?"

I shook my head. "Later."

The look he gave me had me feeling hot and almost regretting walking out of the door.

Twenty-Nine

Zera

No sooner did I close the door to the gym, I stumbled, falling to my knees.

That was why I wanted to get out of there. Something didn't feel right, and I didn't want Knox to think it was related to what I had just done, ensuring I'd never get near his cock again.

A few deep breaths cleared my head a little, but my hands were shaking. I forced myself back to my feet. I couldn't stay here—Knox could walk out at any moment.

Feeling like I was walking through a fog, I made my way through the garage, using the cars to keep myself upright.

Outside, it was snowing. I could barely see it. My vision was dark and the blurriest it had ever been. The only reason I pressed on toward the house was because there was a low wall to follow.

My hand was freezing from being dragged through the snow on top, but the cold was also keeping me conscious.

By the time I got to the stairs, I was crawling, wondering what the hell I had swallowed.

Somehow, I made it into my bedroom, shutting the door, before collapsing onto the floor.

When I opened my eyes, I wasn't in my bedroom.

I wasn't even in the castle anymore. There was a familiarity about where I was, but I couldn't place it. It was too dark.

And then a door opened, the light on the other side illuminating the room as a skunk ran in.

No, not a skunk.

A honey badger.

"You will leave my wine alone you evil whore. My wine," it screeched, running straight through me.

"It's not wine you fucking kleptomaniac idiot." Liberty's voice echoed down the hallway before she appeared in the doorway. The second she saw me, she screeched and jumped backwards, slamming her hand on the light switch. "Motherfucking blackout. *Aotrom*." The room burst into light, but I couldn't figure out where the source of it was coming from.

Clutching at her chest, she looked around. "Whoever decided a witch needed a familiar would have been better off with a dragon-shifter sized cock butt plug, because *that* would be a lesser pain in the ass."

I stared at the witch in astonishment. She was wearing shorts and a strappy top, her hair currently in pigtails on the side of her head.

And she was looking straight through me.

"Pinot, where the fuck are you?"

She walked through me, before marching to the other side of the room, snatching a small bottle out of the honey badger's hands.

"My wine," it screamed, like she had just stabbed it.

"It's slug entrails, you fuckwit. Goddess be

damned, if you drink this, you'll make yourself ill."

The honey badger stood on its back legs, placed its hands on its hips, and narrowed its eyes. "You're a shit witch." And then it ran back out the door it had come in.

Liberty let out a long and weary sigh as she rubbed at her temple. "And I deserve that butt plug for fucking up that spell and letting him speak." With her hand gripping the neck of the bottle, she walked toward the door. "*Dorcha.*" The room went black as she stepped out of the room.

I glanced around the room. Why was I in Atlanta, and what the hell was I doing in the hair salon? More importantly, how come the witch couldn't see me?

Just as I was wondering how I was going to get out of there, the door opened up again. Liberty stood in the doorway, cocked her head, and stepped inside.

"Look, I don't know what Mingi told you, but I don't help ghosts. I don't need a poltergeist protection, and I sure as hell don't specialize in exorcisms, but if you don't get out, I will give it a good old college try, and you'd best hope I don't send you to the underworld, because I pissed off the Reapers and that won't end well for you."

Can you see me?

I heard the words in my head, but they didn't seem to leave my mouth.

Liberty left the room, closing the door behind her.

Then the room went completely black.

Thirty

Zera

I could feel my head pounding before I opened my eyes. When I did, I found myself on my bedroom floor.

The lights weren't on, but the moonlight reflecting off the snow outside made the room bright enough to see reasonably well.

Clutching at the side of my head, I rolled onto my side and then sat upright.

I had very, very limited experience with men, but I

was one hundred percent certain, that was not supposed to happen.

Why had I gone to Atlanta?

Had I gone to Atlanta, or was that a dream?

Why on earth would I *go* to Atlanta?

Groaning, I pulled myself to my feet and switched the lights on. Whatever had happened, I was cold. I moved over to the bedside table and picked up the clock, peering at its face.

We usually ate around the same time every evening, and I didn't have enough time to be able to bathe—not after telling Knox that was why I was leaving. Plus, the smell of something delicious was drifting through the castle.

What had happened hadn't made sense. While there was a possibility that it had been a dream, I was sure the likely answer was actually something supernatural related which the others would easily be able to explain.

I would tell them after dinner.

With my mind made up, I pulled the bags off the floor and emptied them onto the bed. The vampire's blade fell out. I picked it up and put it back in the bottom of the bag. I was still a ways off from being able to fight with it.

I pulled the dress Knox had mentioned out of the pile, setting it to the side as I put the remaining clothes back in the bag.

The dress wasn't like anything else I'd chosen. Almost everything was dark, but this was scarlet. It was long enough that with my height, the bottom would sweep the floor as I walked.

But it was so pretty.

I quickly changed. When it came to footwear, aside from a few pairs of boots and a pair of gym shoes, we'd not bought anything that would go with the dress. I put on my slippers to keep my feet warm, not really caring that they didn't match as the dress covered them.

After running a brush through my hair, I stepped in front of the mirror to examine myself.

Never had I imagined that I would ever wear anything like this.

But then again, I always thought I was going to die in that cell.

Leaving the bedroom, I made my way downstairs to the kitchen. As I got close, Javion seemed to appear from nowhere. Instead of the dark jeans and hoodies he favored, he was wearing a suit. It was dark blue with thin lines of silver and green running through it and silver buttons that looked decorative. Underneath, he had on a white turtleneck top.

The twists in his hair had been styled to one side, revealing a sharp undercut with two lines running through it. I didn't like the guy, but even I could admit he looked good.

Javion stopped as soon as he saw me, his eyes casting an appreciative glance over me before they narrowed. He sniffed the air before walking up to me, stopping so close I could see the silver in his eyes.

"What do you want?"

The next thing I knew, Javion's hand was on the back of my neck, and his lips were over mine, forcing his tongue into my mouth.

I shoved my hand on his chest and let out a large charge, sending him flying backwards. "Don't touch me."

From the floor, he looked up at me, shaking his head. "You taste of him."

I stuck my tongue out, trying to wipe the taste of the vampire away on the back of my hand.

"Knox?"

He could tell that from a kiss? "You needed to stick your tongue down my throat to find that out?"

Javion stood, smoothing out his suit. When he looked back at me, he had a grin on his face, showing off one of his fangs. "I was curious what your reaction would be if I gave you the same attention the others are."

"I've already killed one vampire. If you ever try that again, it won't be the last."

The grin disappeared from Javion's face. "If you mess with vampires, you want to learn how to sleep with one eye open, little sparkler. And if you hurt Knox—or DB and Hunter—you won't need to worry about being asleep."

"What does that mean?" I narrowed my eyes.

Without giving any further explanation, Javion turned and walked into the dining room, the door slamming shut behind him.

I stayed in the hallway, staring at the closed door while I waited for my hands to stop shaking. *What was that?* I didn't like Javion, and Javion didn't like me. Did he need to stick his tongue down my throat? And could he really taste Knox?

Strangely, that was . . . intriguing.

And then the shiver shot down my spine.

Ugh.

Not wanting to be alone with Javion, I bypassed the dining room and went to the kitchen. I barely got three steps in when my mouth fell open.

The only other person in the room was Carter. As he was busy whisking something in a pan, he hadn't noticed me as I stopped dead in the middle of the room. Like Javion, Carter was also wearing smart clothes: dark pants, a crisp, white dress-shirt, and a bowtie. Over the top, to protect his clothes, he had donned an apron.

Javion's rude behavior was brushed aside as I stared at the mature man in front of me. Carter looked good in a suit. *Really* good. I wasn't entirely sure why he was dressed up, but I wasn't complaining.

"You can go wait in the dining room." As though he could sense me staring, he turned.

And promptly dropped the whisk.

"Gods be damned . . . Zeraora, you look . . . incredible."

It took him three strides to cross the room to reach me. He promptly swept me up in his arms and kissed me.

I kissed him back, wondering if he could also taste Knox, but when he set me back on the floor, he didn't mention it. Was it simply because Knox and Javion were together that Javion could tell? Or did vampires have a better sense of taste?

"It won't be long before dinner is ready," Carter said, moving to pick the whisk up off the floor. He rinsed it off under the tap, and then quickly cleaned up the splatter from the tiles. "You can go wait in the dining room, if you like?"

With Javion? I shook my head and took a seat at the counter. "I'm fine here." I looked over the array of pans and dishes. "What are you cooking?"

The kitchen in Castle Viegls was huge. The oven range had space for ten pans to be cooking at the same time, and most of them had something on it.

"Do you know what date it is?" Carter asked. When I shook my head, he smiled. "Winter Solstice: the longest night of the year. We celebrate with . . ." he turned to me, smiling again. "You know what, you'll find out soon."

He refused to tell me anymore than that—not even what we were eating, even though it smelled delicious.

Hunter turned up just as Carter was getting ready to dish out plates, and in the name of everything tasty, if I hadn't watched Carter cook the food, I would have put money on Hunter being the meal.

His suit was black pinstriped, and unlike Carter, his wings weren't hidden, and his horns were out. I caught a glimpse of his tail hanging behind him and instantly, my cheeks went hot.

The gargoyle sauntered over to me, as though

knowing exactly what reaction he was having on me. He leaned in beside my ear. "Later, Zee."

And then he promptly ushered me out of the kitchen so that he and Carter could serve up meals.

I wandered into the dining room, expecting it to just be me and Javion.

Javion wasn't alone.

He was pinned up against the wall by Knox. Neither of them seemed to know I was there. Javion's eyes were closed, but his mouth was open, fangs on display. He was holding tightly to Knox's hair.

Knox was preoccupied with Javion's neck, just below Javion's ear. I could hear the sucking over Javion's moans.

Was Knox drinking his blood? Did gargoyles do that, too?

All I knew for certain was that watching them caused an ache between my legs. I swallowed, licking my lips.

And then I shook my head, trying to shake the feelings away. This was Javion. I hated Javion, and he hated me.

So why was I getting so turned on?

Javion's eyes opened, and they locked in on me. But instead of saying anything, he just smirked. Without breaking the gaze, I watched as his hands ran down Knox's body and started rubbing at the bulge in Knox's pants.

Knox jerked into him before pulling his head back. "Javion?" he groaned. "We said—"

"We have an audience."

Knox turned, his eyes wide as they settled on me. "Zera."

My name came out as a moan as Javion's arms wrapped around Knox's body, pulling him back. Held in place against Javion's chest, the vampire's hand returned to Knox's cock, this time, slipping under the waistband of his pants.

My attention was on Javion stroking Knox's cock, and I couldn't look away.

All of a sudden, a tray was placed on the table with a clatter, and before I could react, two hands were clamped down over my eyes. "Not in the dining room, and not in front of Zeraora."

I batted Carter's hands out of the way, but Knox and Javion were already separated and moving over to take the tray Carter had set down.

"I don't think she was complaining," Javion muttered, shooting me a dark look.

"Complaining about what?" Hunter asked as he

walked into the room, pushing the cart with the rest of the dinner on it. He ushered me to sit down at the table, and I did so, taking the seat before Javion could get there.

Ever since our first meal together, we had been engaged in a silent battle to claim the seat I was in. Hunter had mentioned that Javion normally took that seat with Knox beside him, but from what I could gather, it was habit.

Knox didn't seem to care where he sat. Even Hunter didn't complain about swapping sides—he was happy to sit beside me. But because it irritated Javion, I'd tried to beat him to the seat whenever I could.

With Javion already in the room, I was sure he was going to beat me, but instead, here I was, feeling smug.

This time, he didn't frown or cuss me out like he usually did. Instead, he sank into the seat diagonally opposite without saying a word.

Weird.

Plates and dishes were spread out across the table in front of me. Carter placed one piled up with food in front of me, and instantly, my mouth started watering at half of the items I recognized, and the other half I didn't, but it all looked equally as delicious.

Carter, Hunter, and Knox all had similar looking

plates of food, whereas Javion had his usual pint glass of blood. He took a sip, a smile spreading across his face as he turned to Carter. "You found A negative?"

"Helena came through."

"Who is Helena?" I asked between mouthfuls of food.

"A crone in Greenville," Carter replied. "She runs the general store, but she also keeps some supplies for supes."

"She does special orders too," Hunter added. "Seeing as it's winter solstice, we wanted to make sure the meal was special for Javion too, because even if he is acting like a vampire with a toothache, he's still family. And that's what we do at solstice."

"The longest night of the year?" That was what Knox had said earlier.

Carter nodded. "There aren't many supes in this county—or the surrounding ones—but we all celebrate it. The locals think it's like Christmas."

I nodded, but I had no idea what that was. It might have been mentioned a time or two on the various Netflix shows I'd watched, but my captors had never spoken about it. Then again, they'd never mentioned Winter Solstice.

"I prefer to drink directly from the artery," Javion

said, suddenly, making me look over at him. He leaned back in the chair, reaching over to play with Knox's hair as he took a sip of his meal. "Arteries have more blood in them than veins. It's fresh from the heart. And it always tastes best during sex."

A grunt of disapproval came from the head of the table.

The vampire ignored it. "But I'm not allowed to have sex on the table during dinner, and even gargoyles need to recover from the blood loss." His eyes locked on mine, somehow knowing that I was replaying a certain memory involving him and Knox, as he smirked at me.

"Javion." That was Carter's warning tone again.

"And going hunting in the local towns is frowned upon because the population knows everyone and everything—except that vampires are real." Javion rolled his eyes. "And seeing as though it's just not practical to drive to Atlanta or Raleigh and back every day, we stock up on blood. But it's usually O or A positive as they're the most common types. A negative is my favorite."

I continued eating my dinner, trying not to show how confused I was at the conversation. I'd been curious about his blood supply. Early on I'd found a fridge dedicated to his dinner, filled with medical looking packs of blood. But I'd never asked, mainly because I didn't want Javion to ever have the satisfaction of knowing I was curious.

This was possibly the longest conversation we'd had—if you could call this one-sided exchange a conversation. Considering our earlier exchange in the hallway . . .

There was something odd about the atmosphere that I couldn't quite put my finger on. It wasn't unpleasant. Even the scowls I would get from Javion didn't seem as irritable as normal.

Actually, I was wondering if A negative stood for 'asshole negative' seeing as though he was almost . . . tolerable.

Maybe whatever Carter had said last night had an effect on him?

Then again, the smug look he'd give me every so often left me feeling uneasy. I didn't know Javion, and nor did I have any desire to get to know him. But there was something odd in his behavior tonight that had me suspecting he was up to something.

Until he did whatever that something was, there wasn't much I could do about it.

Doing my best to ignore him, I continued eating

my meal, listening to Hunter recount a story from a previous Winter Solstice when they'd gone out hunting deer.

We finished eating and I started to gather plates up, but Hunter put a hand on my wrist and shook his head. "We have a present for you."

"Come through to the living room," Carter added.

I glanced over at Knox and Javion. The way Knox smiled at me, I knew he was clued in as to what the present was. Javion, on the other hand, was shooting looks of suspicion at Hunter.

Hunter stood, holding his hand out to me. I took it and we walked into the living room where he sat me down on one of the armchairs. While he disappeared, Carter, Knox and Javion sat down on the couches, all with their attention fixed on me.

"Why have I got a present? I didn't do anything."

Carter gave me a sad smile. "You don't need to do something to deserve a present."

"Call it a Winter Solstice gift," Knox suggested.

"But I didn't get any of you anything."

"Nor do you have to," Hunter said, reappearing with a large, brown cardboard box with a smile on the side of it. "If things hadn't gone to shit in Atlanta, I was going to take us to Walmart on the way home to do this anyway." He set the box down in my lap.

I eyed the box, curious. "What is this?"

"Open it and find out," Carter told me.

The seal on the box had already been broken, so I lifted the flap and moved the protective paper out of the way.

The box was filled with eyeglasses.

I stared up at Hunter and arched an eyebrow. "What are these for?"

Hunter perched on the coffee table in front of me, taking the box from my lap and setting it on the floor beside him. "Now, don't get offended, but I noticed that you squint at everything unless it's right in front of your face." He plucked a pair of glasses out of the box and passed them over. "Try these."

"There's nothing wrong with my eyes," I protested. Supes had enhanced strength, healing, and senses—including sight. Hunter had told me that. "I'm not broken."

Carter stood and walked over. Instead of taking the glasses away, he crouched down beside my chair to look at me. "You sleep with the light on."

My mouth fell open. "How do you know?"

"I've seen the light under your door."

It wasn't needed every night. If the sky was clear,

the moonlight would reflect off the snow and make the room bright. But I'd quickly learned that it only took a few clouds, and with my room in the back of the castle, overlooking nothing but mountainside forest, the room went black.

If I slept with the light on, when I awoke in the night, I wouldn't have to control my pounding heart—or the electrical charges.

The truth was, although I hated the painfully bright lights always being on in the cell, in the last few weeks there, when they'd turned them off, the darkness had become more terrifying.

But that didn't mean there was something wrong with my sight.

"Your body is still healing from what you had to endure," Carter said, softly. He reached out, his fingers, a hair's breadth above my bandages.

I shifted uncomfortably, unable to look any of them in the eyes. Despite my admission to Knox, I hadn't been able to remove the bandages.

"We put two and two together and figured you'd been kept somewhere under a bright light, or the constant electricity being forced from you damaged your eyes," Hunter said. He held the eyeglasses out again.

Carter nodded. "I'm sure, with time, your eyes will catch up once your body has finished healing everything else. Until then, these are just to help you out."

"And if they feel too uncomfortable, once we work out your prescription, we can try contacts."

I had no idea what most of that meant, but I took the glasses off him and put them on. "These just made everything worse." I took them off and thrust them back at Hunter.

"I bought one of every strength. There are plenty to try." Hunter gave me an encouraging smile as he took the glasses back from me and swapped them for another pair.

"And if none work?"

"Then we got it wrong. If we could take you for a health checkup, we would, but supes generally don't have vision problems, so we don't tend to get supernatural optometrists. Until you can control that power inside you a little better, we're improvising."

I was convinced there was nothing wrong with my eyesight... until the eighth pair I tried on, and suddenly, things had defined edges.

Lifting the eyeglasses, I looked at Carter's face, and then I dropped them back on my nose.

When I was close to Carter, I could see the lines

around his eyes and the silver hair at his temples. With the glasses on, I was two feet from him, and I could see them clearly.

I leaned to the side, looking past him, at Knox. From here, I could see the scars on his face. My mouth dropped open.

"And we have a winner," Hunter muttered, looking at the label which had been attached to the glasses.

"What?" I asked, seeing his raised eyebrow.

"Nothing," he said, before shutting the lid on the box. He held his palms under his face. "How do I look?"

"You're not fuzzy." I knew it was a strange answer, and I could see Hunter's smile completely clear—right down to his perfect set of teeth—but he wasn't.

In fact, as I looked around the room, nothing was.

I hadn't thought there was anything wrong with my eyesight because I hadn't realized this was how clear things were supposed to be.

With my heart feeling like it was going to burst from happiness, I leaned forward and kissed Hunter. He chuckled against me as he wrapped his arms around me.

"What the actual fuck?" Knox demanded. "Get your hands off her."

Hunter pulled away. "I'm sorry," he whispered,

before turning. "Well, I hadn't wanted to share the news quite so suddenly, but Zera and I—"

"What the fuck do you mean, Zera and I?" Knox demanded, getting to his feet. "I claimed Zera."

With a snarl, Hunter took a couple of steps towards his brother, his hands clenched. "Like fuck you do. You have Javion."

I watched the two of them, confused as to why they were arguing. Frowning, I turned to Carter, expecting him to share in my confusion, but the look he was giving me . . .

Carter's shoulders were slumped, and there was disappointment in his eyes. "I should have known," he told me. "But I understand. I concede."

Hunter and Knox fell silent as they turned to face their alpha. "Concede to what?" Hunter asked.

From the far side of the room, Javion burst out laughing. "Oh, come on. She's been playing you all against each other, and you haven't even realized? I've been telling you from the beginning that she can't be trusted—"

"Javion, you need to check yourself before—" Hunter snarled.

The vampire jumped to his feet, amusement disappearing from his face. "Don't get pissy because I'm the one saying *I told you so*. It's not my fault that she waltzed in here and wrapped her pussy around your cocks."

"Javion." Carter's warning rang across the room. "Do not talk about Zeraora that way."

Holding his hands up, Javion shrugged. "You know what, I'm just going to sit here, regretting the fact that vampires don't eat because popcorn would be great right about now."

"Hang on, are you saying DB and Zera...?" Knox asked, looking at Javion like he was crazy.

Did he think Javion was crazy for suggesting that I had been with Carter, or because it was Carter I'd been with?

Why were either options crazy? Any of them?

"Why don't you ask the elemental who she's been fucking?"

Moving so slowly that it seemed like time had slowed instead, Knox turned to face me, his eyebrow arching as he looked at me in confusion.

"I haven't fucked anyone."

"But you kissed Hunter."

I nodded. "Yes."

"Wait, you've been with Knox?" Hunter asked, whirling on the spot.

"Yes."

Why was this a problem?

Beside me, Carter let out a long sigh, earning him a sharp look from Hunter. "And DB too?"

Carter nodded.

"Zee, you can't do that!" Hunter exclaimed in exasperation.

"Why are you getting mad at me?" I asked, contemplating removing my glasses just so I wouldn't have to see each of their angry expressions.

"They're pissed because you're fucking about with all three of them," Javion unhelpfully informed me.

Why would that make them mad?

"While I understand and concede to Hunter or Knox, you're still going to need to make a choice, Zeraora," Carter told me, softly.

This conversation was making less sense the longer it went on. "But I've made my choice."

"Who?" Hunter demanded.

Thirty-One

Javion

I'd been a vampire, immortalized as a thirty-year-old, for nearly forty years, and in all that time, I'd never missed the ability to eat 'normal' food as I did right then.

For years I had been listening to the gargoyles tell me that their sense of smell was as good as mine, but not *once* had any of them picked up the smell of Zera on the other. Nor had they picked up the scent of each other on her.

I'd known Knox had been with the female before he'd told me he'd claimed her. I'd smelled her all over him, for fuck's sake.

Knox could fuck whoever he wanted. Hell, if he finally found a female to claim, I was happy for him. One day, I hoped to find my betrothed too.

But *that* female was not his mate.

I don't care what sob bullshit story she'd given DB. No one just *escaped* from the Lycans.

"I'm claiming all of you."

The female's response had me wondering if I was hearing things.

What the hell did that mean?

I glanced over at Knox. His nose was wrinkled up the way it did when he thought about things that didn't make sense. It was cute as fuck.

And then I let out a long sigh, rolling my eyes as I worked out the new twist in the game she was playing.

Now I really did wish I had popcorn. At least this would be a quick end to whatever the fuck Knox thought he had going with her.

"You can't do that," DB told her, far more gently than I would have done.

The female looked at him. Her bottom lip was poking out—was she actually pouting? "Why not?

Knox claimed me."

I had a lot of respect for DB. He had earned that a long time ago, and he was an alpha I was prepared to follow—a huge thing considering I was a vampire and he was a gargoyle. It was only because of our history together that I was even still here, waiting for him and Knox to see that they needed to think with their brains and not their cocks.

DB shook his head. "Zeraora, that's not . . . Claiming, with gargoyles . . . it's not something to joke about. It is claiming a mate, a partner, a lover."

The female looked at him like he had just pointed out snow was cold. "Yes. And I'm still claiming all of you."

"You can't." Hunter took her hand, encouraging her to sit back down as he lowered himself back onto the coffee table. "Gargoyles can only have one mate. If you have feelings for more than one of us, you have to choose one of us."

The female wrinkled her nose up—it was definitely not a cute action. "Who the fuck made up that stupid rule? And I'm not a gargoyle."

"Yes," DB agreed, still with more patience than I could muster. "But we are."

"And yet Knox claimed me *and* dickhead in the

corner."

The smile slipped from my face as I raised my hand and flipped her the bird. Annoyingly, she also had a point with her first comment.

The female folded her arms and settled back into the chair. "I like all of you. So . . . I'm choosing all of you. I'm *claiming* all of you." She frowned as her gaze settled on me. "No, that's not true. I don't like you."

I clutched at my chest. "Oh wow," I said, my tone drier than the Sahara. "My heart bleeds. However, will it recover from this devastating news?"

"You're dead." The female cocked her head. "Does it even still work?"

My eyes narrowed. "Fuck you."

"No, thank you. You can continue doing that with Knox."

With a groan, Hunter slapped his palm over his face.

I smiled, amused despite the fact that I despised her.

DB rubbed at his temples. While my body had stopped aging several decades ago, DB's hadn't. Despite this, I'd never thought of him as older than me—until now. He looked completely out of his depth. "Zeraora, you can't just . . . You have to choose."

The female shrugged. "I did. I chose all of you." She glanced at me and turned up her nose. "All but Javion."

I cocked my head, watching her as she switched her attention between the three gargoyles.

She was being . . . sincere?

She genuinely seemed to think she could claim all three of them as mates? They were gargoyles for fuck's sake. Gargoyle's didn't share their mate.

"Do you know what it means to claim a gargoyle?" I asked her.

Okay, maybe I was stirring the pot a little with that loaded question . . .

"To be their mate, partner and lover," the female said, reciting what DB had told her. "Why are you making that out to be a big deal?"

"Because it is," Knox answered. "It's a commitment to be with someone and love them and protect them."

"It's a lifetime," Hunter added.

The female pursed her lips, considering what they were saying. "Is this because I am leaving in the spring?"

"You can stay longer than spring, Zee."

"What?" Knox demanded.

"Thank fuck," I muttered under my breath, earning

me a dark scowl from Knox. I just shrugged at him.

"I think this is our fault," DB said, bringing both mine and Knox's attention to him. "Through no fault of your own, you've been locked away with no experience of the real world. In only a couple of months here, all you've known is us, and whatever shows Hunter has been watching with you."

"Mainly the wholesomeness of the DC and Marvel universes. And Supernatural and Buffy the Vampire Slayer," Hunter informed him.

"You went for the show about *vampires*?" I asked in disbelief. "Not just vampires, but a vampire *slayer*?"

"Don't worry. I already asked and you, unfortunately, won't burst into a cloud of dust if I stake you," the female shrugged. "But firsthand experience tells me decapitation is very effective."

I jumped to my feet, ready to march over there and tear a chunk out of her neck, but Knox was in front of me.

There was a reason I lived with gargoyles, and it wasn't just Knox. I hated the man who sired me, along with his entire House. But there was an ingrained *thing* in me—in all vampires—that we banded together.

We might have been supernatural beings, but we were the only ones who couldn't have offspring.

Consuming blood kept us alive, and it let us fuck who we wanted, but no amount of blood would allow babies to be created.

When someone threatened us, vampires stuck together.

And considering I already didn't like or trust the elemental female, the only thing stopping me from painting the room with her blood was the man in front of me.

I was banking on at least one of the three gargoyles coming to their senses and seeing her for the threat she was because I didn't want to be the one to hurt Knox. But if none of them worked it out quickly enough, I was going to do what I needed to in order to protect him.

Staring Knox in his beautiful eyes, I sucked in a deep breath, curled my hands into fists, and walked away, putting the chair between us.

I looked over at DB, finding him watching me. "Marvel and DC?"

"My point is," DB said, turning back to the female, "we've not taught you anything. You're a beautiful, smart woman, and I think it's easy to forget that you've not experienced anything near what you should have done for someone your age."

"You know you're making yourself sound really

old," Hunter said.

"I am old," DB told him. "And I also should have known better," he said to the female. "No matter how I try to convince myself otherwise, I took advantage the other night. And it sounds like the twins have too."

"Fuck you, Carter," Knox snarled. "I've never done anything that Zera didn't want to do."

"If she doesn't know any different, how does she know what she really wants?"

"Because he asked me," the female said, frowning as she pushed her glasses up her nose. "Like you did. Like all of you have since I got here. And for some reason, even when I give you an answer and tell you all exactly what I want, you all still tell me I don't know what I want."

"How can you know what you want?" DB asked. He sucked in a deep breath. "There's a lot for you to learn. You were locked away for twenty years."

"She's sheltered, not stupid," Hunter told our alpha, giving the female a sympathetic smile.

When DB didn't respond, the female stood, taking her eyeglasses off as she did. She folded the arms and set them down on Hunter's knee.

"What's wrong with them?" Hunter asked, his eyes wide. He scooped them up, trying to pass them back to her.

The female held her hand up, shaking her head. "If the choice is between seeing everything with a fuzzy edge or seeing the expressions on all of your faces right now, I don't want them."

She maneuvered herself around the coffee table, avoiding the gargoyles as she walked to the door.

"Where are you going, Tric?" Knox asked.

"The dishes still need doing." She didn't look back as she walked into the dining room and closed the door behind her.

I sucked at my lower lip as I stared at the door. I didn't like the female. I didn't *trust* the female. So why the fuck did her being upset feel like someone was twisting a wooden stake in my heart?

"DB," I said, slowly turning back to face him as I rested my forearms on the back of the armchair. "As far as I'm concerned, you're one of the most level-headed, sensible people that I know. I think I can count on one hand the number of stupid things you've said over the years we've been together. But that was harsh. Even by my standards."

"You haven't made her feel welcome in this home since she arrived."

"Maybe not, but I've also never pretended to like

her. She wants to claim you, and you called her a naïve idiot."

DB shook his head. "I never called her that."

I stood, folding my arms, and fixed him a look. "Not in so many words."

With a long sigh, DB sank back into the couch and rubbed a hand over his face. Once more, he seemed to have aged in front of my eyes. "But it's not wrong. The naïve part, at least."

Knox snorted. "You're a dick."

"Excuse me?" DB's hand fell into his lap as he cocked his head and fixed Knox a look of disbelief. "What did you say?"

"She's inexperienced, but that doesn't mean she's incapable of making her own decisions."

"And you think claiming the three of us is a reasonable decision?"

Thankfully, Knox shook his head. "No, but I think she's fully aware of whatever it is she has chosen to do with each of us. As far as I can tell, I'm the only one who has even mentioned claiming to her, and I've got Javion, so why the fuck wouldn't she come to the conclusion that multiple mates are acceptable?"

"It doesn't mean it is." DB rested his arm over the back of the sofa as he looked at Knox.

I was surprised to see the anger had left him, and resignation had set in.

"She needs to choose one of us. As I said, I concede. I had my mate; getting a second one won't happen. You two are closer in age and have more to offer than this old man."

"Oh, for fuck's sake, DB," I exclaimed, rolling my eyes. "You're forty-two. That age-gap is nothing."

Knox whirled around to face me, his eyes narrowed. "I knew you weren't happy about my claim to Zera."

"Of course I'm not happy: I don't like the damned female, and I sure as hell don't trust her." I stood upright, gripping at the back of the sofa as I glared at Knox. "I don't want her anywhere near any of you. But I'm also not going to let DB sit there and wallow because he's *old*. Fuck me—forget the popcorn. I want to go back to my room and play Fortnite."

I fully expected that the female would be the demise of this group. But not in such a pathetic way like this. The attack was supposed to come from outside, not within.

Even if there was a genuine hint of her wanting to be with the three of them, if her choice was going to turn them into a worse blubbering mess than this, fuck them all. I was going to rip her beating heart out of her chest and crush it before she crushed theirs.

I was halfway to the door when Hunter spoke. "You're assuming she has to."

"What the fuck are you talking about?" Knox asked.

"Zera—making a choice."

"What? Because DB is too old, and I'm too broken, we should both walk away? Because fuck you."

Hot-headed Knox . . .

My hand hovered above the door handle, but only because I was sure either the handle or the door was about to get ripped off if I touched it. "That's the opposite of what he's saying," I said, my words coming out as a growl.

Forget the door. I wanted to rip their heads off.

"Javion is right," Hunter agreed. "Why do we need to make her choose?"

"Because we're gargoyles and gargoyles have one mate."

I turned just in time to see Hunter raise a shoulder. "And technically, we'd still only have one mate, it's only Knox that would have two." He moved over to the couch, sitting down beside DB, but making sure he was still facing Knox too. "She's right. We keep asking her to tell us what she wants and when she did, we dismissed it. I think it's fair to say we all like Zera—"

I cleared my throat, throwing the gargoyle a pointed look.

"—And she still seems to be of the belief that she's got to leave us come spring. Why don't we give this a try? Maybe we can get her to stay—"

"Are you fucking serious?" My mouth dropped open. "I'm done with this bullshit."

"Javion—"

Fuck him.

I didn't even pause to hear what Knox had to say.

Fuck DB. Fuck Hunter. Fuck the fucking female.

And fuck the solstice.

I went directly back to the basement, bypassing my room and heading straight for my lab. The room was lit with the glow of the large monitors at the far side of the room, and the various neon green LEDs inside the towers.

Settling down into the large leather seat, I allowed myself a moment to close my eyes and listen to the background hum and whirr of the various fans, and then I leaned over and put a drum and bass playlist on, cranking up the volume.

A distraction was what I needed.

Usually, the best form of distraction was Knox, but seeing as though he was currently colluding with the other two on their own twisted demise, I was going to go for my next best option.

Games.

Picking up the control to the PS4, I brought it out of sleep mode—only to discover it needed yet another update installing.

My fingers drummed on the desk in time to the beat of the Andy C song as I waited for the update to install, and instead, turned my attention to one of the computer screens in front of me.

Although I had the ability to link them all up into one mega-screen, they were currently running different programs and scripts. Three were searches I'd set up since DB had brought the female back to the castle. One on the regular internet. One on the dark web, running on its own dedicated server. And the third on the red web—the version of the dark web which had been created for supes.

I gave the three searches a cursory glance over to make sure there were no new hits—there weren't.

How was it possible that *no one* had any information on electric elementals? In seven weeks, I'd found fuck all.

Whispers.

Rumors.

Nothing concrete.

Fire, earth, air and water—I could find tons of information on the red web about those elementals. The human internet, as expected, classed them as mythical creatures. The dark web was empty of information. That was an area used mainly by unscrupulous *humans*.

But there was a massive void when it came to electric elementals.

And somehow, no matter what I told DB, he dismissed it, claiming she was a unicorn of the supernatural world.

Fuck that.

Unicorn shifters existed—at least there was information on them on the red web.

The PS4 finished restarting, and I turned my attention back to that. With my headset on, I loaded the game, happy to see DoNtGiVe_a_CoLbY was online.

"Jav, bro, where you been?" Colby asked, his deep voice coming through my headset crystal clear.

"Is Atlanta back online?" The last I checked, they were still trying to figure the cause of the EMP out and the city was still a mess.

"Nah, bro. We shipped our House out. Shit went

down, and we got out."

Colby was a vampire from the Atlanta clan of the Golatt House. I'd met him not long after I'd been changed, and then it had been years later when we'd met again—when games started going online.

"Yeah, I saw on the news. Have they still not figured out what caused the EMP?"

"Humans blaming humans. Nothing that affects us."

I nodded although he couldn't see me. We'd teamed up together to take on two other players, and one was creeping up on Colby. I waited for him to get between the crosshairs of my sniper and took him out.

"Fuck, cheers, bro."

"I got your back."

"Speaking of, did you hear anything about one of ours being murdered the night of the blackout?"

Running a tongue over a fang, I took a moment, killing an enemy before responding. "What's that, Colby?"

"Vamp killing. Apparently, they'd been attacked by gargoyles, and we all know you're fucking one."

I growled into the mic. "My mate didn't kill any vampire. "

"Wasn't specifically blaming yours, bro," Colby

said, sounding far too casual. "Heard it was a female anyway. But you live with more than one—they know anything?"

Female gargoyle?

This was it.

This was my opportunity to rid this castle of the elemental vermin that had taken up residence.

If I told Colby it was her, the House would be here within a couple of hours.

Problem solved.

"You know," I said, reloading the weapon. "If there's one thing those other gargoyles need, it's to get laid. Desperately. But they're thankfully lacking in the female gargoyle territory around here, and they're too focused on finding the Lycans."

"You're still on that mission?"

Before I could answer, there was a knock at the door.

"I gotta go, Colby. Knox is here. But you're welcome any time."

"Sure. Laters, bro."

Although I refused to turn around, I did stick my mic on mute. Knox's reflection appeared in one of the monitors as he slipped into the room.

"DB is going to light the fire soon."

I ignored him, pretending I couldn't hear him over the music and the game.

Knox walked over, turning the music down. "I know you heard me."

I pulled my headset off and tossed it on the desk. "Unless that elemental is going to be on top of it, I'm not interested."

"You are jealous, aren't you?"

I shoved myself, the chair rolling backwards, away from him. Getting up, I put more space between us. "I'm not jealous. I don't know how many times I have to tell all of you: there is something not right about that female. Supes don't just *leave* the Lycans. Dammit, we've been hunting them for decades, and we still can't find them. Then one night, she turns up?"

"She escaped."

"And she's just going to bring trouble to Castle Viegls. Dammit, Knox, there are vampires hunting her because of what she did to Aella. They already know there's a gargoyle involved."

Knox took several slow steps towards me as though trying to figure out if I was going to walk off. It was tempting, but I stayed where I was, arms folded.

"Jay . . ."

I closed my eyes, fighting with my own body not to

react. Knox only ever called me that when I was making him come from drinking his blood. Just the low grumble of his voice was already making me hard.

"Imagine she hadn't escaped the Lycans, and she was just an average supe who I was claiming."

"I've already told you; I don't care that you're claiming some female. I care because she isn't your average supe." I wasn't blind. She might be barely more than skin and bones, but she wasn't unattractive. There wouldn't be any objections from me if they occasionally brought me in on that action. Three types of supe sandwich and I'd be more than happy being any part of that meal.

If it wasn't *that* female.

Finally stopping in front of me, Knox draped one arm over my shoulder while the other rested on it to play with the twists in my hair. "Just imagine the fun the three of us could have together."

The problem was, I was.

"I'd rather imagine taking you against that door," I muttered.

Knox leaned into my ear. "Why imagine it?" His tongue ran around my lobe.

Keeping my arms folded despite the erection in my pants, I stood firm. "Don't you have a bonfire and a mate to get to?"

"The bonfire and my other mate can wait for a quickie. I already have a mate in front of me who I'd much rather have behind me," he whispered as the hand draped over my shoulder slid off and moved down my body. Over the fabric of my pants, Knox cupped my erection, rubbing it. "We both know you've got some lube hiding in here."

To hell with it.

With a snarl, I slammed him against the door, smashing my mouth over his to swallow the sound of his laughter. My fang caught his lip, and his blood joined our kiss.

It was a good thing Knox liked it rough, because that was what he was going to get. I tore at his pants, unbuttoning and unzipping them, then forcing them to the floor. His cock was as hard as mine, but I wasn't going to touch it.

Instead, I placed a hand around his neck. I pulled him over to the side so I could reach a set of drawers. As my mouth dominated his, I opened the top drawer, my hand searching until it wrapped around a familiar bottle.

I pulled it out and shoved it in his hands. "You'd best lube my cock up because you've got about thirty seconds before I fuck you against that door, just like you want."

With a grin which made me want him to put that mouth to better use, Knox squeezed a generous amount of the cool lube on my cock, making sure to coat the full shaft, twisting his hand around me.

When his hands started to get a little less focused on that task, and more on running up and down my cock, I reached down, taking the lube from him, and tossed it back inside the drawer. I wrapped my hands around the collar of his shirt. Pulling him up, I turned him around and shoved him against the door. "If you want to get off, you should do it yourself."

Giving him just enough time to brace himself, I lined myself up and pushed the tip of my cock into his asshole. There was a moment of resistance as Knox gasped.

And then I was fucking him, taking my frustrations out on his ass as Knox repeatedly called out my name while he jerked off.

Next time, we were doing it in my bedroom, up against a mirror. Instead, I had to imagine it. And then I was coming.

Fuck, that was just what I needed.

I rested my forehead against Knox's back, finding

the spot between his wings, curled up beneath his suit. "Just because I don't trust her doesn't mean I don't love you," I muttered into his jacket as Knox continued to work towards his own release. "Now hurry up and finish, or you're going to be late to the bonfire."

Thirty-Two

Zera

My hands were shaking so much, I had to stop stacking the plates because I was sure I was going to break them. I'd already broken enough things—like an entire city—and Carter already seemed disappointed in me.

I moved over to the window and looked out. Although it had stopped snowing, the moon and stars were still hidden by a thick blanket of clouds, so low, it looked like mist was creeping over the snow outside.

Even though the security lights on the side of the building were lighting up certain parts of the large garden, there wasn't much out there to see anymore.

I leaned forward, resting my head against the cold glass. A shiver ran down my spine.

Had I been hoping for too much?

Was I becoming too settled here? Too comfortable around the men who lived here? Attracted to men that I ultimately had no chance with?

Why was it so hard for them to understand that I liked all three of them?

So what if gargoyles only had one mate? I wasn't a gargoyle. Or was that enough of a reason for me not to be a mate at all?

Maybe Carter was right, and I didn't have enough knowledge and experience of the real world—or the supernatural world.

It's not that, and you know it.

The evil voice in the back of my head, which had started sounding eerily like Javion, had other opinions.

Why would any one of them want to be with a freak who spent all her life locked in a cage? A freak who had no contact because she was too dangerous.

I sighed, my breath fogging up the glass.

Maybe Javion really was right.

My hands had stopped shaking enough for me to continue stacking the dishes, transferring them off the table and onto the cart. Once the table was clear, I wheeled the cart through to the kitchen.

Trying to keep myself occupied, I scraped what was left off the plates into the garbage disposal as I filled the dishwasher.

Humans didn't think the supernatural world existed unless it was on television or in books. To them it was made up. But even if they found out it did exist, they would still consider supes as monsters—threats to humankind.

Javion thought I was a threat to all of them. Carter was trying to keep me hidden in this castle so the other supes didn't find out about me.

I was the monster of the supernatural world.

Before I could stop them, sparks of electricity appeared at my fingertips. They bounced over the plate in my hand, zapping the garbage disposal. It ground to a halt.

Closing my eyes, the plate slipped from my hand into the empty sink, landing with a clatter. I ignored it, trying to get the power surge under control before I wiped out every appliance in the kitchen.

Beside me, there was a small pop. When I opened

my eyes, the digital display on the dishwasher was dead.

No wonder they wouldn't let me claim them. I would destroy everything they owned if I stayed here.

Javion was right.

I would destroy all of them.

On the television shows, when the girl got dressed up, the night usually ended up with a kiss. Back in my prison, the movies Ruben watched had the night ending up with more than a kiss . . . to be fair, the night usually started with the girl losing her dress.

There was a knock on a door, and I turned to find Carter in the doorway to the dining room. "Can I come in?"

What kind of question was that? "It's your kitchen."

Carter walked in, stopping by the breakfast island. "It's your kitchen too."

"Good. Because I broke the garbage disposal." I sighed. "And the dishwasher." I glanced in the sink. "And a plate."

"Can we talk for a moment?"

I frowned, about to tell him that we were already talking, and then I realized what he was saying. "Yes."

"Zeraora, I owe you an apology. You were right." Carter rubbed his hand over his jaw. "Since you arrived here, I've been telling you to do things at your own pace and do what you are comfortable with. I've asked you to tell us when you're happy, or when you're feeling uncomfortable."

"And I have," I told him.

Carter nodded. "I know you have . . . I know you have, *now*. You've been honest about everything, and I completely ignored that because of my own insecurities."

"What do you have to be insecure about?"

Carter was smart, handsome, knowledgeable, patient, a good chef, and incredibly talented with his mouth. If I wasn't so surprised by his statement, I could probably have listed off another dozen reasons as to why he couldn't possibly be insecure.

"There aren't many supes who naturally have more than one mate, and while it's not uncommon in the supernatural world, it is for gargoyles. Actually, it's normal for gargoyles to fight for the mate."

My eyes quickly scanned his appearance, but there wasn't a stray wrinkle in his suit, much less an indication that the three of them had been fighting. "Wait, you aren't going to—?"

"No," Carter said, quickly. "It would never have come to that because I would have conceded. I *had* conceded. You asked about my insecurities . . . I'm older than you—"

"I don't care about that."

"I also had a mate. Manon . . . she was French. She left her clan in Aurillac to be with me. And she was killed twelve years ago." Carter took a deep breath, leaning his hip against the breakfast counter. "A gargoyle's mate is for life, and I have spent the last twelve years thinking that was it. And then you appeared."

Biting the inside of my cheek, I stared at him, unsure what to say because I wasn't sure what kind of response was required. Truth be told, I wasn't entirely sure what he was telling me.

"With all that said, Hunter, Knox, and I are going to listen to you. If you want to be our mate, we've all agreed that's what we want too."

"Of course that's what I want," I blurted out. "That's what I've been trying to tell you."

"I know." Carter moved over to me, smoothing my hair behind my ear as he looked down at me. "We will find a way to make this work."

My heart felt like it was swelling inside my chest and a wave of dizziness hit me. As I swayed, Carter's hands held my hips. "Zeraora?"

"I'm fine," I told him. "I'm better than fine." I slumped against him, wrapping my hands around his body. Carter held me, saying nothing as I clung onto him. I felt . . . happy.

"Zee?"

I pulled back, finding Hunter behind us, my coat in his hands. "What's that for?"

Hunter's gaze dropped to the coat before he quickly shook his head. "Would you like to come outside."

I looked up at Carter who nodded.

"Okay," I muttered, curious.

Carter released me and I walked over to Hunter, putting my coat on.

A short while later, the three of us were in coats and boots—the latter looking a little strange with our formal clothes. Carter led me and Hunter outside to the middle of the garden.

From the dining room, the bushes and trees had hidden the large mound of snow in the middle of what was a lawn. Hunter held my hand, keeping me back with him. Carter strode forward, sticking his hand into the snow mound. Moments later, he was pulling back a plastic sheet to reveal a pile of logs and branches underneath.

"What is he doing?" I asked Hunter as Carter knelt.

Hunter moved behind me, his arms sliding under mine before joining in front of me. He held me against him, resting his chin on my head. "Three of us, huh?"

I shrugged. "If I like you, I don't see why it's a problem."

"No, but if you liked us, maybe you could have told us?"

Turning in his arms, I looked up at him and frowned. "I did tell you."

Hunter tilted his head, looking down at me as he pursed his lips. "I suppose you did." He leaned down, pressing his lips against my forehead.

"Where is your brother?" Carter asked, coming to join us.

"Probably with Javion." Hunter looked down at me. "Are you really okay with that?"

"Why wouldn't I be? Knox claimed Javion before he claimed me." I turned, finding the pile of logs was now alight, a fire starting to spread from the side closest to us. "What are we doing out here?"

"It's our family tradition, and we want you to be a part of it," Hunter said.

"Every Winter Solstice we have a special meal and then we come out here and light a fire. Weather permitting, of course," Carter explained.

"Last year, we had a blizzard so bad, the fire was off the cards."

"It's not big and extravagant, but it's our time to be together," Carter added. He glanced at his watch. "What is taking Knox so long?"

"Sex?" I suggested.

While Hunter burst into laughter, stepping back when he started shaking me, Carter coughed and spluttered.

"What's so funny?"

Hunter cleared his throat, wiping at the corner of his eyes. "DB's of a more reserved generation."

I looked over at the more mature man. "But you were married. Didn't you have sex?"

"Zeraora, that's . . ." Carter's mouth flapped open a few times.

"What's going on here?" Knox asked, finally joining us. Javion was beside him, putting the twins between me and him.

"Zee just asked DB about his sex life."

Javion's eyes seemed to bulge out of his head.

"Don't worry," Hunter added. "She was asking about yours before then."

"No I didn't," I told them. "Carter asked what you

two were doing and I—"

"Suggested each other," Hunter finished before bursting into laughter again.

With pink cheeks, Knox held up a box he was carrying. "Can we just make the S'mores now?"

"Yes, excellent idea," Carter declared, loudly.

He walked over to Knox and the two of them busied themselves with sticking white things onto sticks. Carter walked back to me, handing a stick over.

I gave it a sniff. Whatever it was, it was sweet. I opened my mouth, ready to take a taste, and suddenly, Hunter's hand was on mine, stopping me from eating it.

"Wait."

"I can't eat it?"

"You need to stick it in the fire," he said, leading me over to the growing fire. He gently eased the stick into the flame, doing the same with his own. "But you have to turn it to keep it from burning."

Knox appeared at my side with something in his hands. "Okay, take it out now."

I looked back at the fire just in time for the white thing to fall off the stick. "Oh."

"Here, have mine." Hunter pulled his out as an edge caught on fire. He quickly blew it out, holding the stick out to Knox.

Knox sandwiched the blob between two sheets of something, pulling it off the stick and holding it out to me. "Here. Careful, that will be hot. Blow on it first."

"What is it?"

"Of course, she's never had a S'more," he muttered.

"Two Graham crackers, some chocolate, and marshmallow," Hunter told me.

I blew on the S'more and then took a bite. The sugar rush hit me, and I moaned. "That's amazing."

"Considering you have a sweet tooth, I'm not surprised you like it," Carter said. He was busy making his own snack.

I devoured what was left of mine, seeking out a fresh marshmallow. Hunter stuck one on my stick, and I promptly set it alight.

In the end, Hunter and Knox alternated making them for me, mainly because I was too impatient and wanted to eat them.

Eventually, Carter closed the box. "You're going to make yourself sick."

That was a strong possibility as I already felt nauseous, but I wasn't about to admit it. Instead, I nodded, using Carter's arm as a rest as we watched the fire burn. Hunter stood on the other side of me, holding my hand, while Knox was wrapped up in Javion's arms.

I sucked in a deep breath. The icy air, tainted with smoke, made my nose tickle. Despite the fact four of us could see our breath on the air, the fire—and the men—were doing a wonderful job keeping me warm.

With nothing above me, confining me, and the men around me acting as a security blanket instead of glass walls, I finally felt like I was where I was supposed to be. Sure, there was a pain in the ass vampire whose feelings were as mutual as mine, but everything else made that small thing seem insignificant.

"What's wrong?"

I looked over at Knox and Javion. The vampire had stepped back and was looking towards the far wall.

"We're not alone."

Thirty-Three

Zera

As I started to look around, Carter pulled me behind him.

"What do you mean?"

"He means, you have visitors."

I whirled around, just in time to see a group of men walking towards us, coming out of the smoke and mist like ghosts materializing. The one who had spoken was tall and looked around the same age as Carter.

"Virgil? What are you doing here?" Javion asked,

sending Carter a sideways glance.

"Just following up on a lead concerning the murder of a vampire from our House."

I thought I was pale, but I looked tan compared to Virgil. He had a thick bushy mustache, and a strong jaw. His clothes were old-fashioned though. They looked more like some of the outfits I'd seen in one of the Captain America films, and if I remembered correctly, that was set in the 1940s.

There were about fifteen or sixteen other vampires, most standing with Virgil, but the others were spread out around the garden. I glanced over my shoulder, catching more figures in the mist.

"Murder?" Hunter asked.

"Yes, one of our scouts was murdered in Atlanta the night of the blackout. Rumor has it, her killer was a gargoyle."

"The rumors are wrong," I said. Before I could say anything else, Carter draped his arm over my shoulder, and squeezed my arm.

"No gargoyle here committed that act," Carter told him. "Unlike vampires, we only kill if absolutely necessary. And seeing as though you are trespassing . . . how did you enter Castle Viegls?"

"We had an invitation," Virgil replied, gesturing

towards Javion.

Javion's eyes went wide as he looked at all of us, shaking his head. "DB, I swear, I never—"

"He invited me. It was vague enough that I extended the invitation to the rest of my House." The owner of the voice looked a couple of years younger than me. Blue eyes, and golden hair, with broad shoulders and a football jersey. He gave Javion an unapologetic shrug. "Sorry, bro."

"That wasn't an open invitation to your whole fucking House, Colby," Javion told him with a snarl.

Colby shrugged. "Shoulda been clearer with the invite then."

"What's going on?" I asked.

"Vampires are not allowed to cross the threshold of a private residence unless invited. They got cursed by witches centuries ago," Hunter explained. "Apparently, they never get the hint when they're not welcome."

"Now, who would you be?" Virgil asked, zeroing in on me. He clicked his fingers before his eyes narrowed into thin slits. "The one who murdered Aella?"

Once again, Carter's hand squeezed my arm before I could answer.

"She's a friend," Knox told him, as Hunter stepped

forward, blocking me slightly.

"Is that code for fuck buddy?" Virgil grinned. "Or elemental?"

Electricity crackled over my fingertips. Whoever this guy was, I didn't like him, and I had no reservations when it came to blasting him with as many kilowatts of electricity that I could manage.

"Looks like she could be both," Colby said.

Virgil laughed. "Thank god we got here before the Lycans." He set his hand on his hip and nodded his chin at Carter. "Did you know the Lycans have a good price on her head? Lucky for you, we don't put a price on a life, so hand her over and—"

"Not going to happen," Carter said, also stepping forward to put himself back between me and the vampires.

"There's three of you, and twenty of us," Virgil told him.

"Four," Javion corrected him.

"Bro?" Colby arched an eyebrow. "You'd side with the walking rocks over your own kind? To protect that. . . thing? I thought she was trouble, coming between you and your mate?"

Knox took a step away from Javion, looking at him like he didn't know him. "You told them about her?"

"No, I—"

In front of me, Carter calmly shrugged his coat and suit jacket off, folding them in two and placing it on the ground.

"Virgil, this is your last chance to walk away," he said, his wings unfolding from beneath his shirt, poking through two slits that had been cleverly worked into the fabric. His skin darkened, looking more like the stone of the castle. Finally, his tail, claws and horns appeared. "Or we won't be held accountable for what happens next."

"You mean like no one will be held accountable for Aella's murder?" Virgil asked before shaking his head. "So be it."

And then it seemed like everything was happening all at once.

Hunter and Knox both pulled their coats off. Hunter's suit jacket followed, just as his wings appeared behind him. Although I knew Knox still had his wings, he kept them tucked away, hidden beneath his suit.

In their full gargoyle state, the three of them were something to see. I was sure that they had all grown; they seemed taller and their shoulder's, broader.

They looked lethal.

Knox and Javion darted over to me, replacing

Hunter and Carter as they leaped into the air, diving towards the small army of vampires that had already started racing towards us.

"Whatever happens, stay behind us," Knox told me.

"I can fight them too." I had the electricity at my fingertips, ready to send everything I could.

"That's a pointless waste of energy." Javion snarled at me as Knox started fighting with two vampires that had reached him. "Just stay there and don't do anything stupid. They're here because of you, so if you don't want your *mates* to get hurt, do as you're fucking told."

Although the electricity continued to build inside of me, I did exactly as Javion said. Not because I was scared of him—and he was terrifying when he turned on me—but because I didn't want to do anything to get anyone hurt.

I'd never seen the four of them fight before.

Whatever Hunter had been doing with the two female vampires that had led to this, I realized it wasn't really fighting. His intentions back then had been different. There had been more defensive moves, avoiding the attacks, or retaliating to the blows.

Now the four of them were attacking. Claws swiped at skin, tearing chunks and limbs to the soundtrack of screams that had my toes curling. Although it wasn't hurting me, my body recognized their pain.

This was a battle between predators.

The vampires seemed almost as strong as my gargoyles, but only when they banded together. Something they quickly discovered when Carter and Hunter decapitated the vampires attacking them with just their claws.

Knox, although limited with flight, was fast and just as lethal on the ground. He tore through the vampires with strong kicks, and then punched through their chest as though his fist were a stake.

Javion was the only one not fighting. Not unless the vampires got past the others. He remained by my side, his hand gripping my arm firmly, stopping me from leaving.

"They need help," I told him, trying to pull my arm free.

The vampires had already worked out that if it was two or more of them attacking the gargoyle, without taking it in turns, Carter, Hunter and Knox were easier to subdue.

"You can't do anything. You are weak. You are unarmed. You have no idea how to fight. And the second the vampires get their hands on you, Knox will drop to his knees in surrender. I know how vampires work, and that surrender might as well be his death sentence." Javion's grip on me tightened as he pulled me to look at him. "And I refuse to let *you* be the reason he dies."

"I am not unarmed." I held my free hand up. "I have this."

"We are dead, you stupid female," Javion snarled, baring his fangs. "Your power works by frying people—by short-circuiting their heart. Ours don't beat. Using your power is a waste of your energy and does *nothing*."

For the first time since leaving the captivity of the Lycans, I felt trapped. There might have been no glass cage around me, but I was just as helpless.

I watched as a vampire pulled a blade out from under his coat, charging towards Carter who had his back to him. "Carter!" I screamed.

Carter turned at the last moment, grabbed the vampire by his wrist and used the momentum to stab the blade through another's heart.

And then a third vampire stuck a blade in Carter's side. It was clear that the stone skin offered some protection, but the blade penetrated it. Carter yelled out in pain, stumbling.

"Then what will do something?" I asked turning to Javion.

"What?"

"If my powers are useless, what will work?"

Javion sneered. "For you? Nothing. Vampires die one of three ways. Decapitation, sunlight, or fire."

From one side, I heard Hunter cry out. Then, as a vampire charged at me, and Javion was distracted, I dove out of the way, pulling a burning stick from the bonfire. Decapitation and sunlight, I couldn't help with but there was a ready-made weapon burning behind me.

Turning, I discovered the vampire was the one Javion had called Colby.

Now armed, I swung, smacking the vampire attacking Javion around the back of the head. Colby yelped in pain, brushing his hands over his head and putting out the few locks of hair that had caught on fire.

Instead of rounding on me, Colby continued to attack Javion, kicking and punching. There was something about their fighting that seemed more brutal than watching the vampires attack my gargoyles. Maybe it was because in their gargoyle form, they seemed bigger and more imposing. Here, Javion looked more evenly matched, and each blow that landed, I could see it as it their bodies gave way . . . their fighting seemed more human.

I swung again, trying to put more force into my attack, but Colby lunged forward and I missed. The momentum sent me spinning and I stumbled, dropping my burning weapon.

As I scrambled around, trying to grab the stick while also getting to my feet, a shadow loomed over me. I looked up, just in time for Colby's fist to hit the side of my head.

My head whipped to the side, sending my glasses flying from my face. It felt like my jaw had been knocked out of place, and I could taste blood.

Before I could figure out what was happening, Colby's hand was around my throat, lifting me from the ground.

Javion was right. I was useless in a fight.

I tried desperately to get him to loosen his grip: clawing at Colby's arms, kicking wildly, but my blows did nothing.

The pain in my face, and the spots dancing across my vision were only working against me.

The burly vampire sniffed the air. His eyes zeroed in on my mouth. Then he pulled me close.

With the lack of oxygen, I thought I was hallucinating.

Colby's mouth moved towards mine, and then, at the last moment, his tongue darted out, licking a spot just beside my mouth.

I was back to hallucinating again. Colby's blue eyes seemed to light up. Like a lightbulb was switched on behind them. "Sweet mother-fucking peaches. Your blood is like the ambrosia of the vampires. It's like drinking champagne."

"Help," I yelled.

Or tried to.

The hand around my throat didn't let much oxygen get in, and it certainly didn't let my cry for help come out louder than a whisper.

Colby looked over at the other vampires before looking back at me. "They want justice for Aella's murder. They won't care what state we present your body in."

I had no idea what that meant. And then he turned, still clutching at my throat. The motion was enough to let up the grip on my throat, just enough to let a little air through, but I was too busy trying to stop him from dragging me across the ground as I lost a boot.

Then we were under the trees at the edge of the garden, away from everything.

Colby flung me against the tall wall that bordered

the grounds. My head smacked the stone. His hands grabbed at the collar of my coat, ripping it as he tore it off me.

The blow to the head, along with the sudden rush of oxygen, left me feeling disorientated with a pounding head. I knew I needed to fight him off, but my body didn't seem able to tell the urgency of that need.

My arms flailed wildly, occasionally hitting his chest, but not doing any damage.

From how it had been described, and from what I had seen with Javion and Knox, a vampire taking the blood of another was supposed to feel good—orgasmic, by all accounts.

The idea of Colby biting me and giving me that made my stomach churn and my mouth taste like bile.

And then his teeth clamped down on my neck.

There was nothing even vaguely pleasant about it. Pain radiated from my neck as his fangs tore through my skin. He might as well have taken a blade to me. Even as he drank greedily, the sensation that radiated out from that spot was agonizing.

The whole experience *hurt*.

I screamed, the noise loud and shrill.

Colby didn't stop.

And no one seemed to be coming.

The power inside me might have been useless, but it was all I had.

I pressed my hands against the vampire's chest and sent a charge of electricity to my fingertips.

With an irritated grunt, Colby pulled back, the motion tearing my skin even more. I stared in horror at my own blood, dripping from his mouth. "No wonder they've kept you hidden away here." With a smirk, he returned his mouth, this time, to a lower position on my neck, once more, tearing at the skin.

Focus.

With each noisy slurp, I could feel the blood draining. If I didn't come up with something new, quick, I was going to be dead.

I closed my eyes, picturing all the electricity inside of me.

The big blasts—the EMPs—they had always been targeted at everything around me. Here, the best it was going to do was kill his cell phone.

But what if all that energy went into one place? Whenever the energy left me, it did so in dozens of bolts of lightning. Maybe it wouldn't be enough to stop him, but if I could concentrate it into one blast, *maybe* I could at least get him off me long enough to get away.

Placing one hand back on Colby's chest, I

summoned every bolt and spark inside of me, channeling it through me and out of the palm of my hand.

I felt it.

One massive bolt of lightning.

It latched onto Colby, and he pulled back, staring at me with his eyes wide.

And then I couldn't see him as the lightning bolt glowed white hot and the vampire ignited with a woosh.

Bacco had gone up in flames, but it hadn't been anywhere near as fast as Colby.

With the last bit of energy in me, I shoved him backwards, putting some space between us.

He dropped to the ground as I did.

Clamping my hand down over my neck, I climbed back to my feet.

I had a weapon now, and if my gargoyles were still in trouble, I was going to use it.

More stumbling than running, I hurried back out of the trees, heading for the bonfire.

There were three of them on Carter.

After going so long without eyeglasses, although my vision was fuzzy again, I was used to this. I held my hand up, squinting as I took aim. And then I let the electricity bolt loose.

Unlike last time, there was an enormous crack that echoed around the walls of the grounds.

Lightning shot across the snow, hitting the vampire square in the back. As he burst into flames, Carter and the vampires turned to look. Without any acknowledgement, Carter spun, taking advantage of the surprised vampires still attacking him. Seconds later, a head flew through the air.

Leaving Carter to fight the last one, I ran to the back of the bonfire, finding Virgil holding an unconscious Javion by his hair. There was a blade in his hand, hovering by Javion's throat.

In front of him, Knox was dropping to his knees.

"Good little pebble," Virgil said, smirking.

"What are you doing?" I demanded as I came to a stop a few paces behind.

"Zera, get the fuck out of here, now." Knox's order came through gritted teeth, but he refused to look at me.

Virgil's eyes locked on my neck. "Who did that?"

Knox turned. Seeing the blood, he growled. The look he gave me was filled with rage.

"Colby," I said, for both of their benefit.

"I'll kill him," Knox told me.

"He's already dead."

"Who . . .?" Virgil arched an eyebrow. "There's no

way a little thing like you killed Colby."

I shrugged.

"That's my girl." Although Knox still looked pissed, he gave me a proud smile before turning back to Virgil.

"I guess you won't mind that I kill someone in return," the vampire told me.

We didn't like each other, and I wasn't entirely sure if the whole reason all the other vampires were here because of Javion or not.

But Javion had tried to protect me.

He was part of Knox's family.

He was a part of Knox.

I didn't have anyone outside of these castle walls.

Family didn't necessarily mean blood.

Family didn't necessarily mean you had to like everyone.

But Javion was my family too.

Besides . . . if he had brought the vampires here, I would kill him myself for letting Knox, Hunter, and Carter get hurt.

I knew how to do that now.

"You can," I told Virgil, ignoring the roar from Knox. "But only if you're quicker than lightning."

I raised my hand and let it rip. The lightning bolt

not only hit him in the face, making the side of his head explode, but it also sent his body soaring backwards into the bonfire.

Knox lurched forward, grabbing Javion and pulling him back before he got dragged in with him. With Javion pressed against him, holding him tightly, Knox looked up at me, eyes wide.

I barely registered it.

The fact I had only one boot on and my bare foot was so cold it felt like hundreds of knives stabbing at it was insignificant. I could no longer feel the pain in my neck.

All I could focus on was blinding rage.

These vampires had invaded Castle Viegls and attacked the only people in the world who cared about me. Not only that, I was sure that if any of them left, they would only return with more vampires.

Or worse.

The Lycans.

Not on my watch.

I marched around to the other side of the bonfire, back to where Hunter and Carter were working with each other to fight the last three vampires. As one of them went for Hunter, I raised my hand. Seconds later, the vampire had been blown backwards, exploding into flames.

As I went to take aim at a second, the world wobbled.

Or maybe I did . . .

I clutched at my head, trying to shake off whatever it was.

Raising my hand again, I took a couple of steps forward for a better angle.

And the world seemed to flip upside down.

The last thing I saw as my body slumped to the ground, was Carter's mouth moving. Whatever he said, I didn't hear it.

Thirty-Four

Zera

I was back in the prison.

Only this time, I was on the other side of the glass walls.

This was a dream—a nightmare.

It had to be.

I wasn't sure when this was. In the whole time I'd been there, I'd had three changes of 'clothes.' This was the last thing I'd been given—the same scruffy slip I had escaped wearing.

Based on my appearance alone, this could have been any point in the last seven years until the last week of me being there when I'd had my chains loosened.

With the bright, harsh lights on, I couldn't tell what time of day it was either.

The vision of me was conscious and damp. That meant my last drenching had been some hours ago, and I was due a fresh round of torture.

Just the idea of that made my knees wobble. I reached out for the wall to steady myself. I was surprised when I didn't slip through the wall, but it felt more like I had pressed up against a bubble of air, than something solid.

I could *feel* it? I thought you weren't supposed to feel things in dreams?

"Wakey-wakey, Battery."

Bacco's voice made my blood run cold.

Slowly turning, I faced the control room.

It was just him.

Which meant . . .

Sure enough, Bacco settled into his chair, pulling out his already hard dick.

He was dead, but I wanted to rip that thing from

his body and use it to choke him.

I turned away, the sight repulsing me. I'd seen it enough times that I never needed to see it again.

Only, as I turned, Bacco released the water.

It was one of the occasions when, not only was my body exposed, but it had arched backwards at the pain. My head was facing the water at it gushed out from above, half-drowning me as it poured down.

My screams were gurgles, masked by the water.

All the while Bacco was making moaning noises in the other room, the sounds coming through the speakers loud and clear.

I could feel it all over again.

It was like I was back in that glass cell with the metal chains clamped around my wrist. I could feel the agony as well as watch it, reliving the nightmare all over.

My legs felt weak, and I slammed back into the wall. This time, Bacco looked over, and I swear, for just a moment, he saw me. But he shook his head and continued rubbing his hand up and down his thick shaft.

The pain in my own body intensified, until finally, I screamed. The noise echoed around the room.

And then I blacked out.

I awoke with a start, only just stopping myself from screaming. Lying there with my heart racing, feeling like it was going to explode, I tried to calm myself.

A bed.

I was in a bed.

My bed.

My heartrate slowed. It *was* a dream. I was safe, and I wasn't back there.

It was dark outside still, but someone had left the lamp on.

Closing my eyes, I laid there, taking stock of myself. My head was pounding, my neck was unbelievably sore, my throat was dry, and my wrists . . .

My wrists felt like they had the first day after taking the cuffs off.

I tried to raise my arm to see if there were fresh wounds there, but I realized something was holding it down.

A brief moment of panic tore through me before I looked and saw Hunter. He was fast asleep in a chair beside the bed, doubled over, using the mattress as a pillow as he held my hand.

Gently, so as not to wake him, I tugged my hand free. The bandages were fresh. I unwound them, but underneath, was nothing more than the hideous red, black and silver scars. Nothing new.

Relief filled me.

It was just a dream.

Although I desperately needed a drink, I lowered my hand, threading my fingers through Hunter's scruffy hair. It was damp, like he'd not long since taken a shower.

That had images of water being poured over me again, and I had to fight back the electricity which had returned and was crackling over my body.

The door to the room opened with a soft click, and Carter walked in. Seeing I was awake, he sighed in relief. "Thank the gods." He hurried over, stopping beside the bed. "How are you feeling?" he asked, quietly.

"I don't feel right."

"I'm not surprised. The amount of power you . . ." Carter rubbed at his jaw. "Where did you learn to do that?"

"I didn't know I could," I told him, trying to sit up.

Carter stepped forward to help me, and then slid a

pillow behind me. "You should rest."

"The vampires—is everyone okay?"

"The vampires are all dead."

"What about Knox? And Javion?"

Taking in a long breath, Carter stepped back. "We should discuss this in the morning when you've had some rest."

"What happened? Who is hurt?"

"No one is hurt," Carter quickly told me.

"Huh? What's happening?" Beside me, Hunter sat up, and like a switch had been flicked, the sleepiness had gone. "Zee? You're awake? How are you feeling?"

"I want to know how Knox and Javion are, and Carter won't tell me."

Hunter and Carter shared a look before Carter perched on the edge of the bed. "Both are fine. We all got a few cuts and bruises from the fight, but we're healing. You are the only one who fell unconscious."

"Then why do you look like someone died?"

Carter looked away. "Javion left."

My mouth fell open. "Why would he do that?"

"Because I told him to."

I stared at Carter's profile, sure I was hearing things, but when I looked at Hunter, it was obvious I'd heard perfectly clearly. "Why?"

"Because the reason the vampires came here was because he invited them." Although there was a sadness to his voice, it was also calm. Eerily so. "He brought them here, and you nearly died."

My hand flew to my neck. There was a bandage covering the area Colby had bitten, but it was sore to the touch.

Javion had brought the vampires to Castle Viegls to get me.

I had expected him to do something like this. I knew he didn't want me around.

But for some reason, it didn't sit right with me.

Trust them all.

There had been a ghost—the ghost who helped me escape—and she had told me to trust them all, *including* Javion.

"You need to stop him from leaving," I said, pulling back the covers from the bed. My feet touched the floor, but as I tried to stand, they gave out.

"Zeraora?" Carter gasped, lunging to catch me. "You need to rest."

I shook my head. "You need to stop Javion from leaving."

Instead of helping me, or even lowering me back into the bed, Carter held me. "It's too late. He's gone."

"What about Knox?"

"He chose you," Hunter told me.

I looked over at him, frowning. "What do you mean?"

Hunter shrugged. "Exactly that. Javion left and Knox stayed."

I shook my head. "Carter, you need to get Javion back. I don't think—"

"Zeraora," he said, using that tone. "Javion brought the vampires to this castle. I will forgive him of many things but allowing the enemy into our home and allowing any of us to be hurt is one of the lines I will not allow anyone to cross. Javion has gone."

"You've made a mistake."

"Well, it can't be undone. Now, get back in bed and rest. Your efforts in fighting must have drained all your energy because you are the only one of us whose injuries haven't begun to heal yet."

I wanted to fight against him, to get out of the room and find Javion before it was too late, but Carter was right. I had no energy. I could barely stand on my own. "Where's Knox?"

Hunter leaned over and took my hand. "Knox is going to be okay, but I think for tonight, he needs to be alone."

Trust all of them.

This wasn't right.

I wasn't completely sure that I really did trust Javion, but if he wasn't here, I wasn't going to be able to.

And Knox.

This must be killing Knox.

Tonight, I could do nothing but tomorrow, when my energy would return, I was going to make this right.

Something told me my life might actually depend on it.

To be continued . . .

ACKNOWLEDGEMENTS

First up, if you're a colleague and you're not reading this, you're awesome and I love you, even if you don't know it because you're not reading this. (That's not true, the Toxic Two are not awesome). But if you are a colleague, you suck and you will no longer be able to make eye contact with me in a meeting. At least there's one benefit to working from home and being able to choose who you look at in a meeting.

Now I've gotten that off my chest . . .

I started this story with a goal: to be able to write a standalone, fast-burn reverse harem with a 40K word-limit.

I failed.

I mean, I got the reverse harem part . . . but yeah, it's a failure.

That being said, I'm happier with how this has turned out. If you've gotten this far, I'm assuming you're happy too. Or maybe you're a little annoyed with that cliff-hanger? Trust me, there was a point where it was going to be much worse.

But in all seriousness, I do hope you enjoyed Grounded. Thank you for giving this story a chance and sticking with it. I hope you're sticking around for the sequel.

This book wouldn't be half as good as it is without my editor. Caia has a talent for not only polishing a manuscript and making it waaaaaaay better, but for explaining the changes and basically being the English teacher I didn't have at school. And don't get me started on the translations. I'm English but I lived in Louisiana for a couple of years. Turns out I'm not as fluent in American as I thought I was and half of our conversations are me sending a photograph with the caption, *what's this?* Plus, she's kick-ass and I'm happy just to know her, never mind have her editing my work. You all need a Caia in your life! But not this one. I'm too needy.

A huge shoutout goes to my girls Sarah and Ji Soo. These are the two who get the random pestering questions and help me hash out sticking points. You know the friend you have to call when you're in trouble? That's Ji Soo. And the friend sitting beside you—that's Sarah. But she's also the person I turn to for everything.

I also need to say a huge thank you to Sarah for helping me move the furniture out of my office so that I could decorate it, then move it back in. Then move all the crap out of the spare bedroom to turn into the second office, before moving the office stuff in that room. Yes, it is as ridiculous as it sounds. And my desk is the heaviest piece of furniture I own.

Thank you to the eagle eyes of by beta readers: Mayara, Karissa, Sandi, Megan, Marisa, and Tanisha. I was confident that this would be the book with no typos. I was wrong. Thankfully, you guys saved this author!

To all of you who received an ARC copy of this and left a review, thank you. It took me months to get this book ready and somehow you manage to devour it in hours. Hopefully you enjoyed it enough to stick around in my ARC team? But either way, thank you.

I'm sure I've missed someone out. I hope I didn't. But if you're sat there thinking I don't love you, I do. I suck. But you don't and you're awesome!

Serenity Ackles

NEWSLETTER

The best way, hands down, to stay in touch with me, is through my newsletter.

Facebook has a terrible habit of suppressing posts, and as for notifications, I don't get them half of the time either!

While I will post occasionally on FB, and I will try to be active in my group, you can guarantee an email from me once a month.

What's more, each month, there will be a giveaway to win—it could be a signed paperback, gift card, or some other fun goodies.

So please sign up using the link below:

Find out more at:

http://eepurl.com/gJhECL

ABOUT THE AUTHOR

Serenity Ackles writes both contemporary and paranormal romance stories. With a long-standing inability to choose a book boyfriend, and always rooting for the 'second lead', she mainly writes reverse harems.

As such, Serenity's stories contain a lot of men, just as much cock, and a liberal sprinkling of profanities.

More importantly, the contain (eventual) happy endings, where, if the girl doesn't want to choose between the men who like her, she damn well doesn't.

WAYS TO CONNECT

Facebook:
Page: www.facebook.com/SerenityAcklesAuthor/
Group: www.facebook.com/groups/SerenityAcklesRebels

Bookbub:
www.bookbub.com/profile/serenity-ackles

Amazon:
www.amazon.com/Serenity-Ackles/e/B081F8D5FK

Newsletter:
http://eepurl.com/gJhECL

Made in the USA
Monee, IL
02 June 2022